CHASING THE KNIGHT

A STEALTH OPS NOVEL

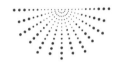

BRITTNEY SAHIN

EMKO MEDIA, LLC

Chasing the Knight

By: Brittney Sahin

Published by: EmKo Media, LLC

Copyright © 2020 EmKo Media, LLC

This book is an original publication of Brittney Sahin.

Chief Editor: Deb Markanton

Editor: Arielle Brubaker

Proofreader: Judy Zweifel, Judy's Proofreading

Cover Design: LJ, Mayhem Cover Creations

Photography: Eric Battershell Photography

Paperback ISN: 9781661671501

❀ Created with Vellum

To my new friends C. and M. - thank you for answering all of my questions to help make this book as accurate and realistic as possible.

Dublin Nights

On the Edge
On the Line
The Real Deal
The Inside Man (4/30/20)

Hidden Truths

The Safe Bet
Beyond the Chase
The Hard Truth
Surviving the Fall
The Final Goodbye

Contemporary Romance
The Story of Us

PART I

PROLOGUE

When they first met

2013

CHAPTER ONE

San Diego (January 2013)

"I thought I'd find you here. You always did prefer to be outside."

Wyatt kept his eyes downcast on the roaring fire, which was surrounded by stacked river rocks to keep the flames at bay. It was a bit too rustic for this setting and seemed more fitting of his place back in Colorado than California.

"I guess some things never change." His words drummed up reminders of why he and Clara had never worked out—but the main reason: he couldn't change. He couldn't be what she'd needed.

He slowly turned toward the bride on the terrace, not sure how he'd feel when facing her one-on-one tonight.

As a sniper, his job was to pay attention to the minutest detail. It was a skill that'd become ingrained in him over the years and was impossible to turn off. But hell if he didn't want to shut it down right now. He didn't want to notice details.

The way her raven-black hair fell over her shoulders in tight curls, lying in stark contrast against the neckline of her off-white ball gown.

The layers of fabric sparkling with crystals sewn into the skirt of the dress, making her look like a Disney princess—the antithesis to her usual get-up: cutoff jean shorts and a ribbed tank top stained with dirt from playing ball with the guys.

He swiped at his trimmed blond beard and blinked a few times before redirecting his focus to her blue eyes. "I should've given you a proper wedding like this." He nodded toward the banquet hall off to his right where the band played and couples danced inside.

Their wedding had been at the courthouse. Impersonal, almost clinical.

No white dress. No tux.

They'd even had swimwear on beneath their clothes so they could go surfing right after they said their vows.

"We were young." Her voice was soft, a hint apologetic.

He reached out, taking her hands into his, then leaned in and brought his mouth to her cheek. "Congratulations. You look stunning." He held on to her for a moment, probably a moment too long, as memories of their life together catapulted to mind. The good and bad times.

"I didn't know if you'd show."

He finally let go of her and forced his hands into his pockets. "I did RSVP, didn't I?"

Had the invite not been via email, he'd never have seen it. He'd been wrapping up five months of combat deployment in Afghanistan when he'd learned Dale Franklin was tying the knot with Clara.

"Most guys wouldn't come to their ex-wife's wedding."

True, but . . . "So, why'd you invite me?"

"Because we're friends now."

Friends? Yeah, he supposed they were, even though they didn't talk all that often. "Right," he said on a sigh.

She smoothed her hands up and down her biceps, a sure indication her nerves were about on point with his. Clara could easily handle the chill in the air, and sixty degrees for January wasn't that bad.

He turned and looked out at Mission Bay, the boat lights bobbing on the dark water, and his thoughts drifted to his training at BUD/S, specifically to his second attempt at earning his trident.

"You're happy with Dale?" That's all he wanted for her. Happiness. The kind of life he hadn't been able to give her since he was too screwed up.

At the feel of her hand on his arm, he stiffened. "Yes, but that doesn't mean what we had wasn't real."

She let go of him, and when he stole a glimpse of her out of the corner of his eye, her gaze was on the fire pit. "You remember the first time we met?"

"How could I forget?" He focused back on the orange-red flames that swayed in the gentle breeze. "You did save my life."

"Did you ever tell the boys you used to be shit in the water?" She'd never let him live that down.

He smiled. "Sure, tell my mates I got whacked over the head by a surfboard and you had to give me mouth-to-mouth? No damn way."

Clara had been a beast in the water when they'd met. A badass surfer and also a kick-ass Marine.

She chuckled, but then fell silent, and it was as if they were both watching a flag lowered to half-staff. "Try not to work too hard. Maybe settle down and find someone who makes you happy."

She knew him too well to suggest he'd ever find love. But he was already happy, wasn't he? His work was all he needed. His brothers in the Navy. But he offered her a, "Yeah, maybe," since he knew she still clung to the dream that one day he would realize he was worthy of love. Somehow Clara had remained an optimist over the years, never letting war taint her outlook on the world or her opinion that people were inherently good. She still believed in him, even if he didn't deserve it.

"I should probably get back to the guests." Her voice was as powdery soft as a fresh blanket of snow.

She patted his chest and walked away, the fabric of her gown dragging behind her.

"Wyatt?" She twisted back around. "Don't die."

"You stole my line." Those had been his words to her each time they said goodbye when she deployed. A simple but honest request to return home. "I'll do my best," he mimicked the response she used to give him. Also simple. Also honest.

After a few minutes, he went back inside, in desperate need of a drink to get through the night. The banquet hall had a coastal chic vibe to go with the outdoor landscape. Overall, the room was uncomplicated, which was much more Clara's style than the wedding dress she had on.

He navigated through the crowd, doing his best to avoid conversation, especially with Clara's parents, and made his way to the second and smaller bar, which was tucked off to the side near the coat check.

"Whiskey. Whatever kind you've got." He dropped his elbows onto the counter and lowered his face into his palm.

"You hate weddings as much as I do?"

The woman had the kind of voice that could sell car insurance to a man without a car. Like velvet or silk, her tone was smooth and low. A hint of Southern.

When he pivoted to his right, his eyes cut straight to a pair of pale green irises. "I'm not the biggest fan of weddings," he admitted.

Her bluish-gray dress was *not* a bridesmaid gown, thank God. It flowed from the waist down but fit tight at the top, and he did his best not to focus on the deep V that offered a hint of cleavage.

She pushed her golden blonde hair off her shoulder and smiled, drawing his eyes to her very kissable lips.

"What about you? Most women like weddings, right?"

"Not all women. Why do you think I'm hiding over here in the corner?" The playfulness in her tone got his engine revving, and his body went from zero to sixty.

He had just returned from a five-month stint in Kabul. Five months without any hook-ups. And this was his only weekend in California before he headed back to Dam Neck. Maybe he could . . .

Wyatt let go of his thoughts when she brought a cocktail glass to her lips, and he spied her G-shock watch, which should've looked out of place paired with the dress, but for some reason, it suited her.

"What?" She arched a brow and lowered the glass to the counter off to her right.

"You military?"

Her light green eyes dropped to the watch, and her lips twitched as if she were battling both a smile and frown. "My brother was in the Army. It was his."

Was? "Shit, I'm sorry."

"No, no." She waved a hand between them, nearly hitting his chest. "He left because of a medical injury, but he's okay. Doing better than ever, actually."

Thank God.

"But wearing his watch, knowing by some miracle he survived, it makes me feel"—she shrugged—"grounded or something. Protected. I don't go anywhere without it."

He could understand that.

He reached for the tumbler the bartender had slid his way, and when his sleeve shifted a touch to expose his Casio, she pointed to his wrist. "Seeing as though you have one on, does that mean you're in the service? British?"

"American Navy. Don't let the accent fool you."

"Aw. Navy versus Army. Great rivalry. Love watching the football games."

He absorbed her words. Took in the sight of her full lips. Her gorgeous eyes.

She had that sweet girl-next-door look. The *sexy* girl next door. An innocent smile that could destroy a man's thoughts.

"So, uh, why don't you like weddings?"

One eye closed as if she were hesitant to spill the truth. "You've heard about runaway bride syndrome, right?"

No way did she jet off and leave some poor chap at the altar, did she?

"You're a runner?" he asked, nearly choking on his whiskey.

"Instead of runaway bride—picture runaway groom."

"What man in his right mind would leave you?"

"No idea. I'm a great catch," she said with a teasing smile. "But I plan on being forever single, and I'm fine with that."

"Well, the arse that left you is a bloody fool."

Wyatt peered around the room and caught Clara dancing with her husband to a slower song. Not far away was Admiral Chandler, covered in chest candy, dancing with his wife. He wasn't sure of Chandler's connection to Clara or Dale. It wasn't every day an admiral of his stature showed up to a wedding.

"Tell me your brother kicked the shit out of your ex, at least."

"My fiancé was my brother's best friend."

Shit. "All the more reason to box the head off him."

Her eyes flicked to the vaulted ceiling before moving back to the dance floor. "Anyway, you feel like going outside? There's a fire pit no one is using."

My kind of woman. "Absolutely." He followed her through the crowd, laser-focused on her fit body as they traversed the room of two hundred people.

Once on the terrace, she held her palms open and did a three-sixty as if relieved to be free of the reception. "Much better."

As Wyatt strode closer, the scent of burning wood, mingling with touches of vanilla from her perfume, wafted his way on a sudden breeze. "I'd give you my jacket, but I don't have a bloody clue where I tossed it earlier."

"Oh, this weather's perfect. I'm fine." She dropped onto one of the four rustic chairs that surrounded the fire pit, the slit of her dress shifting to expose one long, tan leg. But it was the silver-colored flip-flop that had him smiling.

"Nice touch."

"The whole beauty-is-pain thing never worked for me," she drawled.

"You a Texan?" he asked while occupying the chair next to her, but he repositioned it to face her instead of the fire. He worked with a lot of Teamguys from the Lone Star State, so the accent was fairly familiar.

"Dallas. Born and raised." She offered her hand. "Natasha."

He reached for her palm. "Wyatt." He cleared his throat when she'd yet to retract her hand, but he wasn't in a hurry to let go either. "You still live there?"

"Virginia now. D.C. border."

"You in politics?" He didn't get that vibe from her, but then again, aside from getting a read on her Texas roots, he couldn't figure much else out about her.

"I work at the State Department," she answered. "Telecommunications specialist." She slipped her palm free of his, her gaze moving to the flickering flames.

Most people he'd met in that role at the State Department were actually CIA officers. Surely, she wasn't, but he couldn't help but joke, "Ah, so you're with The Company?"

"You're a comedian, huh?" Her eyes landed on his.

He waved a finger at her with a slight nod and continued to tease, "Yeah, I can see it now. You work at Langley." He brought his forearm to the wide plank chair arm and made a play of taking a long look left, then right. "Here on official business?" he asked in a low voice. "You undercover now?"

She leaned closer and whispered, "Not tonight, but I do have a gun strapped to the inside of my thigh in case Dale tried to run on Clara." Her brows knitted as she said in a serious voice, playing along with the charade, "But you got me, I'm most definitely a CIA agent."

He settled back in his seat and let go of the chair arm. "Well, that confirms it." He kept his eyes on her, his mood much better than it had been earlier. "You're not really in the CIA."

She pressed a palm to her chest, feigning surprise and indignation. "And what gave me up?"

"No spook would call themselves an agent. CIA *officers* recruit foreign nationals to be agents." *Why am I talking about this?* He was off his game. Damn those five months without sex. Plus, well, the setting was most likely messing with his head. Ex-wife's wedding and all.

Her lower lip trembled as if fighting a chuckle.

He glanced in the direction of the banquet room, realizing he'd left his drink at the bar. Of course, he wouldn't need alcohol to get through the night now that he'd met Natasha. "So, how do you know the bride and groom?"

Her hands went to her lap, and she played with the jersey fabric of her dress. "You'll think I'm crazy if I tell you."

"I doubt that."

She looked up at him. "Remember my ex-fiancé?"

"Brother's best friend?" Wyatt nodded.

Her chest lifted and fell from a deep breath. "Well, he just married Clara."

If he'd been drinking, he would've spit the whiskey right out. "That's rubbish. Dale and your brother may have been best friends, but why didn't your dad kill him?"

She shrugged. "Dad loves Dale like a son."

"And you're his daughter." Maybe they were both a little crazy to be there? "So, why'd you come, then?"

"I've known Dale for forever. Family friends. How could I not come?"

"You really were half-expecting he'd run tonight, weren't you?" And if Dale had jetted off on Clara, Wyatt would've broken his legs.

"Dale never looked at me the way he looks at Clara, so no." She waved a dismissive hand as if trying to block out

11

memories from her past. "But um, what's your story? I'm betting you're friends with the bride since I've never seen you before."

He gripped the wooden chair arms since it was his turn for a dose of the truth. "The bride's my ex-wife."

There was no sense of shock on her face at his answer. She actually responded with a laid-back, "We're a pair, huh?"

He peered at her, and her long lashes fluttered before her green eyes connected with his. "Looks that way."

She tipped her head to the side, observing him with curiosity in her eyes. "Can I ask you something?"

"Sure." And maybe he'd be able to answer. It was a coin toss.

"How long have you two been divorced?"

He didn't talk about Clara with anyone. Failing was unacceptable, and no matter how much distance he put between him and his father, he couldn't get the man's voice out of his head. The nagging *You always disappoint me* ringing in his ears like the sound of that damn BUD/S bell whenever one of his brothers bowed out.

Failing in his marriage had made his father's voice louder. More high-pitched.

And when Wyatt had to roll back at BUD/S to finish with the next class, it'd nearly been his undoing. He'd managed to convince himself the sole culprits had been pneumonia and a shoulder injury and had nothing to do with the fact Clara had dropped the big divorce bomb on him right before indoctrination. But the jaws of disappointment had sunk into him deep just the same.

"Legally, back in oh-seven. But we separated in the fall of oh-five shortly after I officially became a citizen."

Her mouth rounded in surprise. "You didn't marry for citizenship . . . did you?" She covered her face for a brief moment before her hand dropped to her lap as if embarrassed. "For all I know your parents moved here when you were younger. Sorry to assume."

"No worries." He'd gotten the marriage-citizenship question a lot, and eventually, he began giving off the same short answer: *Moved to the U.S. for marriage and became a citizen.* Not exactly the truth, but it worked, and most people didn't know the rules for citizenship so they didn't question him. He preferred to keep his past out of sight and out of mind.

Unlike the Navy, he couldn't get a SEAL contract until he became a citizen, and part of him would always wonder if Clara had waited to separate until his citizenship processed, knowing how important being a Teamguy had been to him.

"I chose school in San Diego instead of London much to my parents' dismay." More disappointment from them that'd led to the fight of the century with his father. "I met Clara the summer before I started uni, and Clara and I married a few months later right before she deployed." When was the last time he'd actually told the truth, and to a stranger no less?

"So, she was already a Marine stationed at Pendleton at the time?"

"Yeah."

Clara was four years older and so different from the women he'd dated in London. Part of the appeal.

"What made you join the Navy, if you don't mind my asking?"

"When I was a kid I'd thought about joining the Royal Navy in the U.K., so I guess I always had the desire to serve." He scratched at the column of his throat, still trying to digest the fact he was opening up. "I dropped out of San Diego after Nine Eleven and joined the Navy. As long as you're on a path to citizenship, you can serve."

Her gaze lingered on the fire and then cut his way a moment later. "Well, Clara does seem nice."

"She's a good person."

Her mouth tightened briefly before she whispered, "So is Dale." One shoulder lifted and fell. "Just not the right people for us, huh?"

He swallowed. "Right."

"You, um, seeing anyone now?" She pointed to his left hand. "These days, most men I know don't wear a ring, so it's hard to ID a married guy anymore."

"Is this your way of asking if I'm available?" If it hadn't been forever and a day since he'd had sex, maybe he could've suppressed the cocky grin on his face.

"Maybe."

"And if I'm available?" he asked.

"Then I'll ask you to dance with me."

"Out here?"

"Better than inside, right?" She shifted the skirt of her dress out of the way to stand. "So, are you forever single like me, or totally attached?" The playfulness in her tone had returned, replacing any hints of somberness that would've taken a K9 to sniff out.

"Forever single." He stood and reached for her hand, and she gasped when he yanked her into his arms and held her to his chest, nearly forgetting the glass walls of the reception area off to his left. Forgetting his ex was now happily remarried.

She braced his biceps and stared into his eyes as he held on to her. They only moved side to side, but it suited him just fine.

He reached between them and cupped her chin, unable to stop himself. Gorgeous was the tip of the iceberg. His gut told him there was a hell of a lot more beneath the surface, too.

"I love this singer, but not-so-great memories come with his music," she whispered like a confession.

"Oh?"

"The song *I'm Yours* by Jason Mraz was my ring tone for Dale when we were together. I was twenty-two, what can I say?"

His hand moved to her cheek and damned if he didn't want to lean in and taste the gloss of her lips, to let his tongue ease into her mouth—to give her a new memory to go with the music.

"Well, at least it's not that song playing now." He didn't think it was, at least. He wasn't too knowledgeable of the current beats. Most of the guys on base usually listened to more old-school tunes.

Her bottom lip rolled between her teeth, her nerves slipping to the surface. He wasn't so sure if it was the talk of her ex or the moment they were sharing that had her pulse fluttering at the side of her neck and her pupils dilating.

"You know, I can't tell if your eyes are blue or gray," she said after the DJ switched to a faster-tempo song. They kept slowly swaying side to side anyway. As long as he was holding her, it didn't matter what kind of steps they took. "Out here, they're sort of a slate blue, like the color of my dress, but inside they looked gray."

"DMV couldn't decide either," he said in all seriousness, unable to pull his eyes away from her.

They continued to dance for another ten minutes or so without saying anything, and it was bloody perfect.

"You really want to kiss me, don't you?" Her lips crooked at the edges, and a dimple popped in her left cheek.

"You have no idea how much," he admitted, his voice husky, "but—"

"But you're another heartbreaker?"

Lately, yeah.

She stepped out of his embrace when he didn't respond and offered her hand. "How about we take a walk on the beach?"

He was drawn to her in so many ways that went beyond attraction, which scared the hell out of him. Almost enough to turn and walk away.

He didn't, though. He accepted her palm and laced their fingers together.

"You always so nervous about going for a walk?" she asked. "I won't try and take advantage of you on the beach, I promise."

He caught her smirk from over his shoulder, and he playfully flipped his eyes to the sky dotted with stars. "Well, I won't resist if you do." He tightened his grip on her hand.

"Tell me something about you," she said softly as they walked at a slow pace.

"What would you like to know?"

"When'd you become a SEAL?"

He stopped walking and faced her. "What makes you think I'm a Teamguy?"

"I've been around enough sailors to know a SEAL when I see one. The accent threw me off at first." She smiled when he'd yet to confess. "Virginia Beach or Coronado?"

He let go of her hand to palm her cheek. "Virginia."

She turned her cheek, and her soft lips dragged across his warm skin. He wanted nothing more than to feel those lips on his mouth.

His balls tightened, desire gripping him like a tight hand around his shaft.

"The exes of our exes hooking up," she whispered. "That'd be wrong, right?"

She was straightforward, and damn did he like it.

"I thought you weren't going to make a move on me out here?"

She wet her lips, and he lowered his hand from her face before securing his palm around her waist to bring her flush to his body.

"And I thought you wouldn't object?"

"I'm pretty sure that'd be impossible to do," he admitted.

She pursed her lips together as if in thought, then murmured, "Hot sex on a California beach is on my bucket list."

"Not Virginia Beach? Or somewhere else? Just California?" He raised a brow.

"Okay, so I don't have a bucket list," she began, "but if I did, I think that it would include sex on a—"

He united their lips, and she relaxed into him as he kissed her.

His tongue dipped into her mouth, meeting hers, and he let out a low hiss, a sort of growl from pent-up need. But hell, it was more than that. Something inside of him had awakened.

He was on a beach with a stranger, not far from his ex-wife's wedding reception, but all the noise in his head grew silent. He could barely remember his near-death experience three weeks ago when an insurgent had set off an s-vest. Or the attack against his convoy a month before that.

The last several years became a blur with her lips on his.

All he could feel and taste was her. His entire awareness was Natasha.

Her nails biting into his back. Her fragrance. Her body pressed tight to him as if hungry to be even closer.

He nipped her lower lip after coming up for air even though he hadn't wanted to stop kissing her.

"I want you, but in a bedroom," he rasped before grinning

like a kid with a golden ticket to the Willy Wonka Factory. "I have pretty strong memories of having sand in places it doesn't belong when at BUD/S, and I'd prefer not to relive that while—"

"Understood." She stepped back and offered her hand.

And was this really happening? Was he going to get laid at Clara's wedding?

But fuck if he could stop himself.

Clara and Dale were happy, so why couldn't two single people enjoy themselves?

"Your room or mine?" he asked as they started for the hotel.

"Yours," she sputtered.

He dug his hand into his pocket in search of his keycard, but when he looked up toward the terrace and the glowing fire pit, he stopped in his tracks, practically yanking Natasha to an abrupt stop as well.

"What's wrong?" she asked.

"I, uh." He resumed walking, and they climbed the steps to the terrace so he could face a man he assumed was there for him.

What in the hell was Luke Scott doing there? He'd recently, and very unexpectedly, quit his position as a Tier One operator, so this couldn't be a *grab your shit, we're spinning up* kind of visit.

Luke coughed into a closed fist at the sight of Wyatt and Natasha's clasped palms. "Sorry to drop in on you like this. Can I have a word?" He tipped his head in apology to Natasha, and his blue eyes moved back to Wyatt.

"I can go back into the reception and wait," Natasha offered.

"I actually need him to come back to my room," Luke said in his stern, no-shitting-around Teamguy tone.

Wyatt turned toward her, disappointment thick in his tone when he said, "I'll find you after."

"Yeah, okay." But something in her voice said she was doubtful he'd come back.

And he honestly didn't know if he would return, but damn it, he didn't want to leave a woman like her hanging. He leaned in and whispered, "If I can't come back . . ."

She nodded as if she understood completely. There was forgiveness in her eyes. She was one hell of a woman, wasn't she? And he hated walking away from her.

She pressed a quick kiss to his cheek.

Luke remained silent as Wyatt watched her cross the terrace and pull open the door to the banquet hall. Music spilled out into the evening air for a brief moment, then vanished along with Natasha as the door closed. She did, however, steal one last look at him through the glass.

He wanted to go after her. To chase after the moment they'd been having and allow it to continue into the morning.

But he couldn't turn his back on Luke even if the night with Natasha had promised to be one he'd never forget.

Wyatt matched Luke's quick pace as they exited the terrace and walked down the path to the second hotel building adjacent to the banquet hall.

"I would've waited until tomorrow to show up, but I'm short on time. Sorry to interrupt like that."

"It's fine," he replied as they moved.

They stopped outside a first-floor suite a minute later, and Luke popped his keycard into the slot, then pushed open the door. "I'm not alone, by the way."

Wyatt followed Luke into the room and halted at the sight of the woman sitting on the couch opposite the king-sized bed. "Jessica?"

19

She stood and extended her hand. "Good to see you again, Pierson."

"You two related?" Wyatt's gaze shifted between Jessica and Luke. Same last names, but Luke had never mentioned . .
.

"He's my brother." She motioned for him to have a seat on the bed as she lowered herself to the couch again.

He dropped down, the soft mattress sinking beneath him.

Luke remained standing next to his sister. "Jessica told me you've worked a few operations together."

"Just last year in Somalia, in fact," Wyatt replied.

At first, the Navy had wanted to go kinetic on the site where a bunch of al-Shabaab terrorists had been housed, but Langley wanted the men brought back for questioning. Jessica had been the CIA liaison between AFRICOM and his team, advising the best course of action to ensure they got in and out of the country fast. And, more importantly, without any of his people dying. Her intel had been spot-the-fuck-on.

All his guys had swooped in on a super-stealth bird instead of a Chinook and grabbed seven terrorists, which had ultimately led to the major takedown of additional players.

The After Action Debrief, the sanitized version of what had happened in Mogadishu, had left out the majority of the details of what had gone down, including the fact Jessica Scott was a badass and should've been awarded a medal for that op. It'd been damn perfect because of her planning.

So, did her presence right now mean Luke was back in the game and in need of Wyatt's help?

"I didn't know she worked at The Company," Luke commented. "Just found out."

"What's going on?" His pulse should've climbed, should've picked up, but he was used to being thrown into unknown situations and forging ahead on reflex. This was nothing new.

What *had* spiked his pulse was when he'd first learned Luke-the-Legend-Scott had quit. Now—well, hell, he was just curious what was going on.

"Mind if I take point?" Jessica peered at her brother, and he nodded. She stood and walked toward the windows, then faced Wyatt. "After Neptune's Spear, Tier One guys have been thrown in the limelight, and it's been making your jobs increasingly difficult."

Neptune's Spear—one of the most famous SEAL operations in modern history because it was the op that took down Osama bin Laden. And yeah, she'd been right. The media had been relentless in their pursuit to learn more about DEVGRU, or Team SIX, operations. What bloody part of *clandestine* did they not understand?

"I've had an idea rolling around in my head for a while since that op," Jessica began, "and I decided, what better time to implement the plan now that we have a new president. Fortunately, President Rydell agreed to the proposal."

"Which was?" Wyatt rose, unable to remain seated any longer at the mention of POTUS.

"To assemble a team specifically earmarked to carry out operations for a few high-ups, including the president. Operations for which our DEVGRU people can't get a green light. Both foreign and domestic," she explained.

"Doesn't POTUS already have dark money for his Delta guys who handle shit like that?"

"Yeah, but there are still proper channels the president has to go through for those ops as well," Jessica countered. "We'll be even more off-the-books."

"We have approval for ten SEALs. Jessica and I have been tasked to lead this group." Luke folded his arms. "But

I'd like to break us up into two units. I'll head up Bravo, and I'd like you to take command of Echo."

"I've seen you operate as an assault leader, and you're also one of the best snipers out there," Jessica added. "We think you're a perfect fit for this role."

He blinked a few times, trying to wrap his head around the offer. "So, you didn't actually quit?" His brows lifted in surprise.

"I need the world to think I retired, but no, I'm still active," he explained. "Listen." He held a palm in the air as if sensing Wyatt's concern since they were vague as shit. "We'll be working directly for POTUS. If Washington can't approve an op but intel says our people are needed, we'll be the guys he sends."

"Unlike POTUS's Delta operations, we won't have QRF on standby," Jessica noted.

"No one's coming for us if we're captured," Luke reiterated.

Because we won't exist. Wyatt turned toward the wall, which had a picture of Mission Bay hanging above the bed. It had been one of Clara's favorite places to go when they'd been married. But now he was pretty sure his kiss with Natasha would forever be burned into his mind whenever he thought about the bay.

"I know it's a lot to ask, especially without too many details, but we can't disclose much until you agree and sign some NDAs," Luke said. "We'd be operating under the alias Scott and Scott Securities."

"And we'll probably take some private security gigs between ops to keep up with appearances. Those jobs might also be a great way to fund us, too. We'll be working on a limited government budget to prevent anyone from discovering we exist." Jessica's voice remained confident. Determined, but not overly pushy.

"You can help pick four guys to be on your team." Luke's words had Wyatt twisting back to face the two of them.

"Why not recruit retired Teamguys?"

Jessica and Luke exchanged a quick look. "We want younger guys who can move up with us," Luke said. "The risks will be great. And most of our retired SEALs are older and have kids."

"I guess that makes sense," he responded.

"Luke's convinced me to hire some vets to work at Scott and Scott, though. It'll help maintain our cover."

"But they won't know the truth?" He could practically feel his pulse pricking at his neck now.

"No one can know. The truth is too dangerous, especially if we want to make this last long-term." She edged closer, her eyes set on him to get a read.

Jessica was blonde and blue-eyed. Attractive. Late twenties. Young for someone in such a high-powered role. And had he not seen Jessica in action firsthand, or hadn't witnessed Luke operate in war, he'd probably already have left the room.

The idea of the team bypassing red tape and congressional approval was both appealing and terrifying.

"You're thirty-one. In the prime of your career. To ask you to leave your men, it's a lot, I know." Luke was right, especially about leaving his brothers behind.

"Can I have some time to think about it?"

"POTUS has a mission he needs us on, and we're scrambling to round everyone up." Luke's calm tone was a contradiction to his statement. "We don't have much time."

"My life has been filled with making quick decisions."

Leaving England.

Marrying Clara.

Dropping out of uni for the Navy.

"And that means?" Jessica asked him.

He extended his hand to Luke and shoved away any doubts from his mind. "I'm not quite sure what I'm walking into, but that also excites me. Story of my life, anyway." He gripped Jessica's palm next and smiled. "So, why the hell would I do things differently now?"

CHAPTER TWO

Natasha pulled her gaze from the outside terrace where the gorgeous SEAL had disappeared with another man who had Teamguy written all over him.

Did I really almost break my "no sex with a stranger" rule?

Wyatt probably wouldn't come back. There was something in his friend's eyes that gave off the "you're about to spin up" vibe. And she wasn't going to stand in the way of a man and a mission. She lived and breathed the life.

But maybe she'd dodged a bullet? That man could probably turn her heart to dust in the palm of his very large and rough hand.

Normally, she wasn't one to fall fast. She erred on the side of caution these days when it came to men. Which might have something to do with her fiancé walking out on their wedding day, leaving her standing in her wedding dress like a sad cake topper missing the groom. But there was something about Wyatt. She'd been instantly drawn to him, and his kiss had been earth-shatteringly amazing.

She returned her focus to her handsome friend, Jack London. Jack had moved to Dallas when she was seven and became best friends with her brother, but she'd always loved that he'd never treated her like Gray's annoying little sister, even though she liked to tag along wherever they went. Building forts in the woods and having Nerf gun battles had always been preferable to her over Barbies.

Jack stood before her with an amber-colored drink in hand. Most likely the same as what Wyatt had been drinking. A whiskey neat—free of anything mixed with it.

"I know we're all friends with Dale, and it's been almost three years since you split, but part of me wants to break his legs for what he did to you."

She smirked at his comment. But . . . the breakup wound up being the push she needed to finally apply to her current job. So, some good had come from being jilted at the altar, she supposed.

And thinking about her line of work right now had a spark of guilt warming her cheeks. Two years in hadn't made lying about working for the CIA any easier, especially not to a man like Wyatt.

"I'm just surprised you're handling this so well." Jack's attention moved to the happy new couple, Clara and Dale. "Marines," he grumbled.

Jack had nothing but love for his Semper Fi brothers in arms, but the guys from other branches loved to poke at each other any chance they got.

Natasha's father never let her brother live down the fact he'd chosen the Army instead of the Navy, choosing not to follow in his footsteps.

"I'm fine," she said, hoping to dismiss the topic. When his hand went to his chest, and his gold band caught her eye, it was a reminder she hadn't seen his wife at the reception. "Where's Jill?" And yes, they were "Jack and Jill," and their friends never let them live that down. Fortunately, Jack was more of a fun and laughable guy than a broody and pensive one, so he had quips prepared for every instance of heckling.

"Jill said she wasn't feeling great. She went back to the hotel room after the ceremony." He gulped back the rest of his drink and lowered the tumbler to the bar top. She knew there was more to it than that. It was her job to pay attention to details after all.

Jack lifted his gaze to hers when she placed a hand on his forearm.

"We may have gotten into a fight."

"I thought the only thing you two fought about was how much your life was consumed by the Army. What's there to argue about now that you've resigned your commission?"

He turned on his heel and went to the main bar. Natasha considered that code for *Let's not talk about Jill*, so once she caught up with him, she chose to follow the silent request to drop it.

They ordered another round of drinks, and her brother, Gray, made his way over, clutching his leg to assist with his movements, which usually only happened when he was overtired or drank too much.

Grayson, who she called Gray, joined in on their conversation, diving right in about which *Rocky* movie was the best. "'If he dies, he dies,'" he cast his vote, reciting a line from the movie. "Gotta go with Four."

"Agreed." Jack toasted with him.

"But—"

"Nope, that's the final answer," Gray cut her off and slung his arm around her shoulders.

"Uh, I can't even with you two. Add Dale to the mix, and you're practically the *Three Stooges*."

At the mention of Dale, Gray leaned in and asked in a not-so-subtle voice, "You doing okay, Sis?"

And that was code for—*Do you want me to kill Dale? Speak now or forever hold your peace.*

There had been a bit of a scuffle following the runaway groom situation. Gray had hunted Dale down, but he'd wound up forgiving his friend, deciding, like her father, Dale wasn't the right man for her.

"Where's Jill?" Gray snatched the olive out of her freshly made martini, and she whacked him in the side for such thievery.

"Don't ask," she warned.

Jack tossed back another whiskey like he was in a drinking competition. Yeah, that couldn't be good.

"Who was that guy you were talking to outside?" Gray swung his arm free of her shoulders and ordered his own drink.

"He's just someone."

He exchanged a look with Jack. "Like a someone I need to hunt down and give the third degree?"

She rolled her eyes and playfully swatted her brother's chest. "Not any of your business." *And he probably won't be back.* Her desire to have sex with Wyatt had definitely trumped her need to prevent the oh-shit moment that would inevitably follow due to breaking her "no sex with a stranger" rule.

Maybe if she was still feeling adventurous tomorrow, she'd call him. She needed his last name to look up his digits, though. There had to be someone there that knew the sailor. Well, someone other than the bride and her parents. Shit.

There were no doubt a lot of *someones* who may have been in attendance at Wyatt and Clara's wedding.

And now she couldn't help but wonder what kind of ceremony and reception they'd had. She knew virtually nothing about the man, but she doubted it'd been similar to this Boho chic vibe.

"I know that look," Jack announced after he'd ordered yet another round. These boys were going to get themselves into some trouble if they didn't slow it down. Basically—the norm for them. "You like this mystery man?"

"He's a Teamguy." Maybe she shouldn't have disclosed that information, but she trusted her brother and Jack.

Gray grunted. "Enough said."

"You do have two former SEALs on your payroll." She did a mental eye roll, chastising herself for continuing to babble. She'd been trying to get Gray off her back, not justify the stars in her eyes for Wyatt.

"And I give them hell for it every damn day," Gray said.

"Cheers to that, brother." Jack clinked his glass to Gray's.

"You two." She flipped her eyes to the ceiling, memories of the empty banquet hall at her own wedding invading her thoughts.

The chairs had been covered in a baby blue satin. The centerpieces full of lilies.

Lilies are for funerals, anyway, right? It was never meant to be, love, her friend Alexa had said to her. Alexa worked for MI6 and was all work and no play, and if Natasha didn't slow down soon, she'd wind up on the same path.

Natasha had been going strong in her job since 2011, not yet hardened by the evils of the world. Not yet jaded. She'd been warned it would happen eventually, but she'd do her best not to lose herself in her work, not to become numb.

She wanted to feel every loss. Remember every win, too. To always be her best and never give up.

Staying forever single would keep her heart guarded, but in doing so would she transform into the kind of officer she didn't want to be, so driven by the chase, the hunt, that she missed out on everything else in life?

Her focus moved back to the happy couple now sharing another dance at the center of the floor. Clara had once been Wyatt's other half. He'd had his lips on her. His hands. And for that reason, ridiculous as it may be, she felt a stab of jealousy. Because she now knew what Wyatt's touch was like.

But she felt nothing, no twinge of jealousy or regret, as she watched Dale and Clara together.

What was it about Wyatt?

If he didn't come back—maybe, just maybe—she'd do it . . . she'd ask for his full name, and she'd Google the hell out of that man and find him. Finish where they left off on the beach.

"Is the sailor the reason for that smile on your face?" Gray jabbed her in the ribs with his index finger.

Yes, she wanted to blurt. "Could you do me a favor?" she asked instead. "Could you get his last name from Clara?"

"And does your SEAL know her?"

This would be the hard part. "He's her ex-husband."

Jack's brows shot up in surprise.

Gray blinked twice as if he couldn't have possibly heard her right. "You're serious. Her ex came to the wedding?"

She pointed at her chest. "I'm here. Why is it such a shocker that he showed up?"

"If you really want to know the sailor's name, Lady Macbeth"—a name Gray just looooved to call her since she'd played the role in the high school play, and he knew it pushed her buttons the way all good brotherly nicknames were meant to—"you'll need to ask Clara yourself."

Fine.

She could do it.

No problem.

Well, maybe . . .

PART II

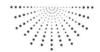

THE RESCUE

Three and a half years later

2016

CHAPTER THREE

ALGIERS (JULY 2016)

"I DON'T LIKE THIS." JACK TAPPED HIS INDEX FINGER ON THE table next to Natasha as if his trigger finger was itchy. They were at an outdoor café in the city center. The buildings around them dated back to the French colonial days with their whitewashed walls.

The overpowering smell of local spices hit her nose, and she stifled a sneeze with her hand when a breeze kicked up a touch of cumin her way from a vendor.

"Of course you don't like this. You never like when I'm out in the city." Less than a month in Algeria tracking down a lead, and every time she stepped outside the safety net of the Station, Jack became grouchy with worry about her.

She toyed with the ends of her headscarf, which served to hide her blonde hair. Aside from a touch of mascara, her face was clean of makeup.

This part of the world posed a significant challenge when it came to creating a legend—a fabricated background or biography for a deep-cover officer. Options were limited, especially for women.

Peace Corps, religious figures, and even journalists as cover stories were off-limits.

To make it even more problematic, a lone businesswoman didn't add up in this region. Therefore, her companion played the role of businessman and, to make it more believable, her brother.

Jack *was* practically her brother, though. After he left the Army Special Forces, he wound up serving in another way, by landing a paramilitary contractor gig with the CIA's Special Operations Group (SOG), also known as the GRS (Global Response Team). The CIA often hired former military guys to assist in the world's hot zones.

And this CIA Station in Algiers qualified as a red-hot zone right now. Tensions were rising due to the police-state repression, not to mention the presence of the terrorist group AQIM (Al-Qaeda in the Islamic Maghreb), whose main goal was to overthrow the government and insert the rule of religion throughout the country.

Jack side-eyed her as he brought his coffee to his mouth. "Don't even think about it," he warned as she fidgeted with the knot of her hijab, contemplating removing it to allow her blonde hair to flow free as a come-and-get-me beacon. "I know what you're thinking."

Jack, the man who'd never lost his humor, even after five deployments, was edgy today. Borderline broody even.

She heeded his warning and let go of the knot that anchored the red silk headscarf in place beneath her chin, dropping her hand to her lap.

He tapped at the comm in his ear. "What's your position, G? Any movement overheard?"

The paramilitary contractors became widely known after

the tragedy that went down in Benghazi a few years back. Those thirteen hours they'd held down the fort at the CIA annex had become front-page news.

Jack was one of the best men she'd ever worked with, and she'd been relieved to learn he'd landed a contract in Algeria shortly before her arrival. She'd also immediately phoned her father to question whether or not he'd pulled the strings to make it happen, given this wasn't the first time Jack had been assigned to her location. Her father denied it, of course, but she had her suspicions. Her father would do anything to keep her safe. Maybe he'd even been the one to nudge Jack to serve again.

A year ago, Jack's wife decided to call it quits. In Jill's defense, he'd promised not to go back into military work once he'd gotten out of the Army. In his defense, the real estate business didn't quite do it for him after the kind of life he'd lived. Also, this was what he loved. Helping people. Taking down bad guys.

"What'd G say?" Garrison was on Jack's team. Former Army Special Forces. Another man she'd trust with her life any day of the week.

"All clear from his vantage point," Jack replied, his voice tense.

She shielded her eyes from the sun as she looked up at the rooftop in the distance where G was located. He had a sniper rifle positioned on them. Even though she couldn't see him, she knew he could see her.

"But something doesn't feel right. The air is charged."

"The what is what?" She pitched her voice low and held on to the laugh that wanted to escape. It wouldn't be good to call attention to herself and Jack by smiling and flashing her white teeth. No, she had to blend in as the sister of a businessman.

They were there to meet a potential asset, a man she hoped had valuable intelligence. Someone who was willing to sell out his group, the AQIM, in exchange for a hefty payout from the Agency.

He was her best chance to not only take down the terrorists, but to find the hacker who supplied the AQIM with the coordinates that led to the Black Hawk being taken down in the Atlas Mountains six weeks ago, killing two soldiers and severely injuring two more.

She closed her eyes, fighting back the memory of her own brother's helo going down six years ago, which had led to his exit from the Army. The road to recovery had been long, but he survived, and she had to remind herself of that whenever fear and nerves threatened to cut through. The watch he'd given her, which she always wore, was hidden beneath her black sleeve on her left wrist.

"Something is going to happen, I'm telling you. I've got a feeling."

She opened her eyes at the urgency in Jack's words.

He was observing the streets, looking left and right. The area around them buzzed with conversation in Arabic, plus snippets of French here and there. A donkey hauling large bundles of trash strapped to its sides lumbered past just as their waiter delivered a plate of dolma, couscous, and lamb.

She gave her thanks in Arabic and eyed the food in front of her with uncertainty, her stomach knotting in protest. Jack's sixth sense kicking in only served to make her nerves more tangled.

"I think your man is on approach."

Natasha followed Jack's gaze to the busy street off to their side, crowded with vendors selling local food.

A man with a thick black beard wearing dark denim jeans and a loose-fitting, white long-sleeved shirt headed their way.

His eyes were focused. More observant than the men and women he passed.

It was her potential asset. Farid, with the AQIM.

He stopped a foot shy of their small, round table and flipped his gaze to the building off to their left, the one opposite of G.

"You came." She offered a slight bow of the head to show subservience to the man to maintain her cover.

"We cannot talk here." Farid's dark brown eyes, the color of the soil from her mother's tomato garden back home, met hers. "Follow me." He turned back toward the street he'd come from.

Jack secured a grip around her bicep, attempting to stop her from rising to her feet. "We can't blindly follow him. We need more coverage."

Yeah, well, the Chief of Station didn't think they needed additional support. He didn't think Farid would actually show. He'd thought she'd wasted the last four weeks trying to turn him. *This is a bullshit lead,* her boss had said before she'd left the Station thirty minutes ago.

"I have to go. You know how important this is." And damn it, they were already losing him.

Jack snarled but nodded for her to follow. "G, we're moving."

The steep, winding streets made it harder to keep up with Farid. "Where's he taking us?" She brought her hand to the Sig Sauer P226 holstered at her hip beneath her top, and a sense of comfort washed over her knowing it was within reach.

Many officers in the field weren't equipped for battle, but Natasha had completed the more rigorous courses at the Farm. She'd earned her silver jump wings, too. As an operations officer and part of the Directorate of Operations

(DO) it was her job to develop, ID, create, and handle sources. To acquire information to protect Americans and U.S. policy. Most people who joined the Agency wanted to be in the field recruiting spies, turning foreign nationals into agents. And she'd been lucky enough to land the gig.

CIA officers were notorious for walking a line between right and wrong, though, which was her least favorite part of the job—also, one she happened to be good at. She often pissed off the wrong people, like last week, and she'd nearly gotten herself PNG'd (declared persona non grata and thrown out of country).

But if she wasn't willing to offend the upper echelons of government every once in a while, she'd never catch as many bad guys.

So, following Farid down the streets, even if gun-wielding men skirted each corner with AKs, she was doing what she'd been trained to do.

She didn't need Jack whispering in her ear every minute like he was currently doing, *Are you sure?* Sometimes he still saw her as a kid sister, as the girl who could kill a deer like the best of them but would cry over the kill later and mourn the loss of life. Yeah, *that* girl. Out in the field, he could forget she was an officer responsible for taking down multiple HVTs over the years and preventing terrorist attacks from happening.

But it was the attacks that had slipped through the cracks that would haunt her every day, like the Black Hawk that'd been taken down. If she'd stopped the hacker after his last act three months ago, maybe those men on the chopper would've made it home to their families. Guilt plunged like a knife in her chest, and another to her gut, which twisted for an extra zing of pain.

Jack tugged on her arm, bringing her to an abrupt stop,

and a strange kind of energy surged and slammed into her. A feeling of danger.

Jack had been right. There was some sort of charge in the air.

Farid stood ten feet away facing them.

"What if he has an s-belt beneath that shirt?" Jack's voice cracked as a looming threat filled the air. "He might set it off."

"He's not going to do that." Jack's protection was top-notch, but right now, she didn't need that. She needed answers. Information. Actionable intelligence.

That was what she needed, and she believed Farid had it.

"We should stop following and abort mission, G," Jack said into his comm.

"Absolutely not." She started for Farid who was still staring at her as if . . . as if he was going to betray her.

She stilled when she got close enough to practically see the dilation of his pupils as he mouthed, "Sorry."

Oh fuck.

"We've got tangos up ahead," Jack said, catching her by the elbow. "Five by my count." He touched his ear. "G says there are five more behind. We're boxed in."

Farid had already turned and was sprinting the opposite way, heading straight for the five armed men barreling at them.

She secured a hand on her weapon as Jack thrust her into an alley off to his right.

Her best lead was gone.

How the hell had she let this happen? She'd been played, and she was better than this.

Her father's voice pushed into her head. *I don't know if you can handle this,* he'd said when she applied to the CIA. *What if you get yourself or others killed?*

41

"Come in, G. I can't hear what you just said. Repeat." Jack covered his ear, then cursed. "They're converging on our location. We need to get out of here," he said as they continued to bolt down the alley, but there was a wall obstructing their path. A dead end. "There's a door up ahead on your left. Try it."

Warning shots rang in the air and someone shouted in Arabic from behind.

He kept his chest to her back, serving as a shield as she gripped the knob.

The blood rushed to her ears as she twisted, as her chest squeezed with worry.

She pushed the door open with her Sig in hand, knowing full well they were about to be shit out of luck.

And she'd been right.

Three armed men were there waiting.

CHAPTER FOUR

IBIZA

"WE'RE SPINNING BACK UP." LUKE SIMULATED THE BLADES of a helo and twirled his finger in the air. "Five or six of us are needed for this one." Luke stood alongside his sister inside the lavish estate on the island, standing before Bravo and Echo Teams. Luke had awoken the guys just as they'd fallen asleep and lassoed them into the main living room.

Only two hours ago, they'd taken out a terrorist cell that'd been using the cover of a nightclub to traffic high-powered weapons and explosives. Bravo and Echo Teams had managed to take out seventeen tangos without killing any clubgoers. They'd consider that a win, especially since no one on their team had been clipped.

But now where were they heading?

Jessica pushed her black-framed glasses up to the bridge of her nose as she viewed the tablet in her hand. She was in her standard white fitted tee and dark jeans. Not much makeup. She did her best not to stand out with a so-called plain look. But Bravo Three certainly had been paying a hell of a lot of attention to her since the moment he joined the team last winter.

"Two hours ago," she began, her voice solemn, "a CIA officer and a member of SOG were taken in the Cabash area of Algiers. Chandler was there to meet with an asset that had possible intelligence on the AQIM, as well as the hacker responsible for selling the intelligence to them that caused the downing of a Black Hawk six weeks ago."

A few muttered curses rumbled around Wyatt from his buddies. "You know the officer?" he asked.

It'd only been a few years since Jessica left the Agency, so it was possible.

"We met a few times," Jessica replied. "A bit of a hell-raiser."

"Like you, Peaches?" Bravo Three and his love to get under Jessica's skin . . .

Wyatt hid a laugh at the sight of Jessica's scowl directed Asher's way.

"Anyway," she said as if biting on the word, "the guy she was meeting up with betrayed her. From the sound of it, she and her partner were ambushed by at least ten armed men."

"Their man on overwatch managed to take out several tangos, but he couldn't prevent the abduction," Luke added, his voice grim.

"And why are we going in? Why not send in additional paramilitary forces or—"

"They're still waiting for the green light," Jessica cut off Owen, who served as Bravo Two. "They're trying to coordinate with the Algerian government, but they're assuming if the AQIM is responsible, this is a ransom situation."

"The request for us to move in and now is coming straight from POTUS. Not only is Chandler an operations officer, but she's the daughter of Admiral Warren Chandler," Luke said, his tone graver than if the words had been delivered by the Grim Reaper himself. "And the man with her was a Green Beret before joining SOG. Family friend of the Chandlers as well."

"This should be a quick in and out rescue and recovery operation." Jessica flipped her iPad screen around to showcase the man and woman they'd be going after.

Wyatt's brows pinched, and he took a step back. *You gotta be bloody kidding.*

Natasha Chandler. *The* Natasha. The woman he'd thought about tracking down after Clara's wedding to pick up where they left off after that kiss on the beach.

He'd resisted finding her because she seemed sweet and innocent, and he was the exact opposite of what she probably needed—a shag and nothing more.

He'd joked she was CIA, but she'd easily tricked him with a little spy tradecraft.

He wasn't sure if he was pissed at her lie, though he had no right to be given his current line of work, or, if possible, even more turned on and intrigued by the woman.

But she was also being held captive by a terrorist group, so he'd have to put his thoughts on hold.

"Echo's got this," Wyatt volunteered his team, working the words loose around the knot forming in his throat.

Luke nodded. "Then Owen can serve as extract."

Owen spun his ball cap around and his hands went straight to his hips. He'd been a naval pilot before becoming a Teamguy, choosing to follow in his brother's footsteps, who'd died serving their country as a SEAL. Owen's flying skills came in handy more times than Wyatt could count.

45

Jessica showcased an aerial view of Algiers on her tablet. "Chandler's wearing a tracking device, so we have her GPS coordinates. The military has a drone up monitoring every move of their abductors. Six enemy combatants have them held at a house about a klick away from a historic Ottoman palace. They're north of the beach near the Caves of Jijel. The landscape is rugged, which makes it pretty isolated. You should be able to get in without any eyes on you."

"Too bad they didn't take them back to their compound, it would've been nice to track them there and take out their entire base upon arrival." He'd love nothing more than to get revenge for the men taken down on the Black Hawk.

"Unfortunately, they're not dumb enough to do that," Luke commented.

"What's the infil plan?" Wyatt asked.

"You'll insert in a few kilometers offshore," Luke ordered. "Take a Zodiac craft with you, then when you get close enough, swim in. Hide your equipment in one of the caves."

Wyatt looked around at his teammates, who stood stoic, prepared despite the lack of sleep. A.J., his right-hand man as Echo Two, gave him a firm *We got this* nod.

"Rules of engagement?" Roman asked, who served as Echo Four and their comms chief when he wasn't rotating as main sniper with Wyatt. He hadn't gone to sniper school like Wyatt, but every man on their team was well-equipped to be both an assaulter and sniper. Hell, medic and breacher when needed, too.

"I'm pretty sure you're not getting in and out of there without taking some lives," Jessica said. "This is Admiral Chandler's daughter, after all. Do what you have to do."

"These the same assholes responsible for taking down the

Black Hawk in Algeria, or are they hired help?" Bitter anger crawled through Owen's tone, mimicking the rage Wyatt felt on the inside at American lives lost.

Luke let go of a deep breath. "Looks like they're with the AQIM, so engage as if they shot the missile at the Black Hawk themselves." The guys began to disperse to prep for the mission, but Luke shot a hand out to stop Wyatt from leaving with his team. "You sure you want to do this? You've been up for almost two days. I can head this one up."

The sultry sound of Natasha's voice floated to mind, and he had to blink a few times to pull himself back to the present.

If anything happened to that woman . . .

He shook his head, and Luke released Wyatt's arm.

"No, I'm good. And if I've been up for two days, you're probably looking at day three without rack time."

"One more thing." Jessica's blue eyes, the same shade as her brother's, landed on Wyatt. "The admiral wants his daughter brought back here, and she's not to leave until he arrives."

"Holding her prisoner, huh?" He had no idea what Natasha was like in the field, but he couldn't imagine she'd be thrilled about a bunch of secretive former SEALs telling her she had to stay put and wait for her dad. "And what about the contractor with her?" he asked when Jessica's silence served as response enough to his prisoner quip.

"He's to catch the first flight back to Algiers per the Chief of Station's orders," she answered. "Natasha will most likely not be a fan of this plan. If she's anything like me, she'll be pissed her cover was blown."

"What, she won't be happy to see our handsome faces?" A.J. joined in on the conversation and threw an arm around

Wyatt's shoulder. "I'm sensing this Natasha woman is a feisty one?"

"Don't get any ideas," Wyatt grumbled, not meaning to let the order slip through, but like hell would he have A.J. hitting on her, especially now that he knew she wasn't some telecommunications specialist at the State Department.

No, not only was she CIA, she was the admiral's daughter.

"You good, Chief?" A.J. dropped his hand when Wyatt faced him.

Not really. "I know our target," he said once Jessica and Luke were out of earshot. "Hell," he added, "I've even kissed her."

* * *

A FEW HOURS LATER, ALL FIVE ECHO GUYS WERE INSIDE A plane similar to a C-130, prepping to jump off the coast of Algeria. Luke had hired the same pilot they'd used on the op in Ibiza, a former Air Force officer who lived in Spain.

Their team didn't have the luxury of operating with official military planes given they didn't technically exist, but they did have friends with access to fun toys.

One, in particular, was an expat living in Spain who had a rare collection of military vehicles. It was his plane they were currently flying in, and it'd be his customized Black Hawk Owen would swoop in on for Echo's extract.

The wealthy expat had somehow designed the helo to be on point with the stealth bird used to infil Bin Laden's compound. The tail rotor had extra blades to reduce the noise, along with modifications to the main rotor for sound reduction. And a paint job to make it difficult for infrared sensors to spot. Plus, a few more mods.

Admiral Chandler knew Luke's team was being sent in to rescue his daughter, but the president had explained they were being hired as private military contractors, similar to SOG.

Having the cover of Scott & Scott came in handy for operations such as the one tonight. And apparently, the admiral didn't care what enemy lines were crossed as long as his daughter returned alive. He didn't want her spending weeks in some cage until the government chalked up a ransom, or even worse, was killed with her death broadcast online.

"Ready to save your girl?" A.J. asked while standing in preparation to exit the aircraft.

"Shut the bloody hell up." He rolled his eyes and moved his goggles into place.

A few minutes later, the guys dropped the Zodiac CRRC (combat rubber raiding craft) out before jumping.

Parachuting into the sea in the dead of night wasn't exactly Wyatt's favorite activity, but he'd do what needed to be done, especially to save Natasha.

"Good to go," he said once they were in the boat.

They anchored eight hundred meters from shore and changed into their black skin suits and put on their fins.

A.J. stared out at the water. "Any jaws of death out there?"

"This is the sea," Roman reminded him. "But there have been a few shark sightings in history."

"You could've lied to me, brother," A.J. said with a shake of the head and secured his goggles in place.

"Then you shouldn't have asked him," Wyatt retorted with a laugh, then hopped into the water first.

He peered over his shoulder every thirty seconds or so as they swam, checking to make sure his brothers were good. No surprise sea attacks, thank God.

Once on the beach, they got rid of their fins, peeled off their wetsuits, and hid their gear inside the closest cave with the use of camo netting.

"Tracker is set," Roman announced after placing the device in their gear inside the cave to transmit their location to Owen for pick-up.

"The house is less than one klick north." Wyatt eyed the GPS tracker for Natasha's location and pointed in the direction they needed to head. "Heads on a swivel, guys."

"Roger," the guys said in unison, then lowered their night-vision goggles into place and moved into formation.

Normally on an op, he wasn't thinking about the target. Not about her hair, smell, the sound of her voice. He couldn't help but wonder if Natasha would recognize him. And would he feel guilty when he pulled the classified card and lied about who he was and what he truly did for a living? *She lied*, he reminded himself.

And he'd lied to every woman he'd met since he started working directly for POTUS in 2013. But the night he'd met Natasha, he'd opened up, allowed more honest words than normal to roll smoothly from his tongue.

Wyatt returned his focus to the op and held up a gloved fist while stopping, signaling to the guys to stay put. He checked the satellite feed on the screen on his wrist. "Two vehicles parked outside the building, and we've got movement on the east side of the home and near the north entrance."

Wyatt set his eyes on the property up ahead, which appeared as if it'd barely survived a drone strike or a bombing in recent years.

"The place looks like it's being held together by some strong-ass glue and maybe prayers," A.J. said over comms.

"Yeah, keep that in mind when we go in," he responded into his mic. "I don't want it collapsing on anyone." Wyatt directed his guys to filter out to their designated positions. The plan was to storm the home as quickly as possible to maintain the element of surprise. "This is One. North guard down," he announced after firing a suppressed shot.

"This is Four. East guard down," Roman said next.

"Infil now," Wyatt gave the order, and his team breached as planned.

A rickety old ladder was perched at the backside of the house, and Chris, Echo Three, maneuvered up the thing like a damn ninja to get to the second floor. Once he was in position, the rest of the team split up to infil the home from the front and back.

It was a classic ambush. A quick in and out before the sons of bitches knew what hit them.

Just another Friday.

His guys popped out rounds with precision with their suppressed M4s, taking down three tangos inside. Where was the last guy?

"This is Three. Second level clear," Chris announced.

Wyatt did a quick scan of the interior. The building was free of furniture. The definition of open concept. Half the roof, including part of the second floor, was missing when he glanced up to see the pitch-black sky.

He moved his NVGs out of his way and used the light on the rifle to guide him as he maneuvered around the empty space.

"First floor clear." *Where the hell are they?*

"Shit, there's a tunnel back here," A.J. said over comms. "Going—" He let go of his words, and Wyatt rushed to his location.

A.J. yelled out something a moment later, then Wyatt spotted him walking backward out of the tunnel entrance with his hands up.

Wyatt lowered his M4 at the sight of Natasha and the contractor exiting the old arched tunnel entrance side by side. Jack London had a rifle aimed at A.J.

With Echo Two in his camo gear without the American flag on his chest, it'd be harder for Jack to recognize A.J. as one of the good guys.

"We're Americans." Wyatt let go of his rifle, allowing the sling to catch it, so he could demonstrate he wasn't a threat. "Admiral Chandler sent us."

Natasha's eyes darted his way, and she stepped forward, mouth agape.

She looked unharmed, thank God.

"So, definitely not a telecommunications specialist, then," he mused, doing his best not to smile given the situation.

"And you're *not* retired." Her voice cracked in surprise. He didn't exactly blame her. He'd come in looking like Rambo—okay, he wished he was Rambo because the man was basically a badass and who wouldn't want to be him?— but yeah, surely seeing a guy she'd almost slept with at her ex's wedding had to be a surprise.

But . . . how in the hell had she known he'd retired? "You, uh, okay?"

Jack lowered the shitty modified AK with a 100-round drum attached to it he'd probably swiped from the AQIM soldier. "We're not injured."

Wyatt peered back at Natasha who was still staring at him. Not quite a deer-caught-in-headlights look but close enough. She had a red headscarf hanging loosely around her neck, which accentuated her blonde hair. Her clothes were about on point with Jessica. Plain long-sleeved shirt and denim. Barely any makeup.

"We're fine," she murmured. "Who do you work for?"

"Private contractors," A.J. replied before Wyatt had a chance to lie. "There wasn't time to get another team here, and we were nearby." He extended a gloved hand. "Glad to see you both alive."

"What happened in the tunnel?" Wyatt asked.

"Some asshole shoved us in there, but Jack handled him and got our zip ties off." She peered around the open space. "I assume you killed everyone?" A bite of irritation moved through her tone.

She wanted someone alive to interrogate. Of course. He didn't blame her, but his priority had been to rescue her and Jack.

Natasha crouched next to one of the dead arseholes and patted him down. "Nothing."

She was alive and safe. Didn't appear to be shaken up at all.

How long had she been with the Agency?

"We're ready for extraction, Bravo Two," he alerted Owen over his radio.

"Five mikes out," Owen answered.

"We need to get a move on it. Got a helo coming in to pick us up a klick from here." Wyatt motioned for Natasha and Jack to exit.

"Someone might have something of use." She'd already moved on to her second body, checking the man's pockets.

"We don't want to wait around and see if these arseholes might have had a chance to send for backup." Wyatt crouched across from her and extended a hand. "Please."

She ignored his palm and sputtered, "Just one more

second." She pushed upright and started for the other body before he could protest.

"Hey, just got word from Jessica," Chris said, barreling toward them. "It looks like we're going to need to do a rapid extract. Got three heavily armed Jeeps heading for our position."

"Time to go." Wyatt swirled a finger in the air, motioning for them to head out. "Now," he added when Natasha was still bent over a body.

"Tasha!" Jack snapped.

"I got a phone!" She stood upright and peered at Wyatt. "Now we can go."

He shook his head while keying in his mic. "Bravo Two, prepare for a rapid extract."

"Roger that, One," Owen answered over the radio.

"Stay between us," Wyatt ordered once outside.

The rocks and sand kicked up beneath their boots as they sprinted. "What's the status on our incoming, Three?" he asked Chris as they closed in on the beach.

"Two mikes out, let's make this snappy," Chris responded.

"Whoa! Wait," Natasha said once they'd made their way to the beach. She spun around to face Wyatt. "You can't be serious."

A thick black rope dangling from the Black Hawk wiggled just above their heads, and he pointed to it, signaling for her to attach herself. "We can't land. Just clip on, and the pilot will take you to a nearby naval ship."

"You did paramilitary training at the Farm, you can handle this." Jack tapped her in the side as he took the harness from Wyatt. "You can clip to me. I've got you."

Wyatt eyed her as Jack secured Natasha to his body and clipped himself to the rope. He did his best to fight the odd feeling swirling around in the pit of his stomach. What in the hell was that?

He barely knew her, but damned if he swore jealousy was kicking him in the nuts at the sight of her breasts smashed to Jack's chest as he positioned his other hand around her back.

"They're ready," he said into his radio, alerting Owen they were prepared to exfil.

Natasha looked back at Wyatt as he began slipping into his wetsuit. "You guys aren't coming with us?"

"We've got a boat." Part of him wanted to stay back and handle the Jeeps full of bad guys, but his orders had been strictly for a rescue op. "We'll meet you at the ship," he said before he changed his mind, "and we'll all board the bird and fly into Ibiza together."

"Spain?" She brought her hands to Jack's chest and pushed as if she could get away, but they were strapped together, and the helo was beginning to lift. "No, I can't go to Spain! Let me down! Damn it, guys. Let me . . ." Her words died in the air as Owen swept them away.

"Shit, brother. She's gonna kill us on that ship," A.J. said with a laugh.

"We might have to knock her out with something to get her to Ibiza," Finn remarked as they prepared to go into the sea before the AQIM reinforcements got to them. "Looks like the extract part is gonna be a walk in the park compared to keeping her captive on the island."

"You gonna tell the admiral we couldn't get his daughter to follow orders?" Chris held both palms in the air and then turned for the sea. His fins slapped the sand as he moved to the water. "Good luck with that."

"Well," A.J. started, "now that I've met her, I'm betting that woman's one hell of a kisser. Maybe you can use your tongue to convince her to stay."

"A.J.," he warned just as the pop-pop-pop of gunfire sprayed in the distance. "I guess since they found us," he began while securing a hand on his rifle, "we should stick around and take out these terrorist arseholes before we go."

A.J. grinned. "Hooyah, brother."

CHAPTER FIVE

IBIZA

"YOU'RE GONNA TWIST YOUR ANKLE. WOULD YOU WAIT UP?"

Natasha shot a quick look back at Wyatt trailing behind her as she made her way down the rocky path. The access to Aguas Blancas was difficult. Actually, getting to the beach wasn't as difficult as trying to get the hell out of the area where the estate was located. It was perched at the top of a steep cliff in the middle of nowhere, and she'd spent an hour trying to get away.

Since she couldn't manage to escape, she'd been pissed and needed a moment alone.

But no, Wyatt, the hot guy from her past with the most incredible blue-gray eyes ever, wouldn't leave her the hell alone. He was too afraid she'd attempt to make another run for it.

Maybe she could hitch a ride with one of the early morning beachgoers doing a little body surfing with the wind kicking up today. Head back to Algeria and finish the job she'd started.

Damn her father and his connections.

Damn the Chief of Station who did whatever the hell the admiral wanted because her dad was golf buddies with POTUS.

"Would you, at least, let me walk next to you, so if you start to fall off the bloody cliff, I have a shot at saving your arse?" he rasped, his smooth and sexy English accent sliding through his words a bit more.

She ignored him and kept moving along the winding trail. Sweat bloomed between her breasts even though it wasn't that hot out yet. She was still in the same jeans and long-sleeved shirt she had on from when she'd been abducted yesterday.

The sun was only beginning to rise in the distance like a ball of fire. She spied the stretch of sand up ahead. The waves were white and frothy, whipped up by the wind like the top of a latte.

The beach was empty as far as she could see, but maybe if she waited, someone would show up.

When she reached the sand, she snuck another look behind her, but he was still there.

Actually, he was right freaking there. She smacked into a muscled wall, AKA his chest, and he snatched her biceps as if she might float away in the breeze.

A scowl marred his lips, lips that were fuller than most men but definitely not feminine—lips she'd never forget kissing.

There was a slight scar that cut through the edge of his blond brow, and it became more pronounced when curiosity crossed his face.

"I need to get out of here, and you guys have me trapped

like a prisoner." She remained rooted in place, wanting to get out of his grasp as much as she wanted to stay in it.

He'd saved her. Saved her friend. But she was a trained operations officer, and she didn't need a babysitter. And if Jack hadn't been ordered back to Algeria the second they'd arrived in Ibiza, she would've begged him for help out of this SEAL prison.

"My father is overstepping, and by keeping me here under his orders, so are you," she bit out, still not moving. Still not able to detach herself from the warmth of his hold. She could feel the heat of his palms even through the cotton fabric of her shirt.

"I don't work for the CIA. My job is to keep you safe, and I'm going to do that, even if it means keeping you safe from yourself." A familiar sound echoed throughout his tone—a hint of her father's concern about her safety.

"I can handle myself." She lifted her hand to his chest, intending to push away, but his heartbeat was steady beneath her touch, and she was once again confused by the feelings this man evoked in her. "And it would've been nice if you could have brought one of those assholes back alive so we could interrogate him for information."

A lazy smile crossed his face, an indication he was holding out on her.

"What aren't you saying?"

"I can't tell you now, but I'm sure you'll find out soon enough." His smile stretched after his cryptic words, and she wanted to—well, she wanted to kiss him, damn it.

She did her best to return her focus to the mission. "Well, I appreciate the save, but I have work to get back to."

"Your legend, or whatever you people call it, was blown. You go back to Algiers and you'll have a target on your head." His words were low. Smooth. Soft like the sand.

She stole a look over at the sun above the turquoise sea. If she wasn't so pissed about being held against her will, she'd take a moment to admire the gorgeous sheet of oranges, pinks, and reds slicing across the sky in layers. As that ball of fire lifted higher and higher, it was as if God had scooped it up and cradled it.

With her tongue pinned to the roof of her mouth, she considered her plan, her next words. How could she convince this rock-hard former operator to give in to her? To break the chain of command and ignore the admiral's orders?

If he was truly retired, he didn't owe anything to her father.

"You don't understand, I can't abandon my mission."

"And I can't abandon mine," he countered in a deep, husky voice. A tone of authority, one that said *Don't try me, honey*—or whatever people who weren't from the South would say. "Tell me what's so important that has you willing to risk your life."

Light continued to stream the area, throwing streaks of gold onto the high cliffs that sheltered the beach. "Classified."

He released hold of her arms and tucked his hands into his pockets.

She removed her shoes, peeled off her socks, and started for the water. Water so clear it begged to be swam in, but she only took one step in.

"Why'd you retire?" she asked when he stepped alongside her, water splashing onto his military-style khaki-colored boots. He lacked the regulation haircut, but most SEALs never followed typical Navy regs, especially DEVGRU guys, which, in her research after the wedding, she discovered he'd been.

His hair was longer, nearly flipping up beneath his plain

black ball cap. His beard full. His eyes still as magnificent as she remembered, that gorgeous shade of blue-gray.

"Classified." He released the word like a breath, a long hiss of *I can play that game, too*. "How'd you know I retired?" He had her there. "A Google search or your spy computer at work?" He peered over at her.

He had eyes that could penetrate steel. Melt titanium. Put Henry Cavill as Superman to shame.

"Why didn't you come back the night of the wedding?" she asked instead.

"And why didn't you call me if you went to the trouble of looking me up?"

"You still live in Colorado? I only found one residence, and it was pretty well hidden from public record. Hiding something from Uncle Sam?"

"What is it about this mission that has you willing to risk your life so freely?"

She faced him, the water still running over her toes. Her feet sank into the soft, wet sand. Her imprint would fade soon after she left. That was her life. It was her job to come and go without being noticed.

She'd been noticed in Algeria, though. Weeks of work lost. Her cover blown. Farid had set her up, and it was her fault for being so determined to get her mark she'd missed the telltale signs of manipulation.

"Who do you really work for?" she asked.

He angled his head and folded his arms across his chest, his biceps straining against the fabric of his olive-green tee. She resisted the impulse to view the ink on his right arm that edged close to the top of his elbow.

"Are we going to keep answering every question with a question?"

She lifted her chin and captured his eyes. "That's another question."

He released a long sigh. "I got called away to work after the wedding. I do have a place in Colorado. It's my only permanent home, and I like my privacy. I work for a security company, and we're contractors for hire." A whisper of a growl pushed through his lips. A rumbling that stemmed from deep within his chest. "Your turn."

Her defenses, normally indestructible, were crumbling with his eyes on her. "I asked Clara for your last name." She'd covertly worked it into conversation since neither her brother nor Jack had the stones to do it. "I used Google until Google wasn't cutting it. I was going to call but then I got pulled away for work."

"And the other part? The mission?" He stroked his thick beard, a beard she couldn't help but imagine gliding along the inside of her leg as his mouth met the sensitive area of her—

"Still classified." His question should have served as an effective buzzkill to the highly inappropriate thoughts swimming around in her head, but it didn't.

She'd been working nonstop and somewhere along the line had forgotten the art of a good fantasy. This man, standing before her like temptation personified, had woken up her libido and pushed it onto a runaway train. She'd gone months without orgasms, even self-induced, and her body needed one. Being held hostage—this wasn't her first time, either—had never left her feeling horny afterward. Why would it? But this was the first time she'd been rescued by a sexier and taller version of Tom Hardy, or maybe that Scottish actor she'd pined over a few years ago. *What was his name?* And even Wyatt's presence had her forgetting famous men's names? *Great.*

"You're after the AQIM members responsible for the

Black Hawk crash. And the hacker who sold them the intel." Wyatt's knowledge of her mission startled her back to reality.

"How the hell do you know about the hacker?" This time, she was the one grabbing hold of his arm.

"Classified." He winked and turned back toward the sea, and she lost her hold of him. "While I respect your desire to complete your mission, I feel like there's more to it than that. Like it's become personal." His voice grew deeper. Gravelly. A *don't try me, I'll pin you down* kind of tone.

"It's my fault." Her admission slipped through the cracks, flowing almost too freely for her comfort, and yet, she felt compelled to share more. "My failure to apprehend the hacker resulted in the deaths of those men. If I'd caught him, he never could have sold that intel, and those men would still be alive." She faced the rocky cliffs. The estate was off in the distance in a strategically remote location. It was more like a rich man's compound with concrete walls and gate cameras.

"You can't blame yourself."

"Tell me . . . if you hadn't rescued me in time, and I had died, would you have felt guilty?" She stole a look at him, and his mouth became a tight line. She didn't need or want pity or forgiveness, she was fine with understanding, and she had a feeling if anyone got her, it'd be him. "Why was your team sent for us?" She fully faced him, and the hard line of his bearded jaw tightened.

"We were local."

She drew in a breath when his gaze lifted to find hers. A shadow of grief darkened his eyes and washed over his features before he looked away. "What is it?"

His hand went back to his beard as if he were buying himself time to get the words out, or to try and keep his thoughts locked away. "I lost someone on my team not too long ago. Pretty sure intel was leaked because of a hacker. How long have you been tracking this guy?"

Ohh . . . "Six months. He'd been on the FBI's radar first, but when he started selling intelligence to terrorists, his case landed in my lap." She was quiet before asking, "Was Marcus Vasquez who you lost? Was he on your team?" She couldn't imagine what it'd be like to lose someone like that. She'd never lost a teammate, and she hoped she never would.

His eyes locked on hers at the mention of Marcus's name, and he slowly nodded.

"I don't think the hacker I'm chasing was responsible, but I heard about what happened to him." She crossed the short space between them. "I'm so sorry."

He was quiet for a solid minute, taking the time to tuck away his emotions where most Teamguys she knew usually kept them—behind fortified walls guarded by fire-breathing dragons.

When Wyatt spoke again, his voice was clear and steady. "I'm sure you'll get your man. From what I've seen, you're not one to give up, and I respect that. But do everyone a favor, don't get killed in the process of going after him." He was quiet before adding, "We wouldn't want your father going all *scorched-earth-policy* on the world, burning everything down in the name of revenge, right?"

"He wouldn't go to that extreme." Well, hopefully not.

"He's a dad. If someone hurt my daughter there wouldn't be a hole or a hell he could hide in."

"You have a daughter?" That hadn't turned up in her research.

"Not that I know of," he said with a smirk before it quickly faded. "I don't plan on having kids because I don't think I could handle bringing them up in this nightmare of a world we live in."

"How can we ever fix the world if we don't have kids, ones we can raise to hopefully make things better?" And most days, well, she actually believed her own words.

He briefly dropped his eyes to the sand. "Does that mean you're looking to have a bunch of little ones running around in the future? I thought you were going to be forever single?"

"I can still have kids on my own." She released a shaky breath, her lungs refusing to work properly as emotion weighed heavy. "But first, I need to find this asshole before he hurts anyone else."

"And you will. But if you head back to Algeria, I'll have to go in and save you, and what if I take a bullet in the process?" There was a sparkle in his eyes, a touch of humor in his tone despite the grave words he'd spoken. A request to get her to back down by trying to find some sort of Achilles heel to use against her.

"We wouldn't want that," she whispered as he brought his face closer to hers like he might dare kiss her.

He cocked his head, and his lips parted.

No words.

No kiss, either.

Silence stretched the length of the sandy white beach until he suggested, "Why don't you get some rest?"

"Sure," she murmured, partially wishing this moment had gone a different direction.

She put her socks and shoes back on without saying more, and they kept the quiet going as they made the journey back to the estate.

Her one-bedroom villa was surrounded by palm trees, colorful hibiscus, and fragrant orange trees. She breathed in the citrusy aroma as she took in the view and wondered what it would be like to take a vacation someday.

Once inside her temporary quarters, she moved along the

terracotta-tiled floor to get to the four-poster bed, which was draped in sheer linens. The bed, the luxurious satin comforter, it all fed into her ridiculously romantic fantasies.

Overhead were olive wood ceilings, and two thick wooden beams served as the sole divide between the bedroom and living room. The setting could've been from the show *The Bachelor,* which she'd never admit she watched, but it was her guilty pleasure, a way to forget the evil of the world for an hour or two.

"Meet your standards?" He leaned against one of the beams and crossed his ankle over his foot.

She sat down on the bed and smiled. "Are you going to be keeping post outside to make sure I sleep and don't make a run for it?"

"*Another* run for it, you mean?" He smirked, flashing his straight white teeth.

Fair. "I won't." Although she wasn't eager to face her father, either. He was going to try and get her sent back to Headquarters.

"Full disclosure, there are cameras outside this villa. If you do try and jet off, we'll know about it."

She held a palm in the air. "I'm solid. I promise."

"Good."

He turned and started for the door, but she couldn't stop herself from asking, "Do you have to go?" She wasn't ready to be alone yet. Last night was still an echo in her ears, in her mind, too.

He stilled, and the fabric of his tee cinched tight down the middle of his back as the muscles drew together. "Not yet."

She stood. "So don't."

Natasha wasn't sure what in the world she was doing, but there was some primordial stuff swirling around inside of her.

See hot guy.

Do hot guy.

A sudden spike in her hormones had her wishing he'd pull her into his arms and make her his in every way.

It'd be nice to swap her memories of last night for new ones.

As Wyatt slowly pivoted to face her, her lip went between her teeth as she observed the indecision on his face.

The tiredness in his eyes was slowly lifting like a curtain to expose his desire.

"If you leave me alone, I might break my promise. I don't always think clearly when I'm hell-bent on getting what I want." Honesty and truth imbued her words, but her stomach clenched tight at the risky use of such bold speech.

"And why else do you want me to stay?" He traversed the room as if it were littered with landmines. Cautious steps. A careful assessment of her. "I thought you were mad I was keeping you a so-called prisoner."

"There's nothing 'so-called' about what you're doing," she quipped.

He planted his hands into his pockets and remained a good two feet away. "So, why should I stay? Tell me." His words rang with command. With a gentle ease of authority it was clear he still had in his line of work, even in private security.

Her heart palpitated, but she did it. She closed the space between them. "You know what I'm thinking."

"Maybe I need to hear it? Maybe I need to know you're as crazy as me for wanting to have sex . . ." He sucked in a sharp breath when her fingers slid up the center of his chest. ". . . after what happened in Algeria."

"I think we're in the same boat of crazy, don't you?" She angled her head, and he brought his palm to her cheek. "I could've died last night, and I wish I could say that's not the norm for me, but I have a tendency to get myself into shit situations, but I also think that—"

His mouth captured hers, and she relaxed into his arms.

He groaned before deepening the kiss, before slipping his magnificently skilled tongue into her mouth.

"Damn, Natasha," he murmured a few heartbeats later.

He knocked his hat loose as he reached behind him, peeled his shirt over his head, and tossed it.

Muscles. More ink. A work of art, and she ran her greedy hands all over his body before he pulled her closer.

She surrendered to his next kiss. A harder one. More intense. The perfect amount of pressure and sweeping of tongue.

His beard scratched her face a little, but she didn't care. She was too caught up by lust, by her need to be his after years of wondering what had happened to him. She'd almost begun to think that night on the beach in San Diego had been a figment of her imagination. But he was indeed real. He was there and holding her. Kissing her.

The same electric energy from the night of the wedding still raged between them hotter than ever.

Leaning back, he guided her top over her head, his fingertips dragging along her heated skin.

She fell onto the bed, and he climbed on top of her without missing a beat.

Her black bra wasn't lacy or sexy. It was standard. Boring. Plain Jane in the CIA. But the way he held himself over her, his eyes devouring her, it was as if he were standing at the end of a Victoria's Secret runway, and she was striding toward him with a confident strut and bright red angel wings attached.

Not a lick of makeup. She'd had her wrists zip-tied last night, and a bandana wrapped around her mouth.

And here she was now in a romantic setting while Jack was back in Algiers, where she should've been and . . . *damn it.*

"You want me to stop?" He'd read her thoughts, her sudden nerves. Somehow he'd known the creep of doubt trying to break in.

"I should've been on the plane with Jack," she admitted as her palm raced across his pec.

He started to pull away, but she snaked a hand around the back of his neck to keep him in place.

"I mean, I should be working," she clarified in case he'd thought Jack was more than a friend and co-worker.

"So should I." He brought his mouth back to hers and nipped her bottom lip. "We can stop."

But her response was to lift her hips, desperate to be closer. To have him inside of her. She wanted to grind herself against the erection in his heavy-duty cargo pants.

Her nipples strained against the fabric of her bra as she shifted and rotated against his hard length.

She was about to ask if he had a condom by any chance when an unfamiliar voice met her ears. "Ahem."

She opened her eyes, and Wyatt stilled on top of her. They both turned their heads to the side to see who was there, who was watching them lose control.

A man she recognized from the rescue was standing in front of the glass door with a giant grin on his face. "I knocked, but you didn't hear."

"What's up, Finn?" Anger, mixed with an *I don't give a fuck what you want, just go away,* filled his tone.

"Thought you'd want to know Admiral Chandler caught an earlier flight than expected. Luke and Asher went to pick him up."

Her father showing up would be a nightmare. Wyatt could

handle himself, but she didn't need for him to be on the receiving end of her father's wrath.

Finn turned and left, and Wyatt dropped his forehead to hers. "Well, shit."

"You prefer my dad not go all *scorched-earth* on ya, huh?" Humor was her go-to in the face of disappointment.

Maybe this Finn guy had saved her from making a mistake, though? Could she have handled a one-morning stand—*is that a thing?*—or would she have wanted more after?

She could talk a big game, vow that she was forever single, but sex without strings had never worked for her during college. Why would now be any different, especially with a man like Wyatt?

"I really don't want to stop." He pushed up and held the brunt of his weight above her with his palms positioned on each side of her body. "But it's not ideal for the admiral to walk in on me devouring the daughter I was hired to rescue."

He rolled off her and stood to snatch his shirt and hat.

She grabbed her shirt as well and pulled it over her head. "Probably not, but it'd make for great TV," she said with a laugh. *More joking. I'm just batting a thousand.* "I'm super out of practice with the sex stuff. I've been living up to my whole 'forever single' thing as you can see."

She'd had sex since she'd seen Wyatt at the wedding, but her biyearly teeth cleaning appointments were more regular than her orgasms.

"I would've loved to do a hell of a lot of practicing with you today." He smiled. "But maybe it's for the better?"

"Wrong place, wrong time." *Again.*

"I really hope you don't stay single forever, by the way," he said while putting on his hat.

"Why is that?" she asked, her voice soft, the promise of something more still hanging in the air between them.

"You're one hell of a woman." He tugged on the brim of his ball cap. "I don't have to know you well to see that. And any man would give his left nut to have a chance at even one night with you, let alone a lifetime."

"Not his right one?" she joked. "But what about you? You thinking about ever settling down?"

"Marriage won't happen for me."

"You married Clara." *Why am I such a buzzkill?* That was supposed to be her father's job.

"That's because I was young, and I hadn't yet realized I'm not cut out for marriage." His voice was low, flat. Sheltering her from hearing any possible emotions. Keeping her from seeing inside to get to the truth about why he didn't want to remarry.

A cold shiver rolled over her skin at his words. "I assume it's not because of the monogamy part." She was reaching. Poking. It was in her nature to push and prod. To get sources to turn and divulge info, and it was so second nature she hadn't realized she was even using her tradecraft on him.

He shook his head. "The knowing how to love part is where I'll fail."

An achy pain crawled into her chest. "That's really sad," she admitted before she could catch the truth from slipping past her carefully crafted defenses that today were made of sticks and straw, no slathering of cement between the cracks like normal. "I'm sorry, I didn't mean—"

"It's quite alright." He stepped away from her. The demarcation line now drawn. His boundaries had been reset. Rescuer. Rescued. "I thought I loved Clara, but she, uh, made me realize that I'm just not capable of that."

71

She couldn't stop herself from reaching for his wrist, and his pulse climbed beneath her thumb.

"Those guys who were with you when you rescued me— you care about them? Would you die to protect them?"

"Of course."

Her brows knitted. "Then I think you're wrong. You're not incapable of love."

"That's different. They're like brothers."

"Mm. I don't know. I think there's a difference between capability and want. And maybe you don't want to love. Maybe you're like me, and loving is just too scary. You're afraid of getting hurt again."

She was about to get kicked back to Langley, and here she was having some profound conversation about love and sharing her own fears with the man who killed a bunch of bad guys to save her. What was going on?

"Maybe you're right." He pressed his lips into a hard, almost unforgiving line. She'd expected more to follow, but he left his thoughts unfinished. Perhaps like her, he didn't really have a damned idea what else to say on the matter.

CHAPTER SIX

"As tired as I am, I was thinking about heading to town and hitting up a club to see what all the fuss is about." Finn stifled a yawn, sitting on the retro flower-patterned couch in the living room across from Wyatt and A.J.

"*You* go to a dance club?" A.J. laughed. "Since when are you some raver?"

"I can be diverse in my choice of music and hobbies," Finn shot back.

"He's kidding, brother," Wyatt said before A.J. could respond. "And since when do you let Finn pull one over on you?"

"Must be my lack of rack time." A.J. tugged at the brim of his hat and settled more comfortably on the couch.

"How's, ahem, Chandler?" And great, maybe Wyatt would prefer joking about a nightclub than answer Finn's question.

Because Natasha was fine. More than fine.

She'd tasted and smelled incredible. Her lips had fit perfectly with his. Her body, too. She was funny, and her humor in crazy situations matched his own. They were both

BRITTNEY SAHIN

probably messed up from their own past experiences—war and relationships. They were perfectly imperfect together, and that scared the bloody hell out of him.

"Why do I feel like I'm missing something?" A.J. spoke up.

"Our boy was getting naked with the pretty CIA officer, and I had to rain on his party." Finn rolled his lips inward to hide a grin.

"It's parade," A.J. quipped. "Rain on his parade."

"Whatever." Finn rolled his eyes.

"But hell, I shouldn't be surprised since you two have swapped spit in the past." A.J. swatted Wyatt's leg with the back of his hand.

Finn lowered his elbows to his knees and leaned forward. "Whoa. What happened now?"

Wyatt looked skyward, wishing he could make both his mates disappear right now.

Natasha in that black bra blew back to mind. Her fit body. Her amazing smile. Those eyes—damn, now he understood how Helen of Troy had launched a thousand ships. Natasha could easily be his Helen, the woman to make him lose his senses.

He needed to calm down. To get his mind, not just his dick, to ease up. To back off.

She's Admiral Chandler's daughter. She's CIA.

I'd rather jump off a cliff than end up like my parents.

Divorce.

People fucking die all the time. It hurts.

Love sucks.

More reasons buzzed to mind as he attempted to squash his feelings, feelings he didn't know he was still capable of having.

"Wyatt met Chandler at his ex-wife's wedding a few years

74

back, ain't that some shit?" A.J. was talking, divulging the details he'd shared last night before the rescue. Damn him. "Luke showed up and made him the offer to join the team, and he never got a chance to close the deal."

His abbreviated story summed it up—tie a ribbon and put a bow on it.

But he needed to shut down the part of his brain that kept yelling to get her digits so he could see her again. "Why the hell did I tell you that?"

"Looks like I ruined it for you today. Sorry," Finn said as the sliding glass door opened, drawing Wyatt's attention to Jessica entering the room.

Saved by the boss.

"And?" Wyatt stood, hoping they'd have some good news to deliver Natasha.

"CIA Director Rutherford spoke to the COS at our embassy in Algeria, and between the phone recovered, and the tracking device you tagged that guy with on the beach—"

"We got a location on the AQIM compound?" A.J. interrupted, on his feet as well. "Tell me we get to go in and take those fuckers out ourselves? Get some payback for that helo crash."

"Wait, what?"

Wyatt's attention swerved to Natasha now stepping up alongside Jessica. The woman had stealth-like skills to sneak up on them like that.

Jessica's forehead tightened. She was usually more careful than to let an outsider hear intel, but they hadn't slept in days, and was Natasha really even an outsider?

"The military isn't planning a drone strike, are they? I was hoping to find evidence that could lead us to the hacker who sold them the intel," Natasha spoke quickly, worry in her tone. "I mean," she sputtered, "I want those guys taken out, but I also have to think about the hacker's next target—prevent another attack from happening."

"I get that," Jessica began, "but this is out of our hands. And as for the operational plan, we're not being clued in since it won't be our team handling this."

"Damn it." A.J. dropped a few more curses, removed his hat and slapped it against his leg.

"But these bastards will be taken down, try and focus on that." Wyatt wished he could make her feel better, but he also understood her concerns. Payback was one thing, but stopping the next attack and saving more lives was the number one priority.

Natasha folded her arms, standing her ground. "Who will be calling the shots? Who do I need to talk to?"

Damn, this woman had balls of steel.

She was a hardened CIA officer after her target once again and not the soft woman who'd writhed beneath him earlier. All business, no sex. He had to get his head back on straight and focus, too.

But her lips.

Her stubbornness.

Her gorgeous smile.

Her damn everything.

It was like he'd painted her with infrared, and she was all he could see in his scope. Bang straight in his crosshairs.

"You know how these things work," Jessica said, her ice-blue eyes fixed on Wyatt for an assist as if she sensed there was a connection between him and Natasha.

He brought a fist to his mouth and tapped it there as he tried to figure out what to say.

"I need to go back to Algiers and find my source. He betrayed me, but if he's still alive, I might—"

"He's dead," Jessica cut her off. "Farid's body turned up outside the city."

Natasha cursed under her breath, crossed the room, then brushed past Wyatt and swung the door open to get outside.

"She's like someone else I know." Finn bit back a smile, eyes on Jessica. "You two make a pair."

"I'll talk to her," Wyatt offered.

"Thanks. Wheels up in an hour. We're heading back to New York," she replied. "The admiral should be here soon."

Wyatt wrapped a hand over the doorknob and looked back at them. "She's gonna be angry."

"More than she already is?" A.J. joked.

"I can't say I blame her." Jessica glanced at her wristwatch and then twirled a finger in the air to get a move on.

He nodded and went outside in search of Natasha, hoping she hadn't attempted to run again.

Thankfully, she'd parked herself on a bench near the perimeter of the estate. He slowly strode toward her, searching for her gaze, and she finally lifted her eyes to meet his. Her shoulders relaxed, and she pressed her back to the metal bench, which was wedged between two palm trees.

"Sorry. I'm just upset."

"I get it. Trust me, I do." He pointed to the bench, and she slid to the right to let him take a seat next to her. "But like I said earlier, I know you'll find him. And I'm sure whoever is dispatched to go after the AQIM will be successful in taking them down."

"This hacker, he's good, though. Really damn good. And I'm worried he's only just getting started—that this is the beginning." Her voice trembled slightly. "And if I don't stop him sooner rather than later, how many more people will die?"

He eyed her palm on her thigh and slipped his hand on top of hers. "You have to focus on what you can do, not what you can't control."

"But I like being in control." A tight-lipped smile crossed her face.

He gently squeezed her hand. "Believe me, so do I." He continued to hold her eyes, and she shifted on the bench to better face him.

They were caught in some type of cosmic moment, and they stayed that way for a little while, sitting in the quiet, listening to the sounds of the sea off in the distance, somehow understanding each other without speaking.

They were one and the same, weren't they?

"You'll find him." He finally released her hand and forced himself to stand, to break free of their shared moment. He didn't usually allow himself to have such moments, not that he'd ever found anyone who'd managed to freeze time and make the rest of the world disappear until her.

"And what will you do next?" She stood and rubbed her arms as if chilled.

He angled his head, the sun hitting him in the eyes. "Sleep on the flight back to the States."

"And after that?"

"Kill some more bad guys."

She grinned. "Thought your specialty was hostage rescue."

"They go hand in hand." He brought his focus to her luscious lips. "I guess I'll, uh, see you in another two or three years, then? And hopefully, next time won't be for a rescue." He started to turn but then peered back at her. "And, uh, go easy on your old man. He just cares about you like any father should."

She nodded solemnly. And then she flashed her gorgeous

smile, the one that traveled all the way to her eyes. "Take care of yourself, Lord Wyatt Edward Frederickson, the third."

Her words were a shot to the balls. Of course she'd discovered his given name. She was with the Agency, after all. "See ya, Chandler." He winked, then turned away, hoping he'd see her a hell of a lot sooner than three years.

PART III

OPERATION ROMANIA

Three years later

2019

CHAPTER SEVEN

LONDON (SEPTEMBER 2019)

THE RAIN WAS UNRELENTING. THE TORRENTIAL DOWNPOUR seemed fitting for a funeral, holding everyone in a pall of gloom, battering umbrellas and beating against the oak veneer of the casket in which Arthur Montgomery lay. The white lilies had succumbed to the onslaught.

Wyatt stood awkwardly on the perimeter of the gathering, doing his best to avoid everyone, including his parents. He no longer fit into the fabric of their society, which was marinated in tradition and steeped in arrogance.

He'd never belonged there. Never understood the need for peerage. The only ranking of importance to him was in the military. Respect that was hard-earned with time put in.

So, why he was about to go to the wake at the Montgomery Mansion, where he'd have to talk to people, was beyond him.

His black dress shoes, which were reserved for weddings and funerals, now carried him through the front entrance. He took slow, cautious steps as if he were in formation to assault a mudbrick home in Ramadi that had possible insurgents inside with AKs.

He'd rather be in Iraq than walking into the home of his childhood best friend. Nonetheless, a friend now gone.

The place was more of a castle than a home, though.

The stone exterior was a throwback to the medieval times. It was no Kensington Palace but the grandeur wasn't too far off. The seventy-million-dollar property sat on a private enclave at the edge of Hyde Park. Period craftsmanship. Sweeping ceilings. Pine paneling. A blend of old and new since the property had survived a fire in the 1800s, only to be partially burned down again in the 1970s.

Memory after memory surged to mind like a storm wave building higher and higher—on the verge of cresting.

He stood a few steps away from the double doors inside the front entrance, and his eyes connected with the family portrait painted by some well-known artist. Arthur had been fifteen in the painting.

Fifteen had been when Wyatt lost his virginity to the daughter of the gardener in the private cottage out back.

Sixteen had been when he and Arthur had played rugby inside the house, and he'd plowed right through the wall in the drawing room.

Sixteen had also been when they'd taken Arthur's father's Rolls-Royce out for a ride to pick up girls. One speeding ticket later . . . yeah, they'd been in deep water after that night.

Arthur's old man hadn't been amused when they'd passed out drunk in the wine cellar when they were supposed to have been grounded. And, oh yeah, two eighteen-year-old girls had been with them, too.

They'd planned and plotted their escape from London.

They would attend school in America where no one gave a damn about peerage, and women would throw themselves at them not because of their names but because of their good looks and muscles (well, back then they were both a bit lanky, but they were more built than most of their mates).

But when Arthur turned eighteen, he changed his mind about leaving London. He fell for their mutual friend Charlotte Walsh. The daughter of a marquess. Their parents had pushed for the union—a marriage right out the gates of high school. Wyatt wasn't sure if they'd been in love, not yet, at least, but a fall wedding had been planned.

More memories hurtled to mind as he remained rooted in place inside that entrance hall, not ready to step in farther and face the fact Arthur had died of cancer.

"I saw you standing at the back of the gathering during the funeral. I didn't expect you to come."

Wyatt's attention moved to Charlotte standing off to his right. She threaded her fingers through her ash-blonde hair before smoothing her palms down the sides of her black pencil skirt. Knee-length. Black shoes to match. A black silk blouse tucked into the skirt beneath a black blazer. Proper. Always proper when it came to the Walshes.

"Lady Montgomery."

"It's been twenty years, but when have you ever addressed me as lady?" Her lips twitched into a slight smile, but her eyes were watery, more so than he'd expected. It wasn't like the Walshes, the Montgomerys, and certainly not his family, to show emotion in public, not even at a funeral.

"I'm sorry about Arthur. I, uh, should've visited when I first found out." He scratched at his shaved face. He wasn't used to being without a beard, but given the day, he'd gotten rid of the facial hair.

When Wyatt learned of Arthur's cancer diagnosis, he'd

been in the middle of an op. And when that op had ended, another took its place. And then another. But he should've made time. Despite what had happened to tear their friendship apart, he'd known the guy since they were born.

"And what would you have said?" She brought her manicured nails into her palm at her side. "You hadn't spoken in twenty years, and I'm afraid that's my fault."

At her words, his focus flicked to her green eyes.

He should never have had drunken sex with Charlotte the summer before he left for San Diego . . .

"I destroyed your friendship. I'm sorry." It was the first time she had acknowledged the consequences of their actions all those years ago. She'd gone straight to Arthur the next day to tell him she had sex with his best friend, no doubt hoping it would stir up some jealousy, make Arthur stop cheating and keep his dick in his trousers before he lost her for good and pissed off both their families.

She'd used Wyatt, but he'd let himself be used. If anyone was to blame, it was him and his own fucking stupidity.

And when Arthur had come swinging at him in a public show of outrage, gossip had spread like wildfire as it always did within their social circles.

Arthur had demanded he get the hell out of London and never come back. Not so hard as far as demands went. Wyatt's bags were already packed for San Diego, which led to fight number two, this one with his old man. *You leave, don't ever come back*, had been his father's words before he'd left for Heathrow.

Over the years, he and his parents had made a pseudo-amends, but they never forgave him for taking off. He was their only child. Their miracle baby since his mum was told she couldn't have children.

Who will carry on the family name? his father had roared

when he'd discovered Wyatt had legally changed his name to Pierson, his mum's maiden name, to avoid ridicule in the Navy from the guys.

"I heard you were in London this summer," Charlotte added when he'd yet to speak.

Of course. Rumors. Gossip.

The nobles loved a good scandal as long as they weren't at the heart of it.

"I should've visited then." He'd been in town on assignment, which had led to his brothers on the Teams discovering his real last name and his peerage. "I was here for work, and—"

"Your mum is proud of you, you know. The work you did in the Navy, and now as a paramilitary contractor . . ." She forced a closed-mouth smile. "My son, Richard, Googled the term paramilitary for me so I could understand what it is you do."

"Yeah, I, um, help people." As vague as vague could get, but she seemed to accept it with a curt nod.

But also, why was his mum talking about him? She never showed much interest when they chatted on the phone, which was a rarity in itself, but to hear his mum was "proud" of him —was Charlotte mixing his mother up with someone else?

He shifted uncomfortably in his dress shoes. Regret poured inside of him, filling his lungs, making it hard to draw in a decent breath.

"Arthur was a good father, but he wasn't always the best husband." Her admission took him by surprise.

Honesty, and so out in the open, was also not very common for a Walsh or Montgomery. He wasn't sure why she felt the need to confess to him, no less.

"I heard you have tattoos." The abrupt change of topic could've given him whiplash. Her eyes lingered on the sleeves of his black jacket as if she'd be able to see through the fabric to learn if the rumors were true. Yup, he had ink, also a sailor's mouth. "You got married shortly after we did that summer."

And she was two for two on the quick convo change. He'd need airbags if it kept up.

"To a Marine, right?"

He nodded. What was he supposed to say?

"Sorry about the divorce, but I'm sure you'll find someone that makes you happy again."

Funny. Same thing Clara said to me.

A few guests cut around where they stood near the main door, and Charlotte turned to welcome them.

He tucked his hands into his pockets and eyed the room open to his left where most people were gathered to pay their respects.

He caught sight of Charlotte's father talking to two teenage boys, and he couldn't help but wonder if they were Arthur's children. From what his mum had said, they had three kids. *Two sons to carry on the name.* His mother's tone had rung with jealousy.

His eyes journeyed back to Charlotte once she'd finished welcoming the guests. "How old are your kids?"

She glimpsed her father and nodded toward the two boys talking to him. "Arthur Junior is fifteen. Richard's twelve." She angled her head to get a better vantage point of the other room, as if searching for her third child, but then straightened, giving up. "Gwen turned nineteen in March. I'm sure she's here somewhere."

Gwen. The pregnancy Charlotte had attempted to hide by moving the fall wedding to the summer. Scandal broke out. Rumors flew. She'd denounced them, and from what his mum had told him, Charlotte had declared the baby simply came six weeks early.

"Gwen goes to uni in Canada." She tightened her hands into a knot, ringing them together. Her shoulders sank a touch even though it was obvious she was doing her best to maintain the dignified posture expected of a lady. "She and Arthur had a horrible argument last summer before she left."

Another confession in public. Really?

"She wanted to follow her dreams. Reminds me of someone I know. She majors in computer programming and philosophy."

"That's great. You must be proud."

"It wasn't the path I would've chosen for a lady, but Gwen has never been much like me." Charlotte's lips pursed, and her eyes fell to the floor. "Can we, maybe, talk in private later?"

He lifted a brow. "How much later?" He wasn't planning on staying very long. In fact, he hoped to get out of there within the hour.

"After everyone leaves?" she suggested as his mobile began vibrating in his pocket.

It was his work line, which meant Jessica or Luke needed him ASAP. They wouldn't call him during the wake otherwise.

"I'm sorry," he said while producing his mobile, "but I have to step out and take this."

"Oh-okay."

He turned and brought the mobile to his ear as he went back outside. He moved under an overhang to stay out of the rain that had refused to let up.

"I'm so sorry to call right now," Jessica said when he answered.

"It's fine." He didn't want to be there anyway. "What's up?"

"Can you hop on a flight to Romania within the hour? It's a time-sensitive operation."

"Of course," he answered, not needing any more details. Anywhere was better than London. "Leaving for Heathrow now."

"You're a lifesaver, thank you. The rest of Echo Team will meet you there. I'll message you the flight details," she said. "The guys will fill you in when you arrive."

"What kind of target are we talking?"

"Remember the guy who sold intel that brought a Black Hawk down in twenty-sixteen?" she asked.

How could he forget? It was also the guy Natasha Chandler had been after.

"We think we found his location. Still don't have a name, but if the intel is correct, he's in Romania. Three hours north of Bucharest. POTUS needs him taken in alive. He's also sold intel to multiple terrorist and criminal organizations over the last few years."

"So, a gold mine. Got it." He started down the steps after ending the call, in a rush to get to his rental, but then he paused and glanced back at the home.

Could he leave without saying goodbye? Yes, but he also didn't want to be a royal prick, so he pivoted back around.

He had five minutes. He should see his parents and say goodbye to Charlotte before jetting off.

He swiped the water from his hair once he was back in the entrance hall.

He spied Charlotte talking to a cousin of hers. "Charlotte."

She turned to face him, her brows pulling together as if sensing something was wrong.

"Listen," he began, reaching for her elbow once he'd closed the distance between them. "I'm sorry, but we're going to need to have that conversation another time. I have a work emergency." Before he could say more, he spotted his parents en route to his location.

"Call me?" Charlotte asked, and he nodded, no idea what she wanted to talk about.

"Wyatt." His dad's voice was low and growly, full of spite. "You actually came."

"I thought I saw you at the funeral." His mum squeezed his arm, her version of affection, and he nodded, not sure what else to do.

His dad adjusted the knot of his black tie, and his brows moved inward as he studied him. No hug. No warmth. Not expected, anyway. If his mum didn't hug, his dad sure as hell didn't.

"I'm on my way out," he said, not in the mood for dissecting his life, which would be inevitable if he stayed.

Charlotte had caught him off guard with his mum's "proud" comment, though, because he usually heard the opposite from her.

If you're going to serve, you should've gone with the Royal Navy.

But really, why do you kill people?

Don't you worry you'll end up in hell?

I think there's something quite wrong with you. You seem to enjoy killing.

Maybe you should see a therapist. No, never mind, someone might hear about that, and the gossip would be . . .

"I came to pay my respects, but I have to head out."

"Sure. Just pop in, let people see you and whisper about—"

"Mum," he cut her off, his voice a soft plea. "I *have* to go.

91

I'm sorry."

"I don't even recognize you," his father said, his voice stiff, his eyes cold. "You dishonored me by changing your last name. We've seen you a handful of times in twenty years. Why even show up here today?"

And here we go. Why in the bloody hell would he want to stick around and engage in a conversation with them?

He pushed his hands into his pockets to hide the curl of his fingers into fists. To restrain his anger. He'd told himself over and over again their comments didn't bother him. Expecting something different from them was like being surprised to find out a terrorist set off an s-belt after promising not to.

He stabbed a finger at his dress shirt beneath the dark jacket. "It's my name now, get over it." Wyatt hadn't intended to snap at his father like a surly teenager, but he refused to get involved in a pissing match.

His mum stretched a hand out and pressed it to Wyatt's chest. "Don't make a scene."

He didn't miss this life.

Not at all.

His team was his family, and he was good with that.

"I have to go," he said through gritted teeth, doing his best not to let his irritation take another misguided route out of his mouth. He swallowed the knot in his throat and ignored the swell of pain in his chest. "Goodbye," he said as casually as possible and took off.

It'd been a mistake to come back, to try and pretend he could be the man they wished him to be for even five minutes.

He was Wyatt Pierson now. He'd shed his title, his name, and his past. If his family couldn't accept that, then he'd go be with his brothers who would.

CHAPTER EIGHT

"I DON'T UNDERSTAND. WE'VE BEEN STUCK ON HOLD, waiting for the green light to send a team over there." Natasha stood on the other side of her boss's desk at Headquarters, still trying to wrap her head around the info he'd just dropped on her.

They'd been sitting on the location of the target package for a week, not too long given how slow Washington moved, but it'd been seven days too long for her.

But was her number one target for years really dead?

"Most of the details of the operation are classified. But I thought you'd want to know he's been taken out." Her boss flattened his long, thin fingers on the maple veneer and stood to his height of five-eight. Dan was a study in brown— coffee-colored slacks, beige dress shirt, russet tie. His dark brown hair was combed to the side, with his equally dark brown eyes directed straight at her.

"The plan was to bring him in alive." Dead was

unacceptable. It was like a gaping chest wound that would forever bleed out. "Was any evidence recovered confirming it was even him who—"

"The guy had a fail-safe. He rigged the place with explosives to destroy everything while trying to make a run for it."

"But how do we know he's really dead, that he didn't escape?" Her throat constricted and her stomach burned.

"The team dispatched tried to get to him, but it wasn't possible. They had to retreat before they suffered casualties. But there's no way he made it out alive."

"And that home dates back to before World War Two." She had done her research, and she'd added all the details to her report, hoping to give the operators their best chance to secure the target when they got spun up for the mission. "The original property records listed a bunker as well as tunnels. A lot of homes in that region had them built in preparation for potential air raids." It was most likely why The Knight chose the damn location. "Did the team have the tunnels covered?"

"Within seconds of fast-roping onto the property, the place blew up."

"So, they didn't secure the tunnels?"

"Damn it, Chandler." Dan dropped back down into his leather chair, a scowl on his lips. "The team didn't even have operational authority to be in Romania. When the bastard exploded the home, they were ordered to evac immediately. It'd been an unanticipated move, and the decision was made to pull the team out rather than risk exposure."

She needed to sit now, too. She stumbled back into the chair opposite his desk.

"There was no opportunity to confirm the identity of the man inside *or* check out the tunnels. They did manage to look into the bunker and it was empty. And since we weren't "officially there, we couldn't ask the Romanians to pull DNA. To check dental records."

"Shit. So, we don't even have a name?" She was back on her feet again. "Is there some way we can get the records now, at least?"

"That's the thing." He settled farther back in his seat. "We did some checking into the Romanians' handling of the case, and it's not good. The home used to belong to a businessman, Alexander Rothus, and after he died in a car crash the property was turned over to the city, and it's been vacant ever since. The Romanians assumed it'd been a squatter who died in the explosion. There wasn't much left of the body, so the remains were cremated and labeled as unidentified."

"You're shitting me! A *squatter* rigged the home to blow, then killed himself? Give me a break!" She hadn't meant to raise her voice, but she was in no state to refrain—her emotions were going to tear her up. "There's no way we're dealing with a John Doe situation."

"What do you want me to say?" His lips flattened before he let out an exhausted sigh. "Our intelligence supports the idea The Knight was hiding there, a perfect place for someone like him. And the assumption is that when our boots hit the ground, he tried to destroy evidence and make an escape, but he died in the process. We wanted him alive, but we couldn't have predicted he'd—"

"With all due respect, sir, you're not actually telling me he's really dead right now, are you, not after this bullshit cremation story? There was probably never a body recovered at the crime scene." She dragged a hand through her hair, processing what she knew about her target.

"His strategy was to blow up the house."

"And use that as a distraction to get out through the tunnels, which surely he did!" Natasha exclaimed.

"The operators said they did see a man inside on fire, which is why we believe he never got a chance to make it out."

She shook her head. "That doesn't mean he didn't get away and pay someone off on the police force to say they found a body." How many times had they seen that? "No way is this just over, not after years of us chasing one of the most calculated and elite hackers in the world. No way did he accidentally kill himself."

"And maybe I agree with you, but the higher-ups want a win, and they like the idea this guy is dead."

"Of course they do, until he hacks the Pentagon again, or helps terrorists steal bioweapons or—"

"Chandler!"

She clamped her teeth together, frustration ringing in her ears, a hollow pit being carved out in her stomach every second the CIA believed this cocksucker was actually dead.

"If he shows up again, we go after him."

"And until then?" she asked.

"We assume he's dead."

"Because that's what the big guns want?" She huffed and spun away, unable to look at someone she used to respect before he became a spineless pawn for Washington elitists.

"You've been preoccupied with this man for over three years. And for now, it's time to move on."

She whirled back around, her temples throbbing. "He hacked *our* secure records last year, sir. He gave up the identities of agents in the field, our own officers—they were murdered! And I couldn't stop him." She held her palms open, her heart pounding, her body shaking. "There's blood on my hands, and I can't just walk away without knowing he's truly dead."

Three and a half years of chasing him. Too many innocent lives lost.

Enough was enough.

"But he kept you alive."

Guilt wrapped like a tight ribbon around her spine, and it had her bowing forward, her eyes dropping closed.

"He knows your name. It was in the case file he hacked. Be thankful you're alive, and if it was him in Romania, you got him. It's finally over."

"He kept me alive because it's a game to him, and I'm just a player. He knew I was close, and he wanted to make me suffer—to punish me by killing others and making me powerless to stop it." Emotion choked her words, but she forced herself to stand all the way upright and open her eyes. "And this was probably just another game. What if we found him because he wanted us to?"

Dan stood and circled the desk to confront her. "I think you need a vacation."

"What I need to do is talk to the team sent in after him. I need to know exactly what happened."

He pocketed his hands. "It's classified. POTUS can't divulge more than I already told you."

That was par for the course, but in this instance, she refused to take no for an answer. "Any clue who went?" she pushed. "His top-secret guys?" The president had dark money for such operations, and word was they were a group of Delta Force guys. Rumors were usually true in Washington.

"My guess is that they were in the private sector if you want to hear the truth. The mission was over and done while we were still waiting on approval to put together a team. I-I don't know who could have done this that fast, not even Delta. But it's all the more reason POTUS would have wanted the operatives to get the hell out of Romania and fast after that explosion."

Her thoughts drifted back to Algiers, to her quick rescue.

Wyatt. Private contractor. Stellar kisser. Sinfully seductive accent.

It was a stretch, but was it him? His team?

"Take a vacation, and when you come back, I'll see about putting you back out in the field."

"Yeah, um, okay," she mumbled, her mind now buzzing with questions and possibilities. "I, uh, have to go." She whipped around and started for the door.

"Chandler," he croaked out. "Don't do anything stupid."

She peered back at him. "Never, sir."

CHAPTER NINE

BOULDER

I CAN DO THIS. KNOCK ON THE DOOR. IF HE'S IN HIS CABIN banging someone, no big deal. He's not mine. Never was. Never will be.

She was there for work. For answers. Not for him. This was not an excuse to see him, to see if he still looked as good, smelled as good. *Kissed* as good.

The cabin was nestled in the woods in Colorado, and if snow was on the ground, it'd look like the set of a Christmas Hallmark movie. The two-story log cabin with a wraparound front porch was a slice of heaven. Pure paradise.

A swirl of smoke pushed into the night sky from the fireplace for dramatic effect. Perfectly romantic.

When the door opened after a few firm knocks, she bit down on her back teeth at the sight of the sexy SEAL shirtless in only worn-out denim jeans.

Her eyes lifted to meet his as if following the shot of a flare into the sky. Like an explosion of fireworks lighting up her senses. He was every bit of color in the rainbow in that one moment as she stared deep into his eyes. The familiar insane pull she'd felt around him the last two times they breathed the same oxygen hit her.

He glanced at his wrist as if checking a watch that wasn't there. "You're about on schedule. Been three years. Although, I was hoping for sooner if I'm being honest." His quip had her smiling. His lack of shock at her presence also meant he'd been alerted she was coming.

"Jessica called?" And if so, why the lack of shirt and the tantalizing tease of the start of a happy trail leading to oh-so-happy places?

She blinked out of her hot-British-now-American-commando stupor to remind herself why she'd flown to Colorado.

If she hadn't been so busy ogling his chest, then falling captive to his eyes, it wouldn't have taken her so long to notice the bandage spiraling around his left arm from the wrist to the elbow. "What happened? Are you okay?" She had a pretty damn good idea, and if she was right, it'd confirm his presence on the operation in Romania.

"Minor burn. No big thing. Kitchen fire."

"Oh yeah, what were you making?" she challenged.

He leaned into the frame of the door, casually crossing his arms and blocking her entrance. "Eggs."

She rolled her eyes. "You gonna let me in or what?"

"If I do," he began, his captivating lips slowly curving into a smile, "you gonna ask more questions about this burn?"

"Is the burn classified?"

"Maybe," he replied, but his arms relaxed, and he stepped aside.

She moved past him and looked around the open-concept cabin. High ceilings with a crisscross of thick wooden beams overhead. The second floor was open to the downstairs. Three doors up there by her count. A couch in front of a roaring fire and a kitchen off in the back overlooking the living room.

"Why are you here? Vacation?" She set her overnight bag and purse down and unzipped her jacket.

He closed the door and faced her, his eyes going to her bag. "You planning on staying the night?"

"Not here-here," she sputtered. "I'll get a place at an inn." She tossed her red, lightweight jacket on the back of the couch. "I need to know what happened in Romania. Did you see him die with your own eyes? Get a good look at him? Any identifying details you can tell me?" She'd decided it'd be best to cut through the bullshit and get straight to the point.

He strode past her without answering, without any change in his expression, and went into the kitchen and opened the fridge.

"I have no idea what you're talking about." He draped his uninjured arm over the top of the door as he kept his back to her, staring into the fridge as if searching for answers.

There were a few scars on his back, which pained her to see. Iraq? Afghanistan? His current line of work? Did he have any combat PTSD?

"Please tell me what happened." She wasn't above begging, not when it came to this topic. "It's classified, I get it. But it was my intelligence that sent you to Romania."

He faced her, armed with two beers. "Why would I go to Romania?"

She stalked into the kitchen as he removed the tops to the beers. He extended one, but she shook her head and folded her arms, standing her ground.

He set her bottle on the kitchen island off to his side and brought his drink to his mouth and took a few swigs. She tried not to let his tanned throat distract her as he downed the liquid. "Please. I can't move on from this. I don't think he really died. I need to know exactly what happened."

He lowered his beer to the counter. "Tash."

"So, it's 'Tash' now?"

"I'm tired. It's been a long week, and so yeah, it's Tash. You okay with that?" A cut of pain moved through his tone. More sadness than irritation.

"What's wrong?" she asked, unable to bury her concern for him.

"Nothing," he said, but he hid his eyes by peering at the floor.

"Then can you please tell me what you know?"

"Hypothetically speaking, if I'd been in Romania, no one on my team got hurt. And we didn't get the chance to smoke anyone, either." He cleared his throat and dragged his eyes up to her face. "Hypothetically, it looks like he had the place rigged with multiple explosives. Probably a thermite charge on his mainframe along with accelerants, based on how fast the place went kaboom and burned white-hot. Remote and command-detonated."

Her stomach squeezed at the news. "But you saw him? Had the exits covered?"

"Whatever was in that house, he wanted to make sure it was destroyed. I assume the explosion was meant to cover his tracks." He gripped the bridge of his nose, and her attention moved to the bandage on his arm. "I did see a guy, but he was on fire, and I couldn't get a good look at his face or save him." He let go of a long sigh. "But he was nice and toasty. Could roast marshmallows on the fucker."

She maneuvered around the island to stand closer to him, which had him pivoting to face her, arms dropping like anchors to his sides. "Same war humor as my brother's, I see."

"I'm not in the military anymore."

"Neither is he. But with what you both do, every day seems to be a battlefield."

He leaned in closer, dipping his head a touch, eyes straight on her. "That'd imply there was some competition on the other side."

"Says the burn on your arm."

"That was my own stupidity. Going in after your man because I knew it'd eat you up if I didn't bring him out alive for questioning." He straightened his spine. "Hypothetically speaking."

"Nice of you to think of me."

"How could I not? You've been in my bloody head since the last time we saw each other." His eyes thinned as if he hadn't meant to let the truth slip, but now it was out there dangling between them, and she found herself trying to remember how to breathe again.

"Is it possible he got out alive?" she asked, choosing to focus on her problem at hand and not the way this man made her feel absolutely every possible emotion whenever he was near her.

"The guy had the place rigged with the kind of shit we use to blow up a downed drone, so yeah, he was prepared. I assume he chose that place because of the tunnel system, too." He angled his head. "But you know about the tunnels since you provided the operational details, right?"

"But could he have survived that fire to make it out of those tunnels alive?"

His mouth pinched tight for a moment. "I don't know. I thought the police found a body."

"They said they did, but I'm not buying it." She shook her head. "Do you think he's dead?" she asked softly.

"What do you want me to say?" he asked, his voice grittier this time. "I hope for your sake, for the world's sake, the guy you were after, who I'm now calling Mr. Crispy, did die." He crossed his arms and leaned his hip against the kitchen island. "And if he's dead, you gonna slow down? Maybe stop being forever single?"

What made him think she wasn't already dating? Had he been keeping tabs on her the way she had on him?

"You still only having sex?" she shot back.

Maybe she shouldn't have brought that up, but she couldn't exactly redact her statement, mark over her words with black ink.

He was in no hurry to hide his smirk, either. "We back to playing the question-with-a-question game?"

"That's another question," she replied without dropping the ball. A repeat of their conversation on the beach three years ago.

"Yes." He'd practically breathed out the word, and his eyes darted to her mouth. "Just sex."

She'd been thinking about the hacker, the possible end to her three-and-a-half-year pursuit of the man. And now it was as if she were crawling out of her skin with the desire to have Wyatt take her into his arms and go all caveman on her.

She'd never felt this way with another man before, certainly not with Dale. No one had ever made her feel the desire to be thrown over a shoulder and carried to the bed, to a carpet, to some type of surface to be properly fuc—

"You still the admiral's daughter?" His thumb made small, sweeping circles over her cheek, and the action had her sex clenching.

"That doesn't ever really change. He'll always be the

admiral." But he knew that back in Ibiza, and he'd pinned her to the bed beneath him anyway.

"There's talk he'll be the next Secretary of Defense."

She nodded. "And that means?"

His attention moved to her powder blue long-sleeved shirt, to the scoop-neck that didn't feel all that sexy, but with his eyes drawn to the bit of cleavage there like a magnetic pull, it was as if she were naked.

"Why are you out here in Boulder?" she asked when he didn't respond, and her words had his hand falling from her face, and he took a step back.

A chill grabbed hold of her, and she was grateful her sleeves and jeans hid the rise of goose bumps on her body.

"I come here when I need space." He turned and went back to the business of drinking his beer.

She took a moment to study the ripple of abdominal muscles, which tightened for a moment as if he'd taken a gut punch in a UFC ring.

"Something's wrong," she said softly. "What else happened during your mission?"

He set his drink down and stared at the floor for a long minute. "A friend of mine, well, he used to be a friend, died."

Her chest caved in at his words. At another loss he had to endure. "I'm so sorry."

"It's complicated," he said, his voice deep, eyes back on her. "And I didn't expect to be quite so fucked up about it, but I guess I am. I came here to get my head on straight." Grief and pain hollowed out his words, dragging his husky voice even lower.

"Want me to go?"

He shook his head but strode past her into the living room to stand in front of the fireplace. She slowly eased up beside him, glancing over to see his focus lost to the burning logs.

Her gaze whipped to his bandaged arm, and guilt punched her in the chest, knocking the wind out of her. If he had gotten killed going after the man she'd been chasing, she would've never been able to live with herself.

"Do you want to talk about your friend?" she offered, keeping her voice as soft as possible. She used to be better at this—sharing emotions, comforting a friend—but she'd begun to harden over the years. The missions, the losses, they'd started to take their toll on her no matter how much she'd resisted.

He slowly turned to the side, the glow of the fire throwing a shadow on his profile. "I wouldn't normally want to talk, but something about you—"

"Has you opening up?"

He huffed out a deep breath. "When I left London at eighteen, I also left everyone behind, including a good friend of mine. My best mate."

She wrung her hands together in front of her, trying to work up the courage to be the ear, the shoulder, the whatever he needed at this moment. If this tough man was prepared to open up to her, she wanted to be there for him.

When she'd done her research and checked up on him—and she refused to call it stalking because her job was all about intelligence gathering, so it was totally in the realm of normal—she'd learned he'd changed his name to Pierson. He'd shed his English nobility before becoming a Teamguy. The *why* hadn't been hard to come up with. He'd get a lot of shit for that kind of name as an operator. But was there more to it?

She relaxed her shoulders, took a breath so she didn't faint from locking the oxygen in her lungs for so long, then moved to stand before his muscular frame. "What happened?"

He lifted his eyes to the high ceiling, his chest rising in the process. Upon an exhale, he said, "I slept with his fiancée."

His words should've had her backing away from him, but the guilt in his tone was so heavy, so strong, it was clear it was tearing him up, especially now that this friend of his was most likely the one who'd died.

He faced the fire again, and she took a moment to observe him. His hair had been chopped since she'd seen him last. Close-cut and tapered at the sides, a bit longer on the top and purposefully messy—or maybe he'd been clawing at it. His full beard was gone. More like a week's worth of new growth, the beginning of a beard if he didn't shave soon. His nose appeared to have been broken once or twice in his life. Not perfectly straight, but it fit him.

He was ruggedly sexy with his ink and his muscles. Nothing like the British aristocrats she'd seen on TV or in movies.

She crossed one arm over her chest and braced the bicep of her other arm, patiently waiting for him to open up more, to reveal whatever it was he wanted to get off his chest.

"Clara is the only person who knows everything that happened before I left England. And to be honest, I'm more upset at how I handled the aftermath than I am ashamed of what I did." He cupped his mouth for a brief moment. "Arthur and I grew up together. Got into trouble together. We had plans to move to California at eighteen. Applied to unis there."

He strode to the couch and dropped down. He leaned forward and brought his elbows to his knees, maintaining eye contact with the fire as if it made the truth easier to disclose.

She sat next to him and contemplated whether or not to reach out to him. A hand on his knee. A touch on his arm.

Something to let him know she was there, that it was okay. That this big Teamguy could be honest without judgment.

"Arthur suddenly got nervous. Too scared to walk away from everything. The title. Money. His father got into his ear. Plus, he began to fall for the woman his parents wanted him to marry." He peered over at her, and her hand went to the top of his thigh. He paused for a moment, his gaze moving to her touch, before continuing, "I wasn't sure if he truly loved her because he was sleeping around a lot. But when Charlotte, also a friend of mine, showed up at my door crying about his cheating . . . I was piss drunk, and we ended up sleeping together. At the time, I didn't realize she was using me to make him jealous, to try and get him to stop screwing around with their wedding approaching."

"Oh." The tiny sound popped free from her mouth. As far as she was concerned, what Wyatt did wasn't all that bad.

"Arthur was upset. Attacked me in public. Came at me swinging. Guess he really had loved her." He shook his head. "But let's just say, the only scandal the nobility despise is a scandal about themselves. My father, sure as fuck, was angry at me. We fought as well, then I decided to drop the news on him I was going to San Diego. I'd said I was done with the life, with being his son." His fingers tore lines through his hair. "I was never cut out for being some bloody lord, anyway."

She replayed his words in her head, then whispered, "From the sound of it, I can't say that I blame you for what happened."

"Arthur fired me as best man at his wedding, a wedding that had to be scheduled sooner than planned because Charlotte got pregnant. And Arthur had every right to hate my bloody guts for sleeping with his fiancée."

"How'd he die?" Death was such a regular occurrence in

her life now. She resented that fact, but in her line of work, she'd been naive to think she could go unscathed, remain untainted by the things she'd witnessed, the criminals she'd failed to stop.

"Cancer, and I should've visited him before he died. Made amends, I don't know. I can be stubborn, too. But I did go to the funeral, and seeing everyone there, well, it was harder than I thought it would be. I got the, uh, hypothetical call about Romania at the wake, and I guess I just didn't have time to process his death until now."

Was she crowding his space? His need to mourn?

"It's been a crazy year. Crazy few years." He stiffened. "I'm not sure if you remember Liam, but he almost died this past summer. And I wouldn't have survived that. None of us would've—losing another guy . . ."

"Marcus," she whispered, remembering the teammate he'd mentioned losing before. "I was happy to learn the men who were responsible for Marcus's death were finally taken out."

"How'd you know?"

"CIA intel provided the location of the terrorists who killed him. I wasn't involved, though."

He looked to the wood floors beneath his bare feet. "And I also heard about what happened to some of your team members last year." Regret carried through his words. "I'm so sorry."

"How'd you know about that?" She removed her hand. "I mean, I'm not surprised given who you are, but the true details were buried deep. Cover stories were fabricated for the public."

To the world, the men and women who were assassinated by hired mercenaries were regular people living their everyday lives. The stars were on the wall at Langley to honor them, but as far as the media was concerned, the deaths were unrelated.

Hit-and-run. Wrong-place-wrong-time robbery. Home invasion. Suicide.

The only commonalities? All of the murders happened at the same hour on the same day, and to people who worked with her on the case chasing the most wanted hacker in history.

"I have high-level security clearance." His answer didn't quite cut it, but she didn't feel like pushing for more information. "I think my heart stopped when I heard about it, and I was also so damn relieved you were okay. If your father hadn't assigned pretty much every serviceman stateside to keep an eye on you afterward, I would've dropped in to see you, to look out for you." He gripped the skin at his throat. "I should've called, though. I should've reached out. I keep fucking up." His hand slipped around to the back of his neck, and he squeezed. Unease crossed his face and moved into every line of his body. "I, uh, thought it'd be better if I kept an eye out on you from afar."

"And why is that?" She knew the answer, though. She remembered their conversation in Ibiza. How could she forget? He didn't believe he could love.

Was he worried she'd fall under his spell, and he'd break her heart?

It was possible it would happen, too. Sex was one thing, but would sex with this man turn her feelings into something more?

His eyes shifted to the floor, and a beat of silence the length of the Rockies stretched between them before he said, "Maybe we save this conversation for the next time we bump into each other?"

Her eyes wandered to his chest down to his navel, to the

slight trail of hair leading beneath the top of his jeans. "Not sure if this qualifies as much of a bump," she joked, hoping to somewhat lighten their exchange before they said their goodbyes, which she could feel was about to come.

He angled his head, his eyes darkening to a midnight blue-gray when he'd caught her checking him out. "Or maybe we should stick to the status quo of our run-ins, where I put my tongue in your mouth and feel you up? Well, until someone interrupts us, at least."

"Like a bear?" She couldn't stop the grin on her face. "And is sex really on our minds right now?" Somehow, it was for her.

Her desire for him had been present since before he even opened the door, it'd only been placed aside because of her pursuit of the truth about the op in Romania.

He shot her a crooked smile, and her heart squeezed. "It's always on my mind. I'm good at two things. Shooting and sex."

A pulse of need surged between her legs, and she swallowed before choking out, "I'm sure you're good at more than that."

He inched closer, invading her personal space, and when she sucked in a breath, his cologne met her nose. Strong hints of spice. A touch of pine. Something else there she couldn't quite put her finger on, too absorbed by the closeness of his naked chest. "There are so many reasons why I shouldn't touch you right now."

Tendrils of desire continued to spin tight inside of her at his closeness, at the husky depth of his tone. The raw and intense beat of pressure that had been building between them since they first met. Well, it had for her, at least.

"I was prepared to be yours the night of the wedding," she admitted. "And that morning in Ibiza."

"We were kept apart both of those times," he said, his voice still deep as ever. "Was it for a reason?"

She tipped her chin up, wishing she could open her mouth and offer him a taste, but would it be too dangerous? And when she moved her hand to gently touch the bandage on his arm, and the realization he could've died going after her target struck her, it had her desire dialing down, replaced by guilt.

"I guess." He was suffering a loss, and she was reeling from the mish-mash of facts about the Romania op . . . perhaps those were more than sufficient enough roadblocks to prevent anything from happening between them tonight.

He continued to stare at her, unblinking. The passion still kindling.

"The spare bedroom is out of the question, right?" she teased, because why wouldn't she make a joke right now? The real her could be awkward and rambly compared to covers she donned. There was no CIA glam on the inside.

"If you stay here, you know what will happen," he responded as if he hadn't caught on it'd been a joke.

But he was right. If she stayed, she'd forget their roadblocks, and she wouldn't be able to resist having his hands trace every line and curve of her body before his mouth did the same.

And the next day she'd want to do it again, but she had a job to do, and so did he. An entanglement with this man would be messy.

"I should go, but I hate leaving you here alone."

"It's the way I should be."

Her shoulders sagged. "No one should be alone." She squeezed his good arm. "Thank you for everything."

"Thank you for what?" He held her eyes as she continued to maintain a grip on his bicep.

"For Romania," she said softly. "And for looking out for me last year, even if from afar. It's nice to know you have my back."

"Well, that's something I can promise I'll always do."

She smiled and forced herself to let go of him to grab her phone to order an Uber.

"I can drive you to a hotel," he offered.

"I think it's best if I just catch a ride." Any more time with him and . . .

He remained quiet as she put in the request for a vehicle, then she stowed her phone in her purse and lifted her eyes to find him studying her.

"What's the name of this hacker anyway—his handle or whatever he calls himself, I mean—the one who may or may not be dead?"

"They didn't tell you?"

He held his palms in the air. "It was need to know."

"He goes by The Knight," she said, removing the guilt from her voice at sharing classified intel.

"The Knight? Any idea why?"

"He treats his hacks like a game of chess. Each move is strategic and calculated. And his goal is—"

"Checkmate," he finished for her with a nod, and an eerie feeling crept up the back of her neck, spelling out in vivid letters that The Knight's game was far from over.

PART IV

PRESENT DAY

The chase continues

2021

CHAPTER TEN

MOSCOW (JANUARY 2021)

"I NEED ONE MORE MINUTE."

"Like hell you do," Jack said into Natasha's ear. "Boris is coming in hot. He'll be inside the hotel in two minutes."

"Which means my one minute is good." Her fingers raced over the keys as she continued to work. She wasn't the best coder at the Agency, but she was the best currently on assignment in Russia, and she had to know—she had to take the one damn minute to follow the trail to see if her gut was right. The Knight had been off the radar since his supposed death sixteen months ago, but like hell was he really gone.

"You got what we needed. Get out now," Jack ordered.

His team had been assigned to Moscow three months ago, only one week after she'd been delivered orders to report there for six months (or longer) of deep-cover work related to the recent string of anti-Western terrorist activities.

Her father clearly stepped in, pulling strings to get Jack

assigned there. Her dad's worry for her had no boundaries, and his influence rang high in Washington.

"One more second," she said under her breath, quickly inputting a string of commands into the laptop, hoping to open Pandora's box and discover the source of the intel—the person, or group, behind the hack.

Whenever a hacker was found to be connected to terrorist activity anywhere in the world, Natasha always pushed the Agency to double-check the code to ensure it wasn't The Knight's handiwork.

Each programmer had a distinct coding style, a sort of digital fingerprint, and in the case of The Knight, he'd always left an electronic calling card behind as well.

Since this latest hack involved her targets, there was no way she could pass up the chance to check a connection to The Knight herself.

"You're out of time. Boris is in the elevator. I'm catching the next ride up."

"Stand down," she shot back her own order. "I've got this."

"If he finds you in that room, the mission is blown," he said in a low voice. "Out. Now."

She executed another set of commands, a string of ones and zeros—binary code . . . *I'm close. I can feel it.*

"He's on your floor. You're done."

A swirl of green letters and numbers flashed onto the screen. Encrypted. But that didn't matter. She got what she was after—evidence to prove she wasn't crazy, evidence that her mark was still out there and living freely.

She whipped out her phone and took a photo of his online handle, an image of a knight chess piece bouncing around in the corner of the screen. It'd almost been too easy to find, almost like candy had been set out for her . . .

He knew I was here. He knew I was following Boris.

Her heart slammed harder and harder, adrenaline pumping. She exited the program with shaky fingers and finished deleting all evidence she'd been on his laptop just as the slow scrape of the door against the worn-out, frayed carpet announced Boris's arrival.

She spun around and took in all six and a half feet of him as he caught sight of her from where he stood in the doorway.

A litany of angry Russian words struck her, and Boris's thick fingers dug into the side of her throat. She wasn't allowed to kill the bastard, and even a suppressed shot to the leg to get him off her could go upside down.

He maintained a firm grip on her neck as she opted for hand-to-hand combat. She was rusty after spending most of her time behind a computer screen. She should've gotten out more. Trained more.

She lifted her arms, moved her wrists outward against his forearms, and applied pressure to weaken his hold of her throat. At the same time, she wedged her knee between their bodies and connected her kneecap to his groin. A maneuver that'd never get old, especially when a five-seven female was up against a man double her size.

But the son of a bitch held on tight and didn't even let out a groan. Did he have balls of steel?

She positioned her elbows on top of his arms and used the weight of her body to drop, then pivoted to the side as quickly as possible.

His hands slipped free, and he lost his grasp, giving her enough time to shift to the side and plant a roundhouse kick to his cheek.

He stumbled, nearly falling backward onto the bed, but he quickly regained his balance and was moving in her direction when Jack arrived.

It was now two against one.

Boris caught sight of Jack and pivoted his way, but he didn't stand a chance. Jack was too fast.

A blur of movements followed as Jack took the guy down to the ground.

He zip-tied his hands behind his back, then stuck a needle in the side of his neck to knock him out. "This was not the plan," he hissed, barely breaking a sweat while standing over the sleeping Russian.

"I have the buyer information," she said with relief. "The weapons deal is two days from now."

"But we don't have the location," Jack said while bringing his phone to his ear. "We need cleanup in room two-twenty." He listened to the other person on the line. "Yeah, he's still alive," he said before ending the call. "You're gonna get your ass chewed out for this, and you know it." He pocketed his phone. "And you could've gotten yourself killed."

"Yeah," she said with a shrug, "and what else is new?"

* * *

Natasha had a good idea what to expect as she approached the SCIF, which was pronounced "skiff" by everyone. The Sensitive Compartmented Information Facility was a secure room for discussing sensitive info, and the bold black letters of the acronym on the door reinforced the significance of what went on inside.

She entered her passcode, swiped her badge at the scanner, then pushed open the heavy door.

The Chief of Station caught her eyes the moment she entered, and he abruptly rose from his seat. He stalked straight at her and pointed to a closed room off to her right.

She followed orders and went inside the room usually reserved for getting your ass chewed out. Today was her lucky day. Given what happened at the hotel earlier, she'd been expecting it.

"What in the hell were you thinking?" Raulson pushed his tie out of the way as if it were an inconvenience, but the skinny fabric swung back in place.

"I couldn't just walk away without knowing for sure. It was The Knight. He hacked the weapons facility. Look at Boris's laptop, and you'll see. I think he's in Canada, too." Since Boris had been unconscious while they waited for an extract, she'd taken the time to download the files from his computer to a USB drive before heading back to the Station.

It'd only taken her three hours, but she'd traced the hacker IP address to Montreal. She'd be due for another ass chewing once her COS found out she'd gone ahead and decrypted the message and traced it without permission.

"He's been off the grid for sixteen months. If he's really alive, why surface now?" He tossed a hand through the air. "And for that matter, why use the same handle and tip us off he's alive? That'd be a rookie mistake, which we all know one thing the asshole wasn't, was a rookie. Maybe we're dealing with a copycat, but—"

"It's not a copycat. The Knight wants me to know he's alive. For us to know." She stepped closer to her boss. "Don't you get it, it's all a game to him." Over a year of searching for this bastard and now there was proof she wasn't crazy. He *was* alive.

"And how'd you find out he was in Montreal? Why would The Knight make it that easy?" He tightened his arms across his dress shirt and stared her down.

Because he's baiting me. He wants me there. And how could she not go, trap or not?

121

"Come on, Chandler," he said when she didn't answer. "You're chasing ghosts. You've got to stop. You're killing yourself trying to find this guy. And you disobeyed orders earlier. You lost sight of the mission because of your obsession with this man."

"We have Boris. We can get him to lead us to the weapons sale," she challenged.

"That wasn't the plan. If the buyer learns the meet has been blown and that Boris was picked up, what then? If he doesn't show, we lose the buyer. The terrorists will go somewhere else to buy weapons, and then we won't be able to stop whatever attack they're planning." He turned toward the door and hung his head. "Everyone warned me you were a loose cannon. I didn't listen, but they were right."

"What are you saying?"

"You're getting back on a plane tomorrow. Hell, tonight if I can swing it." Raulson slowly faced her, the angry draw of his lips quivering as if he were resisting spewing words he might later regret. "Not even your father can get you out of this mess."

This could not be another Algeria. Another instance where she got kicked out of Station, letting The Knight slip through her fingers.

"And those orders came from the ambo, right?" She tsked. "He's been looking for any reason he can find to get me out of Moscow."

"No, Chandler. This is because of your lone wolf shit." He let go of a long, drawn-out sigh. "We're done here. You'll be lucky if you ever get another field assignment again." He left the room without another word, and she slammed her palms against the wall by the door.

"You okay?" She peered to her right to see Jack in the doorway.

"It's over. I'm getting PNG'd back to Langley." *Algeria all over again.*

"This about earlier, or about you pissing off the ambo by turning down his request for you to screw him?" His brown brows lifted in question.

"How'd you know the ambassador hit on me?" Her arms crashed to her sides as he shut the door so they could be alone.

"I overheard him, and it took all my restraint not to take him down. It sounded like you had it handled, anyway."

"He's an ass, but he's not my problem right now. I should say that I screwed up by breaking orders, but—"

"You still feel you did what was right?"

"I got confirmation The Knight is active again, and I even have a location."

He gripped hold of her bicep. "Maybe it's time you turn this over to someone else?"

"How can you say that? You know how important this is to me. You know what he did to our people. I can't let this go."

"Tasha, you've been going nonstop these last few years. You don't make it home at Christmas, you never date, you—"

"You've been talking to Gray?" She perked a brow.

"I don't have to. I see you more than your family. Your brother worries about you. Everyone worries about you." He dragged a hand through his brown hair. "And there's something you should know."

"Yeah?"

"I'm finally getting out. This was my last contract."

"Really?" She'd heard that before. He was addicted to the work, and it was why he hadn't been in a relationship since his ex-wife left. He was too worried a woman would try and force him to choose her over the job again.

"Your brother finally convinced me to work with him."

"Ah." She smiled. "So, you're not really out, just not working with the Agency anymore."

"Pays better," he said with a wink. "And it'd be nice to work with Gray again."

"He could use a guy like you on his team."

"But that means I won't be out here to have your back anymore."

She hung her head. "Sounds to me like I won't even be allowed in the field for you to worry about anyway."

"What are you going to do now?"

"Maybe I need a vacation?"

"You serious? You'll let the Agency handle the lead?"

"Sure," she lied, not even flinching. No poker bluffing signs on display.

"Tasha." Her name rumbled under his breath.

She opened the door and shot him back a look. "What?"

"Do me a favor, I have two more weeks here before I'm out, don't go getting yourself into trouble before then."

"So, you're saying wait two weeks?" She flashed him a smile.

"Or how about don't get into trouble at all?"

"Now you know I can't make a promise like that."

CHAPTER ELEVEN

New York City

"I can't believe our first op for the new POTUS is in the freeze-your-balls-off cold," A.J. complained. "I'm gonna have a word with Knox about this when we get back."

Their new president just happened to be Knox's father. Former President Rydell left big shoes to fill, but if anyone could do it, it was Isaiah Bennett.

It was still hard to wrap their heads around, even three weeks into his presidency, but the alternative would have been unthinkable. If Isaiah Bennett had lost the election, Bravo and Echo Teams would've been out of a job.

It had been eight years since Luke recruited Wyatt.

In that time, they'd lost a man and had several close calls for the rest of their team, including almost losing Jessica.

They'd also grown in more ways than Wyatt could count during those eight years. Well, most of his team had. He wasn't so sure about himself. All of Bravo Team was in love, which was something Wyatt still didn't believe would ever happen for him, even though there was one woman who had him questioning his chosen path of singledom and strictly sex whenever he thought about her.

Natasha had roped him in with her smoldering eyes, gorgeous smile, and her sultry voice the night of Clara's wedding. But it was Ibiza, with her beautiful mind, badass skills, and giant-sized heart, that officially had him tripping all over himself.

But she deserved more than what would've been a failed attempt on his end to be the man she needed.

Maybe she'd finally found someone? The hacker she'd relentlessly pursued for years had been off the grid since Romania, so he could only hope she'd decided to move on and find her happily ever after.

But maybe if . . . *Shit, no maybe ifs.*

"What'd you say?" Wyatt directed his focus to A.J. who'd said, well, something, a moment ago. He was sitting opposite him at the conference table in their headquarters for Scott & Scott Securities.

Jessica had called to inform Wyatt they had an eleventh-hour mission in Norway and to get his team to headquarters. "I had said it sucks our first op with President Bennett has to be in the colder-than-a-witch's-tit cold." A.J. purposefully trembled as if outside.

"The cold will be worth it to see you shit in your pants at the sight of a polar bear," Wyatt said with a laugh.

A.J. waved a hand in the air. "Like you'll be any better, brother."

"I'm not worried about the polar bears even though I think they outnumber people up there." Finn drummed his fingers on the space-gray tabletop. "It's the fact that everyone off settlements is required to carry a gun. I don't want to be mistaken for a bear in our snow camo."

"You actually did research?" Roman, sitting off to Wyatt's left, joked.

"Not everyone is a walking encyclopedia like you," Finn casually shot back. "But Jessica said she's sending us just south of the North Pole, so yeah, I'd like to know what I'm walking into."

"So, aside from bears that should only be seen on the side of a Coke can—what else should we worry about when we head out?" A.J. leaned back in his leather seat.

"For starters, you're not allowed to die there. Bodies take forever to decompose because of the climate. The permafrost will mummify you." Roman maintained a straight face, but hell, it was true.

Wyatt had also done his due diligence on their assigned target location: Longyearbyen, a coal-mining town in Norway's Svalbard archipelago. What Roman said was true about permafrost and mummified bodies, but the main reason the rule was put in place long ago was the fear that cryogenically preserved bodies might still contain traces of deadly viruses, like Spanish flu. These days, all corpses were shipped to the mainland for burial.

"I quite like that policy. Don't fuckin' die on me out there." Wyatt gripped the chair arms, anxious to get a move on it once they'd been briefed.

"I don't know about you," Chris began, "but I'm ready to get out there and operate."

A.J. flipped his American flag ball cap backward. "Of course you'd say that. You act like an FNG. Kicking our asses whenever we run like you're back at BUD/S with something to prove."

"It pays to be a winner, brother," Chris repeated a common SEAL motto. "And really, if you're worried about your abilities to operate in the cold, maybe you ought to head back to Kodiak Island and get some training in."

Cold-weather SEAL training in Alaska had become mandatory after 9/11 for Teamguys. Most civilians thought of the Middle East as hot—they didn't realize it got damn cold in those mountains in Afghanistan, too.

Their missions hadn't been in the Arctic polar-bear-cold in years. Looks like they were due. It'd been forty-five days since they'd gone on a mission, and Wyatt would go wherever the hell POTUS wanted.

"You think you're funny, don't ya?" A.J.'s Alabama drawl kissed the syllables as he spoke.

"Well, my trigger finger is itchy," Wyatt admitted. "I need to get the hell out of the city." He needed to do what he did best, which was operate. Hunt bad guys. Wipe them off the planet. It wasn't like he had anyone to go home to. No one on Echo did, so he preferred his guys go out whenever possible, let Bravo stay home with their loved ones.

A.J. stabbed a finger in the air Wyatt's way. "You volunteered Echo Team, didn't you?"

His team didn't have a choice but to suit up, but he loved to give his brother a hard time. "Of course. And you're grateful, don't pretend otherwise."

The door to the conference room opened a moment later, and Jessica walked in, followed by Harper Brooks.

Like Jessica, Harper had been with the CIA. She'd worked on the op that brought Luke and his now-wife together. She'd nearly died in the process, too. It wasn't until after Luke tied the knot in 2019 that they'd brought Harper on to help out. Harper accompanied Echo Team every time they spun up, usually every mission where all ten guys were on an op as well.

"And what were you boys talking about?" Harper set her

laptop on the conference table and Jessica synced it with the screen on the wall.

"They were bitching about the cold." The guys loved to joke around, but Wyatt preferred that any day of the week to being uptight, especially in their line of work.

"Some of us were, not all," Chris corrected and shot Harper a wink.

Harper rolled her eyes at Chris's lame attempt at flirting. He didn't have a chance with her, but hell, he wasn't a quitter.

Harper was smart and gorgeous. Long and wavy dark hair with a few new reddish-toned highlights. High cheekbones. Full lips. Wyatt didn't blame his guys for being attracted to her, but he'd prefer they keep things platonic. It'd be better for his men to stay single. Mission-focused.

Harper shifted her hair behind her ears, her lips teasing into a smile, then crossed her arms over her graphic tee, this one sporting a black-and-white picture of Einstein. She usually dressed more casually and hip than Jessica.

Well, lately, Jessica was donning pregnancy clothes. She and Asher finally became a couple after years of back-and-forth tension. Six months pregnant with twins, and on her petite frame, she was more stomach than anything else.

"Maybe sit down?" Wyatt stood and pulled out Jessica's chair for her.

"Aren't you the gentleman?" Finn smirked while folding a piece of paper into a stealth fighter.

Wyatt shot Finn his notorious *Bite me* look as Jessica slowly lowered herself into the chair.

"Thanks for getting here so fast. Bravo's scattered all over the East Coast right now, and we need you guys on a jet within the hour," Jessica explained as Wyatt sat back down. "Luke won't make it to the office in time, so we'll go ahead and get started."

Harper clutched the back of the chair and peered around the table at the team. "Technically, we're being hired as Scott and Scott. Unofficially, this mission is a personal request from POTUS."

"What's the mission?" Wyatt straightened in his chair, intrigued.

An architectural design of a facility mostly buried in a snowy mountainside appeared on the screen that occupied the main wall in the room.

"The 'doomsday' vault," Roman said, clearly recognizing the structure. "The place stores seeds in protective chambers in the event of natural disasters or war."

"Right." Harper clicked to another aerial view of the facility. "The world's agricultural practices have improved as technology has advanced. We've accomplished larger-scale crop production, but in the process, we've decreased biodiversity. Today, as few as thirty crops make up ninety-five percent of the world's food supply, which makes our agriculture susceptible to threats like diseases and drought. While there are more than a thousand of these gene banks throughout the world, many have been destroyed by natural disasters or war. Svalbard was chosen specifically because of its remote and safe location —an icy wilderness. Their goal is to eventually house a copy of every seed that exists. In addition, other countries use the vault as a backup storage facility. To put it simply, this place is basically our insurance policy against starvation."

"Yesterday morning, Roland Nilsson was taken from his hotel room. He's an American contractor with Cyber X Security who'd been conducting a security systems update to the seed vault," Jessica said as Harper showcased a male in his mid-to-late forties. Brown hair with threads of silver throughout. A trimmed beard and mustache. Sharp blue eyes.

"The hotel cameras caught a partial image in the lobby of his abductor, and we're running his face through our systems to see if we can get a match."

"You thinking someone is planning to force Nilsson to hack the vault's security to get inside, and what, steal seeds?" Wyatt asked.

"Bioterrorism is the new trend for bad guys," Roman noted. "Pathogenic fungi destroy a third of all food crops every year. Imagine if someone coordinated and induced an attack on the most important global crops—wheat, soybeans, rice, potatoes, maize. Or introduced a species of seeds not native to a land, allowing it to invade the host crop and destroy the existing food supply. Massive starvation would be the result."

Harper's gaze connected with Roman's, and she nodded in agreement. "Which is why this facility was designed to be one of the most impenetrable sites in the world."

"So, if the bad guys aren't able to hack the security system, the next best thing is kidnap the man who designed it," A.J. pointed out.

"Surely, their security protocol will be updated given his abduction." It'd be the first thing Wyatt would do if he were in control of such an invaluable facility. "But why send us for something like this?"

"The Norwegian government would prefer not to have their fingerprints on this case for a few reasons," Harper began. "And the Crop Trust and Nordic Genetic Resource Center, who also manage the seed vault, want discretion. They don't want to draw attention to a potential breach and scare off countries from utilizing their bank."

"Are they alerting the other companies Roland Nilsson has designed security systems for? Shouldn't they all know they could be at risk, too?" Roman asked, and it was a damn good question.

"That call is out of our hands. We're under direct orders not to share any information about this case with anyone," Jessica responded, clearly sharing Roman's concerns about other security breaches as well. "The area you are flying to is under Norwegian control for the most part, but other countries were granted access to mining minerals there. One particular location, an old coal mine, is under Russian sovereignty."

"Russian?" A.J. mumbled. "And here's the other reason we're going, brothers."

"We've already begun coordinating with Norwegian authorities on what they know about the abduction," Jessica said, "and there's been a sudden spike in electrical activity in a place that currently only has two occupants. Tourism there is shut down right now, so the activity is a red flag."

"Pyramiden, the ghost town? The forgotten Soviet city?" Roman asked in surprise, catching everyone's attention.

"Yup." Harper flipped to an aerial view of the town. "Pyramiden is about a four-hour journey in the winter by way of snowmobile from the largest city, Longyearbyen. The place was mostly deserted in ninety-eight, but to maintain sovereignty, Russia needs at least two citizens living there at all times."

"And you think our bad guys took the security specialist to this place?" Chris stood and edged closer to the screen to view the map.

"If they're planning an attack, it'd make sense. A perfect place to hide out before they attempt to go into the seed bank," Harper answered. "The governor of Svalbard tried to reach out to the two men living there, but it was radio silence."

"And the Norwegians don't want to take a trip there themselves for a little looky-loo?" A.J. asked.

"A looky what?" Finn threw his paper airplane straight at him, but A.J. snatched it with his quick reflexes before it hit his face, tossing it right back at him.

"The Norwegians would prefer not to have to ask the Russians for permission to head there, nor do they want to go in without it," Jessica continued, ignoring the boys' typical goof-off behavior.

Wyatt played out the possible infil situations for a hostage recovery operation in his head. "No available LZ's to cut down the travel time?"

"I wouldn't want to fly there," Roman said. "In ninety-six a plane crashed, killing everyone. And a couple of years ago, a Russian Mi-8 helo carrying three scientists crashed after take-off from Pyramiden, killing everyone, too. The place is doomed."

Chris faced the team. "Well, personally, I'd rather take my chances on a helo than a Ski-Doo."

"The heliport is too close. Our abductors would hear you coming. Plus, the site is owned by Arktikugol, a Russian company. I doubt it's even operational this time of year, anyway," Jessica said as Harper showed an image of the terminal and a Mil Mi-8 helicopter parked outside. It'd been taken in the daylight, which meant it wasn't a recent image given the area was experiencing its dark days.

"And what are the odds our targets will still even be there by the time we arrive?" Wyatt asked. "The Norwegians have a better chance if they infil now instead of waiting for us."

"The seed bank is in the process of altering their security protocol, so if the abductors managed to get anything out of the American contractor, the information will be useless— that's *their* priority," Harper explained. "*Our* objective is to recover the American, and if we can, take the abductors in for questioning."

"And we're bringing them all back with us on our snowmobiles?" A.J. asked in surprise.

"We're coordinating with the Norwegian authorities. They'll have everything you need for any given situation when you arrive," Jessica said. "There's an ambulance attachment you can use to bring back Nilsson and any abductors."

"Yeah, and who's pulling that back?" A.J. asked. "I suggest the youngest here."

"I'm not that much younger," Chris retorted.

"Then stop acting like a new guy all the time with that bullshit over-the-top working out you do, and you won't earn yourself these Captain America challenges." A.J. shot him a shit-eating grin.

"I do not look like Captain America, by the way." Chris swiped a hand over his short dirty blond hair.

"Since daylight's not an issue, we'll head in, get our hostages, then exfil." Wyatt spun his chair to the side to better view Jessica. "We flying private or commercial?"

"Private jet. We need you there as quickly as possible." Jessica slowly rose and braced the table at her side.

Good. He'd prefer to bring his own long gun on the op.

"Shit, we'll have to use muzzle caps for the rifles if it's snowing," Finn said.

"Nah, just grab some condoms." A.J. peered at Wyatt. "Sure Boss Man has some we can use."

Wyatt was on the verge of responding, but shit, A.J. was right. He *did* always have condoms on him. Not enough to cover everyone's rifle muzzle so snow didn't get into their long guns, though. Shooting rounds downrange in the intense cold was always tricky.

"You'll only have twenty or so minutes before comms go on the fritz because of the temperature." Harper frowned. "I'll be staying in Longyearbyen, so I won't be right there with you all, which I hate, but hopefully, the satellite phone will work so we can remain in contact."

"Good call," Roman cut her off. "It's going to be a dangerous trek out there, and I'd prefer you stay back."

"Nah, this op should be a walk in the park. It'll just be," Chris said with a shrug, "really damn dark, filled with bears, and you know—in a cold Soviet ghost town."

"So, like any other day, really," Finn deadpanned.

CHAPTER TWELVE

PYRAMIDEN

IT WAS JANUARY, AND THE ARCHIPELAGO WAS EXPERIENCING its Polar Nights. The sun was always six degrees below the horizon, and the only light came from the moon, stars, buildings, and of course, the famous greenish-hue in the sky —the Northern Lights.

It was dark, but Wyatt could make out the outlines of the towering rocks in the distance. The dramatic icy peaks looked surprisingly similar to pyramids, giving the town its name.

Overhead, the mystical green lights flickered and danced. A shooting star raced horizontally, and the green glow waved, seeming to intensify before his eyes.

It was an amazing sight, but after a four-hour ride on the snowmobile, his legs were stiff—the effects of his near age of forty creeping up on him, not that he'd ever admit it to the guys.

Wyatt adjusted his headlamp so he could better see through his Klim Viper snow goggles as the guys forged a path through the snow to get to the main part of town, which was half a klick away. They were decked out from head-to-toe in Arctic gear to keep them as warm as possible in the subzero temperatures, but it was still bitterly cold out.

They'd re-zeroed their weapons in preparation for shooting in the cold, as well as lubricated their rifles. A shot could easily go wrong with the denser air creating an increased drag on the projectiles. Not to mention how shit could go south with optics.

The team had gone over possible infil options on the plane ride to Longyearbyen and had come up with a half-dozen contingency plans, too.

Wyatt slowed once they reached the red, white, and blue town sign just outside the entrance. The lights appeared to be on in the old government headquarters building. "Stick to the plan. Clear the surrounding structures and wait for my go-ahead to insert," Wyatt ordered in a low voice.

Echo Four would be on overwatch even though it was normally Wyatt handling the long gun. They had no idea how many enemy combatants they'd be going up against, so Wyatt preferred to have his boots on the ground with his men.

The team scattered to their assigned breach points and made their way into the town within a matter of minutes.

Wyatt turned on his comm. "Radio check, Four. Are you in position?"

"This is Four," Roman responded. "I'm in location across from the government HQ building. There's definitely activity inside."

"Roger that," Wyatt answered.

The entire town appeared frozen in time. A mini Soviet Union. The Russians probably had other reasons for choosing such a location aside from mining coal, most likely to maintain a foothold in the west.

Either way, it was as if the Iron Curtain had never lifted even after the fall of communism in Russia. As to why the Russians still wanted to maintain sovereignty over the land, well, their resident conspiracy theorist, A.J., had churned up a dozen reasons on their flight from New York.

Wyatt exited the first site he'd checked, the gymnasium.

No signs of life. Only withering plants.

He dimmed his headlamp, hoping the lens didn't fog up and crack, then in a low voice said, "This is One. The gym is clear. What's your location, Two?"

"This is Two," A.J. came over the line. "I'm in the children's nursery, and I feel like I'm in a horror movie. Empty cribs. Little shoes lined up along the wall. Fucking creepy. It's like everyone just abandoned the place."

"People left their stuff everywhere," Chris chimed in. "Found someone's stash of Playboys, too."

"How the hell did you manage that when we're only checking for a hostage and our targets?" A.J. asked.

"I opened a closet door, and I swear the magazines just fell on my head," he answered.

"Fell right open to the centerfold piece, too, right?" A crackle from A.J.'s laugh cut through the comms.

"This is Four," Roman popped into Wyatt's ear. "Just got a call from TOC on the SAT phone."

"What'd she say?" Wyatt went still, waiting for Roman to continue. Harper wouldn't have risked calling unless it was serious.

"She said someone must've tipped off the Russians. The Norwegians said they flew into Longyearbyen before us," Roman added. "And I've got a positive visual on three FSB agents exiting the HQ building now. Heavily armed."

"Charlie Mike, Boss Man? Or we getting out of here?" A.J. asked.

Damn it. "We need to exfil. Now." He dimmed his headlamp to the lowest setting. "We are *not* going to war with the Russians. The FSB work directly for the Russian president. Do not engage. Understand?"

"Roger that," Roman responded.

"Shit," Chris barked out. "You hear that? Helo somewhere overhead."

"The heliport is close by. You have a visual, Four?" Wyatt exited the building he'd been in to put eyes on the sky. It was too dark from his vantage point, but he could hear the familiar sound of blades.

"Fuck," Roman rushed out. "They've got an RPG. The FSB agents are about to shoot down the chopper. They must assume the kidnappers are trying to make a run for it."

"So, they're just gonna kill them?" Chris asked in surprise. "And are we going to let that happen? What if the American is on that bird?"

"Don't make a move, Four," Wyatt ordered, even though it pained him to do it. They did not have orders to fire at Russian agents. "Hold your position. We can't get into this fight."

"We can't let that helo go down," A.J. hissed.

"Stand down, Two." Wyatt bit down on his back teeth. "Rules of engagement are clear. We do not engage with the Russians under any circumstances."

A whistling sound tore through the air, then a moment later, the helicopter exploded. A burst of red and orange sprayed the sky before gravity pulled the chopper to the snowy ground.

"This is Three. We need to get to that bird before the FSB agents do and confirm who was on board," Chris rushed out. "I can head there now."

"No, it's too—"

"I can do it!" Chris cut off Wyatt. "Someone might still be alive."

"You've got company, One," Roman informed Wyatt.

At the sound of boots crunching across the snow, Wyatt hurried back into the building, shut off his headlamp, and hid in the shadows of the gymnasium. "Go, Three. Do not engage with anyone, not even a fucking bear. Got it?"

"Roger," Echo Three said in a rush, his breathing already labored as if he'd started on the move before he'd been given orders, and if they weren't in a hurry, he would've given him hell for it.

"The rest of you, don't move a damn muscle until the Russians are out of sight," Wyatt said after the sound of boots in the snow faded.

"The men outside the HQ building are exiting the town, probably heading for the crash site. As for if there are more here, I don't know," Roman updated the team.

"Hold your positions until we have the clear from Four to move," Wyatt instructed, fear fast-tracking up his back as he worried about Chris outside.

"This is Three," Chris's voice popped over the line two minutes later. "I have visual confirmation of the American. He was in a body bag, already dead. Tortured, and he bled out from the looks of it."

"Maybe the Russians knew that." At least Wyatt hoped they wouldn't have risked the life of the American. "Who else was on board? Any survivors?"

"They're all dead," Chris answered. "I'm snagging photos of the men so we can run them through facial recog when we get back."

"Better hurry. The Russians are coming in hot on your location," Roman rasped.

"Don't be a heroic son of a bitch," Wyatt shot out. "Get to our exfil point, Three," Wyatt commanded.

"Two other FSB agents just left the side entrance toward the helo crash," Roman announced.

"Now's the time to exfil," Wyatt responded. "Move out."

"Roger that," A.J. answered, followed by Finn and Roman.

"Three?" Wyatt called out once all of his team, except for Chris, were back where they'd left their Ski-Doos. "Come in, Three."

"Three, where the hell are you?" A.J. asked next.

Static filled the line for a moment. "I've got a situation," Chris said. "My path to you is a bit blocked."

"By what?" Wyatt asked.

"Eh, you know, a giant fucking polar bear." The line went quiet for a moment. "If I fire, or throw a 9-Bang, the Russians will hear me."

"Do whatever necessary to keep yourself from getting eaten," Wyatt told him. "A suppressed shot will be fine."

A suppressed shot would still be heard, but it'd be more like a loud clap. A firm spank in the arse. Hopefully, the sound would be chalked up to something other than a gunshot, and the Russians wouldn't pursue.

"Just shoot the bear. Drop your animal-loving bullshit for tonight," A.J. urged.

"I can't risk exposing you guys," Chris answered in a steady voice.

"Don't even think about sacrificing yourself," Wyatt ordered. "Get yourself here and alive, right the bloody hell now!"

The line went dead.

"Three, come in?" Wyatt saddled onto his Ski-Doo when he heard a thunderous noise in the distance and saw a flash of light. Chris had thrown the flash-bang grenade to scare off the bear instead of shooting the thing.

"We're coming for you," A.J. said. "We didn't spend half our lives dodging bullets to have one of our guys taken out by a damn bear."

CHAPTER THIRTEEN

New York City

"THIS FOOL WAS PLANNING ON DOING SOME KUNG-FU MOVES on a nine-foot polar bear, all because he didn't want to kill the thing." A.J. cracked up laughing, clutching his stomach after he'd retold the story of what happened in Pyramiden back at the office.

Chris snatched an apple out of the bowl on the table in their kitchen and threw it at A.J.

"You're lucky the Russians never caught up with us," Wyatt added, "that's all I'm saying, or we might've all been served up as bear food for being there." He adjusted the brim of his plain black ball cap, doing his best not to smile.

It'd been a close call for all of them, and it could've easily gone the wrong way, so he shouldn't smile, but A.J.'s reenactment for Asher of Chris versus the polar bear had been too comical to maintain a straight face.

"I'm just glad you're all okay, and we didn't start a damn

war with Russia," Asher said before Harper peeked her head into the room.

"Hey, I think we've got something." She flicked her wrist in a come-hither motion. "Head to Jessica's office."

Chris saluted her. "Yes, ma'am."

The guys filtered out of the kitchen and to Jessica's room three doors down. She was at her desk with her black frames on, and Harper stood off to her right. "We've got news," Jessica said once Echo Team had settled at the circular table in front of her desk.

Asher strode behind her chair and nuzzled his nose by her cheek. "Took you long enough," he joked.

"Real funny, my love."

Asher gave her a quick kiss, then joined the guys at the table.

Wyatt brought his focus back to the two genius women in the room, waiting for more information.

"We got a hit on one of the men from that chopper, and he matched the profile shot we pulled from our vic's hotel—a highly trained mercenary. He was hired on the Dark Net, and he assembled a team to carry out the job." Jessica removed her glasses and straightened in her chair. Her eyes traveled around the conference table before falling upon Wyatt last. "According to the Norwegians, the Russians claim when they arrived in Pyramiden, surveillance footage showed the American being tortured to death."

"They had cameras inside?" Finn scoffed. "Or are they covering their asses for shooting down the bird without knowing if he was already dead?"

"They won't share the footage, so I guess we'll never know," Jessica responded.

"Why bring the body with them on the bird if the

abductors were trying to make a quick exit?" Wyatt gripped the chair arms, trying to prepare himself for whatever news Jessica was about to drop on them.

"Insurance, maybe? They assumed they wouldn't get shot down with the American on board, and they didn't anticipate the cameras inside Pyramiden proving Nilsson was already dead," Harper answered.

"Still doubting the camera theory, but why do you two ladies look like you've seen a ghost?" A.J. asked. "We're the ones who nearly got our asses smoked by the Russians in a ghost town."

"Because the abduction had nothing to do with the seed vault. It was a case of misdirection. Using Pyramiden as a location benefited them in two ways—it tricked the Norwegians into assuming the kidnapping was about breaking into the seed vault, and it provided a safe haven to torture the contractor for information."

"If the kidnapping wasn't related to the seed vault, what kind of information were they hoping to get from Nilsson?" A bad feeling began to worm its way into Wyatt's gut. A.J. had nailed it when he said the women looked like they'd seen a ghost. Given that Jessica and Harper were badasses in their own right, it took a lot to shake them.

"While that helo went down in Pyramiden, the Pionen Data Center in Sweden, one of the world's most secure and supposedly unhackable facilities in the world, was simultaneously hacked," Jessica said.

"And let me guess, our American contractor with Cyber X was also instrumental in setting up their security system?" Wyatt asked.

"Close. Some of the top companies around the world, including the Pentagon, hire Cyber X to hack into their systems," Harper answered. "If Cyber X can't get in, virtually no one else can. But if they're successful . . . time for a security upgrade."

"And I'm guessing Cyber X makes bank providing those upgrades," Finn commented. "So, Nilsson was the Cyber X guy sent to try and hack the data center?"

"Last year," Jessica replied. "We're thinking because of his insider knowledge of the site, he was needed to help breach the facility."

"So, while everyone was worried about the seed vault, our bad guys were really targeting the data center." Wyatt released his grip on the chair arms. "Do we know what data was stolen?"

"The Swedes won't tell us, saying the matter is a private issue. They won't be making the hack public knowledge. Even the Norwegians are running with the story that Nilsson was killed in an accidental crash," Jessica explained. "These kinds of situations tend to cause more panic and damage if the truth gets out about what really happened."

"I'd still like to know what the hacker was after in Sweden. All that setup had to be for something big."

Jessica grabbed her pen and jotted down a note. "I'll see if there is any chatter."

"We need to find out who the hell hired these men. The hack of the data center clearly wasn't done in Pyramiden," Asher said, his voice low and grumbly.

"We know who hired them." Jessica pushed back from the desk and brought a hand beneath her stomach.

"Saving the best news for last," Wyatt said, forcing a smile because it still wasn't clear why she was so spooked. And when Jessica's gaze cast down to the floor, his stomach dropped.

"We think it was the hacker you supposedly took down in Romania back in twenty-nineteen, known as The Knight. Well, he left his electronic calling card behind, at least," Jessica said when looking up.

"Or we're dealing with a copycat," Harper added.

The blood rushed from Wyatt's face, and he closed his eyes at the news. Now he knew why Jessica had been avoiding looking at him. She was well aware Natasha had sought him out in Colorado for answers about the operation in Romania, an op that had gone the wrong fucking way. Natasha had told Wyatt the hacker's online moniker when she visited, but this was probably the rest of the team's first time hearing it.

"Where are we at on tracing the location of the hacker?" Wyatt's eyes flashed open, and he pushed away from the table.

He wanted to phone Natasha, to find out if she knew The Knight was back again, or at least, someone making it look like he was.

"That's the thing," Jessica began, "he made it way too damn easy for us. We traced him to what appears to be an abandoned mill in Montreal."

"So we go to Montreal," Chris said while standing, no hesitation whatsoever. "I don't like leaving a job unfinished."

"Easy there, Captain America," A.J. drawled. "It's clearly a setup, or a loser copycat."

"No shit, but did you see a corpse in Romania?" Chris asked A.J. "Because I didn't, and I never felt good about hauling ass so quickly out of there without confirming Mr. Crispy died with our own eyes."

Wyatt agreed, but orders were orders. His people had to immediately evac or risk exposure.

"There's more," Jessica said before Chris or A.J. could continue any type of back-and-forth. "Right now, about every hacker worth his or her weight in the hacker world is currently convened in Montreal."

"What?" Wyatt's eyes traveled straight to Jessica.

"The Bug Bounty Competition," Roman murmured, drawing Wyatt's attention his way for more information. "And I saw in the news that Cyber X Security is the main sponsor for the event this year."

"Right," Harper replied. "I'm surprised the owner, Felix Ward, is still showing up given what happened to Nilsson, but then again, Felix has never missed an event, not with the world's best hackers gathered there."

"The winner gets bragging rights and a huge financial payout," Jessica noted. "It's also considered a safe-from-arrest zone because in exchange for providing agencies, such as the FBI, with their knowledge and skills, the hackers don't get cuffed."

"And many hackers are recruited to work for the sponsors, too. If they're gonna hack, the Feds would rather them do it on the side of good," Harper said. "These events are where Cyber X gets most of their top-notch hires, and Felix Ward likes to handpick the cream of the crop."

"And our hacker could use this event to hide in plain sight." Wyatt dragged his palm down his face and gathered in a deep breath before letting it go.

"This asshole wants to let everyone know he's still around and back in business." Based on Jessica's comments, it was clear she didn't believe this was a copycat situation like Harper had hinted at. "There was also a recent systems security breach into a weapons facility, which enabled a Russian criminal to steal weapons. The arms were slated to go to terrorists, but the CIA stopped it."

"And that hack was traced to The Knight?" Wyatt asked.

"Yeah, and to Montreal," Jessica confirmed. Thankfully, she still had plenty of contacts at the Agency. Plus, it didn't hurt that the CIA director was on their team as well. "The officer who tracked the lead didn't follow protocol, and she got kicked back to HQ because of it."

Bloody hell. "Natasha Chandler." So, Natasha already knew. And if she thought for a minute The Knight was alive, she'd knowingly take the bait at the shot of finding him.

Wyatt could feel A.J.'s eyes on him at the mention of Natasha's name, but he kept his focus on Jessica.

"Where is she now?" Wyatt asked Jessica.

"Natasha took a two-week vacation." Jessica's brows shot up. "So, where do you think she is?"

"She's gonna get herself killed." Wyatt went to the window and brought his balled fists to the glass. "We need to follow this lead and head to Montreal."

"And that's exactly what he wants," Asher said, and Wyatt didn't want to hear it right now.

"Asher's right. We need to get more information before we send a team straight into the guy's trap." Jessica kept her voice calm.

"This hacker might be doing things differently now." Wyatt bowed his forehead to the glass. "Having Roland Nilsson kidnapped, that's a change from The Knight's MO, right?"

"And what is his MO?" Roman asked.

Wyatt slowly turned around to face the team. Arms drawn across his chest, his heartbeat steady like a drum, but the beats were slowly intensifying the longer he thought about Natasha in Canada. And since she was there on vacation, she was without the Agency backing her up.

"I didn't work the case, but from what I remember, his

MO had always been to try to one-up himself. In the past, he grew gutsier with each hack. It was a game of escalation," Harper explained, taking the reins since she was the only one active during the height of The Knight's so-called career of hacking. "He'd steal intelligence, or help terrorists breach secure sites to obtain weapons. And when the CIA was getting close to figuring him out in twenty-eighteen," she said while reaching for the gold chain around her neck and rubbing the cross between her fingers, "he hacked the Agency. Leaked the identities of several officers and foreign agents involved in his case, hired an assassin on the Dark Net, and had them murdered."

The Knight had kept Natasha alive, but why? What sick game was he playing? Or worse, *still* playing?

"Then somehow Chandler," Jessica added after clearing her throat, "tracked him to Romania, and you guys were sent in."

"And everything went FUBAR," Chris commented.

Jessica's blue eyes connected with Wyatt. "If it's really him, and he's behind all of this, we'll get him this time."

"But we need more intel before we go jumping into the deep end without knowing how to swim, brother." Since when was A.J. the voice of reason?

"We're SEALs, remember? We're fucking great swimmers." Chris lifted his chin Wyatt's way, letting him know he was on his side no matter what he decided to do, and of course, Chris would be game. He lived for this shit.

"Although, I wouldn't mind if you all have a chat with Felix Ward, seeing he's sponsoring the hacking competition, and it was Nilsson who worked for him," Jessica said, and Wyatt agreed, especially if it meant he could go to Canada and ensure Natasha was safe.

Luke opened the door and entered the office a moment

later. "Sorry I'm late. President needs our ear. He's calling the secure line in a few." He looked back at the guys in the room. "Looks like you filled them in based on the sour looks on their faces." Luke shut the door behind him and leaned against it.

"Before we get back into the gloomy stuff, is there anything you want to tell us?" Jessica's lip caught between her teeth as she eyed her brother, and Asher stood next to her and looped an arm around her waist, holding her tight to his side.

Harper gave them some space and crossed the room to stand with the rest of the guys, eyes directed on Luke while they waited for news, and based on the starry look in Jessica's gaze, it'd be some good news, thank God.

Luke hooked his thumbs in his front belt loops. "I, um." He cleared his throat, and a touch of red crawled up his neck and to his cheeks. "Looks like Eva is pregnant."

"Another baby? Hot damn!" A.J. cut through the room to get to him, and Luke grinned. "I'm gonna start calling you all the Bravo Baby Factory." He hugged him and slapped him hard on the back, so loud you could hear the sting.

Everyone on Bravo but Knox, who'd only recently married, either had children or were about to.

Emily, Bravo Four's wife, was expecting. They'd also adopted a daughter in 2019.

And Owen already had a little guy not too long ago.

Jessica was due with twins.

And now Luke was having another baby.

A.J. was right. The men of Bravo were racking up the baby-making mileage.

"Congratulations, brother," Wyatt said. "I didn't know you were even trying."

"Neither did I," Luke answered with a laugh. "But hey, Eva will want to wait on an official announcement, so—"

"No baby talk until then. Mum's the word," A.J. said with a nod and zippered his lips shut. "Okay," A.J. began while reaching into his pocket and pulling out a twenty. "We placing bets on what POTUS has to say?"

The guys dug into their pockets and whipped out a few bucks to place bets. Typical.

But Wyatt couldn't think about anything right now but the fact Natasha could possibly be in danger. He once made her a promise he'd always have her back, and he wasn't about to leave her hanging now.

"Guys," Jessica said a minute later, "we've got incoming from President Bennett."

After a moment, the president's face filled the screen on the wall. "Gentlemen, ladies. As you may have heard the rumors, I'll be announcing the new Secretary of Defense soon —Admiral Warren Chandler."

Natasha Chandler, the admiral's daughter. The woman on his mind right now. Did her father know she was in trouble?

The president shifted his screen to showcase Admiral Chandler sitting next to him in the Situation Room. The last time the guys had been in that room was when they'd learned an assassin had taken aim at Isaiah Bennett last year during the election season. A swing and a miss.

"President Bennett filled me in on what you all do for him, for the country. I can't say I'm surprised given your involvement in rescuing my daughter in Algeria, though."

"In case you're wondering, he's on board," Bennett added as if there'd be any doubt. "Actually, that's why we're talking to you today."

Wyatt took a step closer to the screen on the wall, his curiosity piqued.

"Luke filled me in on what happened in Pyramiden," Bennett began. "Thank you for not starting a war with Russia, by the way," he said with a small smile. "He also informed me the hacker responsible appears to be the man supposedly taken out by your men in Romania."

"Technically, we didn't kill him," Luke noted. "The house was rigged, and it was command-detonated to explode."

The president nodded. "The Agency strongly believes this is a copycat and not the real deal. Either way, he, or she, needs to be found, but CIA Director Spenser is obviously cautious about assuming the hacker is in Montreal."

The team had yet to meet the new CIA director in person, but from their interactions on the phone with Director Spenser, he seemed to be less of a dick than the last guy they'd had to work with.

"Or he is there and wants the Agency there, too. Payback for Romania? Maybe even to finish the game he started," Jessica interjected.

"Or looking to set up someone in Montreal since the world's best hackers are there," Luke noted. "Either way, it'd be a safe location to work from given the Bug Bounty Competition starts Friday. The place is literally crawling with hackers. No pun intended."

"I honestly don't know," the admiral began, "but my daughter was just sent back to Headquarters. Fortunately, the Agency was able to complete the op and prevent the weapons sale, but because Natasha disobeyed orders so she could verify whether or not The Knight was the hacker involved, she was put on a desk. She's currently using vacation time. Although, if you remember her back in Ibiza, she's not a fan of being pulled away from a case. So, I have a hard time believing this vacation to Montreal is to sit back and relax."

"What are you asking of us, Admiral Chandler?" Luke cut to the point.

"We're giving you operational authority over this matter," the president stated. "If we send anyone with the Agency to Canada, someone in Montreal—in the hacker community—is sure to get wind of it. It'd be better for your people to head up there and take a look. Keep this mission off-the-books."

"And your daughter, sir?" Wyatt swallowed.

"I'd like to keep her alive and out of a Canadian jail if possible."

"We can do that," Luke answered before Wyatt could get the words out.

"Keep us informed. I want regular updates," the admiral added. "Due to the personal nature of this operation, I'll be holding off on announcing my new position until this situation is resolved."

"Understood." Luke exchanged a few more words with the president and admiral before the call ended.

Wyatt tore his fingers through his hair. No way in hell would he try to convince Natasha to back down from this case. They'd need to work together, which meant she'd find out soon enough he wasn't really a private contractor for hire, but at the moment, that was the least of his worries.

"We can get a list of hackers who signed up for the competition and are at the conference. Narrow down the list of suspects in case the hacker we're looking for is one of them," Harper said, and she was already on her laptop working before she'd finished her line of thought.

Wyatt continued to watch Harper work, doing his best not to let his mind race, to wander to thoughts of Natasha. To her sun-kissed blonde hair and her killer green eyes.

"That's a lot of names to go through," Finn said when Harper brought the list onto the screen.

Wyatt moved closer and began reading through them to see if anyone stood out. When he spotted a familiar name near the end of the list, his eyes widened. "Shit, it can't be her."

"Can't be who?" Asher asked, coming up behind him.

"Can you pull up what you can find on Gwen Montgomery?" Wyatt pointed to the name on the screen. Charlotte had mentioned her daughter was in school in Canada and studying computer programming, but would she really compete in a hacker competition? Her mum would have a bloody heart attack.

"Here you go," Jessica said, and when the girl's face filled the screen, Wyatt stumbled back, and his stomach muscles tightened.

Fuck. Me.

"She's gorgeous," Chris said. "Too young for me, but hot."

"Full name is Gwyneth Diana Montgomery, but she goes by Gwen. She's twenty. Well, twenty-one in March. She attends a school in Toronto. Daughter to Charlotte Montgomery and the late Arthur Montgomery. Nobility, too." Jessica rattled off a few more details.

"You know her or something?" Luke asked.

Wyatt had never gotten a close look at her at Arthur's wake but . . .

"I need a minute." Wyatt grabbed his mobile and rushed out of the office and to a private conference room down the hall.

He dialed his mum, had her give him Charlotte's number without explaining why, then phoned Charlotte before he lost his nerve.

"Charlotte," he rasped when he recognized her voice upon answer. "It's Wyatt Pier—" He stopped himself from finishing his name. "It's me. Sorry it took me over a year to actually call you, but fuck, Charlotte. She has my eyes." He brought his palm to the desk as his stomach tucked in, and his chest constricted. "Hell, she has a lot more than my eyes."

Every fiber of his being burned. It stretched. He was going to break with every moment of painstaking silence as he waited for her to speak.

"Is she mine?" He paused. "Is Gwen my daughter?"

CHAPTER FOURTEEN

"You're going to have to run that by me again." The room was closing in on him, and Wyatt tugged at the material of his shirt. He was too damn hot, and he couldn't breathe. "I don't understand."

"Arthur didn't want to know. And he didn't want you to ever know there was a possibility," she said, her voice flat. Emotionless. How was that possible given their current conversation? He was ready to claw at his skin.

"Start over. From the beginning." He slid to the floor, bringing his back to the wall and propped a knee up with one leg stretched out. "Word for damn word."

There was a crackle over the line like he was on a SAT phone out in the Middle East and just keyed his mic for help. The sound was the result of a shaky breath. Emotion from Charlotte now showing. And it terrified him.

"When the doctor told me I was pregnant, I assumed it was Arthur's because you and I were together only the one time."

"I used a condom, Lottie." He hadn't used her nickname since they were in primary together, but it'd just slipped out.

"Arthur always did, too." Another loud crackle hit his ears. "Doctor said conception was June. I admitted to Arthur after we were married that there was a small chance the baby could be yours. He didn't want to even talk about it. He said she was his, and he forbade me from telling you or anyone else what I'd told him."

"You never found out? Tested her blood against his or something?" How the hell was this happening?

A daughter.

No.

He couldn't have an almost twenty-one-year-old daughter.

A daughter who was attending the Bug Bounty Competition in Montreal. Hell, she might have even run across The Knight, unaware he was the best hacker to date as well as a dangerous and ruthless monster. The same monster Natasha had been hunting down for years. And no doubt the reason she was currently "on vacation" in Montreal.

"As she got older, she started to remind me of you, and I wanted to check. But every time I brought it up to Arthur he'd get so upset. In his eyes, blood didn't matter, she was his. And he's right, I mean—what's blood, anyway? He raised her. He's the only father she's known."

"You were going to tell me at the wake, weren't you?" Arthur had just passed, and what, Charlotte thought it was time to set the record straight, to let Wyatt know he might be Gwen's dad?

He stared at the tattoo reminder inside his forearm of the friend he'd lost twice. Once because Wyatt left England and never looked back and again to cancer. Emotion plowed through him too heavy and fast to handle.

"It occurred to me then that Gwen might still have a father," she said, an echo to his thoughts.

"*Might*." There was still a chance she wasn't his. But the second he saw Gwen on screen, he knew in his heart, in his gut, she had his blood coursing through her veins.

God, he didn't know which way was up right now. The world was spinning.

He squeezed his eyes closed and drew in a breath to try to calm the hell down. He never got like this. Not ever. But this was . . . new. Foreign. *A dad?* He thought about his uptight father, and he gripped his chest.

How could his parents not have realized the similarities? Didn't they see the Montgomerys regularly?

"I'm so sorry. We were doing what we thought was best, and admit it, you wouldn't have wanted to know."

Her words were a cold slap in the face. "I . . ."

"How'd you know? Why the call?"

Because she's on a list of hackers. She might be in danger.

A sense of worry, concern like he'd never experienced, shot through him. It was a vicious sound and it rang so loud he thought blood would come out of his ears.

He'd already made his mind up to go to Canada before the admiral's request to protect Natasha, but now—shit, he also had to go there to protect his own daughter.

Is she mine?

Yes.

No.

Damn it.

"I'm going to Canada for work, and I'll be near the . . ." He couldn't get the words out. His ability to speak was buried deep beneath a pile of new responsibility he'd never in his life shouldered, nor believed he would have to.

"There's a chance she may not be yours," Charlotte said in a soft voice, but she wasn't even buying her own words.

159

"Your mum has seen Gwen a dozen times, and she never made the connection, so . . ."

His mum didn't *want* to see the resemblance. It would cause a scandal, and she'd lose her bloody mind. She had to have some idea, though.

Gwen looked nothing like Arthur. She didn't have Arthur's hook nose, or Charlotte's small button one. No, Gwen's cheekbones, her bone structure was a feminine version of Wyatt's. Even a touch of a cleft in her chin like his, almost unnoticeable, but he'd spotted it on the screen. He'd noticed every detail as if he'd been staring at an image of a much younger sister.

"I have to go." He blinked, working to pull his shit together as he forced himself upright. He braced a palm to the wall at his side to maintain balance, feeling as though he were pissed drunk.

"You're not going to reach out to her, are you? She'd never forgive me, and we still don't know for certain. And you don't want kids, right? Your mum said you didn't."

Of course. His mother had planted seeds in Charlotte's head to prevent her from letting the truth slip, to prevent a larger stain on the family name than Wyatt had already caused.

"I have to go," he said again in a daze and ended the call at the sound of the door opening.

"You good?" A.J. must've sensed something was wrong because he closed the door behind him and approached Wyatt like he'd just pulled the pin on a grenade. Or maybe it was all in Wyatt's head because he was on the verge of a mental breakdown. "Sick?"

He let go of the wall to ensure he appeared as though he had it in him to fly to Canada and take down a hacker while also protecting *two* women. "No, I'm good. Bad sushi at lunch."

"You didn't eat sushi. I was with ya. BLT."

Right. Shit. "Bacon was probably, um, bad. Or the lettuce." He forced a half-smile. "There's always some lettuce recall these days."

I'm losing my mind.

A.J. closed the space and slapped a hand over his shoulder. "We really talking about lettuce right now?" His gaze moved to the mobile clutched in Wyatt's hand. "Or is this about the admiral's daughter?"

He wished it was only about her.

Facing Natasha would more than likely test his resolve. He hadn't done a stellar job at resisting her before, and it'd taken all of his damn strength to do so in Colorado.

But no, this was about the fact he may have a daughter, a daughter that could be in danger. And he didn't have a clue as to how he was supposed to act and feel right now.

"I'll sleep it off on the plane."

"That mean you're volunteering Echo for this mission?"

Wyatt nodded. "Did you really expect anything different?"

CHAPTER FIFTEEN

MONTREAL

BROKEN FLUORESCENT LIGHT BULBS AND PAINT CHIPS crunched beneath Natasha's boots as she carefully moved across the floor. She'd already spent two hours searching the abandoned clothing mill, about a mile away from where some of the other old textile factories were situated. Unlike those buildings, which were beautifully renovated as if the owners had gone on one of those HGTV shows her mom adored, this place hadn't gotten any love. The mill had remained an outcast from the newly blossoming area that now drew in big names in A.I. and tech.

The building was mostly empty, aside from trash and the occasional rodent, but its mammoth size made it difficult to traverse. Even though it wasn't littered with landmines, there was plenty of rotten wood that buckled beneath her feet, threatening to give out with each step.

To make matters worse, most of the giant-sized windows had been boarded up, leaving her to rely on only a flashlight to navigate around piles of garbage. It also came in handy to scare off the critters she heard skittering around.

She'd never been much of a believer in ghosts or haunted houses, but when she reached the third floor, she swore there was a shift in the atmosphere. It had taken on an eerie stillness unlike the other floors, and if possible, it was even colder. Most unsettling were the brushes of what she could only describe as energy that nudged against her body, like people bumping into her in a hurry to get somewhere.

She checked her watch. Maybe it was an echo of the past, people rushing out of work at five to get home.

Her shoulders trembled, and a chill rattled her teeth together. It was damn cold inside, even with her jacket on. But it was January in Canada, what'd she expect?

The creepy sensation continued to move through her as she searched for some sign, some indication The Knight had recently been inside the factory building.

It'd already been four days since she'd run the traceroute program back in Moscow before getting kicked back to Langley. The program allowed her to link the IP address from the weapons facility hack to a physical address. Although getting through the firewall hadn't been easy, and the signal had bounced all over the place before she'd traced the origins —the fact she'd been able to find the location at all and so fast meant The Knight wanted her there. The signal was still transmitting, so at the very least, there had to be a modem in the building.

The Knight had planted the bait in front of her and waited for her to bite. He'd somehow found her in Moscow and used Boris to get to her. Another pawn in whatever sick game he was playing now that he was back.

But she was determined to follow any possible lead, even if it'd been purposefully placed in front of her. She wanted this guy, and she'd do whatever necessary to find him and put him out of commission.

Hell, if she were watching an episode of her own life right now on TV, she'd be shouting *Oh, come on, don't go in there!* and *Give me a break!*

But despite often ridiculous plots, screenwriters got a few things right on occasion. People in her position sometimes did risky things, and this moment was proof of that. She was inside this ghost of a factory that could be used as a set for horror films, and she was unarmed. Another check on the stupid chart. Since she wasn't in Montreal with operational authority, she hadn't been allowed to bring her firearm across the border.

Maybe she should have gone back home to Texas and taken a real vacation. She owed her mom a visit, and she missed her old high school and college friends.

But no, she knew herself better than that. As soon as she'd arrive in Texas, guilt would sharpen its blade and start carving away at her conscience until she hopped on a plane to Montreal to try and catch the bastard. She'd visit home after The Knight was finally out of her life once and for all, and if catching him meant risking her career, then so be it.

Survivor's guilt was real, and it burned through her body like a line of fiery anger down her spine. Her fallen colleagues couldn't chase after him, so it was on her to take the bastard down and prevent any more lives lost.

After another thirty minutes searching through the third level, she made her way up a rickety wooden staircase to the final floor and sent a silent thank you to the universe for not allowing the stairs to collapse under her weight.

She stood still for a moment, allowing her eyes to adjust to the light filtering in through the windows, then turned off the flashlight and stowed it in her bag.

This was the only floor with natural light. Someone had removed the boards from the windows, and if her instincts were right, it was The Knight.

Maybe he wanted her to find something there? *Or maybe he just wants to shoot me.* There could have easily been a sniper on overwatch from the building across the way. *He doesn't want me dead*, she reminded herself for the tenth time since showing up to the factory. *Not yet, at least.*

She took careful steps past the exposed brick wall on her left that'd been turned into a canvas for graffiti taggers.

"What do you want?" she whispered as she slowly walked, nearly tripping on a rusted pipe.

She stilled at the slight twitch of sound, and this was most definitely not a disturbance from the past, no spirit coming to haunt her.

No, the sound was of this world, and it was modern technology.

A camera.

She followed the noise a few feet ahead to find a security camera mounted above an impressive graffiti Statue of David.

The green light glinted like a stereotypical "diamond in the rough" and was an indicator it was actually running.

He was watching her, she could feel him behind the lens. The camera had detected her movement, and the soft, whirring noise was him zooming in on her. He'd chosen this floor because of the light, so *he* could better see her.

The place could be rigged with explosives like the property had been in Romania, but fear didn't strike her as she stared up at the camera. No, she was just thoroughly pissed off.

He'd taken too much from her.

Penny, a CIA analyst with a megawatt smile and huge dreams.

Zach, a husband and father of two who'd given twenty years of service to the Agency.

Xena, a Russian cyber whiz who'd become a CIA agent, providing credible intel for three years.

Yasemin, a Turkish spy and white-hat hacker who'd come the closest to tracking The Knight, a move which most likely had prompted him to take out her team.

"What do you want?" she hissed, looking directly at the camera, palms open, beseeching. "I'm here." She enunciated each word in case there was no sound on the camera and the son of a bitch had to read her lips.

Irritated, she turned back to face the room to search the area within range of the camera lens. He'd brought her there for a reason and not just to get a good look at her.

She cocked her head at the sight of a blinking light near a heap of scraps. A pile of old clothes as if they belonged to a homeless person, fluffs of fabric possibly from the days when the textile mill had been operational, empty spools once used for thread . . .

She edged closer to confirm what she suspected was a modem and router box without an attached computer. The Knight had staged this scene down to the last detail. She noticed more props for his show behind her.

An iPhone about five models too old.

And something else, something that made her stomach burn.

She took cautious steps, keeping her head down to at least avoid a headshot if a sniper was actually in the wings, then swallowed the tight knot in her throat and reached for the object regally sitting on top of the black router box. A chess piece—a white knight.

Natasha closed her eyes as a memory pulled to mind. The day she'd learned team members from her case had been hit in 2018, a package had been delivered containing a cell phone and a chess piece. A piece identical to the one now in her hand.

She'd tried to identify the brand, the age of it, and where it may have been sold. No luck. It hadn't been distinct enough.

Like the previous chess piece, this one was rough around the edges. A slight chip in the side. Worn from use. The only fingerprints she'd probably find on this one would be hers, same as last time.

She set the chess piece down and picked up the phone when it began ringing.

"Natasha," he said as soon as the phone met her ear. "Have you missed me?" He wasn't using a voice-changer app like the previous time he'd phoned her. "It has been too long. How are you?"

She faltered back a step at the sound of his voice, which was far too normal for how she'd imagined him in her head. Unlike a movie villain, whose voice communicated darkness and evil, The Knight's voice was plain. It didn't reveal any hint that he was a monster.

"I did not expect you to show up alone. Where is that guy you always have attached to your hip when you are hunting me?"

Jack?

"You got here much quicker than I expected, but I should not be surprised. There was a reason I kept you alive. You have always been better than your colleagues."

From what she could tell, he was most likely European, a non-native English speaker. A male in his late thirties or early forties. She could be off by a decade or so since he was working to hide his accent, but most native English speakers used contractions, and he was speaking far too properly.

She needed to keep him talking to try and learn more about him, but since he wasn't disguising his voice, this was probably all part of his plan.

She'd studied the game of chess, searching for symbolism in his choice of hacker handle where there may not have been any, hoping if she understood the game better it would somehow help her figure out his next moves.

But maybe he was just a sociopath? Maybe his choice in using a knight had been to throw her off?

"What do you want?" she asked when he'd yet to speak again.

"We never finished our game." The camera lens blinked and clicked as if focusing again, getting a close-up shot of her.

"Why'd you wait so long to come out of the shadows? Why'd you detonate that house before you even left?" She was fishing, hoping he'd bite.

"You want to know if I was at the house in Romania when it exploded? You have been wondering for sixteen months."

Would she believe any answer he gave her?

"I was there, but since I am still alive, you did not win our game." The anger in his tone revealed his accent, offering confirmation he was Eastern European.

"Why do you want me in Canada? If you're looking to continue whatever sick game you think we're playing, sending me on a goose chase isn't in your normal rule book."

"You are right, Natasha. This time is different. But since you have to ask me why I brought you here, I am concerned that you are losing your edge. I provided very solid clues for you these last several days. Two back-to-back hacks should be more than enough to get you started."

She stalked even closer to the camera and tipped her chin, staring as if she could see into his vicious, soulless eyes.

"I went through a lot of trouble to bring you here, please do not disappoint me. It is only a game if I have a worthy opponent."

"You son of a bitch!" she hissed, but he hadn't heard her because he'd already ended the call.

Two recent hacks? What had been the second? Maybe if she'd stuck around Langley another day before taking off on vacation, she would've found out about it. Just because it wasn't in the news didn't mean something hadn't gone down.

She pushed up the sleeve of her jacket and checked her G-shock watch.

There was someone she needed to track down.

Her most valuable asset, Jasper, had gone off the grid after he'd helped her locate The Knight in Romania. Losing her source had been a blow, especially since she'd known in her gut The Knight wasn't dead.

Jasper had pissed off more than the CIA with his disappearing act. MI6 were gunning for him as well.

But she knew Jasper was in Montreal now. And him choosing to resurface in the same place as the biggest hacker convention around the same time The Knight had come out of hiding, well, there was no damn way it was a coincidence.

CHAPTER SIXTEEN

"PASSWORD?" THE MUSCULAR GUY STANDING AT THE DOOR sounded bored and looked like he'd rather be anywhere else but there. Natasha offered him the code, and he stepped aside with a nod, allowing her entry. The two-story, red brick building was one of the original firehouses in Montreal and, in its glory days, had used horse-drawn fire wagons. Today the place was rented out for parties, like tonight's event for a group of world-famous hackers.

The party was in Griffintown, a district of Montreal which had been revitalized over the course of the last decade. From the looks of it, the firehouse had maintained its original charm with the red-trimmed windows and a brass fire pole at the center of the room, with the addition of a fully stocked bar stretching the length of one exposed brick wall. Several black leather couches were strategically positioned around the room, along with high-top tables and stools. The DJ spinning from the second floor, which overlooked the main level, made the place feel more like a nightclub than a haven for hackers to do shady shit.

No one was dancing. Most people were listening to jams

through their own headphones, if that's what all the head bobbing was about, with computers on their laps as they sat working—coding.

There was a diverse mix of people in attendance. Men and women had flown in from Russia, Romania, China, and two guys she'd noted on her list were from North Korea. They'd come for the conference and the competition, all itching to be declared the MEH, the Most Elite Hacker. They had no idea The Knight already held that title, at least in his opinion. Of course, these hackers were competing in a legal setting.

The five hundred K bounty had probably turned a few hackers who normally hung out on the Dark Net into so-called white-hat hackers. And if they were lucky, or wanted a legit future, they might land one of the high-paying jobs with the sponsors of the competition doing what they loved without the risk of handcuffs.

Natasha did another survey of the room, identifying all the men who appeared to be in their thirties or forties.

Half the people there wore hoodies with the hood pulled up, a classic hacker look. The guy on the couch off to her left was no different. She dropped her backpack to the floor and sat next to him.

He was in his mid-twenties and most likely not her target. The hacker looked up from his screen. His oversized burgundy hood surrounded his face, serving as a kind of mask and cape to protect his identity. Lowering the headphones to hang around his neck, he gave her the once-over.

Natasha reciprocated and conducted a casual perusal of his neck, face, and hands—the only areas not covered by clothing—and wondered if The Knight had any burn scars.

"Hi," she said with an easy smile, falling into her role as a young hacker, hoping it was believable.

Black brows, artfully plucked, darted together as he gave her another quick glance.

She had on a short, pink and black plaid skirt, a pink tank top beneath a black hoodie, and black 8-eye Dr. Martens to complete the outfit. It wasn't exactly her typical go-to, especially all the dark eyeliner and eyeshadow, but it worked. Usually, someone at the Agency helped pick out her cover, but thankfully, she'd gone under plenty of times at hacker events in the last several years, so she was familiar with the scene.

She popped a piece of gum into her mouth and began snapping it to shave a few years off her age. "I'm Heather." She tightened her ponytail, which she'd added some pink highlights to at her hotel before heading there.

"What's your handle?" he asked skeptically.

"Crash Override," she deadpanned. He didn't get it, but a woman at a table off to her right chuckled.

"You're for real?"

"You've never seen the movie *Hackers*? It was . . ." She let go of her words at the sight of her source walking through the main entrance.

The saying *Don't judge a book by its cover* couldn't be truer in regard to Jasper Kenyon.

Appearing as if he'd stepped off the pages of an Abercrombie catalog, Jasper looked more like a model than one of the best hackers on the planet. When Jasper's eyes connected with hers, a look she couldn't immediately identify flashed across his face, and he took a quick step back, bumping into the woman who'd come in behind him.

He shouldn't have been surprised to see her. He'd chosen to come out of hiding by entering the competition. But the alarm crossing his face . . . did he think she'd announce to the room he used to make bank selling intel to the CIA?

She tipped her chin, motioning for him to follow her upstairs so they could talk. He held her eyes, then finally nodded before unbuttoning his black wool coat.

Without a further word to Hacker Guy, she grabbed her bag and went for the spiral staircase.

Upstairs, she hurried past the DJ and made her way to what had once been the kitchen where the firefighters must've gathered for meals back in the day. She'd studied the layout of the building upon learning about the party, assuming, and rightly so, that Jasper would show since he had entered the Bug Bounty Competition.

She discreetly removed a device from her backpack to check for any bugs or listening devices. When the small light turned green, signaling the place was clear, she stowed it away in her backpack, swung the bag in place over one shoulder, then waited expectantly.

Jasper rounded the corner a moment later, making a slow, hesitant approach. "Since you're here, I'm guessing you remember how to solve a cipher." He cocked his head and observed her, his gaze cataloging every detail as if triple-checking she was indeed Natasha.

"I still remember how to solve a basic substitution cipher." To find the location of the party and receive the password to get inside, she had to decrypt a code. And, thanks to a class on ciphers used by Russian spies during the Cold War, she was fairly familiar with it—a straddle checkerboard cipher. "I have to say, I was surprised to see your name on the list of competitors. Where have you been? Why'd you ghost me?" A hundred more questions buzzed to mind, but she didn't want to overwhelm him.

Recruiting new assets to work this case after the tragic loss of her sources in 2018 had been next to impossible, especially since The Knight claimed credit on the Dark Net.

So, when she'd learned MI6 had a valuable asset, she'd called in a favor to a friend and requested MI6 time-share him. Jasper was one of the best programmers she'd ever met in person and his willingness to help her had been one hell of a break.

"Are you Heather tonight?" he asked, ignoring her comment, his British accent a reminder of another Englishman from her past—Wyatt.

He crossed his arms, distrust in his eyes when it should have been her distrusting him. He was the one who got rid of his CIA burner and vanished.

"Yeah, I am." Heather had been the alias she'd used when they worked together in the past. Pink hair and all.

His fingers moved through his long blond hair, the color like the sand from the Sahara. He'd let it grow since she'd last seen him in 2019. It brushed against the collar of his black, button-down shirt.

"I can't help you. Whatever you're going to ask, I'm done. I should never have helped you all in the first place."

"You tell MI6 the same thing? Do they know you're here? If I was able to find you, it won't be long before they show up." Last time she'd checked, Jasper had a life-long commitment to England in exchange for a "get out of jail free" card. And because of that, MI6 didn't have to pay him, so the CIA footed the bill when it came to tapping his cyber genius to go after The Knight.

"MI6 knows I'm here."

"You spoke to your handler?"

"Yeah, an hour before I came here. I have a week, then I have to report back to London."

And what, work with MI6 again as if he'd never left? Seven days of free rein? She didn't buy it. She'd call her contacts there to verify his story, but what would she say? She wasn't supposed to even be working the case.

"Well, we need to talk. I don't know where you've been or what's going on, but you made the decision to show your face, so deal with the consequences."

"I had to go into hiding because I helped you." He stabbed at the air, a scowl on his lips. "I ran out of money, hence the reason I'm here." He let out an exasperated breath.

She took a step closer. "I can't imagine money motivating you enough to enter a competition sponsored by Cyber X Security. You detest Felix Ward."

"Well, it's true. And after I win the competition, which I will, because I can out hack everyone here with my bloody eyes closed, I'll go back to London." His jaw tightened beneath his blond stubble, and his blue eyes became cold and vicious.

"Bullshit," she hissed, not buying this for one second. "What the hell is really going on?" Her fingertips curled into her palms at her sides. "Why are you in Canada?"

No way was this a coincidence. No. Damn. Way. When it came to The Knight, everyone was a pawn in his game, and each move had been carefully mapped out in advance, making him her most challenging adversary ever.

"How many times do I have to tell you?"

"Keep working at it until you get to the truth," she snapped.

He huffed out a breath.

"If you were hiding because you're worried someone will find out you were working with—"

"He's not dead!" Jasper yelled, then quickly lowered his voice upon realizing how loud he'd been. "He's alive, and yes, I'm worried. How could I not be?"

Her eyes stretched at his admission. This wasn't just some

hunch. He had proof, didn't he? "And how do you know he's alive?"

His chest rose and fell with a deep breath, but he remained quiet.

She reached for his arm. "Let me help you. This competition will only put a target on your head. Why put yourself in the public eye if you're afraid of him? It can't be for the money."

He spun back around and yanked his arm free of her grasp. "I don't have a choice. Just please, leave me alone. Don't follow me. Don't try and reach out to me again." He closed his eyes, fear shadowing his face. "Whatever game he's up to, you can be damn sure this time you won't be left alive. I suggest you get the hell out of here before you end up dead." His eyes flashed open, and he shook his head, then left in a hurry.

She snatched her backpack and went downstairs a moment later. She didn't see Jasper anywhere, so he probably took off.

No way could she drop this, though. She needed to get to the truth. To find out what he really knew and why he was in Montreal.

"You friends with The Smoking Gun?"

She blinked at the use of Jasper's online hacker handle. "What?" She looked over at Hacker Guy still sitting on the couch, the one who hadn't known about the movie *Hackers*.

"I saw him go upstairs after you. Aside from the DJ, no one else was up there. You two screwing? He's gorgeous, and I was hoping he was into men instead of women. Sadly for me, looks like your short skirt won out."

"We weren't doing anything. Just talking." And Jasper did, in fact, prefer men, but it wasn't her business to share that information with a stranger.

His eyebrows lifted. "Well, in that case, then you should know there's a hottie who is most definitely not checking me out, but he's sure as hell banging the shit out of you with his eyes. You know, if you're interested in men, that is." He tipped his chin, and she turned to follow his gaze.

The hairs on her arms stood. Her body locked tight. She was nearly frozen in place. Her heart pumped double time when her eyes connected with the sexy man across the room.

His back was to the brass fire pole, eyes pinned her way. He hadn't been here when she arrived. She would've felt a presence like Wyatt Pierson's.

"You know him? Based on your body language, I'm assuming you want to, at least."

"Yeah, we're familiar," she admitted in a daze. "Can you excuse me?"

"I'd never stand in the way of a good orgasm," Hacker Guy said as she started across the room.

What if The Knight was watching and saw her with Wyatt?

He was dressed in faded denim and short sleeves that showed off his tattoos. The ink now stretched the full length of his right arm, unlike the last time she'd seen him in Colorado.

His military boots had been traded for civilian ones, and he'd left the top few eyes unlaced. Natasha marched up to him, and when his lips parted, preparing to say God knew what, she fisted the material of his shirt, pressed up on her toes and kissed him.

His mouth was stiff at first. No doubt surprised by the greeting. But then his lips relaxed and he took over, his tongue parting her lips and easing into her mouth as if it were the most natural thing in the world, as if they'd spent a lifetime greeting each other this way.

One paw of a hand went straight to her ass and gripped tight. For a moment, she forgot this was supposed to be an act, something that "Heather" would do. It'd be better for all eyes in the room to believe he was a hookup, a hot lay and not a special operator.

Wyatt deepened the kiss as his other hand went to the back of her head and held her firmly in place. His tongue roamed her mouth, dancing with hers, and her panties were going wet faster than she'd thought possible, especially given the day she'd had.

How did they still have such chemistry? Why was it always so kinetic whenever they were near each other?

She forced herself to come up for air and brought her mouth to his ear. "Go with my lead," she whispered. "Please."

"Got it." His voice was a touch unsteady, a bit undone, the kiss having impacted him as well.

Their bodies were still pressed tight, so tight she could feel his hard length against her. The hand on her ass moved beneath her short skirt and was burning his imprint on her bare flesh. The thong left her totally exposed.

"You okay?" he whispered, worry evident on his face and in the way he studied her. In the current shoddy lighting, his eyes appeared to be gunmetal gray. His gaze lured her in, making her forget why she was even there to begin with.

"I'm working," she whispered once she'd regained her focus. And since he was there, he had to be, too. "The name's Heather." Hopefully he heard her over the electronic beats the DJ was dropping like it was 2001 and they were at a rave.

She finally freed herself of his embrace and turned to see if the hacker from the couch, or anyone else for that matter, was watching them. She had no idea who to trust, and right now, everyone in that room was a suspect until proven otherwise.

"Come with me." She reached for his hand, her heart still pumping hard. The music punctuated each step she took, beat by beat.

Wyatt followed her to the hall off to the left where the bathrooms were located. She turned to face him, placed a palm on his chest, and gave him a quick shove against the red-painted wall. "What are you doing here?" She ran a short nail up his chest, keeping up with the act, but honestly, it didn't feel fake or forced. Her hand on him, her body near his, was about as perfect as perfect could get, regardless of their location.

"I—"

She stole his words with a kiss at the sight of someone approaching the bathrooms.

Following her lead, Wyatt took her into his arms. His tongue swept along the seam of her lips, encouraging her to open her mouth so he could gain access. It was as if they were picking up right where they left off in Ibiza. Maybe like they would have done in Colorado had the timing not been so shitty for both of them.

Now wasn't any better, but this kiss was for her cover. Well, she'd keep telling herself that at least.

"It hasn't been our standard three years since we've seen each other. What brings you here early?" A swell of relief filled her chest at the idea of not being so alone in this search for The Knight, though.

"What makes you think I'm here for you?" There was a touch of playfulness in his tone, and his brow lifted, that tiny scar becoming more obvious.

"Maybe not for me, but you're here for work."

He leaned in and nipped her lip when they caught sight of

a man exiting the bathroom a moment later. The heat gathering between her legs further intensified when he sucked her bottom lip between his, then spun her around so it was her back to the wall now. He propped his hands over her shoulders.

His mouth hovered near hers, and she lifted her eyes to his. "You shouldn't be here," she said, even though it was exactly where she wanted him to be.

"If you're here, I'm here." He moved his lips to her ear. "I told you I'd have your back, and it looks like you need me."

He was right. She needed someone now more than ever. She could lose her position with the CIA if the Agency discovered what she was up to, but how could she not pursue The Knight after everything he'd done?

Wyatt's erection pressed against her, bringing her thoughts back to the intimacy of their position. Without thinking, she rotated her hips, the need to create friction between them, eclipsing her rational thoughts. "How'd you know I was here?"

He pulled back a touch and found her eyes. "Because I think The Knight is alive," he mouthed, causing her heart to nearly stop. "And we need to talk," he said before kissing her again.

CHAPTER SEVENTEEN

THE KISS HAD NEARLY ERASED THE MISSION FROM WYATT'S mind. Her lips had torched his focus. Her mouth on his had almost obliterated every possible danger that surrounded them.

It wasn't until he and Natasha were upstairs, tucked away in a kitchen area of the old firehouse, that he was able to get his shit together. This woman had a tendency to give him tunnel vision, and all he could see and want was her.

But Gwen . . . where was she?

He had checked the party the moment he arrived for both Natasha and Gwen, but there'd been no sign of either of them. When he'd rounded a corner and spotted Natasha striding down the spiral stairs in her get-up, he'd frozen in place and waited for her to notice him.

But still no sign of Gwen.

Almost every hacker worth his or her salt on the list for the competition was present. He'd learned to sharpen his memory at sniper school in his younger years, and it came in handy during operations like this when he had faces and names to remember.

Gwen's face was one he'd never forget. And how could he?

He'd been stone-cold silent on the flight to Montreal while studying the other names on the competition list. He'd gone through a gamut of emotions, including pissed at his mum for most likely suspecting Gwen was his daughter and keeping the truth hidden from him.

A.J. had tried to get him to talk on the flight but failed.

Chris and his wise-ass comments had been a bust.

Roman had just let him be because Roman was Roman.

And Finn had hopped on the same train as A.J. and Chris, which was typical, trying to get him to explain the sudden mood swing.

He'd just waved his buddies off.

His mind had been churning, same as his stomach, thinking about Gwen.

A daughter.

It was still too hard to wrap his head around.

With Harper and the rest of Echo along on the op, they'd need to know the truth, but he wasn't ready to say the words out loud, *I'm a dad.*

Natasha stood in front of him, hands on her hips after having cleared the room of listening devices. "You promise you're not here to make me leave? My dad's not having you hold me hostage again?"

He wouldn't mind holding this woman hostage. Lock her away somewhere to keep her safe, as well as Gwen. Have them tucked away and protected while he hunted down the bastard. But Natasha was a strong and independent woman, a CIA operations officer. She wasn't an untrained civilian unaware of the true underbelly of darkness in the world. No, she lived and breathed it. She could handle herself. But could Gwen?

"No, I'm here to help," he said, his gaze sweeping over her, taking in her current look.

A goth-slash-hacker chick who loved black and pink. Even her hair had pink highlights. She'd look hot no matter what she wore, but the short skirt paired with boots had him itching to bring his hands back to her legs and feel beneath that material again.

And shit. He was gonna get dizzy if he kept flipping back and forth between the two women he needed to protect.

Two women? He brought his palm down his face, trying to regroup. "Good call on checking for bugs." What'd he expect, though? This wasn't amateur hour. She was a professional. More equipped at espionage and cover stories than him.

"I was here earlier, but I'd rather be cautious. We're good, though. We can talk."

He folded his arms across his chest and watched as her gaze lingered on his new ink. He'd gotten the tattoos a few weeks ago when he'd been bored out of his mind waiting to operate.

"Sorry about the kissing, I don't know who might be watching us, and I just kind of went with it." She matched his position but kept her back to the kitchen counter as if attempting to maintain a safe distance between them, from the possibility of him pulling her back into his arms to kiss her.

But hell, part of him wanted to hoist her up onto that counter, wrap those long legs tight around his waist, and take her right there. Not even the DJ's music would muffle the cries of her orgasms.

The other part of him wanted him to get his shit together and remember why he was at this hacker party in Canada—to help and protect Natasha, as well as find his daughter and look out for her.

He wasn't sure which part of him would win, especially with Natasha standing there in a plaid skirt and neon pink tank beneath her hoodie, which was now open, offering him a view of the tight fit of the top, showcasing her curves.

In Ibiza, he'd had her top off, but he'd never made it far enough to unsnap her bra.

"The Knight," she said softly, and her words were a slap in the face, one he clearly needed.

Thank God his buddies weren't on comms, or capable of getting inside his head right now. The shit he'd get for his sudden lapse in coherent thoughts . . . they'd have comedic material to use for days.

"You're here because of him, or because of me?" she asked. "I'm confused."

"Both, but I'd prefer not to get into that here."

"How'd you even find this party?"

"A co-worker of mine just registered to compete in that hacker competition, and she was given some cryptic message to decipher in order to reveal the location. I persuaded her to let me come instead so we could talk."

Her mouth rounded for a brief moment as she came to terms with his words. "It sounds like we have a lot to discuss."

"But not here," he repeated.

"We should get going, then." She snatched her bag in a hurry and brushed past him, but he reached for her arm.

"I can't leave quite yet. I just need . . ." He swallowed. "Need to stay a bit longer."

Because he wanted to see if Gwen made an appearance. Put eyes on her, get a good look to see the truth up close for himself. The truth he had already accepted.

Natasha pivoted back to face him, her lips drawn in a tight line. Worry etched between her brows. "What is it you aren't telling me?"

She was CIA, of course, she'd see through him, just as his brothers had on the plane. He shoved his hands into his pockets and tipped his head to the side. "There's someone on the competition list I sort of know, and I want to make sure she's okay."

"Who?"

"Gwen Montgomery." He tensed as he thought back to his conversation with Natasha in Colorado when he'd dumped part of his life story on her—a fact that still surprised the hell out of him. "My friend who died, well, it's his daughter."

She lifted her eyes to the exposed air ducts above them for a brief moment. "I remember you mentioning him. She's really here?"

"At Arthur's wake, Charlotte told me Gwen attends school in Canada. I saw her name on the list of competitors for the event, and I want to make sure she doesn't get caught up in whatever The Knight is doing here."

Natasha dropped her bag to the ground by her boots and found his eyes. "You're here. I'm here." She gave him a contemplative look. "And a young woman related to your past is here. Why are we all here? Why does *he* want us all here?"

"No." She was trying to connect dots that just weren't there. "No one knows that she's . . . that she's my friend's daughter. Not even my teammates. And Gwen's never even met me. She probably has no idea who I am."

"So, Gwen being here is a coincidence?" she asked, disbelief pushing through her tone.

"I think so." *I bloody hope so.*

"Okay." She forced a smile. "Still, I'm not sure if it's a

good idea for anyone to see you with her. Not without an alias formed beforehand."

"Right." Wyatt obviously hadn't thought this through. He hadn't told anyone on his team he'd planned to seek out and talk to one of the competitors on the list. A competitor who just happened to be his daughter.

"I'm sure there will be another one of these events since the competition doesn't start until Friday. We can figure out a plan, one that enables you to keep an eye out for her." Natasha reached for his arm and squeezed.

She didn't protest, didn't question him. She just accepted what he needed to do and was on board with helping. "You're incredible," he said before dipping in to kiss her. To hell with reason and consequences, he needed that kiss.

She slowly pulled away after a moment, eyes still shut when she whispered, "Was someone coming?"

"No," he admitted, his throat tightening as emotion gathered like a storm in his chest. "That was for me."

* * *

THEY'D KEPT UP THE ACT AS FORMER LOVERS, LEAVING THE party with Natasha's arm looped with his, leaning into each other as if they couldn't bear to be apart.

A minute later, they were sitting in the back of a cab, Wyatt's focus on the passing scenery, his thoughts drifting to Gwen, who was somewhere in the city, and hopefully, nowhere near the danger.

When the cabbie hit a bump in the road, jolting Wyatt's current train of thought, he moved his gaze to Natasha.

Natasha's arm was pressed tight to his left side, and even the thickness of a winter coat couldn't dampen the rush of electricity coursing through his body from that mere touch.

Her bare thigh (and those legs had to be damn cold) connecting with his jeaned leg was causing all kinds of havoc on his senses, too. And, as if that wasn't distracting enough, her plaid skirt had shifted up to an almost indecent level. Wyatt caught sight of the driver peering back in his rearview mirror, no doubt trying to get a glimpse between her legs, even though she'd pinned her thighs closed to prevent such gawking.

Wyatt's mind was about on point with the cabbie, though, because he wanted to steal a look, too. Honestly, he wanted to do more than look. He wanted to bow before her, spread open her knees, and worship at the altar of her body. Take a taste from her other lips.

He squeezed the bridge of his nose for a second. "Fucking whiplash."

"What?"

He dropped his hand and found her smiling. Had he spoken his thoughts out loud? And how would he explain he couldn't seem to keep his head on straight when his mind was bouncing back and forth between keeping Gwen safe as well as both worrying about and desiring Natasha?

"We're here," the driver announced before he could summon a response.

Once on the street, Wyatt motioned for her to move off to the side of the hotel entrance. "One second, I gotta let my people know we're heading inside before we go up."

She quirked a brow. "How'd you figure you'd find me at the party?"

His hand hovered over his iPhone. "Because it's where I would've been if I were tracking a lead on the bastard in Montreal."

"Great minds."

"You certainly have one." He took a second to indulge in

the idea he and Natasha could work together on a regular basis, or hell, just spend more than their standard few hours alone.

His grandmother used to say *Find a lady that makes you feel like sunshine after a rainy day*. He'd taken a more literal approach to her words and chose California as his leading lady, where sunshine was more plentiful than in London. But standing before this brilliant woman, maybe he finally understood what his grandmother meant.

"You okay?" Slender fingers skirted the side of his inked arm.

He cleared his throat and blinked out of his stupor. "Yeah." One extra nod to ensure he came across as believable as the phone line connected. "We're outside," he announced to Harper as Natasha removed her hand from his bicep.

"You found her. A.J. owes me twenty." Harper chuckled. "He thought you'd come back alone. I'm preparing to loop the feeds now."

"Thanks. Be in soon." He tucked the phone in his back pocket. "We'll head to my room first, then Harper will loop the security feeds to hide the fact we're leaving to get to my team."

"Smart thinking."

"If he's watching you, it's best if no one connects you to my team."

"But you think it's okay we're together?" Her back was to the brick siding of the hotel, and he wanted to lean in, to kiss her again. To feel the sun and escape the rain.

"I guess we'll have to keep up with the act that we're old lovers. I'm sure *he* won't believe it, but for the sake of everyone else at the event, the cover story should work." He pressed a palm to the building over her shoulder and angled his head.

A shaky exhale guided his eyes to her heavenly mouth. "Well, I'm damn good at tradecraft. I can keep up with the act if you can." It was as if her words had reached out and physically touched him, and when their gazes locked, he saw the color of his mum's family jewels in Natasha's eyes. An almost crystal-like green.

"I've never had to kiss on assignment before." A nearly audible gulp followed.

"Neither have I." Feather-light words had him dipping his face closer to hers.

"You were a natural back at the club." Those expressive green eyes remained connected with his, continuing to draw him in.

"I don't know, I might need more practice."

"Right." Wyatt's free hand cupped her cheek. "To help with the cover story."

"For the cover," she murmured, then pressed up on her toes to close the space between them.

A soft touch of the lips turned into something hotter. Deeper. Tongues touching. Hands roaming.

But shit. Her legs were freezing. Naked beneath her skirt.

It took all his energy to pull his mouth from hers after their long, sensuous kiss. "We should get you warm."

She smiled as he removed his hands from her outer thighs where he'd been gripping hold of her, doing his best not to let his hands slide beneath her skirt. "Says the guy who doesn't even have on a jacket."

"Trust me, right now, I'm pretty damn warm." She had his blood heated, at least. But he wanted to get her out of the cold before she lost feeling in her hands, so they went indoors.

It took them a matter of seconds to get inside the elevator, and before he even realized what he was doing, he had her against the wall with his mouth tight to hers.

He didn't give a damn if this exact scene was looped and replayed on the security footage that Harper was busy creating. He didn't even care if the boys were upstairs watching them and gave him a hard time later.

In his arms, she made the rest of the world fade away.

There was more feeling packed into her kiss than there'd ever been with another woman.

He couldn't explain what in the hell was going on between them, but maybe if they had more time together, he'd have the guts to decode the foreign feelings he experienced when she was around.

If he was lucky, he could stand in the sun for longer than a few hours before the impending rainstorm would most likely strike and tear them apart again.

"We're here." Her words vibrated against his mouth.

He forced himself to step back, did his best to adjust his dick as she bit back a laugh at the sight, then they went into the hall and took a quick left to get to his room.

Once the door to his suite was secured, he faced her in the foyer. A small gap of space existed between them—her back to the wall, his against the door.

No eyes on them. No reason to kiss. But he wanted to, and he could see in her eyes she felt the same.

"Aside from the wedding, The Knight keeps bringing us together," she said, her voice soft. "I hate him more than anyone I've ever encountered, but the fact that I get to see you every few years . . . it's not so bad. Even when you lock me into a harness and force me to fly away on a rope dangling from a chopper."

"You finally forgive me for that?"

"You did save me. I guess I can forgive being held

hostage on a beautiful island." Her lips teased into a gorgeous smile as she dropped her backpack to the floor, and he took that as a sign to move in.

In two steps, he had her braced against the wall, legs wrapped around his hips, and his fingertips buried into the flesh of her arse cheeks.

Her tongue matched every stroke of his. They were both wild with need. Drunk on lust they'd left unfulfilled for eight damn years.

"What are we doing?" she asked between hungry kisses.

"Practicing our cover story, remember?" He held her pinned to the wall, and when his lips traveled from her mouth to the sensitive skin at the side of her neck, her short nails bit into his back. "You smell so good. Like coffee and vanilla." It was the sexiest smell he'd ever breathed in.

"It's called *Black Opium*," she whispered.

He dragged his lips to her ear. "Yeah, well, it's sure as hell addicting." He wanted to lick, kiss, and taste every inch of her. Drag his fingers from her arse to her clit and see how wet she was for him.

But his mobile began vibrating, and like always, he was cockblocked by the call of duty.

When Natasha lowered her feet to the floor, Wyatt kept her caged in, his palms pressed to the wall over her shoulders. "We're being summoned."

She blinked as if trying to force away the lust in her eyes. "We got distracted, I guess."

"Easy to do around you," he admitted.

She closed her eyes and let go of a deep breath. "And there's something I haven't told you yet."

"Which is?" he asked, his voice nearly hollow.

"I was working a case in Moscow and—"

"Weapons facility hack. I know."

"You do?" Her eyes flew open in surprise.

"I do, and you tracked him here."

She nodded. "And I found the exact location he wanted me to find. There was a surveillance camera, a phone, and a chess piece waiting for me."

"What?" He pushed away from the wall and lowered his hands to his sides, her words an effective buzzkill. The mental image of her being abducted and tortured struck him with an intense blow.

"He called me. He's brought me here to restart his game."

"He could've killed you." Worry broke his words in half. "He could've been there. You knew that, but you still went."

He knew she was stubborn and determined, but did she have a death wish?

"And what would you have done?" A voice now void of desire. The seasoned CIA officer had returned. That woman yelling her wrath down at him while dangling from a helo in Algeria stood before him.

"I wouldn't have gone in alone."

"I didn't have a choice, and I didn't know you were in town."

He leaned against the wall and brought the back of his head to it, willing his heartbeat to dial back down to normal. "My people knew about the building, too, but we were organizing an infil plan to prevent being identified in case he had the place under surveillance. Or get taken out by a sniper on overwatch." Horrible possibilities continued to hit him left and right. "Or blown to hell from possible thermite charges set."

"I'm glad you didn't engage. He wouldn't have hesitated to kill your people." She cared about him, but where was the concern for her own safety?

"You were so sure he'd leave you alive?"

Fiery green eyes met his. "I have been hunting this bastard since before you and I met in Algeria." A searing bite of anger cut through her tone. "I'm not an idiot. I knew he wasn't going to kill me." With her bag back in hand, she turned for the door.

"Damn it, that's not what I meant." He gently grabbed hold of her arm, and she grew still. "I know you're not stupid, but it makes me a little insane to think about you there alone and right where he wanted you . . . in the palm of his hand."

"Then I guess it's a good thing I'm not alone anymore." Softer words met him this time. "We, um, should go meet with your people."

"There's something I need to tell you, too."

She slowly turned to face him, concern etched as a tight line crossing her forehead.

"You should know the truth about me." He'd been granted permission by the Commander in Chief to do so, which removed the burden of guilt for spilling his identity as Echo One for an elite unit of secretive SEALs. "I work directly for the president, and once the Secretary of Defense is appointed, it looks like I'll be working for your dad, too."

CHAPTER EIGHTEEN

HE WANTED THE ADMIRAL'S DAUGHTER. THE SOON-TO-BE Secretary of Defense's daughter, no less.

Actually, it was more than want. It was a need that raced through him at a nearly unstoppable speed. Not even his strong-willed determination and set-in-stone policy about staying single could block out his desire for her.

"Where's the rest of the team?" They were inside Harper's hotel suite after he'd divulged the truth about his work to Natasha, and Echo Team was nowhere in sight.

Harper turned in her swivel chair at the desk in the living room, and her gaze moved to Natasha standing quietly at his side. "They're getting some shut-eye. I didn't think we needed them here right now, anyway." She stood and strode to greet Natasha. "It's been a while. You remember me?"

"Harper." Natasha smiled and let go of her bag. A firm handshake between two badass operatives instead of a hug. "I heard you went into the private sector, but I guess you never really got out, did you?"

"More like a transfer." Harper nodded at Wyatt. "And it

sounds like Wyatt had a chance to fill you in on what we really do."

"I always wondered why you left the Agency. I'd figured you for a lifer like me," she said.

Natasha slipped into "operative" mode, taking a quick tour of their temporary command center and more than likely cataloging every detail. There were 1,000 square feet, which included the bedroom off to their right.

Only one bed, which Harper slept in, but the suite was big enough to serve as their command center while in town. It was hard to cram a bunch of military guys in a small, single hotel room, so the money was worth it.

"Looks like this gig pays better than mine," Natasha joked while stealing a glimpse of the view of Victoria Square outside the two-story windows.

"We're mostly self-funded," Wyatt explained. "It's one of the benefits of running Scott and Scott. We make decent money there, and it helps pay for ops like these."

"That's pretty selfless of you all." Her focus winged Harper's way, who was now back at the desk.

Wyatt stood in the middle of the room so he could look back and forth between the two women. "Natasha went to the factory today." He dropped the news like he was ripping off a bandage, wanting to get it over with, not looking to tangle with her again about a decision that still had his heart palpitating. He trusted her instincts, yes, but that didn't have him worrying about her any less.

"You did what?" Harper shot her a glaring look.

"And you wouldn't have done the same?" Natasha challenged with a knowing smile, then pointed to the backpack she'd set down by the door when entering the room. "There was a camera, modem, and router there. A phone and chess piece, too. Everything is in my bag."

"This hacker person anticipated you'd show." Harper's lips tightened.

"That hacker person is The Knight," Natasha grumbled, clearly frustrated from being questioned for the past sixteen months on her beliefs about that fact. She blinked a few times. "But, um, what brought your team here? Was it the weapons facility hack? Or the other hack, the one I'm not aware of because I went on vacation?"

"How'd you know about another hack, then?" Harper tipped her head to the side. "It wasn't made public. Not yet, at least."

"The Knight," she said, adding a little extra bite to her tone. "We had a little chat on the iPhone he left for me today. He told me there were two hacks recently."

Wyatt tucked his hands into his back pockets. "The second hack is the one that got our attention."

"I'm not sure if you saw in the news about the American security specialist dying in a helo crash in Svalbard?" Harper grabbed her laptop and sat next to Natasha. "He was kidnapped and taken to Pyramiden."

"You're saying The Knight was involved?" Her green eyes lifted and glided straight to Wyatt.

"Or a copycat," Harper casually tossed out, and Natasha appeared to ignore her words, her attention remaining on Wyatt.

"He must have done it to get my attention. He basically confessed to me today."

Wyatt watched as guilt crossed Natasha's face. Blame for Roland Nilsson's death. "Don't," was all he said, knowing she'd understand him.

Harper cleared her throat as if to redirect their attention. "Originally, it was believed the Svalbard Global Seed Vault was the target, but it turns out the Pionen Data Center in

Sweden was hacked. One of Cyber X's security specialists, Roland Nilsson, was tortured for information, at least that's what we assume happened before he was killed. No idea what, if anything, he told them. The men who did it were hired on the Dark Net. We're still trying to trace the payment, but we managed to ping a location to the factory here."

"Do we know what was stolen from the data center during the hack? What *The Knight* was after?" Natasha asked.

"We're still trying to get the Swedes to talk, but while we were en route here, Jessica did manage to hear some chatter," Harper began, her tone steady. "It looks like it was a virtual account belonging to one person and not a corporation or organization. As for who it belonged to and what was stolen, we're still working on finding out."

Wyatt looked to the windows blocked by the floor-to-ceiling drapes, a silvery gray color filling his line of sight. He couldn't stop his thoughts from wandering to the possibility of his daughter getting caught in the crosshairs of this madness—the danger she could be in. A dull, achy throb bloomed in his chest, and his hand moved to his heart.

"Obviously, I didn't work the case when I was back at the Agency," Harper spoke up, "but CIA Director Spenser provided Jessica Scott with all the case files going back to the end of twenty-fifteen when The Knight first popped onto the radar. What's not mentioned is the source name of who discovered The Knight's location in Romania. It's been redacted."

"After the CIA's files were hacked by The Knight in twenty-eighteen, I couldn't risk having my source's name listed in any record," Natasha responded.

"And how'd you find this source?" Wyatt faced the room and squared his legs, firming up his stance as he waited for her to share intel. The pain in his chest remained, so he continued applying pressure with his palm.

"My source, Jasper Kenyon, was on loan from MI6," Natasha answered. "It took a hefty payout to convince him to help us given what happened to my agents in twenty-eighteen, but he's one of the best hackers in the world. Possibly better than The Knight since he managed to locate him in Romania."

"And he's British?" A decent assumption if MI6 had their hands on him.

"Yeah. He got himself into a lot of trouble by exposing secrets from the House of Lords, among other things. A whistleblower of sorts." Natasha's eyes drifted his way. "His online moniker was The Smoking Gun. He became known for providing the best evidence to take down corrupt leaders—Sherlock Holmes's infamous 'smoking gun' kind of thing."

"So, a white-hat hacker who pissed off the nobles?" Harper clarified.

"Exactly, but his tactics were still illegal, which was how MI6 managed to acquire his talents," Natasha explained. "He worked the case with me for five months before he tracked The Knight to Romania."

"But when our people showed, he blew up the house." A memory of his team preparing to infil flashed to mind. The explosion had sent his guys flying. They'd had luck on their side that night since no one on Echo got hurt, minus his burns from going in to try and get their target out.

"If he had his home rigged with explosives, he would've been long gone before detonating. He'd never choose to go out that way. Too stubborn." She'd probably gone over the Romania op in her head even more than he had, which had led her to believe The Knight didn't die that day. "I think he paid off a Romanian official to say a body was found to hide the fact he was still alive."

"Maybe, but what if he wasn't expecting our guys? It's possible he panicked. Maybe hit the button early." Harper was clearly playing devil's advocate, still suggesting The Knight was dead and they were dealing with a copycat in Montreal. "Or someone else hacked his fail-safe and it was murder?"

"Is that possible?" But then, he knew of cars being hacked remotely, why not a home rigged with thermite?

"What about a setup? Someone knew our team was en route, and they waited for you guys to show to blow the place up," Harper pitched another possibility while standing, and Natasha, surprisingly, remained fairly steady this time during Harper's line of questioning.

"If that were the case, and someone else wanted him dead, and all evidence destroyed, who else knew about the location?" Wyatt asked.

Aside from Natasha's people and source, only Wyatt's team had been read in on the classified details of the operation.

"You suggesting an inside job?" A sudden look of insult crossed Natasha's face. "I didn't even know the op had taken place until after the fact. No one did, except the president and your people from the sounds of it."

"What about Jasper?" Harper asked before Wyatt could manage a response. "He gave you the location. He have any reason to want him dead?"

"Jasper has a long track record of taking down bad people. But murder? No." Natasha closed her eyes and sat back down. "But Jasper is in town. He was at the party tonight."

"The guy you were talking to upstairs right before you

came down? I don't remember his name on the competitor list." The guy had grabbed his jacket and blown past Wyatt before Natasha had come down those spiral stairs looking like a dream moments later.

"A late add. Today, in fact," Natasha explained. "I was shocked to see his name on the list when I got into Montreal earlier."

"I only registered today as well. I better get our competitor list updated in case there were any other late adds," Harper said, and Natasha nodded in agreement.

"But yeah, that was Jasper at the party. And when I confronted him, he claimed he'd decided to enter the competition for the bounty since he ran out of funds while in hiding."

"You're shitting me." Wyatt's hand fell from his chest in one heavy swoop of motion.

"I think Jasper's lying about why he's here. He says MI6 agreed to let him enter the competition if he promised to return to London after. But he must know The Knight didn't die that day in Romania, and that's why he went into hiding. He's worried The Knight is out for blood."

"And yet, he's willing to put himself out in the open now?" Wyatt shook his head. "That doesn't add up."

"I can try and reach out to my contacts at MI6 and make sure he's telling the truth," Harper proposed. "Are you sure you don't want to sit this one out, though? Since you aren't here with operational authority, don't you think it might be best to let us handle things?"

"The Knight killed people I cared about, people who were my responsibility to keep safe. I can't walk away. But also, he wants me in this sick, twisted game, and if I bow out, that'll only piss him off, and he might hurt more innocent people because of it. So no, I'm not backing down. And I promise you, Harper, this isn't a copycat. The Knight *is* alive." Natasha pivoted toward Wyatt. "I should get going. If he's watching my moves . . ." A sudden curse slipped free.

"What's wrong?" He stalked closer but resisted latching on to her with Harper's eyes on them.

"I painted a target on you tonight without even thinking," she began when her eyes slowly journeyed up to his face. "That's not like me. I thought it'd make sense for everyone at the party to think you're a past lover. But whether or not The Knight believes the cover story, he may still come after you to try and get to me."

Wyatt reached for her arms, decidedly not caring Harper was watching, and he gently gripped her biceps.

"There's no chance he can ID you from the op in Romania, right?" Natasha asked before he could speak up.

"No, he wouldn't be able to recognize me. And we're not officially working for the president, so if he hacked a government server, he would find a retired SEAL," he added, hoping to reassure her.

"But he's good." Worry filled Natasha's eyes.

"Yeah, and even if The Knight's alive, and he purchased facial recognition software on the Dark Net to try and put a name to Wyatt's face while we're here, well, we've got that covered." Harper added a confident nod. "This is what we do."

"And besides, the last thing you need to do is worry about me, I promise," he said in all sincerity. "And if he does come after me, I'll be ready."

CHAPTER NINETEEN

"YOU DIDN'T NEED TO SPEND THE NIGHT AT MY HOTEL. HE'S not going to hurt me. Not yet, at least."

Natasha's place was in Old Montreal, the historic area of the city dating back to the early French settlers and still infused with their influence. Galleries, cafes, boutiques, and gourmet shops were set in historic buildings dating back to the sixteen-hundreds.

They'd walked down uneven cobblestone streets, the sound of their footsteps a faint echo of history in his ears, the impressive architecture making him feel like he'd traveled back in time. When they'd approached her hotel in what she'd described as *Too quaint and romantic of a setting,* and a horse-drawn carriage trotted by, Wyatt couldn't help but agree. And he'd never been a romantic.

Inside her room, the romantic theme continued. Natasha likened it to the sets of the Hallmark movies she confessed to watching. Apparently, such films provided a welcome distraction from work and kept her mind from spinning out of control at bedtime. He could think of a few other distractions to put her mind at ease, though.

He set his overnight bag down and moved farther into the small space. Where his overly pricey hotel was bright and modern, her room was cozy with warm accents. It was sparsely furnished—a black, antique-looking bed with white duvet against an exposed brick wall, matching nightstand with a small brass lamp on it, and an old-fashioned armoire similar to those inside the rooms of his parents' former home in England. Unlike more modern hotels, the windows in the room actually opened.

She crouched next to the bed and pulled out a small suitcase, then opened it to reveal a false bottom, exposing a small black box hidden there.

"We've got those in our hotel rooms as well," he said at the sight of the small green light on the device blinking steadily, indicating no listening devices were present.

"I don't trust The Knight. I like to ensure my room remains free of any intrusions by him."

Wyatt tapped at the watch on his wrist once she was standing again. "If someone goes into my suite, I get an alert."

"Sounds like your gadgets are fancier than mine." She smiled and tossed her jacket onto the bed. Her hoodie came off next. Followed by her boots.

"We'll have you stay with me starting tomorrow." There wasn't much room for the both of them at her place, and if he was in this tight space with her for long, well, God help him.

"That makes sense."

No argument. He was almost surprised by that.

Standing by her bed in only a skirt, tank top, and socks, it was like all roads led to this woman, and he knew that. Could feel it. Maybe always had.

But this time, could he ignore it?

"The admiral did give me orders to keep you alive and out

of jail, and I'd hate to piss that man off." A smirk touched his lips.

"Knowing Dad, I figured as much." She sat on the bed and removed her hair tie, letting her mass of golden locks, with hints of pink highlights, fall free over her shoulders to frame her heart-shaped face.

One bed. And with her in it . . . "I'll sleep on the floor."

"I won't have you sleeping on the hardwoods. Don't be ridiculous."

"The bed can't be more than a queen." They'd be too close. Their cover story practice might turn into something real. Who was he kidding? Not a single thing he'd done with her tonight had been an act.

"We're adults. It's fine. I didn't pack anything sexy. All cotton and comfort. No worries."

Like her PJs would serve as a forcefield to keep his thoughts at bay? "And you're as crazy as you are beautiful."

"And you're as blunt as you are sexy," she shot back without missing a beat.

"I guess we make a perfect—" *A perfect what?* He was clueless as to where in the hell he was going with that.

She coughed into a closed fist as if trying to remove the tension he'd created with his dangling sentence.

"You really think The Knight is here, and we can finally catch him?" Her mind was back where it should be and not where his thoughts had gone . . . beneath her skirt.

"As stubborn as you are, yeah, my money's on you not him." He would always place his bets on her, too.

"You believe me, right?" She frowned. "I know Harper isn't quite convinced but—"

"She got burned by someone posing as a copycat on a past op while at Langley. I think she's just extra paranoid now." Harper had a few walls up, just like a lot of the guys on the teams. He had to assume her experience at the Agency, before joining Echo Team, shaped who she was—how could it not?

"Oh, I'm not familiar with her casework when she was with the Agency, but I can understand how it feels to be burned. The Knight is evidence of that."

He pressed his back to the closed bathroom door opposite the too-small-for-the-both-of-them bed.

"So, what's your alias going to be?" she asked, maybe in need of some diversion. "What will Harper whip up for you?"

"What kind of man would your alias Heather date?"

"Ohhhh, she wouldn't date." Her playful tease had his quads tightening.

"So, what kind of man would she sleep with?" He'd done his best to refrain from dropping the F word, knowing the use of such language would send an immediate signal for his cock to salute her.

"A bad boy. Someone with tattoos. Good looking but smart. A sense of humor." She secured her lip between her teeth, adding an extra sultry effect before dropping, "But you'll do." Her humor faded away too fast, and he realized why when she added, "If you want to keep an eye on Gwen, I'd suggest your alias also be in the cyber field."

Gwen. My daughter. Well, probably.

"I can hold my own in that department." He wouldn't have been able to say that in the past, but after eight years on Echo, he'd done his fair share of cyber work, and Jessica had been a great teacher. "I doubt I'm at your level, but as long as I don't need to enter that competition, I'll be good." He stroked his beard, which was starting to grow in since he'd shaved it last month. "Can I ask you something?"

"Of course. Whether I answer or not depends on the

question." Her tone was so smooth it was as if the silky lingerie she'd claimed she didn't pack had caressed his skin.

He had to cough. To clear his throat. To do bloody something to get his head on right. "When'd you join the Agency?"

"That's your question?" The teasing grin that showcased her white teeth had him faltering back a step.

Work talk. It was safer.

"In twenty-eleven." She stood. "I was twenty-five, just finished getting my doctorate in international relations, and I wasn't sure what to do with my life, so I thought, why the hell not try and do something where I might make a difference—go outside my comfort zone?"

Outside her comfort zone? Like he was now. "So, I should be calling you Doctor Chandler? You're like a female version of the character from a Clancy novel, huh?"

"I'm not an analyst." Her smile stretched to her eyes.

"Right." He cocked his head. "And are you happy?"

"I don't have any regrets."

"But are you happy?"

A moment of silence lingered between them before she said, "On the lonely nights . . . no."

Hallmark movies to fill the void?

His stomach tightened, because hell, he felt the same, minus the movies.

He wanted to close the space between them, to hold her, but he remained rooted in place, standing in front of the bathroom door.

"Sometimes, I struggle to remember who I really am." A touch of somberness filled her voice. "Separating from my cover story to remember what's beneath it all."

"And what's beneath?" Getting the knot down his throat was harder with her soft green eyes pinned on him.

"Before I became such a badass, I was a complete dork." Honesty, he liked it. Hell, he loved it. "Not a cool girl at all. Someone who says the wrong thing at the wrong time and then wants to hide awkwardly in a corner." She held both palms to the sky as if saying *But hey, this is how God made me, gotta love yourself.* "A girl who wouldn't walk up to a stranger at a party and kiss him like I did earlier tonight, that's for sure."

"You kissed another guy?" He bent his head to the side, studying this incredible woman. Light radiated from her like the sun. "Because I don't think I qualify as a stranger anymore." She made the move he'd wanted to and closed the space between them. "We're dating. Well, our covers are."

"My cover wouldn't date, remember?"

"Right. Just sex." His muscles tensed on reflex. "So, who'd I meet at Clara's wedding?"

"I was still fairly new to the Agency, so you probably got a hint of awkward me with a splash of kick-ass me."

"Is it okay if I am attracted to all of you, not just one part?" he rasped.

The expression *The truth shall set you free* was spot the hell on. Sharing those words with her made him feel like a kid again, back when he would imagine flying free in the sky like Superman. Back before his parents' loveless marriage and the shitty things he'd seen in the world had become like gravity, weighing him down.

"Because I like the woman who wore flip-flops with her formal dress and who sometimes rambles," he admitted. "But I also admire how brave you are. Like really damn brave. And how you're not a quitter, and you're passionate about what you do. Hell, the way you cursed at me when the Black Hawk took—"

She closed the distance and pressed up on her toes to

bring their mouths together, and he dipped his head so she could better reach him.

It was a delicate kiss at first, and he enjoyed every stroke of her tongue, every soft nip and lick. He loved her taking command of the moment. The confidence in her actions was a turn-on.

Her hands moved from his chest around to the back of his neck. Desperate need began to take control of his thoughts—the passionate desire escalating with every pass of her lips over his. With every touch.

But he had to stop. He had to step out of the sunshine. For now, at least.

He tore his lips from hers and held on to her cheeks. "I want you more than I can possibly express."

"But you're afraid of hurting me?"

It'd be a damn dead end with him, wouldn't it?

He bowed his forehead to hers, not ready to let go. "Because I just found out I probably have a daughter, and my head is royally screwed up."

She went still in his arms. "You got someone pregnant?" And she was surely conjuring up images of a woman out there right now with his child in her—but no, that wasn't the case.

"Over twenty years ago I did."

He lowered his hands and stepped back, eyes open, heart thundering as he waited for a response.

"Gwen," she said at the realization. "Are you sure?" She searched his face for answers.

"Charlotte told me earlier that there's a chance she's mine. I called her after I saw Gwen's name on the competitor list and discovered she'd be in Montreal." He sat on the bed, dropping his weight onto the soft mattress. "But the second I saw her picture, I just knew."

Her hand went to his leg once she was sitting next to him. "I don't know what to say."

"Neither do I." He placed his palm over her hand. "I never wanted to be a dad."

"Are you sure no one else knows about this?"

"Aside from telling Arthur her suspicions, Charlotte said she never told anyone else. I was planning to come to Montreal to be here for you, but when I found out about Gwen, and that she was here, it just—"

"Overwhelmed you?"

He peered at her and nodded. "I keep worrying about her, and I keep wanting you, and my head is spinning."

"I can't imagine what you're going through." Her sweet sincerity touched him in the heart. "But I can promise you I'll help you in any way you need. I'll do whatever I can to keep Gwen from getting in the line of fire while we're operating here."

Of course, she'd say that. Because she was a good person.

He let out a soft, "Thank you."

"But I do think you should tell your people. I'm guessing they don't know."

"No, they don't." Guilt hit him. "I can tell them tomorrow." He expelled a deep breath, then wrapped an arm around her back and pulled her tight to his side because it felt bloody right to do so. "You should know that I really do want you." He let the unsaid *But,* followed by a million ellipses, hang between them as chills crisscrossed his body. "You're an amazing woman who deserves a man who has his head on straight, though, someone who can give you what you need, who can be totally present in the moment."

"You told me before that you had my back," she whispered softly, "looks like you're trying to protect my heart, too."

CHAPTER TWENTY

THE BED WAS TOO DAMN SMALL. WYATT HAD BEEN RIGHT TO
be concerned about them sleeping together.

Her body had been up against him all night. Every time
he stirred, he'd found his chest to her back, or her breasts
smashed to his chest. He'd opted to keep his clothes on
instead of changing into the sweats and tee in his bag, hoping
the rough denim would be a better barrier between their
bodies. But when she woke him, moaning in her sleep as if
she were dreaming about sex, he'd found his cock painfully
hard in his trousers, anyway.

This was why they needed to sleep in his suite where
there were two beds. It'd still be near impossible to be around
her without wanting her sexually, but *this* was downright
torture.

And heaven help him, her cotton PJ bottoms were thin,
and the pink polka dots did nothing to prevent him from
picturing what was beneath. It was almost worse because it
enabled his imagination to run wild with inventive ways to
remove her pajamas in under three seconds.

A few hours later, when the sun began to rise, the light slowly spilling through the windows, Natasha appeared to be having a nightmare. At the sight of tears tracking down her cheeks, Wyatt decided to wake her up.

He wrapped her tightly in his arms, the same way he'd always wished his mum would have done to comfort him after a nightmare when he was a kid. In a soothing tone, he whispered, "It's okay. It was a dream." He gently stroked her head and threaded his fingers through her hair. "I've got you," he murmured.

A moment or two later, she tipped her chin to look at him, her green eyes glistening as she rasped, "I was reliving their deaths. I'm never able to stop him."

Wyatt's heart swelled, aching to take away her pain. He assumed she meant her team members who died, who The Knight had assassinated in 2018.

When his buddy Marcus, who'd once been Bravo Three, had died, it'd taken a long damn time for the pain to lessen.

"Have you gotten help? Talked to anyone about it?" He kept his voice low and soft.

She blinked away the rest of her tears and nodded. "It was mandated that I get therapy if I wanted to operate again after what happened."

He maintained his hold of her, not ready to let go, not prepared to lose her.

"I was doing okay, but I think getting confirmation he's still alive has brought all these feelings back up again." She licked a tear from her lip. "But I'm too stubborn to sit this out if you're going to suggest it like Harper did last night." She reached between the tight fit of their bodies and placed a palm on his bearded jawline. "There's a chance I may not be thinking as clearly as I should be, though. It's quite possible you were right to yell at me for going into that factory alone even if I knew he wouldn't kill me."

He agreed with her confession, but he also trusted her instincts. She knew The Knight wouldn't take her out so easily. The man was an insufferable bastard, and he had a game to play.

"I guess that's why I get a little confused being around you." Her eyes dropped closed. "You feel good," she whispered. "But also dangerous." Her lip quivered as if fighting emotions again, and it shredded him all the way to his core. "Apparently, I enjoy safety but also living dangerously. The CIA hires walking contradictions, and I'm that girl."

"Do I scare you?" *Because I should.*

"The way you make me feel does, but you also make me feel safe." Her eyeliner from the night before was slightly smudged beneath her eyes, and when her long lashes lifted, her green irises shone with unshed tears. "I know I'm making absolutely no sense."

She was wrong.

She made perfect sense to him.

Because he felt the same.

She was the sun he never knew he craved, and yet, he kept clinging to the familiarity of the rain.

"I'm sorry. You have a lot on your plate. And I don't mean to be talking about this. You told me last night you're struggling and—"

"And you're struggling, too. We're in the same boat." His heartbeat kicked up the closer he brought his face to hers. "You don't owe me any apologies. If anything, I owe you one because I can't seem to get my head on straight."

Because as much as he needed to stay focused on the case, on keeping Gwen safe, he couldn't disregard Natasha, or how she seemed to ignite something inside of him he couldn't even begin to explain.

"I'm going to do something I've never done." She closed her eyes as if trying to maintain a sense of resolve. "I'm going to follow your team's lead on this case."

"You are?" This wasn't the direction he'd expected the conversation to go, but maybe it was for the best.

"A new perspective and fresh set of eyes might prove valuable. I've been working this case for so long I feel lost. And the last thing I want is to get your people hurt because I'm not in the right state of mind." Her lids lifted. "If anything happened to you or your daughter, I'd never be able to live with that."

Now he was closing his eyes, his body growing still like he was stuck on freeze-frame mode.

How would he survive the constant state of worry that came with being a dad? The fear of something happening to Gwen was already unbearable.

He hadn't wanted kids, or to marry again, for many reasons. But near the top of his list was this very issue—how would he forever ensure their safety?

How had Arthur done it? And he'd had three kids. The tattoo on the inside of his arm drew his eyes, and his stomach burned. He wasn't cut out for this.

He didn't play the *What if?* game when it came to his team and their missions. He didn't think about dying. He was doing his job.

Losing a brother was hard, but like him, they were warriors. It hurt. It hurt beyond belief when one of them died. But that was the life they'd all chosen.

Having a child, or a wife, he'd lose his mind with worry on a daily basis.

"You're quiet. Are you okay? Did I upset you?" Her hand

connected with his chest where his heartbeat thrashed like a wild horse kicking its legs in the air out of fear.

"I can't," he sputtered as if she had a clue what had been going on in his mind. He eased off the bed and surrendered his hands in the air. "I just can't."

She sat and clutched the sheet to her chest, covering herself as if she were naked instead of wearing pajamas. "What's wrong?"

He brought a palm to his mouth, trying to slow his pulse, to calm the hell down.

"Hey." She dropped her legs to the side of the bed, released the sheet, and padded over to him.

"I-I don't think I can do this."

"Do what?" She grabbed hold of his forearm, forcing him to lower his hand from his mouth.

"Be a father." He shook his head, his entire body tensing. The nerves stretching. "I've only known about her for a day, and somehow I already . . ." He brought his hands to his hips and bowed his head as he tried to gain control, to not be a damn coward. He had to man up. "I can't be anyone other than Echo One."

"Wyatt." His name on her tongue should've eased him. The sound of her voice should've comforted him, but he was too far gone. Too out of bloody sorts to do or say anything.

"I can be a sniper. I can hunt and kill terrorists." He pointed to his chest, hating the raw, scratchy sound that came with his words. "I know how to do that." He stretched his arms open wide as she stared at him with sad eyes. "But I-I don't know how to be a father, or how *not* to worry about something happening to her." His arms fell like hard slash marks through the air. "And then there's you. I'm afraid I'll hurt you." He turned and snatched his mobile off the dresser.

"What you're feeling is normal. This is all new. You don't

need to feel bad about it," she said as he grabbed his boots and worked his feet into them, not bothering to lace them up.

"I need some air." He went to the door and threw a quick look at her from over his shoulder. "But maybe it's me who shouldn't be working this case."

CHAPTER TWENTY-ONE

Natasha couldn't let him storm out like that. His heart appeared to be breaking with every passing second, and it was clear he was angry and upset with himself.

"Wait," she croaked out as she approached him in the hall, the word barely audible. "Please, stop." More punch to her tone this time to get him to hear her.

Wyatt stood outside the elevator doors, head bowed, palms on his hips. "I'm okay. You don't need to try and—"

"But I do."

He'd saved her from feeling lonely at Dale's wedding.

He'd swooped in to rescue her in Algeria.

He literally walked through fire trying to get The Knight out alive for her in Romania.

And surely there were dozens of other instances (probably many more) that she didn't know about, where he acted selflessly to help others. So yeah, she did need to do this, because she refused to let this man beat himself up.

Standing a foot away from him, she turned to the side and pointed to her room, knowing they couldn't have this conversation out in the hallway. "Get back in there right now. I won't take no for an answer."

He grumbled something too low to hear but followed her command. Once they were inside the room with the door shut, he whirled to face her, a silent plea in his eyes to let him be. Not going to happen.

Wyatt pinned her in place with a glare, his irises a shocking mix of blue and titanium that robbed her speech and had her heart racing.

Her breath froze in her lungs as silence hung in the air and filled the space, creating an almost visible pressure between them.

"I'm not cut out to be a dad. And she's twenty. She had one already. She doesn't need me filling Arthur's shoes."

"That's a load of crap, and you know it. And men like you don't just give up and walk away when things get tough."

"Yeah, well, maybe I'm not as strong as you think." If defeat were an overflowing river, it'd sweep them both away.

She absorbed some of his pain, and her tone was shaky when she whispered, "That's not true." With a palm to the planes of his chest, the muscles hard beneath her touch, she dared a step closer. "We wouldn't even be having this conversation if you didn't feel a sense of responsibility toward her."

"You think she wants a dad who only sticks around out of honor or a sense of duty?" he challenged.

"You're just scared. You put your life in danger all of the time to save strangers. You do it without any thanks afterward. But knowing Gwen is your blood makes it personal. It changes things. She's no longer a stranger, and if something happened . . ." She drew in a shaky breath and released it. "Walking away from this case and from a child you haven't even had a chance to meet won't change the fact she's your daughter. It won't make whatever hurt or anger or frustration you're feeling inside go away."

"Your shrink teach you that?" He was intentionally hitting her with a verbal left jab, hoping to leave a sting, but it wouldn't work. She was stronger than that.

And she understood his need to fight back. To keep his guard up. She'd done the same when she was ordered to go to therapy. She hadn't wanted counseling then, only revenge.

"When my brother almost died, I never regretted being his sister even though the anguish caused me pain. When The Knight had most of my team murdered, I never regretted my relationship with them or for crying over their loss." Her eyes burned with tears as she relived the tragedies. "Don't you get that? She'll still be your daughter. You can't change that by pretending she doesn't exist."

"I spent twenty years unaware I had a child." His breathing picked up, and his gaze intensified. With every heave of his chest, she witnessed him struggling with his own personal demons. Sometimes the hardest battle to fight was against yourself, and she knew that all too well.

Wyatt wasn't just scared about losing Gwen, he was angry he'd already lost twenty years of her life.

"Maybe her mum was right to keep her from me." More anger directed at himself.

"You don't mean that," she said, keeping her voice soft.

His jaw tightened. "You were right to never reach out to me. To not—"

"No, I was just scared, like you are now." She fought the tremble in her tone the best she could. "I was afraid of falling for you. I wasn't worried you'd leave me at the altar like Dale, but that you'd . . ." Her throat grew thick, the words trapped inside. The truth was unsettling. A truth she hadn't yet faced.

He leaned in. "Say it." His words were hot and fanned across her face. "You were worried I'd die."

"No," she rushed. "Dale was a Marine, but I was still going to marry him."

"I bet you didn't really love him. And that was before the Agency, before you discovered how screwed up the world can be." His hands slipped from the wall as if realizing the implication of his words, at the suggestion there could be love between them in the future.

"Don't turn your back on Gwen." She had to focus on why they were having this conversation to begin with. "She needs you."

"And how would you know?" He drew his hands to his hips.

"Because at thirty-five, I still need my dad, even if I'll never admit it to him."

"Yeah, well, she had a father, and he died way too damn young." He walked to the window and brought a palm outside the frame, even though his view was obstructed by black curtains. "My men will keep her safe, but I shouldn't stay here. What if my actions get her killed?"

"You're a hero and—"

"I'm not. I'm just a guy doing his job."

She walked up to him and brought her hand to his back. "Fathers are often heroes in their children's eyes. Military or not."

"My dad was no hero," he bit out, catching her eyes from over his shoulder.

"But you are." And there was no doubt in her mind. "Maybe you and I don't know each other that well, but I respect you. And whether you want me to or not, I care about you. Please don't write off what I'm saying."

He slowly turned, his eyes softer now as he peered at her. "Tash."

His nickname took her back to their conversation in Colorado. "So, it's 'Tash' again?"

"After everything we just talked about, and you putting me in my place while wearing those polka-dotted PJs, yeah, you're Tash to me." Thankfully, his tone was laced with a lot less anger now. "I need to tell the team and see what they say, and I'll let them make the call as to whether they want me here or not."

"Okay," she agreed. "But since we're now working together, you know my vote."

The back of his hand caressed her cheek before his thumb skirted along her parted lips.

"Which version of you did I get just now? CIA Natasha or . . .?" He stuffed both hands into his pockets.

She shrugged. "I think you got all of me."

A small smile of surrender met his lips. "Just the way I like you."

CHAPTER TWENTY-TWO

NATASHA HAD SHOWERED AND CHANGED BEFORE THEY LEFT for his hotel. Wyatt remained quiet for the most part. She'd offered him the use of her shower, but he'd declined and grumbled something about how being naked while she was in the next room would probably knock his screws loose again, and he was, apparently, still trying to jam them back in place.

She'd chosen to keep her Hacker Girl alias in place by throwing on jeans paired with a white top beneath a pink hoodie with the *Anonymous* hacker group logo stitched to the back of the sweatshirt. One sweeping side braid and her Dr. Martens to complete the look.

Once in Harper's suite, Wyatt jerked a thumb toward four muscular guys who stood upon their entrance. "I believe you met everyone in Algeria. I'll leave you to get acquainted while I grab us some coffee."

"Echo Team, huh?" Last night when Wyatt had given her a brief explanation about his top-secret job, he'd said there were ten guys in total, and it was Echo Team in Montreal.

"This is Captain America." A guy with a Southern drawl threw an arm around the man who did indeed remind her of the movie superhero. She could see a resemblance in the face. Body, too.

"I'm Chris, and A.J. thinks he's hilarious." After a quick handshake, Chris plopped down onto the sectional couch and stretched his jeaned legs out, booted feet on the coffee table.

Her gaze moved to the guy on A.J.'s left, the man who'd been a buzzkill the morning in her villa in Ibiza, interrupting her and Wyatt just as they were about to have sex.

"Finn, right?"

"See, I made an impression." Finn shook her hand, then took a seat on the other side of the L-shaped couch, its modern lines a fitting complement to the blue and purple Picasso-esque paintings arranged on the wall above it.

"Sure, brother." A.J. tipped his head to the last guy in the room. "That's Roman. He's the quiet one." True to A.J.'s description, Roman silently shook her hand and then sat next to Harper at the desk.

"And thank God we have someone like him to make up for the rest of these comedians." Harper turned in her chair to face Natasha with open palms. "Welcome to the circus."

Natasha grinned as her focus darted to Wyatt heading her way armed with two mugs. "Thanks." She clutched the coffee in her palms, and he tipped his head before retreating to the wall of windows on the other side of the room.

"Thank you all for being here." The guys probably expected her to kick things off, right? "I think having your team here will offer new insight into the case. It'll be nice to work together."

"We're happy to provide an assist." Harper smiled. "Also, it's not that I don't trust your instincts about The Knight being alive . . . I mean, you've been working the case for years, but I just needed to draw my own conclusions about it."

"I was a bit high-strung last night, I'm sorry," Natasha apologized. "For sixteen months, I've been told to let this case go. I guess I can get defensive."

"Aw, you ladies need to hug it out?" A.J. grinned, and Wyatt was going to smack the wise-ass smirk off his face.

"But just so you know," Harper said, ignoring A.J., "I matched up the code from some of The Knight's previous hacks, and it's identical. Could it be a really damn good hacker copycatting him? Yes, but I highly doubt there's someone out there who could."

"And does that mean we're officially operating under the notion we're dealing with the real Knight?" A.J. asked.

"I think so." Harper surveyed Echo Team. "You guys?"

"I'm down with that," A.J. announced before the rest of Echo followed suit and agreed. "Well, I guess that settles it, then." He clapped his hands together and shot Natasha a mischievous smile

"So, you happen to pull anything of use off the camera or phone he left behind at the factory? And I assume you scanned everything to ensure The Knight didn't leave behind any tracking devices?" Natasha asked as she took a seat next to Chris, wishing Wyatt was beside her. He still appeared a bit withdrawn, his mind on their conversation about Gwen, perhaps.

"No trackers. Everything was clean," Harper said with a nod. "We traced the call back to the conference center, so he was there. Or at least, he wanted us to think he was."

A.J. settled onto the couch next to Finn. "Even though the hacker hoedown hasn't officially started, there are currently two presentations by bigwigs in the tech industry going on there, plus registration is still open for the competition. It's like trying to find a virtual needle in a virtual haystack."

Chris smirked. "The hacker hoedown? A virtual haystack?"

"You know what I mean," A.J. grumbled.

"Anyway," Harper began, "as we expected, there wasn't anything of use, but if he does call again, maybe we'll get lucky. For now, we're looking over all the case files."

There was still a lot Natasha needed to fill them in on, and she was glad Harper and Jessica had done some speed reading. It would certainly save them time.

"Jessica and I were talking earlier, and we started looking into Felix Ward." Harper pushed up the sleeves of her red long-sleeved shirt and typed something into her laptop before flipping the screen around to show Natasha. "The seed vault, the data center, and the weapons facility, they were all clients of Cyber X Security."

"You think The Knight is targeting Cyber X," Natasha stated. "It's possible."

"Half the world's major companies have hired Cyber X at some point in the last few years, which is why I find it so interesting that out of all these attacks," Harper began while pointing to the long list of names on the screen The Knight had hacked, "none of Cyber X's clients were ever hit. It's like they were immune to The Knight."

Natasha was impressed at how quickly Harper and Jessica were assembling the puzzle pieces. There had to have been a stack of case files a mile long. She set her mug on the coffee table in front of her and leaned forward, waiting for Harper to explain to the team what Natasha already knew but hadn't had a chance to get into with them last night.

"You saying the guy who runs Cyber X is better than The Knight?" A.J. asked. "Because based on what happened to two of his clients this week, I'm gonna say no."

"Cyber X wasn't really well known until twenty-seventeen," Natasha told him. "Felix founded the company in twenty-thirteen, but he declared bankruptcy in twenty-fifteen. However, a year later, things began to turn around." Her gaze moved to Wyatt as he stood with a firm stance in front of the window, a slice of light from the parted curtains creating a halo around his body. She blinked, resetting her focus back to the others in the room. "His company hit a billion in revenue two years ago, and he even published a book, *From Bankrupt to Billionaire in Five Years*. It released this past November."

"How'd he manage to pull that off?" Wyatt crossed the room to join the team and discarded his mug on the TV stand.

"Cyber X acquired a lot of new customers because of The Knight's hacks. Many of the companies ditched their cybersecurity because of the massive breaches. Eventually, Cyber X began to snatch up the business. Not all of them hired Felix's company, but many did, and he quickly established himself as the premier agency since his clients appeared to be the most secure from hackers." She offered what was usually a long-winded explanation in as few words as possible. "The CIA didn't make the connection until twenty-eighteen."

Since Harper hadn't worked the case during her time at the Agency, she wouldn't have been made privy to the classified details. It'd been "need to know" to reduce leaks.

"The FBI placed Felix and his wife under surveillance. Plus, every other employee. Since the Cyber X headquarters are in Seattle, we couldn't operate there." Turning the investigation back over to the FBI had been brutal. She'd hated being left out of the loop.

"Guessing it was hard to nail him on anything since the FBI's always constrained by the pesky U.S. Constitution, having to get warrants for those wiretaps and all," Chris said, humor in his tone.

But he was right. The FBI often turned international cases over to the CIA because the Agency had more freedom and funding than they did. "The FBI believed Felix was actually The Knight, and he was hacking other companies to drum up business as a last-ditch effort to save Cyber X from going completely under. The timeline was a match, too. The Knight's activity started not too long after the company declared bankruptcy."

"And with Cyber X benefiting from The Knight's attacks, I can see how that'd draw attention to him." Finn looked Natasha's way. "But why'd it take so long to see that pattern?"

"Because, in the beginning, Cyber X was a blip on the radar in the industry. It took years to see the trend. And since not all companies went straight to Felix's, it only became glaring later on that something was up since Cyber X was still the *only* company never targeted," Natasha admitted. "Felix claimed The Knight probably tried to hack his clients but due to Cyber X's superior systems design, had failed. Like The Knight, Felix's ego requires its own zip code."

"Since Felix isn't in prison, I'm guessing the FBI's theory was a bust?" Wyatt asked, and Natasha directed her attention to him.

"When The Knight hacked a facility or company, he sold the intelligence or data on the Dark Net. Sometimes, I think he even sold it back to the originating companies," Natasha said. "But the money could never be traced back to Cyber X. To anywhere, in fact. There were no discrepancies in Felix's books, no offshore accounts, nothing out of the ordinary. He and his wife had alibis for several of the hacks as well."

"The Knight became more aggressive in twenty-eighteen, which was when the FBI was surveilling Cyber X," Roman spoke up, "which would be the opposite of what Felix would do if he were on the Feds' radar."

"Well, you're thinking like a normal person and not like a psychopath," A.J. remarked.

"Yeah, but if Felix is our man, why start attacking his own clients this past week?" Wyatt asked.

"Well, I, for one," Chris started, "don't think it's Felix, but The Knight might want us to believe that." He stood and tightened his arms across his chest.

"From my experience, whatever game The Knight's playing, Felix is most likely a pawn." Natasha's gaze moved back to the man capable of making her heart skip beats.

"And I'm still not convinced the dude in the house in Romania was even The Knight. Hell, maybe your source set you up." Chris peered at Natasha. "No offense."

"We could bump into the fucker today and not know it," A.J. griped.

"It's possible," she confessed. "But as for whether or not Jasper set me up and lied about Romania, I don't think so. It wouldn't make much sense unless you're suggesting *he* is The Knight, and he just wanted me off his back. And just so we're clear"—her eyes went to Chris—"Jasper has been under MI6's thumb for years. He was thoroughly vetted by the CIA before we began sharing him as an asset as well. He has an alibi for many of The Knight's hacks, and I'm one of them. We were working side by side at the time of The Knight's very last hit in twenty-nineteen."

Chris's rationale behind throwing Jasper's name out there as a suspect made sense, especially since Jasper ghosted Natasha and MI6 after Romania, but she wasn't a rookie, and she'd done more than her fair share of due diligence when it came to anyone connected to her case over the years.

"I get what you're saying, and I respect that. But the fact

is that Jasper and The Knight both came out of hiding at the same time." Chris clearly wasn't ready to let the idea go that Jasper could've fooled the CIA and MI6. "I just think we need to consider all possibilities given how manipulative this Knight asshole is."

"I don't know. Chris might have a point." Harper grimaced with apology Natasha's way. "Pretty much everyone in Montreal with hacking skills should be a suspect."

"I agree that Jasper lied to me about why he's really here. He wouldn't come out of hiding just for money, and the timing . . ." Natasha gave a hesitant nod. "At the very least, we surveil Jasper in case he's in danger. I don't want anyone else dying because of this case."

"There's, uh, one more person here we need to keep an eye on." Wyatt's deep voice carried her attention his way, and he dragged a palm across his jaw, his nervousness showing. Their conversation earlier raced back to mind.

"Yo, brother, you okay?" A.J. cocked his head.

"Yeah, but you all might want to sit for this." Wyatt's words had the room zipping so quiet you could actually hear the virtual needle dropping in that virtual haystack A.J. had mentioned.

"Normally, it's one of our two lady geniuses that gets my skivvies all twisted up, but shit, man," A.J. said, breaking the silence as he dropped back onto the couch next to Finn.

"Want me to step into the hall?" Natasha asked softly.

"No." His response was immediate, and when she peered at him, his eyes were focused on her as if he were attempting to draw strength to speak.

She gave him a tight nod of approval, sensing he needed it, then he looked around at his teammates who all sitting again.

"One of the names on the competition list is someone I know," Wyatt confessed.

"Gwyneth Montgomery?" Roman was a quick study.

"The woman who had you hightailing it out of the room at the office after you saw her photo yesterday?" Finn's brows drew together. "She's a bit young for you to be"—he looked at Natasha for a brief moment before peeling his focus back to Wyatt—"you know."

"God, no." Wyatt shook his head and looked to the floor. "She, um . . . I'm pretty sure she's my daughter."

"You're gonna have to run that by me again," A.J. said in disbelief.

"Daughter," he repeated slowly as if bracing for impact, his hands wrung tight at his sides.

"But you're not certain?" Harper held on to the chair arms like she was preparing for takeoff.

"Her mother, Charlotte, thinks it's possible. And then there's the small detail that Gwen looks just like me." Wyatt pulled at the skin of his throat as if working to get the words out. "According to Charlotte, Gwen wasn't a fan of taking on the lifestyle or duties expected of the nobility. She left London like I did, and now she attends school in Toronto."

"Have you made contact since you've been here?" Harper asked, still clutching the chair arms.

"No, I haven't seen her yet. And I'm sorry I didn't tell you all before, but I was still trying to wrap my head around it."

"So, are we saying congrats and pulling out our long guns to scare the piss out of any man that tries to date her?" A.J. was back on his feet, ready to throw down with any of Gwen's future dates.

"A.J.," Harper hissed.

"What?" A.J. shrugged. "I mean, we all knew the dating thing would be hard when Bravo's kiddos became teens."

"Are we all believing it's a coincidence that Gwen is also in Montreal and entering this hacker competition?" Finn asked.

"And wow, your daughter is a hacker." Chris scrubbed a hand over his blond beard and stood.

"Daughter," Wyatt said, the word a whisper of disbelief again. "No one knows she's my daughter. So, Gwen being here, competing in this competition, is just a wrong place, wrong time, kind of thing."

"Or the universe's way of letting you know you have a daughter," Finn commented. "I mean, would you have found out otherwise?"

"I don't know." Wyatt's shoulders slumped, the conversation obviously uneasy for him. "But I'm not sure if I should work this mission. The personal connection and all."

The guys all exchanged looks except Roman. He kept his focus steady on Wyatt. "You shouldn't surveil her, but you should stay."

"And I agree," Finn was quick to say, and the rest of Echo fell in line with him.

"I should probably run it by Luke and Jessica." Wyatt focused on Harper as if waiting for her input.

"Want me to talk to them?" Harper finally spoke up, and was that her way of saying *Stay*?

"I should talk to them," he said, "but I might need some air first."

Natasha never gave Wyatt that air he'd needed earlier, so she wouldn't stand in his way now.

Wyatt looked her way. "Come with me?" He motioned for the door, and Natasha followed him out into the hall.

They stood in silence as the elevator took them to his

floor where they'd wait for Harper to alter the security cams and hide the fact they'd been in Harper's suite.

Once inside Wyatt's room, she grabbed her white North Face jacket, and he put on his black winter coat.

"Thank you," he said as they stood by the door waiting for Harper's all clear to move out. "For this morning. For now." A smile eased onto his lips. "Thank you for helping me when I couldn't figure out my left from my right."

"It's always easier when you're not the one dealing with it." That's what her therapist had once told her, at least.

He glimpsed the text on his phone that came in from Harper. "We're good to go." He opened the door, and she followed him down the hall and back into the elevator. He leaned against the wall, hands in pockets, eyes set on her. A million thoughts appeared to cloud his mind. "What are you thinking about?

"The Dallas Cowboys and if they'll make it to the Super Bowl this year." Her awkward joke seemed to work since he returned her smile.

"American football . . ." He followed his words with a playful grumble.

"You are American now. Isn't it time you fell in love with *our* version of the sport?"

He pushed away from the wall and took one step closer, which was enough to have her searching for a deep breath of air.

The sports topic had been meant to diffuse the tension before they suffocated in the small space of the elevator, but now?

"English football—*soccer*—is not my cup of tea." Not that she drank tea. She was a coffee addict through and through. "I'm also from Texas, so basically, it's in my blood to love football."

He tipped his head to the side but remained quiet.

"My brother played football at West Point, so I'm a big fan of their team as well," she went on when he'd yet to speak.

The doors dinged and opened, and he motioned for her to exit first. Her tall brown boots carried her quietly across the tiled floors, and she kept the quiet going once they were on the street. She allowed him to take the lead, and they made their way to Victoria Square across from the hotel.

The ground was covered in freshly fallen snow, but the sky was now crystal clear. They walked to a nearby row of benches surrounded by foliage, and he brushed the snow off one and motioned for her to sit. "Thank you, sir."

When he threw a *My lady* back at her with his sexy English accent, it was a reminder that he was, in fact, a lord. Not that the man seemed to care about peerage. He didn't fit the stereotypical mold of nobility either, but hey, with the setting and the snow, could she for five minutes pretend she was living inside a Christmas movie special?

They sat and observed the people passing by in silence. She'd started people watching when she'd first joined the Agency to sharpen her profiling skills, but it'd become ingrained and was merely a habit now.

The ring of her phone disturbed the quiet ten minutes later. "It's my brother. I can call him back."

"No, you should answer. He's probably worried about you."

"Really, it's okay."

"Please. If I had a sister . . ." And the *I now have a daughter* line hung in the air between them, and she nodded in understanding.

"Hey, Gray," she finally answered before the call went to voicemail.

Wyatt brought his elbows to his thighs and stared off in the distance where cars buzzed by on the road opposite the trees.

"Jack's worried about you," her brother said right off the bat. "He thinks you might do something crazy, so this is me being the best brother ever and checking on you."

She couldn't help but smile—her brother had that effect on her. "Jack's paranoid. I'm fine."

"Sure," he grumbled. "Where are you? You need my help? Baddies to take out?"

"I'm good, I promise." A sound, like a loud clap, popped in the background over the line. Was that suppressed fire? "Where are you?" She hoped he was playing a video game and not in the middle of a real gunfight, but with Gray, either was possible.

"It's nothing."

"Gray," she scolded. "Why don't you call me later? That'd better be a game you're playing."

"I'm totally fine. You know me."

"And if you make phone calls while in the middle of gunfire to women you're dating, it's no wonder you're still single." She could feel Wyatt's gaze on her, and she stole a quick look at him, catching a smile on his lips, and it was a nice sight to see. It did something funny to her insides. "Now hang up the damn phone."

"You sure you're good?"

Am I? Her stomach muscles tightened. "Yes, and now I'm hanging up." She ended the call before Gray could shoot her a rebuttal and tucked her phone back into her jacket pocket. "Sorry about that. He has spectacular timing." She rolled her eyes. "Who makes a call to their sister when under enemy fire?"

He held his palms open, and his eyes glittered as if there was a story there.

She pivoted on the bench. "Tell me."

"I may have been talking to my mum once when I took on some unexpected fire, and I *may* have kept talking while shooting back."

"Trying to worry her, huh?"

"Sometimes I forget getting shot at isn't everyone else's typical Monday." He straightened his spine, bringing his back to the bench and his right ankle over his knee. "My mum, she had to have known about Gwen. How could she not? I knew the second I saw her photo." He looked toward the sky. "Anyway," he said, dragging out the word as if he desperately needed a change of subject, "I thought your brother got out of the Army. Medical injury?"

"Yeah, um, his helicopter was taken down and part of his leg had to be amputated." She'd rushed the words out quickly, hoping it'd make the memory less painful. "We're lucky he made it out alive, though." Not everyone did.

"Damn, I'm sorry." Wyatt reached for her hand, which felt good since her fingers were getting tingly from the cold, and he was a ball of heat.

"I was worried the amputation would destroy him, and it almost did, but he bounced back. But that's Gray, a fighter. He does what you do now. He doesn't let his injury stop him." She managed a smile. "Well, I should say he does what I thought you did. He handles private military contracts, as well as some security gigs."

"We do that, too." He gently squeezed her hand. "When we have time, at least. The side gigs, I mean."

"Sounds like you're one busy man." And she'd bet that was another reason why he didn't want a relationship. "It must be hard keeping the secret of what you do from everyone you care about."

"Is it for you?"

"Pretty much everyone I care about has top security clearance, which makes my life easier."

"And the men you date? Are they in government?"

"I, um, usually date guys who have similar security clearance to me," she admitted. "The Agency hires officers who are honest but can also easily lie—that contradictions thing again."

"Like when you faked me out by calling yourself an agent at the wedding?" He shifted on the bench to better face her.

"Ah, you remember that." Her cheeks warmed, and she was probably blushing. "It was sort of my way of telling the truth without—"

"Actually telling it," he finished for her. "I get it."

And speaking of the wedding night, she couldn't help but whisper, "You really want to kiss me, don't you?"

"I remember you saying those words to me that night very clearly." The deep timbre of his voice had the hairs on her arms standing.

"I, uh, don't know why I brought the kiss up. I'm sorry. Poor timing. I tend to do that, and I—"

"Is this the start of a ramble?" he asked with a sexy smile.

"I'm awkward me right now."

"Not the badass?" He arched his brow, and the scar bisecting it had her reaching for his face as if on autopilot.

"No, definitely not the badass one," she answered in a daze, then pointed to his eyebrow. "How'd you get that?" There were other marks on his body she remembered when seeing his naked chest in Colorado, but this one was in her line of sight at the moment.

He could get hurt.

He could die.

Same could happen to her.

A tightness developed in her chest as she traced the line of his jaw before he captured her hand inside his own and held it between them once again.

"It's not from my time in the service." He lowered their hands to her jeaned thigh but kept hold of her palm. "Someone broke a beer bottle across my face one night at a bar."

Her eyes widened. "Why would anyone do that?"

"He was pissed his football team lost, and I"—he showcased an inch between his thumb and forefinger of his free hand—"may have gloated a bit."

"And this is the sport you think I should watch?" She smirked.

"It's the best damn sport out there. We're passionate about football in England, among other things."

"So, shooting, sex, and football? The trifecta?"

"I can't play the bloody sport, so no. But I'm damn good at betting on who will win." His accent slid harder through his words, deeper than normal, and it warmed her in inappropriate places.

Wrong time, she reminded herself.

"Now I'm the one vibrating." He dipped his hand into his pocket and brought the phone to his ear. "Harper, what's up?" He paused to let her talk, then told Natasha, "The Cyber X Twitter account posted a challenge for the Bug Bounty competitors to try and find where Felix will be tonight."

"What's the catch?" she asked.

"Decrypt a ridiculously complex code to get the time and location."

"It looks like Felix is trying to get an early read on who

the top contenders are." It was Felix's style. He loved to recruit the best hackers in the world to work at Cyber X.

"Harper can go tonight and take one of the guys with her since she's competing." He held the phone to his ear again for a few seconds and then shifted it to the side to say, "We don't know where Jasper is staying yet, so we'll have Finn and Chris on overwatch at the location tonight, and if he shows, one of them will follow Jasper back to where he's staying."

"I'd like to go, too."

"You're not a competitor," he reminded her.

She checked her watch. "I can be. The last chance to register is tonight. I can always drop out later, but if Felix is there, then The Knight might be, too. And if Gwen shows . . ."

His face changed at the mention of Gwen's name, worry flooding his eyes, hardening every line of his already super hard body. "I have no idea how good she is."

Our chance to find out.

He let go of a deep breath and brought the phone closer to his ear. "I guess we're going, too." He exchanged a few more words with Harper before ending the call.

"What happens if Gwen is there. Are you planning on talking to her?"

"Maybe, but I hate lying to her, and surely, I can't lead with the whole dad thing."

"Is Charlotte planning on telling Gwen about you?" she asked once they'd started walking back to the hotel.

"I think she was going to tell me back in London after Arthur's wake."

"But you got called away to Romania." She stopped walking at the realization, and he turned to face her. "I'm sorry."

"Not your fault at all." He reached for her elbow, and his

grip was gentle but firm enough to signal with his touch he truly meant his words. "She wanted me to call her, and I never did, but Charlotte could've reached out. Maybe she was worried I'd only disappoint Gwen."

"Wyatt." She didn't want him going back down that rabbit hole again.

"I had a shit role model for a father," he admitted while letting go of her and stuffing his hands into his jacket pockets. "I don't want to be like him."

She squeezed his arm this time. "I think you'll be an amazing father."

He tipped his head to the side, bringing his gaze to her hand before his blue-gray eyes found hers again. "How do you know I'll be any good?"

"Because no matter what you think, I believe you are capable of love, or you wouldn't care so much about disappointing her. About losing her."

"I—"

She pressed a finger to his lips to silence whatever rebuttal she knew was coming. "It's true, and I wouldn't be standing here, trusting you the way I am, if I didn't believe it."

His eyes turned to slits as he observed her with parted lips. "And maybe it's you who's always showing up when I need someone," he said in a soft voice, "not the other way around."

CHAPTER TWENTY-THREE

Natasha looked nothing like her hacker cover tonight. Standing inside Harper's hotel suite, she could've played the role of a gorgeous woman in a Bond film, and although she was in a form-fitting, red dress that hugged her sensual curves, Wyatt wasn't exactly playing the part of Bond. Jeans and a white long-sleeved shirt. A casual black overcoat. The only upgrade had been his shoes. A pair of dark loafers.

The second Natasha had stepped into the room, she'd immediately drawn the eyes of both Chris and Finn. Wyatt had to signal the command to close their bloody mouths.

Thank God A.J. the Comedian, who liked to get under his skin, hadn't been in the room. He was parked outside Gwen's hotel.

Harper had chosen Roman to accompany her tonight, so he was in his room getting ready.

It was probably for the best Natasha had chosen to change in Harper's room instead of his suite. He would've broken a blood vessel watching her stride out of the bathroom in that dress with her strappy black shoes. The heels were conservative in height, not too tall so she could dance. Her long legs didn't exactly need the extra boost anyway.

Wyatt cleared his throat, loud enough to pierce the air, a signal to his brothers to find something else to do since they were still gawking at Natasha like she was the ceiling of the Sistine Chapel.

"You look hot." Finn tucked his hands into his cargo pants pockets. "You'll get Felix's attention for sure in that thing."

"You sure Felix won't recognize you?" Chris asked, standing alongside Wyatt in the living room. "Even as your alias Heather?"

Natasha had signed up for the competition, using her alias just before the deadline expired while Jessica and Harper decoded the Cyber X Twitter challenge.

"No, I've never met Felix." Natasha turned to the side and peeked back into Harper's room as if waiting for her to come out, too.

The back of her dress dipped low enough to send a quick note to his brain informing him of a detail: no bra strap. Maybe the dress had a built-in bra? He didn't have a bloody clue about women's fashion, all he knew was she was stunning, and she'd have every man at the club tonight staring at her like a walking piece of art.

"Maybe you should trade places with me," Chris said into his ear. "I can play babysitter with the admiral's daughter."

Wyatt ignored him, knowing his buddy was purposely trying to get a rise out of him, no doubt working double time to fill in for A.J. as well.

He checked his watch before pulling the material of his sleeve back in place. It was near eleven at night. "Surprised Felix chose a salsa club. Doesn't really fit the hacker image I have in my head."

"He's an eccentric billionaire." Natasha moved farther

into the living room and away from Harper's bedroom. "It's hard to ever know what to expect with him." She pulled her silky blonde mass of hair over one shoulder. Her green gaze traveled across the room and connected with his, and he immediately conjured visions of her on her knees with his cock in her hand, while those red lips of hers sucked him dry.

Then his brain did a quick switch to thoughts of him on his knees, bowing down before her, parting her thighs to get to her smooth legs. Running the flat part of his tongue up the seam of her sex. He was going to have a hell of a time focusing on anything or anyone other than her tonight.

He was ridiculously attracted to her in that outfit, but he wanted to get the dress off and have her all to himself—the real her, the one beneath her legend.

He may have put the brakes on that happening last night, but he wasn't sure how much longer he'd be able to pause this thing between them.

The main door to the suite opened a moment later, and Roman strode in wearing black jeans and a black pressed button-down shirt paired with Oxfords. His black hair was gelled and parted to the side, and his eyes journeyed across the room, right past Natasha and straight to Harper, who'd exited her bedroom a moment before.

"We ready to do this thing?" Harper had on a hot pink sleeveless dress that molded to her body and was apparently like a magnet for Roman's eyes.

Roman didn't make any quips to irritate him about Natasha, and he wasn't sure if the man had even noticed her. "You look stunning." Roman wrapped a hand tight around the back of his neck.

"Not so bad yourself." Harper winked Roman's way, but he was too busy examining the floor to notice.

"Instead of tailing our marks, maybe you boys could use

some backup," Chris said with a smile. "You might need help when Harper and Natasha get hit on by everyone in that nightclub." He jerked a thumb toward the two women.

"We won't let anything happen to them." Wyatt kept his voice as level as possible, hoping to tamp down the new surge of desire bursting at the seams with her a vision in his favorite color. "Do we need to go over the plan one more time?"

"Like how you four will be dancing at some club while Finn and I will be on overwatch freezing our nut sacks off?" Chris's typical wise-assery had Natasha's dimple popping.

"I thought you didn't mind the cold?" Wyatt shot back, referring to Chris's comments just the other day when prepping for their trip to Svalbard.

Chris grabbed Natasha's jacket off the couch and offered it to her instead of responding. She turned as he helped her into it. "So much chivalry from you men."

"Unexpected, right?" Finn remarked with a laugh while Harper passed out comms to the guys.

"Where'd you get models like that?" Natasha took the comm out of Wyatt's palm, and the slight touch of her fingers, small as it may have been, had him tensing. "I thought the CIA had the latest and greatest tech."

"A benefit of working with two genius women is you get toys like these," Chris said, giving a nod to Harper.

"You should see the pens we carry." Finn wasn't being sarcastic. He reached into his pocket and produced a black ballpoint pen.

New spy gadgets, huh? Got any secret kill pills or pens that double as weapons? A.J. had asked Jessica when she'd unveiled the latest tech before they'd left for Montreal.

"The pen doesn't double as a knife, but it records all conversations up to a range of twelve meters," Roman explained, bringing his focus up when Harper handed over his comm. "We have new software that can discern and isolate separate conversations."

"Unfortunately, if you're planning on eavesdropping on anyone like Felix, or even Jasper, they'll have countermeasures in place to prevent recording devices from working." Natasha glanced around the room.

Finn tucked the pen back into his pocket. "I figured, but you never know, maybe we'll get lucky."

Wyatt motioned for Natasha to exit. "Be safe," he told the guys before leaving the suite.

He stabbed the call button outside the lift a bit too aggressively. He was keyed up about the idea Gwen might actually show at the club tonight. The best of the best hackers would probably have decrypted Felix's challenge, but he had no idea what kind of skills she had.

Luke and Jessica had been shocked when they learned he was a father during their Skype call earlier, but it was decided Wyatt should stay in Canada and only pull out if the mission ever became compromised because of his connection to Gwen.

We trust you, Jessica had said.

But did he trust himself? He could barely stay focused with Natasha at his side. What would happen if his daughter showed up tonight?

"You okay?" she asked as they descended to his floor.

"Nervous," he admitted. "Not sure what to think if Gwen's there."

She pivoted to the side and lifted her eyes to his. "It'll mean she's a genius. That code Felix sent out wasn't easy to crack. It took both Jessica and Harper three hours."

"And I'm not sure if I want her to be some hacker genius."

"As long as she uses her talent for good . . ."

"And if she doesn't?" Once the doors parted, he waited for her to step out, then followed her to his room and texted Harper they'd be leaving the hotel in a minute.

Natasha pressed her back to the wall of the small foyer, and the memory of kissing her in this very spot last night flashed to mind.

He checked his watch, ensuring the device in his hotel room hadn't been tampered with and no one had entered while they'd been gone. The green light signaled they were clear and no bugs had been placed.

"Everything will be okay." She pressed her palm to his chest and slid it up to his shoulder. "I promise," she said softly. "I can't keep up the chase. I'm exhausted from hunting this guy down." Her voice dipped and her words hit him straight in the heart. "I need it to end."

"I've got your back. Don't worry."

"You gonna let me have yours?" Her hand went to his heart, which beat like an intense drum with her so close.

"I'll do my best to let you," he admitted, knowing they were talking about a lot more than just going after The Knight.

* * *

It was as if they stepped into Havana once inside the club in Old Montreal. The club was a hole-in-the-wall place, probably some hidden gem. The decor was a vibrant mix of colors: teals, emeralds, lime greens, oranges, and pinks. The walls, furniture, and artwork were an embodiment of the vibrant country of Cuba.

A band was situated at the front center of the room on a stage, playing lively salsa instrumentals. Between the music and the overflowing amount of mojitos, he couldn't help but remember his last mission in Cuba in 2018.

Chris and Finn had gotten piss drunk and nearly been thrown in jail when they went partying after the mission was completed.

A.J. had joined the band and picked up a guitar and somehow managed to get everyone singing along with him to a Luke Bryan song.

Roman had gone back to the hotel for some rack time, choosing not to party.

And Wyatt had sat at the bar shooting back whiskey, deciding whether or not to head to D.C. and visit Natasha. He'd planned on reaching out to her after learning The Knight had targeted her team, killing some of her agents and colleagues, but then he got spun up for the mission in Santa Clara. He hadn't been sure if she'd even want him to show up, at least that's what he'd convinced himself, so he'd decided it'd be best to keep an eye on her from a distance.

When she'd visited him the following year in Colorado after his op in Romania, it was then he realized he should've gone to see her after his mission in Cuba. He should've done more than just ensure she was safe. He should've buried his bullshit and, at the very least, called her.

Wyatt ordered two rum and Cokes, then pivoted to face the club. "She's making contact now," Wyatt said into his mic as Natasha strode through the room to get to Felix, drawing the eyes of everyone there with each step she took.

Felix was there as promised in the tweet, tucked away in a booth off to the side of the small area where couples were salsa dancing, exchanging partners every so often during songs. The pissed-off-looking woman sitting next to Felix was the president of Cyber X, and also his wife.

Kate was in her thirties, but she looked closer to twenty.

With her wealth, it wasn't any surprise she'd removed more than a decade to obtain her much younger look. Her pale skin was a contrast to her raven-black hair, close in color to Felix's. Her eyes were green, several shades darker than Natasha's.

Before leaving the hotel, Wyatt had studied the dossier Harper had prepared on the Wards. Felix had met Kate at the very first Bug Bounty Competition in 2012. She'd placed second, and he'd landed first. Felix had used his winnings and family inheritance to start up Cyber X Security.

The Bureau had looked into Kate, plus every employee at Cyber X. Many of Felix's hires were former hackers before turning over a new leaf to be on the right side of the law. It made the FBI's job a bit trickier in profiling since over half the employees had a criminal record.

"Contact is being made now," he updated his team over the line once Natasha was standing next to Felix's table, introducing herself as one of the hackers who'd managed to solve his Twitter challenge.

Natasha pivoted to the side, hands on her abdomen as she smiled and nodded at something Felix said.

The plan was to make a quick intro and then head back to the bar to keep an eye on the other hackers who had the skills to attend tonight.

Would Gwen show? The idea of her being an elite hacker . . .

"She's heading back to me." That was fast. "Cleared for phase two," he whispered into his mic, letting Harper and Roman know they were good to enter the club.

He turned back toward the bar and paid for the two drinks, then offered Natasha hers once she returned. "How'd it go?"

She took a small sip of her drink, eyes carefully surveying

the club. "He didn't say much. It was strange. He was off. His wife, too." She shrugged her bare shoulders slightly. "But he was blatantly checking me out, so maybe that pissed off his wife," she said, keeping her voice low while leaning closer to him so he could hear her. "Or maybe they fought earlier. I don't know. Something wasn't right."

"One, this is Three," Chris's voice popped into his ear. "I have visual confirmation on target two entering the club."

Wyatt brought his hand to his ear. "Roger."

"Looks like Harper is about to approach Felix now," Natasha said. Roman had chosen to stay with Harper when she introduced herself to Felix. "And wow, they're getting an invite to sit." Natasha tipped her chin toward a guy with longish blond hair. He was in his late thirties from what Wyatt remembered from the profile. "And there's Jasper."

Jasper paused mid-stride when his gaze touched upon Natasha. He fidgeted with the collar of his pressed salmon-colored button-down shirt that was untucked from his dark-washed denim jeans.

"Looks like he sees you." Wyatt brought his drink to his lips and took a sip.

She linked her free arm with Wyatt's when Jasper approached.

He stopped in front of them, and his eyes lingered on Wyatt before shifting back to Natasha. "What are you doing here?"

"There was a tweet," she responded, keeping her tone casual.

"You obviously got help finding the place." Jasper glanced at Wyatt again, his eyes slowly roaming over his body.

It only took Wyatt a moment to realize he was more Jasper's type than Natasha. "I'm Link," he offered the alias

Harper had cooked up for him today. Link was a well-known hacker, but he'd never shown his face or made any public appearances. It was easier to utilize a handle who had clout in the hacker world than to try and invent an entirely new persona no one would have ever heard of.

"*The* Link?" Jasper arched a brow. "I didn't see your name on the competitor list."

Wyatt set his drink aside. "I'm here to support Heather."

Jasper's eyes tightened on him. "How come you're finally coming out of the shadows?"

"It got a bit too dark in there, thought I might try the light," Wyatt quipped. "You know my friend?" He tipped his head to the side toward Natasha.

"I know her a little too well." Jasper switched his focus to Natasha. "And I'd watch your back with this one." He leaned in and whispered something into Natasha's ear, then turned and started for Felix's table.

"You think he bought my story?" Wyatt asked her once Jasper was out of earshot.

"Maybe. He probably assumed I recruited you, though."

"And what'd he say to you?"

She faced him and positioned her mixed drink on the bar top off to her right. She gently fisted the material of his shirt as if she were going to kiss him and brought her mouth to his ear. "To leave him the hell alone, so he doesn't get killed."

"You believe him?"

"Yes and no. I think he's scared, though." Her lashes lowered, her gaze casting to his lips, and a moment later, she said, "My date would probably kiss me right about now."

He pressed his mouth to hers, happily taking the invitation, even if it was in the name of their cover stories.

"One, we have a problem," Chris announced over comms.

He lowered his forehead to Natasha's after their split-second kiss. He needed more of her touch, a longer taste so he could savor the moment later.

He inched away from Natasha to maintain eye contact but lifted his hand near his mouth. "Go, Three," he told Chris. "What is it?"

"Jessica called. She said Felix wasn't the one who sent out that tweet. She discovered Cyber X's account was hacked," Chris explained. "Someone else sent the tweet."

"Does that mean what I think it means?" Wyatt asked him.

"Yeah," Chris responded. "Keep your eyes peeled, brother. He's probably watching you now."

Wyatt looked over Natasha's shoulder and surveyed the crowd behind her, then peered at everyone off to his six. "We've got a problem." He brushed her hair behind her ear and lightly gripped her shoulder as if this were a sensual moment. He nipped at her lip before his mouth skated to her ear. "The Knight hacked Felix's account. He sent the tweet."

She flinched beneath his touch. "And Felix had no choice but to show and pretend he sent out the invite. Explains the sour mood from him and his wife."

He released her and backed up a step. "They're nervous." Felix and Kate were probably afraid the world would soon find out Cyber X had an Achilles heel, too, and it was The Knight. They weren't so untouchable after all. "Harper's standing," he said a moment later, and she turned to follow his gaze.

Harper had her hand out, requesting a dance from Roman. Her eyes connected with Wyatt as she and Roman moved to the dance floor, giving him a message to meet her out there.

Wyatt guided Natasha to where the couples danced. He lifted her arms and slung them over his shoulders, then secured a grip of her hips.

"He could be anyone," she said into his ear as they moved, her footwork impressive.

"Where'd you learn to dance like this?" He twirled her twice before catching her in his arms and dipping her.

"I could ask you the same thing," she said with a smile.

"If I tell you—"

"You'll have to kill me?" she asked with a laugh. It was almost as if they'd found themselves cocooned in the moment, forgetting where they were and why they were even there.

The Knight brought them to the club, he reminded himself. Time to get focused. But damn if he didn't have tunnel vision with this amazing woman in his arms. The smile on her face went to her eyes, making her simply irresistible.

He had a weakness for legs, but a smile, especially hers, was his ultimate kryptonite.

"Horse-back riding, shooting skeet, piano, and dance lessons. Required by my mum," he finally admitted, moving forward and backward in time with each beat.

Her lips twitched as her palm went to his chest. "A man after my own heart."

He was about to spin her when he caught sight of Roman and Harper nearby. He gave a quick nod, and they changed partners.

Dancing with Harper was like dancing with Jessica—they were both like sisters to him. His hand didn't have a mind of its own like it did when he was with Natasha. It didn't race down Harper's back and to her arse.

"What happened at the table?" he asked her.

"They were both uptight. He was mostly pissed, and she appeared nervous. Afraid, maybe. And I guess now we know why. But that didn't seem to stop Felix from flirting with me."

Yeah, he'd done the same to Natasha. *Arsehole.* Wyatt glimpsed over at Felix's table. Jasper was doing the talking, but Felix had his focus dead set on Harper. "Well, it looks like you've managed to distract him from his bad mood," he said as Felix suddenly stood and came their way.

Felix was about Wyatt's height, more lean than muscular. His legs were encased in dark denim, which he'd paired with a white, pressed button-down shirt.

"Can I cut in?" Felix's green eyes moved to Harper, and Wyatt stepped back.

"Took you long enough," Harper said, her voice soft and flirtatious, even though Felix's wife wasn't far away.

Harper had easily slipped into her alias so fast it'd taken Wyatt a moment to remember the woman used to be with the Agency like Natasha. She must've decided to take advantage of Felix's attraction to her.

Wyatt tucked his hands into his pockets and backed up a few steps, working his way closer to where Kate and Jasper sat.

He peered back at Natasha. She made eye contact with him as she continued to dance with Roman. She moved with graceful ease, and he immediately missed the feel of her body intimately pressed to his when they'd danced.

He reached into his pocket and clicked on the pen, hoping he was close enough to catch some of Kate and Jasper's conversation with the recorder.

After a minute, A.J.'s voice popped into his ear. "Target three is entering the club."

Shit.

Target three. His daughter.

The guys had studied Gwen's social media accounts

before heading to the club tonight. They'd checked out Twitter, Instagram, and Facebook.

Her photos on Facebook dated back five years. Taking a virtual walk through her teenage years had done a number on him. He'd had mixed feelings about seeing pictures of her with her friends and boyfriends.

Regret hung heavy for missing out on so much of her life, but it was also nice getting to know more about her.

Her favorite color had to be red given how often she wore it.

She'd frequented the same ice cream place in London Wyatt had gone to as a kid. A simple vanilla and chocolate lover like him. A scoop of each.

She had excellent marksmanship based on the photos of her shooting skeet back at her family home.

Gwen also wrote several pieces for her high school newspaper that had most likely given Charlotte and Arthur heart attacks. Especially one article, in particular, calling for the abolition of nobility titles.

The tweet she'd sent out a few months after she'd turned eighteen had his stomach turning, though. *I grew up in a house of lies.* **#Gettingoutofhere #Screwthislife #Donewithliars**

He had no idea what had happened, and he probably never would find out, but he remembered Charlotte saying at the funeral that Gwen and Arthur had a blowout right before she went to college.

"You got her in your sights?" A.J. asked, pulling Wyatt's focus back to the club just as Gwen appeared in his line of sight.

"Yes," Wyatt replied, too low for A.J. to have heard him because his vocal cords were jammed at the sight of Gwen walking with confident strides.

Dressed in flowing black trousers with a bright red top that hung off one shoulder, she secured the attention of everyone she passed.

Her blonde hair was pulled into a tight ponytail, and her lips were as red as her shirt. Her heels on the tile floor were made silent by the band.

Felix stopped dancing with Harper when Gwen brushed past him like an angry breeze, sweeping his focus her way.

"Excuse me," he overheard Felix say.

Harper switched places with Natasha, and Wyatt clicked the pen off. He gathered Natasha into his arms to dance again, but couldn't remember the steps, not after having just seen Gwen for the first time. And certainly not with Felix tearing a path to get to his daughter at the bar.

Unless Felix had memorized every name and face on the competitor list, which was unlikely, there was no way he'd make such a fast approach on Gwen unless he'd met her before, and it had his stomach sinking to Titanic-like depths.

"What the hell is going on?" he rasped.

Natasha turned and pressed her back to his chest, then began moving up and down against him, doing a sexy shimmy. It wasn't exactly salsa, but it enabled her to put eyes on their targets.

Targets. In what world did he *A*, have a daughter, and *B*, have a daughter that was a target?

Gwen's arms were tight across her chest as Felix talked to her near the bar. There was no touching. No intimacy. But there was something between them. The absence of touch may have said more than any possible brush of their bodies ever could.

"She's ordering a drink," he grumbled a minute later. "She's only twenty."

"That's legal here. And in the U.K., right?" Natasha commented.

"Yeah, well, it's too young. Hell, so is twenty-one. We need to change the laws."

He stopped dancing, his heart shriveling in his chest when Gwen ignored the drink the bartender offered, instead maneuvering around Felix and toward the side door, which led to a small patio area outside. "I'm going out there."

Natasha's mouth tightened, but she nodded.

Harper's glaring look wasn't enough to stop him, either. He had to see her. Talk to her. Know she was okay.

If the most dangerous hacker in history was somewhere in the club tonight, like hell would he have his daughter standing outside on a patio.

He pushed open the door, and a blast of cold air hit him in the face.

She was standing beneath the heater, and some guy in a dark hoodie offered her a smoke.

"Don't you know smoking is bad for you?" He tucked his hands into his pockets, instinctively pulling his shoulders forward against the cold.

The guy pivoted Wyatt's way but kept his eyes on the ground, then moved past him and went back inside. He didn't want to tango with Wyatt. Smart move.

"What, are you my father?" Her words and sarcastic drawl were a kick in the nuts. Then she rolled her eyes, which he imagined she probably did a lot.

She edged closer to the heater, and he lifted his hand to the knob that was out of her reach and jacked up the flame to increase the heat for her.

"Thanks." Her mumbled appreciation was almost too low to hear. "Did you follow me out here?" Her brows knitted in distrust. "Are you some creeper?"

At least she was cautious, but he couldn't believe his daughter was so close and with her bluish-gray eyes focused on him, the stubborn lift of her chin tipped up. "I saw you talking to Felix, and you looked pissed. I thought I'd check on you."

She looked him over as if trying to get a read on him. "You don't look like a hacker," she concluded.

"Neither do you." *And why in the hell are you one?*

"But, you do look familiar." Her brows remained tight as she assessed him. "You're from England?"

How could he stand here and lie to his daughter?

Probably his daughter.

No, she was his. She had to be.

Same color hair. The same *Are they blue or gray?* eyes. The same . . . "Yeah," he forced out before he became dizzy from his thoughts.

"Do I know you?" She kicked her suspicious glare up a notch. If looks could kill . . .

"We've never met." That was true, so he felt less dick-like for his response.

"I really feel like I know you." She tipped her head to the side and moved closer to him.

He cleared his throat and asked, "What happened with you and Felix?" He needed to turn this conversation around and get it off of him.

His words had her backing up a step. "Felix is an arse." Her teeth clicked together, chattering from the frigid temperature. Her cheeks were rosy from the cold, and her long, dark lashes lifted to meet his eyes. "What's your name?"

She wasn't going to let this go, was she? Stubborn like him.

She's Arthur's daughter. Arthur raised her. I'm only

blood. But then, why the hell did he feel such an immediate connection with her? A need to protect her and to knock down any threats in her way?

"Real or online moniker?"

"You can start with your cyber name."

It took him a moment to remember, to pull his shit together. "Link."

She bumped into the heater, and he extended a hand to catch the thing before it fell over on her.

"Nice reflexes, but you're also a liar." She shook her head. "I don't like liars."

He released his hold of the heater, which should've been recalled for its shit stability and almost falling onto his daughter.

But how in the hell had Gwen known he wasn't Link?

"You're not entering the competition with that name, are you?" The angry draw of her brows was confirmation he was fucked. Of all the names Harper could have picked, somehow, his daughter was the only one who'd met this recluse hacker, Link. What were the odds? With the way things were going lately, why was he even surprised?

"No, I'm not entering."

"Link's a good guy, and he wouldn't like someone using his name. I suggest you choose a different handle if you're going to try and pretend you're a hacker," she said, her tone sharp. She brushed past him, but he whirled around and captured her arm, doing his best to keep his touch light.

"Be safe," he couldn't help but say.

Her gaze cut to his hand on her arm before meeting his eyes. "I have a dad. I don't need another."

Wyatt forced himself to release her, her words creating a gaping hole in his heart—an unexpected and painful blow.

He watched her hurry inside and took a minute to shake off his emotions. "Two," he said into his comm.

"I got her," A.J. answered right away. "She's exiting the club."

"Don't lose her," Wyatt instructed, pushing the heel of his hand to his forehead, hoping to relieve the pain but grateful she had left the club.

"You okay?"

He lowered his hand at the sound of Natasha's voice. "That was hard."

She brought her hand to his back, but he wasn't ready to turn around yet. She'd see the hurt in his eyes.

"She's angry at Felix. And it feels . . ." He didn't want to elaborate because it tugged at his desire to kill, and there was one target in mind—Felix Ward.

"You think something is going on between them." She'd said it for him, but could he answer without breaking something?

"I do." He turned to face her.

"Maybe they're secretly seeing each other. He could've gotten angry she showed up tonight."

Wyatt tried to draw upon Natasha's strength when all he wanted to do was go back inside and snap Felix's neck.

Felix was thirty-eight, a year younger than Wyatt.

Gwen would be twenty-one in March.

She was too young.

And the prick was married.

"I'm gonna kill him." His hands turned to fists, and he gritted down on his back teeth while staring at the side door to the club. "She probably came tonight unaware Felix wasn't the one who issued the challenge."

"And since she's trying to prove herself—how could she resist?"

"But he got pissed she showed up."

"And he was already upset knowing someone hacked his account," she added. "Plus, his wife was there."

"That didn't stop him from flirting with Harper," he pointed out.

"Target One has left," Chris said over comms, alerting the team to Felix's status, and his words had Wyatt's heartbeat intensifying.

He tapped his comm. "What's the status on your target, Two?"

Was Felix going after Gwen?

The line crackled, and A.J.'s breathing came across a bit labored. "She walked three blocks and stopped. She's on her phone. Maybe she's waiting on a ride. I'm ordering an Uber, so I'm ready to follow. I might be out of comms range soon."

"Okay," he said, his shoulders sagging in relief with Gwen away from whatever game The Knight was playing. "Let me know if anything changes."

"Roger," A.J. answered.

"Target One is climbing into a limo that just pulled up," Chris informed him.

"Follow him," Wyatt ordered and motioned to Natasha to head back inside the club so he could put eyes on Jasper and Kate. "Everyone, stay on assigned targets as planned."

"What now?" Natasha asked him.

"We head back to the hotel," he said, his voice clipped from worry. He wished he could trade places with A.J.

"But The Knight, what if he's here?" she mouthed.

The son of a bitch brought them to that nightclub for a reason, but what was it? To toy with Natasha? Another jab at Felix?

He glanced around the place, looking for any other hackers on the list of competitors—no one was familiar. "If he's here, he doesn't want us to know it," he said into her ear. "We can have Harper check the club's surveillance footage later."

"He's too good to let us see him," she said as they started for the coat check, an eerie feeling crawling up the back of his neck and chills crashing over his skin.

He stopped outside the club when A.J.'s voice popped into his ear again.

"This is Two," A.J. said, his tone more breathless than before. "Target Three *was* picked up, and it ain't no Uber. She just got into Target One's limo."

CHAPTER TWENTY-FOUR

"How'd Arthur handle her teenage years?" Wyatt tore his hands through his hair as he paced back and forth in their hotel room.

Natasha had her back to the wall alongside the bed, trying to figure out a way to calm him down. He was acting like her father had the night of her prom. Except the admiral had chosen to be in uniform when her date arrived. He'd also had a selection of his favorite firearms on the kitchen table prepared for cleaning. She'd scolded her father about it, not because he'd been trying to scare her date, but for not being more original.

"If Felix is The Knight's target, maybe he deserves whatever he's got coming," he grumbled.

He'd guzzled the green juice. Or whatever it was that turned Bruce Banner from a scientist into the Hulk. Wyatt had gone from an experienced special operator to a bear protecting its cubs from a threat.

Maybe there was a gene for this behavior? An innate switch that got flipped when a man became a father?

She blinked a few times and decided remaining silent may

not be the best course of action. "And if Gwen gets caught in the crossfire because The Knight attacks Felix?"

He stilled again, his lips a white slash of worry. "Jesus." He dropped down onto the bed and brought his elbows to his knees and his palms to his face.

"I'm sorry." She removed her heels, tossed her coat, and sat next to him, hoping she could talk him down from whatever proverbial cliff he was about to jump from. "Try not to worry, though. A.J. saw them get out of the limo and go into a condo that's rented out to Cyber X. She wasn't held at gunpoint, she went willingly into his place."

When Wyatt lowered his hands and turned his head to observe her, she noticed his skin was much paler than normal.

"The idea of them together . . ." He closed his eyes. "He's nearly eighteen years older than her. If he's using his position of power to"—Wyatt circled his index finger in the air, and if the situation wasn't so shitty, she'd laugh that he'd used the "spin up" hand signal to indicate sex—"sleep with her, then I'm gonna kill him before The Knight can, and then we won't have to worry about her being caught in the middle of anything because Felix will be dead."

He was back on his feet. A man on a mission.

He strode across the room and crouched in front of the safe, which was beneath the TV.

He was going for his gun. Great.

"You gotta calm down. You're dealing with emotions you've probably never experienced before, and you'll get through this. But take a breath, okay?" She went to his side. "A.J. and Chris have eyes on the rental property."

"And the curtains are drawn, and they can't see inside." He clutched a 9mm but didn't stand. "What if she's in danger?"

"Wyatt, she went with him willingly. She was waiting for someone to pick her up. She knew Felix would come for her."

"She's too young to know what she's doing." He shoved the gun back in the safe and cursed, then locked it and stood.

"Gwen was smart enough to get into the competition, as well as be one of the few who decrypted the tweet sent by The Knight tonight," Natasha pointed out.

"And that also scares the shit out of me." His shoulders sagged.

Her gaze flicked back to the safe. "How'd you manage to get weapons over the border? I couldn't bring mine. The Canadians are sticklers about that."

"We have connections pretty much wherever we go. Always need an arsenal at our disposal. I'll get you a piece tomorrow." That tightness in his jaw went slack, but only for a moment. "And by the way, she's apparently the only one on the planet who knows the real Link."

Her attempt to distract him from worrying failed miserably.

But wait . . . "What? Really?" That was hard to believe. "Right now, you should try and rest. Harper and Roman are back upstairs looking into whether or not Gwen and Felix have any prior history. Plus, Harper needs to check out the club's surveillance footage. There's also the matter of tracking The Knight's location when Felix's Twitter account was hacked. Lots of unanswered questions, and hopefully, we'll know more by tomorrow. Let them look into this while you—"

"You think I can sit here and rest?" He dropped back onto the bed and brought his elbows to his knees.

"You don't have a choice. Harper asked me to keep you in this room until we hear something," she confessed while sitting next to him.

He side-eyed her. "I'm your hostage?"

"Tables have turned," she said, keeping her voice light and teasing, hoping to help his mood a little, to at least get him to become less growly. "After Ibiza, it's only fair."

His lips lifted slightly at the edges. "I guess there are worse places I could be than trapped here." His eyes moved over her dress, which was so snug it was hard to breathe. "I assume you're here to supervise so I don't make a run for it?"

"I think it'd be best if I stayed with you." She stood and went to her suitcase. "If I change in the bathroom, you gonna leave and go kill Felix?"

Leaning back, Wyatt supported himself with his palms pressed to the mattress on either side of his body and stared at her, his eyes slowly moving to her legs and down to her red-painted toenails. "I can't make any promises."

"At least you're being honest about it."

There was a slight chance he would run, though. He was a father now, and maybe it was to a twenty-year-old, but regardless, he was new at it, and he wanted to keep her safe. Keep her breathing. And clearly, away from some manipulative billionaire who may have wanted more than her hacking skills.

"I'll change in here." She reached for the zipper at the side of the dress and dragged it down.

"You trying to distract me so I don't do something stupid?" His voice was low and rough and provoked an immediate reaction in her body as if he'd brought a calloused palm over her breast. And why did that idea have to turn her on so much?

The red silk fabric began to slide down once the dress was unzipped, but she held the front in place over her chest. "No, I just don't want to take my eyes off you."

"Yeah, well, you've got my attention now." He cocked

his head, his eyes sharp on her body, and his gaze coaxed goose bumps to pop across her flesh. He rose and closed the space between them. "But you have my word, I won't leave." He tipped his head toward the bathroom. "I won't have you making yourself uncomfortable because of me." His tone remained deep and husky. "You should change in there."

"I . . ."

"Please." The throaty word sounded like a drop-to-his-knees prayer begging her not to undress in front of him.

"I have some experience with having to cycle through changes of clothes in a stealthy manner," she said with an easy smile, hoping to come out of this moment without her knees buckling, or the invisible forcefield they'd attempted to create between them disintegrating. "I wasn't planning on showing you any skin."

"Trust me, you could be as stealthy as Houdini, and I'd still get hard as a rock." His blunt honesty had her sucking in a sharp breath, and doing her best not to look down to see if there was any truth to what he'd just admitted. "I won't go," he promised, his words clinging to her as if he'd touched her instead.

She clutched the dress, ensuring it stayed in place and lightly nodded. "I'll be right back, then."

She snatched a change of clothes with her free hand and hurried into the bathroom. Once she was alone, Natasha let the red dress pool around her feet and braced the counter. *What am I thinking?*

The familiar drum of desire she'd experienced with him in the past reverberated in time with her heartbeats, the pace gaining speed.

She wasn't sure how long she'd stayed in the bathroom to collect herself and button up her emotions, but when she returned to the bedroom, Wyatt was on the bed, arms tight across his chest, and from the looks of it, asleep.

Her lips tucked in, emotion leaking right back out at the sight of this muscular man passed out on top of the covers, so worn out from everything he'd been through.

She quietly discarded her dress and thong in the laundry bag and tiptoed to the other bed to sit in her gray sweats and black tank top. After waiting a few minutes to ensure he was deep asleep, she removed his loafers and snatched the gray throw blanket from the other bed to cover him up.

He stirred a little, his legs hanging off the edge of the bed, but he didn't wake.

The idea of grabbing her laptop and working crossed her mind, but before she had a chance to decide what to do, Wyatt's mobile began vibrating on the nightstand.

Harper's name flashed across the screen. She clutched the phone and hurried into the bathroom to answer, keeping the door only slightly cracked.

"Hey, he's asleep," she whispered.

"Wow, you actually managed to get him to calm down."

"I think all his angry pacing and yelling wore him out." She stole a glimpse of Wyatt through the cracked door.

"I don't want to wake him, but he should know Gwen left Felix's place. She got into a cab instead of his limo. Back at her hotel now."

"She look okay? Were there any sounds of struggling or, um, anything?" She cringed at the idea of Gwen and Felix sleeping together.

"No. She wasn't there long, then Felix walked her out to a cab. No hug or kiss goodbye."

Huh. "Are we misreading the situation, then? Or did they fight and not make up?"

"Not sure yet, but Chris is staying on Felix, and A.J.'s

parked outside Gwen's hotel." She paused. "I did find a connection between Felix and Gwen."

She went farther into the bathroom and leaned her hip against the vanity counter.

"Gwen took a flight to Seattle two weeks ago, paid for by Cyber X."

"So, she had a job interview?"

"Hotel was also paid by the company, which they do for all potential candidates, so it adds up. They posted three summer intern positions online three weeks ago."

"And maybe he didn't think she was qualified, so she decided to enter the competition to try and prove herself to him that way," Natasha suggested. "But their behavior toward each other at the club would suggest there's more going on."

"Even if there is nothing romantic between Gwen and Felix, there was definite tension, and if The Knight had eyes on the place, he'd have noticed."

"So, he might target Gwen if he thinks she's connected to Felix somehow." Her shoulders slumped.

"We can't rule out the possibility, but Jessica and I were talking, and Gwen might prove to be an asset."

"Because she has some connection with Felix?" Her stomach roiled. "Or as bait for The Knight?"

Assets were the bread and butter of a CIA officer's life. But was Harper really suggesting using Wyatt's daughter to get to The Knight?

"No, we'd never risk her life. But it looks like she's more connected in the hacker community than we realized."

"Wyatt said she even knows the real Link."

"So, it's possible she knows something. Maybe she has a clue as to what's going on with Felix, and why he's a target."

Natasha understood what Harper was suggesting, and if it

were anyone else, she'd be first in line to make a deal with Gwen. *But* Gwen wasn't just anyone.

"Turning people is what I do." *What I'm good at.* Usually good at, at least. She'd failed a few times, like trying to turn Farid back in Algiers. "But Wyatt won't do anything to put Gwen in danger. And I don't blame him." She released a long sigh. "I've been going after this SOB for years, so trust me, I want to pursue every possible avenue to get him before he can kill more people, but Gwen's off-limits. We should focus on keeping her safe."

There'd been a time when she would've sacrificed almost anything, including her own life, to catch him. But she cared about Wyatt, and she couldn't possibly further endanger his daughter. She'd never come back from a choice like that.

"I know. I shouldn't have brought it up. But you admit The Knight's not playing the same game this time." Harper's voice softened. "She might be able to help."

"Or she knows absolutely nothing, and *we* inadvertently paint a target on her head by pulling her into this." She looked heavenward. "I can't ask her to be a source on the ground. We can bring her in to protect her and see if she wants to share what she knows, but I won't put her in harm's way. And that's still Wyatt's call. This is his daughter, and it's only a matter of time before he loves her like he was the one who raised her." *If he doesn't already love her.* She lowered her head at the sound of the door creaking, and her breath hitched when she turned to see a pair of blue-gray eyes. "I'll call you back."

CHAPTER TWENTY-FIVE

Natasha ended the call and bumped into the vanity counter behind her.

She set the phone down, swallowing at the sight of Wyatt's lips drawn tight.

"Gwen is safe at her hotel. She wasn't with Felix long. And it looks like we may have misread the situation between them." She rushed out the details Harper had shared as to what she'd learned about Gwen. Quick, fragmented statements. Her nerves cutting through as he leaned against the interior doorframe with crossed arms, his eyes trapping her in place.

How much of her conversation with Harper had he overheard?

"Harper and your people are working on leads. Trying to come up with a plan." She worked the words loose, the beginning of a ramble that would inevitably follow if he kept staring at her like that.

He cocked his head, and a touch of darkness passed over his face. "And one plan is to use Gwen to get to Felix in hopes of getting to The Knight?" His tone was raspy and sleepy, but there was still an unmistakable bite of anger present.

"I don't want that." She drew in a deep breath and studied him.

His muscles were taut. Jawline tight beneath his beard.

"You're obsessed with this hacker, but you . . ." His words trailed off as he pushed away from the doorframe and took one step into the bathroom. "You didn't even take a moment to consider using Gwen." He closed the space between them, pinning her against the counter as he brought his palms down on each side of her. He had her in his favorite position—caged between his arms. "Finding him is everything to you."

"It's not everything if you get hurt. If Gwen gets hurt." Liquid crept into her eyes, taking her off guard. The visible signs of her emotions blurred her sight.

He angled his head when she forced her gaze back up. His eyes were still dark, but they weren't shadowed with anger this time. They were a softer blue-gray, more like the color of the sea in Ibiza, a reminder of when they'd nearly had sex.

"I'll never forget this. I'll never forget you having my back like this." His hand lifted to palm her face, and when he leaned closer, his hard shaft pressed against her.

She swallowed a moan, letting it die inside of her until he secured his other hand in her hair and gently tugged, guiding her chin up. Then, she let the gasp free. Let him see her desire for him, as wrong as the timing may be.

"Are we back in that same boat of crazy?" Her voice was so weak her words nearly crumbled in the air.

Instead of answering, Wyatt asked, "You truly think I'm capable of love, don't you?" He was searching for the truth in her eyes, but she gave it with her heart, hoping he would feel it in a kiss.

Natasha pressed up on her toes and brought her mouth to his. If a kiss were a love poem, a flower unfolding to reveal the brightest red, or the moment a loved one stepped into view upon returning home safe from duty . . . that was this moment. This kiss.

Her lust and desire expanded as she breathed in his intoxicating scent, which could only be pheromones since Wyatt wasn't wearing cologne. It filled the tight space between them as every possible emotion pushed against her rib cage, clamoring for attention.

The kiss was consuming. It was raw and real. Intense.

Teeth clashing. Tongues dueling. Need that'd been held in limbo for eight years suddenly released.

He didn't stifle his groan, he released it freely, and as she surrendered to him, to the moment, her body went lax.

"Natasha." He trailed his mouth to her ear, his breath fanning out and heating her skin, causing her to shudder. Wanting more, she latched on to his biceps to pull herself closer.

A sharp nip on her earlobe. A soft kiss at the side of her neck. She buried her fingertips in the fabric of his sleeves when his thumbs brushed over her nipples before traveling slowly down the sides of her ribs.

When he tugged on the hem of her tank top, Natasha let go of her hold on him and raised her arms to speed up the process of getting her topless.

A step back. A quick once-over. Desire turning his eyes to yet another shade of blue-gray, the color of the sky when a storm loomed overhead.

She planted her lip firmly between her teeth and prayed he wouldn't back down tonight.

It'd been eight years of interruptions and bad timing, and,

hopefully, not even The Knight could stand in their way this time.

He dropped to his knees without warning, secured his hands on her hips, and lowered her gray sweatpants, caressing her legs as he did so, while she watched and tried to remember how to breathe.

Standing only in a pair of plain white cotton panties, Natasha instinctively banded her arms across her body as his gaze, intensely focused on her nakedness, caused her skin to grow hot.

"Please, Tash." Wyatt reached for her wrist, a request to show herself to him.

The knot in her throat went down easier than expected given her exposed state. After eight freaking years of wanting him, what reason did she have to hide?

She wasn't that young twenty-something-year-old standing alone at the altar anymore. She wasn't broken or afraid. Strength and confidence rolled through her like a high tide moving in over the sand, and her hands went to his shoulders.

His lips tipped at the sides. The hint of a wolfish grin. A sexy, the-things-I'm-gonna-do-to-you kind of grin. And God help her, she wanted him to do all of them.

Those storm-gray eyes lowered once again. And if she were the moon and he the earth, it seemed Wyatt could no longer fight the gravitational pull between them. Lifting a hand, he traced one finger down the center of her stomach, over her panties. Her knees buckled, her breath hitched, and a tremble fired straight through her body as his touch burned a line to her sensitive bud.

Strong hands gripped her outer thighs as he leaned in and nibbled at the hemline of her panties, his short beard softly scraping along her skin. His lips brushing across the band of material. Her breasts throbbed, heavy with need. The impending moment was almost too much, waiting for him to kiss her where she'd only dreamed of before.

Wyatt remained steady on his knees, eyes lifting back to hers as if he needed to see the expression on her face while he touched her. Needed to know how he made her feel. She was completely undone. Unraveled like a never-ending spool of yarn.

Barely touching me, and I'm going to come.

She lost his eyes when his tongue circled her navel, and his finger shifted her underwear to the side to gain access to her shaved center.

"Wyatt," she cried when his finger pushed inside and instantly crooked to her G-spot like he somehow had superpowers and just knew where to find it.

"I want my mouth on you, is that okay?"

His request for permission had her blinking. Taking a moment to pause at his sincerity in such a heated moment. She wasn't sure if his question qualified as chivalry, particularly in British aristocracy, but it warmed her heart.

"Please," she said. Then added a nod, worried her emotions, wrapped like a tight corset around her ribs, might have strangled the word.

She fisted his dark blond hair as ecstasy mounted inside of her . . . her breath, her words, her everything frozen in this moment of intimacy.

He removed his finger, and she gasped from the loss, but when he dragged her underwear down, his fingertips sliding slowly along her skin in the process, she swallowed hard, preparing herself for what was next.

His warm tongue slid along the seam of her pussy, and she cried out a shriek of pleasure, losing hold of his hair to grab on to the counter for support.

This man was a lover, that was for sure.

Skilled. Amazing. And right now, all hers.

She pressed her hips forward, her nipples tightening almost to points of pain as he licked and sucked, then brought two fingers deep inside her while his tongue flicked and caressed.

The climax built and built. Her hands flew to his shoulders when she surrendered to the orgasm.

"Holy shit," she muttered under her breath as he brought his lips up to her pelvic bone and then worked his mouth higher until he was standing, and they were kissing again.

His cock strained against his jeans, hard as a rock, and she rotated her hips, ready for him. Prepared to take every inch he'd give her.

Lonely nights wouldn't exist with this man inside of her.

Hallmark movies wouldn't be necessary if she had his kiss. His touch.

In her bed, he'd shield her from the darkness of the world, helping her sleep better at night.

She kicked her sweatpants and panties free from her ankles without disconnecting their lips. Then, with deft fingers, he worked at the button of his jeans and zipper and quickly pushed them out of the way. He stepped out of them, and they only stopped kissing for the moment it took to discard his shirt.

"You tasted so good down there," he whispered against her mouth. "And your lips up here are a special brand of heaven, too. I could kiss you forever." Before she knew it, he'd spun her around to face the shower stall, and she gasped when her breasts met the cold glass.

With her head tilted to the side, a sigh of pleasure left her mouth as he placed her palms high against the glass, then trailed one rough hand from the center of her back down to the curve of her ass.

She squeezed her legs together as need grabbed hold of her, and he fit his naked body tight to hers.

She wanted him.

Needed him.

With eyes closed now, her fingertips curled into her palms against the glass, her adrenaline surging with every moment of waiting for him to unite their bodies as one.

He lifted her curtain of blonde hair, shifted it to the side, and brought his mouth to the nape of her neck before slanting his lips near her ear. "I want to do something different, but I honestly don't know how."

Chills crested and crashed over her spine. "What is it?" she whispered, opening her eyes.

He propped his hands alongside hers. "Make love. I want to make love to you." His voice was raw and scratchy with desire, but a swirl of other emotions cut through, too.

I'm going to fall in love with this man.

And maybe part of her already had.

She'd left a piece of herself with him on the beach in California.

Another fragment in Ibiza.

Then in Colorado.

He already owned so much of her heart, how could she not give him the rest?

CHAPTER TWENTY-SIX

A LAMP CRASHED TO THE FLOOR, ITS BULB BLINKING TO A quick death, but Wyatt barely noticed, too preoccupied with Natasha in his arms.

The second they left the en suite, they'd become even more ravenous for each other.

Her tits against his chest, luscious lips locked with his . . . they'd stumbled across the room, knocking shit over as they took turns dragging their fingers over each other's bodies. Hell, they probably looked like they were practicing hand-to-hand combat maneuvers.

The oil on canvas knock-off of a Jackson Pollock slid to the floor next to the nightstand when Natasha gained the upper hand, taking charge this time and backing Wyatt into the wall. Damn, her passion and physical strength turned him on.

He grabbed her arse, urging her to wrap her legs around his hips. She did it effortlessly, eagerly rubbing her wet pussy against his hard cock.

He had to have her. Right. The. Fuck. Now.

The plan was to make this last. To stretch it out for as long as possible.

He'd wanted to make love because he was pretty sure all he'd ever done was screw, and despite the physical passion they shared for each other, there was something else between them. Something he couldn't quite explain, or maybe understand yet.

"Tell me." He flipped their positions, bringing her back to the wall. Her legs were still tight around his body, but he'd yet to enter her, even though her pussy was a red flag waving in the wind, and his dick the damn bull.

Restraint. He was trying to maintain some shred of restraint.

"Tell me the difference," he rasped.

"Between making love and sex?" she asked between breathy moans as she bucked against him, and it took him a moment to shake off the animal inside so he didn't succumb to impulse and pound into her like a wild, uncontrollable beast.

Sex was one thing.

But what he felt for her right now. . . it was next-level. Something different. Maybe he already had his answer, but he still wanted to hear her say the words. Feel the meaning brush across his skin.

"Yes." He growled, the timbre somewhere between the roar of a lion and the howl of a dying wolf. His dick was going to die a painful death if he didn't plunge deep inside her wet center soon, though.

Natasha's slender fingers threaded through the hair at his temple, and she tipped her head to the side. A sweet smile graced her lips. "The difference between making love and having sex is how you feel about the person you're with."

"And how do you feel about me?" he asked, almost nervous to hear her answer.

"I feel happy. In this world of chaos, the risks that come with my job, the heartache and despair I see . . . despite all that, I feel happy when I'm with you. You make my heart feel good. You make *me* feel good." Her lips crooked into a fuller smile. "Really, really damn good."

He allowed her legs to slip from his waist, for her feet to touch the floor because maybe they both needed to be grounded in the moment. To fully appreciate it. "Can I ask you . . . what kind of person do you think I am?"

She leaned back against the wall, her full breasts lifting, distracting him. He needed to control himself for a moment. But damn, he wanted to reach out and grab hold of her again. Plant his mouth on a rosebud nipple and lightly tease it between his teeth.

"You're this ruggedly sexy guy who saves people for a living and does it without any thanks. You care about your teammates and will die for them without a second thought. You constructed walls, which probably started when you were a kid because of how your parents raised you, and those walls got higher after Clara and continued to rise as you watched people you cared about die."

It was like his heart took a nosedive into his stomach as she spoke. His next breath was shakier than he'd expected as he looked into her eyes and curved a hand around her hip.

"I don't want to knock your walls down, because I've learned they only stay down if you're the one to remove them." Her brows knitted, so much intensity and compassion there. "But I'd love for that to happen. Once the walls are gone, you'll be able to feel everything I feel for you without having to ask me. You'll just know."

"Jesus, Tash." He brought his forehead to hers and held her cheek with his free hand.

"I'm no Freud, but I—"

He kissed her, and not even a freight train barreling his way could stop him.

Not The Knight.

Not any terrorist arsehole in the world could stand between him and this moment.

Right now, it was just her.

She slipped a hand between them and gripped his shaft. Her palm slid up and down from root to tip, and he clamped down on his back teeth, holding her eyes until he could no longer remain standing.

In one swift movement, he released her hand from his cock, scooped her into his arms and carried her to the bed.

She let her head hit the pillow, her blonde hair falling wildly beneath her, the touches of pink a reminder she'd come to Canada to chase a vicious and deadly hacker.

He hastily sheathed himself with a condom, then brought the brunt of his weight onto his forearms on top of her, his chest brushing against her nipples.

"I want you even more than the sunshine," he whispered without thinking, forgetting she wouldn't know what he was talking about. And before she could ask, he kissed her. Harder than he'd meant to. Almost bruising. A kiss meant to punish himself for waiting so long to be with her.

He knew deep inside this was the right time, though. Any sooner, and they may not have been ready.

Her hips lifted as an invitation, and he took it. Unable to stop the bull from charging.

The moment their bodies joined, he raised his head to find her eyes.

A tightness filled his chest. A thrum of absolute certainty

cutting through, touching every space inside of him, from heart to mind.

He drove his length deeper, and each thrust had her moaning, crying out, but never losing sight of his eyes.

He now understood the difference between sex and making love. It had nothing to do with the movements and everything to do with the organ in his chest he hadn't believed still worked.

His heart swelled, and his shoulders lightly trembled as they moved together as partners, as one.

And something inside of him let go and damned if there'd be no turning back now.

He would breach every possible point and blow the hell out of every wall or door if it meant keeping her in his life.

She'd chased The Knight for years, but he could see himself chasing the ends of the earth if it meant even one more connection with her like this.

NATASHA SHOT WYATT A LAZY SMILE AND RAN HER PALM along his inked bicep. "You know, I'm not exactly surprised no one believed you were a hacker. Most hackers spend too much time behind a keyboard to build muscles like yours."

He made a show of flexing his bicep, and she chuckled. "Not the only thing that's hard, sweetheart." He waggled his brows, and her focus dipped between their naked bodies.

They'd run out of condoms two hours ago. He'd only had two on him since his buddies actually had used some for their long guns on the op in Svalbard to keep the snow out of the muzzles.

He was generally more prepared, but he hadn't had sex in a long time, nor had he ever made love, and after doing so with Natasha, it was so damn addicting he hadn't wanted to stop. So, despite all the heavy shit going on in their lives, they'd gone at it back-to-back, taking a shower once in between that had been meant as a chance to catch their breaths.

Her lowering to her knees beneath the water and sucking him dry had left him barely able to walk after that, though, so it'd taken another thirty minutes to get his energy back since he wasn't exactly twenty anymore.

"And by the way, Jasper seemed to buy my Link story," he added when she wrapped her hand tight around the base of his shaft.

"He was too distracted by your muscles and looks."

"Hey, I'm more than a pretty face," he teased and leaned in to kiss her. "Can I confess something?" he asked after breaking their lips apart.

"Will I want to keep jacking you off if you do?" She arched a brow. "You're in a rather dangerous position right now."

He closed his eyes for a second as she shifted her hand up and down, adding more pressure at the base and catching some precum at the head to use beneath her touch.

"I think I'm safe," he croaked out, attempting to withhold from blowing his load impossibly fast.

She tipped her head. "Then by all means."

He cleared his throat and draped his arm over her hip bone to rest his hand on her arse cheek. She definitely worked out. Her glutes were beyond stellar.

And now he was distracted by memories of her a few hours ago on all fours with her arse up and her clit pink and soft and ready for him to penetrate.

What had he wanted to confess? Hell if he knew.

And . . . fuuuuuck. He came all over the bed, and she kept her hand sliding up and down until he was empty.

He collapsed onto his back, his dick slapping the side of his leg, totally spent.

"I completely forget what the bloody hell I was going to say. It's like I went arse over tit and—"

"And that's British for?"

He rolled his head to the side, noting that the room looked like it'd survived a post-rock show party. They were *not* going to get their deposit back. Jessica would kill him.

. . . And it was worth every second.

"Arse over tit?" she repeated as if realizing the signals to his brain were still crossing every which way.

His palms smacked down onto his chest, his elbows resting on each side of him. He was sated. Relaxed. Almost forgetful of why they were in Canada.

"To fall over," he said with a grin. "Sometimes, a bit of London slips back into my words."

"More than sometimes."

He tipped his chin to find her gorgeous eyes, and his heart squeezed to discover a smile on her face as well. His favorite feature of hers.

"My buddy A.J. likes to joke I'm more Yankee—even though I've never lived in the north—when I'm stateside, but when my boots leave the U.S., I become a Brit again."

"He's the comedian, right?"

He smiled. "He's my best mate, even though we rag on each other all day long. But hell, Chris and Finn are quite the comics." Of course, Liam could be funny, too. Then there was Asher and Knox. "Actually, we're all a bunch of wiseasses," he admitted.

"Except the quiet one, Roman?"

"He has his moments."

She propped her head into her palm, resting her elbow on the bed, and he pivoted to face her. Her glorious tits were begging to be touched, so, naturally, he reached out and palmed her breast.

"They're right there, what do you expect?" he asked when she'd dropped her focus to his hand.

"They're sore from you grabbing them all night."

He smoothed her pink nipple between the pad of his thumb and forefinger. "Want me to stop?"

She closed her eyes and sucked on her bottom lip.

"I'll take that as a no." He reached between her thighs. She was already wet for him. "You tender down there, too? I could kiss you—make you feel better."

She went to her back, brought her feet to the bed, and parted her thighs as a direct invitation. Damn this woman was perfect.

He eagerly moved between her legs, avoiding the wet, sticky spot his cum had left on the sheet and settled between her thighs.

Her hands dove into his hair as she shifted and moved against his tongue, grinding her way to an orgasm with his mouth on her.

"No, damn it," she cursed when his mobile began vibrating on the nightstand. "I'm so close."

"I'm not stopping," he said before claiming her again with his tongue and lips.

"They might know something. Harper might need us."

"Thirty seconds won't make a difference. Now shut your brain off and ride this fucking orgasm like you want to."

She moaned at his words. She'd admitted to him last night she'd never been turned on by cursing and dirty talk in the bedroom until him, and his sailor's mouth was happy to oblige.

She jerked against his face, coming hard, and he held her hips down so as not to lose contact while she cried out a string of *Oh, Gods* followed by one long shout of his name.

"I really hope Harper doesn't kill us," she said after catching her breath and sitting up a minute later.

He dialed Harper back. "More than worth the arse chewing to have you come on my face," he said just before the call picked up.

"Hey," Harper answered. "I never heard back from Natasha, so I'm hoping you both got some sleep."

Maybe a total of thirty minutes. "We're about to head to your room," he said when he noticed it was already eight in the morning. "Any news?"

"Yeah," she said. "I'll explain when you come up."

"Give us five minutes to"—he cleared his throat—"get cleaned up, and then loop the security feeds."

Natasha's cheeks softened with a touch of pink.

"On it, thanks," Harper replied.

He set the phone down and climbed on top of Natasha. "You smell like sex."

She ran her hands over his chest. "So do you."

"You said you're stealthy at changing clothes . . . how are you with showers?" He smirked.

"As long as I don't have two hundred pounds of solid muscle in there distracting me, I can get in and out in under sixty seconds."

"So, basically, I need to stay out here."

"Yes." She grinned. "That's an order."

CHAPTER TWENTY-SEVEN

"YOU GOT LAID, DIDN'T YA, BROTHER?" A.J. SLAPPED WYATT on the back as they stood inside the kitchen of Harper's hotel suite.

"Why are you here instead of watching Gwen?"

Worrying about Gwen and his anger toward Felix-the-Arsehole-Ward packed a heavy punch to his gut.

A.J. pressed his fingertips to his eyes before stifling a yawn. "Roman swapped places with me around five so I could get a few hours of rack time." He elbowed him in the side. "Gwen's still in her room. Harper hacked the hotel surveillance cams, so we also have a direct line of sight to her door, which thank the stars above, was close to the elevators where there's a cam."

His shoulders sagged with relief, but he knew Harper had news, and whatever it was might give him heart palpitations.

"And the rest of the team is still in position?"

"Yup."

He wanted to feel guilty he'd been having sex while his team was on watch to keep his daughter safe and eyes on their targets. But when he glimpsed Natasha standing in the living room wearing jeans, a white long-sleeve top, her hair still wet and pulled into a ponytail, he could barely remember to breathe, let alone feel guilty about how he'd spent his night.

"So, I need details, because I haven't gotten laid in like six months, and—"

"What, are we sorority sisters?" He side-eyed A.J. "Your lack of sex have anything to do with a certain redhead FBI agent you're holding out for?"

Wyatt had noticed Natasha drank her coffee black like him, so he filled two paper cups with the stuff, hoping it miraculously tasted better today than yesterday.

A.J. closed his eyes, and the dreamy smile on his face was a clear indication he was remembering the agent he claimed to fall in love at first sight with last year when working the attempted assassination case against Bravo Five's father.

"Damn, brother, I'd stay celibate for another year if I knew she was the light at the end of this dark, sexless tunnel, but who knows if I'll ever see her again."

"There are these things called phones. You could call her." Wyatt smirked as A.J.'s eyes flashed open.

"Nice try on distracting me." The abrupt slap on Wyatt's back nearly caused him to spit out his coffee.

And now A.J. was the one quickly changing gears, not prepared to talk about his own love life.

"You deserve this"—A.J. waved a hand in front of Wyatt —"adorable, doe-eyed look you got on your face, especially with what you're going through."

I'm a father. His thoughts suddenly whiplashed, and he was back to being screwed up in the head, wondering what to do about Gwen.

She was in danger, but aside from holding her hostage, which he was seriously considering, he didn't know what to say without spooking her. He couldn't lead with *I'm your dad,* or I *work for the Commander in Chief of the United States of America, and you need to do as I say.*

"For real, though, how are you doing? We haven't had a second to talk since you dropped the daughter thing on us." A.J. crossed his arms and pinned his back to the small counter off to his left. "Lettuce," he grumbled, reminding Wyatt of his flimsy excuse for looking green around the gills back in New York after he'd gotten off the phone with Charlotte.

Speaking of Charlotte—he should call her, right?

"You understand that if Felix ever hurts Gwen, or takes advantage of her in any way, he dies?"

"Damn right," A.J. said with a nod, and Wyatt was grateful they were on the same page.

"You boys done gossiping in there?" Harper called out. "I have Jess on a secure web call."

Wyatt followed A.J. out of the kitchen and into their temporary command center. Natasha whispered a quick *Thanks* when he handed her the coffee, and he returned her gratitude with a smile.

"I, uh, didn't ask before, but how far along are you?" Natasha's gaze was on the screen as she sipped her coffee.

"Six months, but with twins, I'm hoping to make it to thirty-six weeks before they make their debut." Jessica set her hand on top of her abdomen. "My other half, Asher, would've popped in to say hi, but he's packing."

Wyatt gripped the back of Harper's chair. "Where's he going?"

"Grand Cayman," Jessica answered.

"Aw hell no." A.J. purposefully stretched his words out for added emphasis. "We're up here in the cold, and he's gonna go catch some rays."

"We tracked the Twitter hack," Harper announced,

ignoring A.J.'s whining. "The original IP was traced to the convention center, but he pinged it from there to Grand Cayman, and we're thinking it's because he wants us to go there."

A.J. stood next to Wyatt. "And we're going to blindly follow this asshole?"

"This is all part of his new game. Another clue." Natasha turned and set her eyes on the windows where the curtains were drawn tight. "We need to see what he wants."

"It's probably to find out if you're working solo on this. Or to get you out of here for some reason." And while A.J. was known for his often wild theories, it was possible he was right on this one.

"I'm sending Knox with Asher. They'll keep a low profile." Jessica spoke with confidence, and why wouldn't she? She'd been running the show with Luke for eight years, and for the most part, they'd always had mission success.

Wyatt followed Natasha's gaze back toward the screen. "What's the hotel's number you traced The Knight to?" she asked Jessica while discarding her coffee on the desk to grab her mobile.

Jessica rattled off the number without asking why and Natasha quickly typed it into her mobile.

"Hi, yes, my assistant made my reservation, and I'm calling to confirm the details," Natasha said. "Heather Aleo."

Wyatt set his drink down on the coffee table and stood before her. Did The Knight know her alias?

"No?" Natasha's eyes connected with his. "Maybe she held the listing under my name, Natasha Chandler." Another pause. "Okay, great. One night only? Yup. Thank you. And the credit card number you have on file, can you read it back to me to double-check if she gave you hers or mine?"

Harper handed her a notepad and pen.

No way would the hotel actually . . . Wyatt's thoughts died when Natasha began jotting down the digits. "Yeah, that person needs to be fired," he said under his breath.

"That's my assistant's card. I'll switch cards when I get in tonight. Thank you." She ended the call and handed the notepad to Harper. "The number is significant. I'm sure of it."

"You're not about to suggest that you go to Grand Cayman instead of our guys, are you?" Wyatt cocked a brow, and a tight knot formed in the pit of his stomach.

"He wants me there. I have to be the one to go."

"And if he wants you there to kill you?" Jessica asked, reading Wyatt's thoughts.

"You know that's not the case." Natasha checked her G-shock watch, the one her brother had given her. "But it has to be me."

He reached for her wrist. "Why bring you to Canada, then have you turn around and fly off somewhere?"

"He's moving his chess pieces, right?" Harper spoke up. "Each move he's made has been calculated and strategic, and right now, it looks like he wants us to solve a puzzle."

"Regardless, you can't go." Wyatt released her wrist and held a firm stance before her, not ready to back down. "I can't let you go alone, and I don't want to leave Gwen."

Torn between two women. A woman he . . . well, felt something for. And a daughter he just discovered he had.

Whiplash.

He shoved the sleeves of his black shirt to the elbows, and his gaze connected with the ink inside his forearm. A reminder of Arthur tattooed there.

"Go with her." Jessica's command pulled his attention back up. "The Knight already knows you're connected with Natasha. And you know our guys won't let anything happen to Gwen."

He swallowed the emotion that had pushed north into his throat.

"You don't have to do this." Natasha's eyes met his, her tone soft. "You don't need to pick one of us."

His shoulders slumped. What was he supposed to say to that?

"I can get you on a flight to Miami in an hour, then a connection from there," Jessica said before he could respond.

"Make it for two." Wyatt faced A.J.

"I promise you, Gwen will be okay," A.J. said before he could issue the request.

"Wyatt." Natasha motioned for him to step aside, but he refused to budge. He didn't need her talking him down. He did trust his people, and there was no way he'd let Natasha go to that island alone.

"We're short on time," Jessica threw out the reminder. "The competition starts tomorrow."

Is tomorrow already Friday? How the hell had time flown by that fast? "He only has the reservation for tonight, so book us a return ticket tomorrow afternoon."

"And at this point, there's probably no need for you to even enter the competition." Jessica looked toward Harper. "We need your focus on the case. Natasha can withdraw her alias as well."

"Agreed." Harper looked to Wyatt a beat later. "And what did we decide about Gwen?"

He clenched his jaw and took a moment to formulate his words. "We wait to talk to Gwen until I'm back, and we don't let her go undercover. We see what she already knows about Felix, then we protect her." He wouldn't flex on this, and he'd fight whoever stood in his way, even if it was his own team. "We do not use her." He left off the *Am I clear?*, but the words popped silently into the air nevertheless.

"Okay. We'll figure something out." Jessica ran her palm over her abdomen with a nod of understanding that probably wouldn't have come as easily if she weren't about to become a parent herself.

"I can head to the convention center and keep an eye on things there with the rest of the guys," A.J. suggested.

"I'll keep reaching out to MI6 to see if I can get them to open up about what they know. They've been close-mouthed so far," Jessica added. "I might need to call in a favor to Alexa who used to work there. Maybe she can get them to budge."

"Not Alexa Ryan, right? Well, she's Alexa Summers now." Natasha stepped forward, and when Jessica nodded, it was as if the world got a whole hell of a lot smaller.

"We've worked together in the past," Natasha announced. "She, uh, was even a bridesmaid in my wedding."

Dale . . . if it weren't for that man leaving Natasha at the altar . . . where would Natasha be now?

Everything had come full circle in some strange way.

"I can call her instead. I'd considered the idea after talking with Jasper, but I'd been on the fence," Natasha said. "Have you all worked with Alexa before?"

"Not exactly." Wyatt smiled. "Her husband's sister is now married to Bravo Four, Liam."

She blinked a few times as if absorbing the news and their connection to each other. "So, if they'd had an actual wedding with friends and family instead of running off and eloping, I probably would've met Emily."

"You know Emily?" They were getting off track, but he couldn't believe how connected their lives had been ever since the night of Clara's wedding, and how the universe kept bringing them back together.

"We haven't met in person, but Alexa raves about her.

And I was happy Alexa finally met someone." She looked back Harper's way. "Before I go pack, any chance you pulled anything of use off the club surveillance or that recording Wyatt snagged of Kate and Jasper talking from last night?"

Harper shook her head. "You were right. The recording from the pen was scrambled. Felix or Kate must've had countermeasures in place." She paused. "But as for the club, now I know why The Knight chose it. It's probably one of the only clubs in the area with no cameras, and no nearby buildings had surveillance running, either."

Natasha cursed under her breath. "If he wanted a place with no cameras, it was because he was there. The Knight could've been anyone."

"More like someone he was worried we'd recognize if we saw him on camera, though," Harper pointed out.

"Which would officially rule out Jasper as The Knight, right?" A.J. asked. "No reason to avoid cameras if he was hiding in plain sight."

"We need to figure out who showed up at the club last night while Felix was still there." Natasha stepped closer to the laptop, eyes set on Jessica. "Check Instagram. All the popular social media sites. Hashtags with the club name. The way people are with selfies these days—"

"Why didn't I think of that?" Harper hissed, clearly disappointed with herself. "There *were* cameras. Everyone in that club most likely had a phone, and we can piece them all together and see who was captured in the background. Good thinking." She pulled her keyboard closer and began typing. "Your plane leaves in an hour. You should get going."

Natasha checked her watch. "I'll call Alexa on a burner before we fly."

"I guess I better let Asher and Knox know they're not

going on vacation." Jessica looked to Wyatt. "Be safe. You won't be able to take a piece with you."

"Guns are overrated," Wyatt said, trying to smile even though his stomach was twisted with worry.

"Says the professional sniper." A.J. rolled his eyes. "But hey"—he grabbed Wyatt's bicep—"these are all the guns you need, right, Chief?"

CHAPTER TWENTY-EIGHT

"YOU HAVE TO BE BLOODY KIDDING ME."

"No one can hear you, right?" Natasha hissed over the phone, standing inside the single-person bathroom at the airport in Montreal.

"No, I'm alone. But you gotta tell me, was he a good shag?" Humor filled Alexa's voice.

Natasha's back hit the door as she closed her eyes. "Good doesn't even begin to describe it." She held a fist tight to her chest, needing five minutes to be a woman talking to her friend about sex and not a CIA operative.

"I knew it. He's a wild one, right? I'm betting he was too wild to stay in London and live the life of a noble, that's for bloody sure," Alexa teased, her British accent ringing through, a touch stronger than Wyatt's.

Even though Alexa couldn't see her, Natasha's cheeks heated. Her neck was probably beet red too. "Why did I tell you?"

"Because I'm your friend, and you no longer have to live vicariously through me and my incredible sex life." The line went quiet for a moment. "But, I would like to know why you never mentioned the sailor to me before."

"Hey, you were the one who told me not to go to Dale and Clara's wedding, and look, if I hadn't, I wouldn't have met Wyatt. And I couldn't mention the two other times we, uh, ran into each other because it was work-related." She shoved away from the metal door. "You mentioned Liam marrying Emily, but I had no idea he and Wyatt were friends."

Alexa had been thrilled to have a sister-in-law like Emily, but how small was the world that Emily's husband was on the same team as Wyatt?

"Small world, right?" Alexa echoed Natasha's thoughts. "And if you're wondering why I didn't bring up any of Liam's hot single friends, it's because they seemed like heartbreakers to me, especially Wyatt."

Wyatt thinks he's a heartbreaker. At least he did. Now that they'd made love, she was hopeful he no longer believed that to be the gospel truth. She could tell he didn't want to be that guy. And they *had* made love. It'd been raw and animalistic at times, which she'd loved, but the emotional connection between them was intense and unmistakable every second their bodies had been united.

"Okay, I need to go back to reality. We'll talk about this later." Natasha stood in front of the mirror and caught sight of her reflection. Only eyeliner and mascara for her eyes and a clear gloss for her lips. She hadn't had time to dry her hair earlier, so it was still in a tight ponytail but no longer damp. She was in her regular clothes, jeans and a white cashmere Ralph Lauren sweater since she wasn't traveling as Heather. "Are you sure you don't mind reaching out to your contacts for me?"

"Of course not. I can't promise you I'll get a firm answer, but I'll do my best."

When Natasha had first phoned Alexa five minutes ago from a burner, she'd given an abbreviated version of what was going on in Canada, doing her best not to share too many classified details.

"Thank you. You can call Jessica if you can't reach me because I'm on the plane."

"Sounds good. And hey, if you have time while you're on the island with the sexy, inked bad boy, you should try and have some fun. Enjoy yourself. One shag, at least."

"I'm hanging up now," Natasha said, fighting the smile on her lips. "Talk soon. Thank you again." They wrapped up the call, and she stowed the burner in her purse.

A night in paradise with Wyatt and no other distractions, wouldn't that be nice?

She exited the bathroom a moment later to find Wyatt standing off to the side of the door waiting for her. He had on dark-washed denim, a plain white tee, and a pair of Converse she doubted he'd wear if he weren't undercover as a hacker . . . but it was the smirk on his face that was the sexiest thing he had on.

The door was thick and heavy, but how soundproof were the walls?

Based on the look he was giving her and the cocky grin on his face, he'd overheard the parts of her conversation she hadn't discreetly whispered. "Rambly. Awkward." She shrugged and smiled as her cheeks heated yet again. "Dork."

He lifted his scarred brow, no doubt at the adjectives she'd just used to describe herself, her lame attempt to explain away her embarrassment at what he might have overheard.

Still clutching their one overnight bag, Wyatt leaned in and brought his mouth to her ear. "And you know I love that about you." He pressed his lips to her cheek before slanting his mouth over hers for one quick kiss, completely ignoring the flood of people barreling past them to get to their flights.

"So, if good doesn't begin to describe it," he asked once in their seats on the plane twenty minutes later, "what does?" He reached for her hand over the armrest and clutched it as she carried her eyes his way.

"Oh," she said with a smile, her heart doubling in size, "I think you know." She almost laughed out loud as he bit his lip and shifted on the seat. He glanced up to the luggage compartments, a pained look on his face, and she realized he was probably trying to get his dick to calm down because his jeans were tenting.

"That's all it takes with you." He huffed. "Just the idea of us together, and I'm a bloody teenager again." His British accent was like silk caressing her skin in the most sensitive of places.

At least they were in first class with no other seats next to them, which also gave her an idea. She stuck her head into the aisle. "Excuse me, do you have any blankets?" she asked the flight attendant, and Wyatt gripped her hand even harder, obviously reading her naughty thoughts.

"You are so bad," he said into her ear after the woman handed them a navy blue fleece blanket.

Natasha pushed up the armrest and scooted closer, then covered them both up.

"We haven't even gotten off the runway yet." He smiled as she stealthily unzipped his jeans.

His back slammed against the seat when she pulled his hard length free from his jeans and boxers and gripped his shaft. "And you know you like it."

Blue-gray eyes flicked to hers. "You're incredible, you know that, right?" he asked, and his tone was husky, laced with the promise of so much more.

CHAPTER TWENTY-NINE

GRAND CAYMAN

NATASHA SWEPT THE HOTEL ROOM FOR LISTENING DEVICES and cameras as Wyatt sat on the bed she'd already cleared and popped open the laptop to call Harper.

After grabbing dinner at the airport in Miami, they'd taken the connecting flight to Grand Cayman. The sun had already set, and even though it wasn't that late, they were both exhausted, but hopeful Harper would have news.

"Nothing so far," Natasha announced after checking the bedside lamps and tables.

The desk in the corner of the room, with the LCD screen mounted above on the teal wall, was clean as well.

"Just need to check the bathroom."

"Thank you." He tossed the pillows to the side, stretched out his jeaned legs, and positioned the computer on his lap.

She hurried into the bathroom to finish her sweep, anxious to hop on to the call and learn whatever news Harper might have to share.

Natasha stilled at the sight of the marble-tiled shower when she entered, though. Memories of the previous night in Montreal flooded her mind—of the luxuriously large showerhead raining hot water over her and Wyatt.

Focus. Pushing away the steamy thoughts, she swept the bathroom for bugs and returned to the bedroom. "All clear. If The Knight was ever in this room, he didn't leave anything behind." She hadn't expected it since there'd been no specific room reserved for her, but she had to be cautious when it came to that bastard.

Wyatt motioned for her to join him on the bed. "The call is connecting now over a secure server."

She sat next to him and propped a few pillows behind her back.

"We're here," he announced once Harper's face filled the screen.

"Good. Anything strange yet?" Harper was also in her bed and wearing pink cotton pajamas with ice cream cones on them.

"Not yet. Swept the room. It's clean," Natasha answered.

"How's Gwen?" Wyatt asked. "What happened at the convention hall today?"

A million other questions bumped around in Natasha's mind that they needed to get through as well, but based on the relaxed look on Harper's face, Gwen was safe.

"Gwen's back at her hotel, probably getting ready for the competition tomorrow. No interaction between her and Felix today during the seminars." Harper must have traveled with her own pillow because she had a silky pink one propped behind her back, which didn't match the rest of the bed. "Felix gave a speech. Kate stood on stage looking irritated, and Jasper didn't make contact with anyone. Kept to himself.

The boys are in position and keeping an eye on everyone. But I do have some news."

Natasha leaned in closer to Wyatt, her heartbeat picking up as she focused on Harper.

"Alexa came through for us. MI6 has people on the ground in Montreal. They're going after The Knight, too. Using Jasper as bait, although he doesn't know it," Harper began. "He called MI6 just like he told you. But he didn't reappear out of the goodness of his heart or any sense of obligation. He informed them his presence in the competition was a life or death matter. The Knight discovered where he'd been hiding and left a chess piece at his front door along with a two-part message—attend the Bug Bounty Competition, or his family will die. And, if he cooperates with the CIA in any way, he'll be killed as well."

"Which was the reason for the lie?" Something still felt off, though.

"I guess. It's also why MI6 decided to keep the CIA out of it," Harper answered.

"Jasper's pretty close to his parents and his twin sister back in England. He'd come out of hiding for them. I guess that makes sense." She frowned, trying to digest the news. "The Knight must know Jasper was responsible for tracking his location, and he wants payback."

"MI6 agreed to let him enter the competition and keep him safe if he returned to England afterward," Harper explained.

"But they left out the part about using him as bait, huh?" Wyatt grumbled. "So, now we have MI6 agents in the mix. Not sure how I feel about this. But are we assuming Jasper is innocent?"

"For now, but I wouldn't rule anything out." A line of worry cut through Harper's forehead as if she had the same off-putting feeling Natasha was experiencing. "He could've lied."

"But . . . the chess piece. Jasper wouldn't have known to use that detail in his story to MI6 unless it was true. He had no idea The Knight sent me a chess piece, too." She wanted to stand. To pace while trying to work through the puzzle, but her legs felt like rubber. She was mentally and physically drained. "You learn anything else?"

Harper nodded. "Not only does the data center in Sweden store virtual data files, but they also store cryptocurrency. The account hacked by The Knight contained three hundred million dollars in Bitcoin. Every penny was transferred out of the account."

Three hundred million? "Isn't that—"

"The estimated number the CIA came up with as to how much money The Knight amassed selling intel he's hacked in the last five years," Harper finished for her.

"What, he hacked his own account?" Wyatt asked, a joking tone in his voice. "That doesn't make sense."

"I'm guessing you still don't have the name of the account holder, or you'd have led with that." This was the first time The Knight had stolen money. But then again, he wasn't playing by his usual rules, so why was she surprised by this move?

Harper's shoulders slumped. "We're still working on getting that. Another day or so, and we should be able to find out who lost three hundred million and doesn't want to talk about it."

"So, what's the plan now?" And why the hell did The Knight bring her to an island?

"We're going to keep looking for connections to try and find a way to get a move ahead of this guy for once. And do our best to stay off the radar of MI6 and Canadian

Intelligence." Confidence cut through Harper's tone, but she didn't know The Knight the way Natasha did. She hadn't worked his case for years.

All the setbacks. The failures. The loss of her team members.

Harper hid a yawn with her hand. Had she even slept since arriving in Canada? "Anyway, get some rest. If anything changes on our end, I'll call you. For now, there's nothing you can do but wait and see why that asshole brought you down there."

"We'll sleep if you finally get rack time, too," Wyatt commented, and Harper's nod came across as a sarcastic *Yeah, sure.*

"Stay safe. And thank you for everything." Natasha moved off the bed and stood by the window as Wyatt ended the call.

"You okay?"

She peeked between the silver-colored drapes to steal a glimpse of the resort. The massive pool, illuminated with internal lights, glowed a brilliant turquoise, and lampposts lining the meandering pathways gave the air a soft glimmer. Happy couples strolled hand in hand through the property as palm trees swayed in the breeze. And off in the distance, too dark to see right now but nevertheless a prominent feature in this paradise was the Caribbean Sea.

"I'm just frustrated." She let go of the drapes and turned to find him standing only inches away.

"I am, too." His white long-sleeved shirt wasn't overly tight, but the fabric clung to his muscled arms, and reached out and squeezed his bicep, worried about him. He had so much going on, too.

Her gaze lifted to find his eyes as she released her hold of him. "What are you going to do about Gwen?"

301

It was a conversation that needed to happen sooner or later because if they were going to bring Gwen into the fold in some fashion, he'd need to decide what to tell her.

"Charlotte's not going to let me drop the news on Gwen alone." He moved to the bed and sat. "And I don't feel right about tearing this girl's world apart with the truth, either."

She sat next to him and took his hand in hers, wishing there was something she could say or do to help make it easier on him.

"But I also know I can't look Gwen in the eyes and lie to her again about who I am." Wyatt turned his head to face her, revealing the pain in his irises. "What do I do? Please, tell me."

She leaned her forehead to his and whispered, "I don't know. But you're not in this alone. You have your team backing you up."

"And do I have you?" he asked, his voice shaky, emotion nipping at his words.

She pulled back to find his eyes. "I think you've had me since that night on the beach, I just didn't know it then."

CHAPTER THIRTY

Natasha gradually opened her eyes that morning, her lids heavy after tossing and turning all night.

Wyatt was on his stomach next to her, his muscularly carved arms draped on each side of the pillow with his face turned toward her, eyes closed. Soft breaths left his barely parted lips as he snoozed.

At some point in the middle of the night, he'd woken and found her scrolling through her phone, so he'd made love to her, which had finally done the trick in helping her relax enough to sleep.

He was only in his plain black boxers, leaving the hard lines of his back exposed, and the stunning sight snatched away the appeal of sleep, and the grogginess lifted like a curtain.

She kept the side of her face flush with the pillow as she raced her hand along the edges of his tricep.

He only had ink on his right arm, from shoulder to wrist. Covering his shoulder and upper arm, intricately drawn angel wings folded inward, as if shielding someone beneath them. Below the wings was a coat of arms, but it wasn't like any of the British ones she'd seen. The Roman numerals III, a lion roaring on its hind legs, plus more pictures occupied the interior of the tattoo. There were also patriotic tatts on his skin, like the American flag waving in the breeze. All the ink was black, including the typically red poppy, a symbol for veterans. The Navy SEAL trident was practically hidden among the surrounding tattoos, and Wyatt had probably done that purposely so he didn't stand out as a Teamguy to civilians.

The tattoo that always managed to catch her eye was the one on the inside of his forearm. She couldn't get a detailed look from this angle, but it was a sword in a stone. The design was very Arthurian. It hadn't been on his arm when she visited him in Colorado. Probably symbolic for the friend he'd lost, and now it had to double as a reminder of the man who raised Wyatt's daughter as his own.

Natasha didn't have any tattoos, no artwork on her body to memorialize her losses, but everyone dealt with death in their own way. Her pain was sewn right into her heart, each loss another stitch. She felt it with every beat of her heart, every breath she was still able to take, unlike her fallen friends.

"I should have visited him."

His words snatched her attention, and she looked up to find Wyatt awake, watching her as if he knew what she'd been thinking about based on the direction her eyes had been set.

"Do you think he knew he wasn't Gwen's biological father? Like, deep down knew?" Wyatt rolled to his side and swatted the pillow a few times before settling his cheek back down onto it.

"Given how strongly you know she's your daughter, then yes, he most likely knew she wasn't his blood. But since you were so close growing up, probably like brothers, I'm betting he considered her blood—that he lost you but had her in his life."

"You think he still gave a damn about me after what I did?"

"You mean the cheating?" Natasha propped her head into her palm.

"The leaving and never coming back."

"Didn't he tell you to go?"

"Yeah, but that doesn't mean I should've listened. We, uh, we're both stubborn."

Her hand moved to his heart, its beat steady beneath her touch. "If what you really want to ask is whether I think he'd forgive you for stepping in as her father now that he's gone, then yes, I do."

The pad of his thumb brushed gently over her cheek, then down to smooth over her lips. "Thank you. I really did mean what I said the other day." He leaned in closer. "I think you're the one who keeps saving me, not the other way around." His lips touched hers, and she was hungry for him again.

Wyatt must have felt it, too, because he inched back only to pull off her sleep cami. He palmed her breast, his eyes belonging to a ravenous man. His mouth tight. Desire deep in every line of his body.

She reached beneath the comforter and shoved her pale blue pajama bottoms down. No panties, so that made it easier.

"Get on top of me," he said after removing his boxers, his voice gruff, laced with need every bit as strong and powerful as her own.

Always the prepared SEAL, he'd bought condoms at the airport in Miami. She snatched one off the nightstand and handed it over as she straddled him. She had no idea if they had time for foreplay, and she didn't want to lose this chance.

His cock was rock hard, the tip leaking precum.

He sheathed his length, twirled a forefinger, motioning for her to face the other way, and then leaned back on his forearms.

Natasha scrambled to reverse her straddle, and with her right hand on his hip bone and her left next to him on the bed, she began to move up and down his shaft.

"Best view in the Caymans."

She stole a glimpse back at him, his cocky smile cute and sexy.

Natasha took control of the rhythm and rode up and down his cock at her own pace.

He must've fallen flat onto his back because his hands were on her now.

Gripping the sides of her hips at first. Sending shivers across her skin when his fingers traced the length of her spine.

But God help her, when he lifted his body upright again and brought his chest flush to her back and reached around to strum her clit with his fingers, she came all over him, moaning so loud she barely heard the knock at the door.

"Coming," he called out in a throaty voice.

She wasn't sure which "coming" he was referring to, but when he lifted his hips off the bed, burying himself deeper, taking over and pumping—uniting their bodies—she realized he *was* about to come. "One minute," he yelled through gritted teeth as he orgasmed, holding her back to his chest, his hands on her tits.

He dropped his chin onto her shoulder. "Talk about timing."

"Isn't that how things go with us?"

But also, who the hell was at the door?

Reality had come too swiftly and unexpectedly.

"Be right there," he hollered once they'd disconnected their bodies. He grabbed a tissue off the nightstand, wrapped up the condom, and tossed it in the small trash bin. He grabbed his jeans, then started for the door. "Wait here," he whispered as if there was a chance The Knight would be on the other side of the door.

She nodded as he zipped his fly, then she lost sight of him when he stepped into the small entrance hall.

Wyatt exchanged a few quick words with whoever was outside the room, then he locked up and returned with a box in hand. "You have any tools in that bag of yours to see if there's a bomb in this?" He arched a brow as he slowly set the box on the bed, which looked about as standard as a delivery from an online retail store.

"Unfortunately, no, but that's highly unlikely." Would she bet their lives on that hunch? Probably not. "It's the perfect size for a laptop." She hurriedly dressed and circled the bed to take another look.

"I'll get Jessica and Harper on the phone."

She was too anxious to wait. "I think we should just open it."

He gently grabbed her arm, and she glimpsed him, catching the heavy rise and fall of his chest. His mouth tightened for a brief moment before he said, "Fine, but let me do it, and you stand back."

"This is me we're talking about. My job is dangerous."

"I know." He released her arm. "That doesn't mean I'm not going to worry about you every second of every day from here on out."

Here on out? The tender tone of his voice, and the words he'd spoken, had her heart stuttering, her breath momentarily trapped in the walls of her chest.

She finally surrendered, her palms in the air, because

although she was coming up on her tenth year in the Agency, maybe she didn't mind having him watch out for her.

"I love your stubbornness, but thank you for letting me win this time."

A smile crept up on her, and he brought his mouth to hers for a quick kiss before his gaze journeyed back to the issue at hand.

He motioned her to step even farther away, then worked his fingers along the seam of the brown packing tape, parting the box open. Her name and the hotel address were scrawled in black ink on top of the box.

His shoulders slumped as if relieved. "You called it. A laptop." She abruptly came to his side as he lifted the MacBook Air from the package and powered it on. "You happen to know the password?"

She sat on the bed with the computer on her lap as he dialed his teammates. "It's gotta be something I'd know."

"Try your name," he suggested before he brought the phone to his ear and began filling Harper in over speakerphone about the current situation.

She only had a few shots at the password before she got locked out of the Mac, so she had to be careful. She tried her name, then The Knight's name. No dice.

Wyatt sat next to her, holding the phone between them. "Jasper got the chess piece, too," he suggested. "The Knight also blames him for what happened in Romania."

"No, it wouldn't be the name Jasper." Her brows pinched tight as she worked her fingers over the keyboard. "Maybe his online name?" She released a pent-up breath of relief after typing it in. "It worked. The Smoking Gun."

"There's gotta be some symbolism there," Harper noted over the line as the home screen on the laptop came to view.

Plain black background and only one blue file folder.

"It's labeled *Play Me*." She clicked it open. An MP4 file inside.

"This laptop won't explode if you play it, right?" Wyatt asked, and she wasn't sure if he was joking or serious.

"This isn't a Mission Impossible film," Harper teased, and Wyatt shot Natasha a quick wink.

Even in a situation like this, the man managed to calm her.

"Okay. I'm playing it." She double-clicked the MP4.

"What do you see?" Harper asked, her nerves probably about on point with Natasha's.

"It's the lobby of a hotel from the looks of it." Wyatt leaned in closer to share the view of the screen. "Not *this* hotel, which is kind of strange."

"No, but I recognize it." She closed her eyes as she drew up a memory. "It's the hotel the CIA footed the bill for while Jasper was on loan to us working the case in London."

"There's only thirty seconds of footage, then it skips ahead an hour and only lasts for fifteen seconds," Wyatt informed Harper as Natasha replayed the footage.

Fifteen seconds in, she paused the clip on her third time watching it. "Look." She pointed to a woman with long blonde hair wearing a black pantsuit and sunglasses. "She never looks up. Keeps her face down and away from the cameras. Also, when she enters the hotel, she has a silver briefcase." She forwarded the footage to the second half. "It's not with her when she leaves."

"That could mean anything. She could be a guest and left the briefcase in her room," Wyatt countered, not ready to jump to conclusions.

"But she's the only person who is in both the before and after shots. I think that's who The Knight wants us to see."

309

Her pulse sped up as she tried to process what kind of message he was sending her.

"And the fact she's in Jasper's hotel is the clue to the message, right?" Harper asked. "What's the date?"

"July twelfth. That's about two months before our op in Romania," Wyatt answered. "What the hell is he trying to tell us?"

"The password was The Smoking Gun," Harper said, her voice soft as if working through the puzzle. "Double meaning? It's Jasper's cyber name, but what if The Knight is letting us know this clip is literally the smoking gun, evidence to prove something."

"To prove Jasper is guilty of . . ." Where would she even go with that thought?

"Send me the file," Harper requested, "and I'll work on obtaining all of the footage from the hotel that day to see if I can get a better angle of this woman."

Wyatt stood and brought his back flush to the wall, eyes set on Natasha as he kept hold of the phone. "What I don't get is what the hell we're doing in the Cayman Islands."

Before Natasha could summon a response, the hotel phone rang. She set the laptop aside and answered it. "Hello?"

"The car you requested is here," the woman announced.

"Car?" Natasha shot Wyatt a puzzled look, and he pushed away from the wall.

"Yes, it says here in our system you requested a car. First stop to the Cayman Island Trust Bank, then from there, to the airport."

What the hell? "Uh, thank you. Be right down." She blinked a few times and hung up the phone. "Harper, can you get us an earlier flight? It looks like he wants us at a bank and then back to Montreal."

As much as she hated following The Knight's commands, what choice did she have at this point?

Wyatt scratched at his beard, his eyes connecting with Natasha's. "I guess we know why we're here."

"And the credit card number The Knight provided the hotel before we came," Natasha began, "I'm betting it's a match for an account at the bank."

CHAPTER THIRTY-ONE

THE BEAUTY OF CARIBBEAN LIFE WAS CEMENTED INTO EVERY square inch of the bank, which was located in George Town, where traditional architecture merged with stores like Versace.

Overhead were paneled ceilings, the color of the white sandy beaches, and intricately carved fans, more for looks than cooling. The interior paint matched the azure water that graced the sand not too far away.

An infusion of the local culture popped in the artwork on the walls. Natasha had mostly heard English inside the bank, but a mix of other languages floated around her as well.

Inside the office of the woman who'd finally been assigned to help Natasha and Wyatt, were sketches by a local artist of caimans, or crocodiles. The island's name derived from early sightings of crocs back in the 1500s, at least that's what was explained in the brochure Natasha had flipped through when she'd sat anxiously in the lobby waiting for help.

"You understand we need more than a passport to grant you access to the account since it was first created without you being here on-site, right?" The woman at the bank had a deep Southern drawl. A transplant, someone probably drawn to the allure of island life.

Snorkeling. Lying out on the beach and drinking cocktails. Music and dancing. Yeah, it sounded like heaven. At the very least, like an amazing vacation, one she wished she could've taken opposed to using her time off to hunt a killer.

"I'm sorry." Natasha blinked. "What'd you say?"

"Have you used a biometric print scan before?"

Wyatt reached for Natasha's hand on top of the chair arm next to her. "Dear, I have to go make a call. Would you excuse me?"

She nodded, assuming Wyatt was about to call Harper or Jessica to let them know the Agency might get flagged about a CIA officer inside a bank in the Cayman Islands. Thank God Director Spenser worked with Wyatt's people and could cover for her, or she'd be ridiculously screwed within a matter of minutes.

"Left palm," the woman instructed, and Natasha slipped her hand in position on the flat screen device the woman held in front of her. "Thank you." She moved back to her desk and took a seat. "So, I have your ID, your palm scan, and now I just need your four-digit pin number before I go process your account."

Pin? She sat farther back in the salmon-colored leather chair, doing her best not to look distraught.

"You would've set it up when you created the account."

"Right." *He wanted me to see the security footage before I came here.* What was the connection? "Sorry, I've been traveling. And you know how it can be with a new man in your life, right?" She thickened her Texas accent and wet her lips, leaning forward a touch on the seat, tightening her

313

eyes. "So many orgasms, I can barely remember my own name."

The woman didn't show any shock. Instead, a casual smile crossed her lips. "With a man like him, I can't say I blame you." Her gaze wandered to the open door, and Natasha followed her focus to see Wyatt heading back into the bank and toward the office.

"Yeah," Natasha said in a bit of a daze as Wyatt's long, jean-clad legs carried him her way. The crisp white tee showed his muscles and the ink on his one arm. "He has the ability to steal my thoughts." *Like now.*

"We good?" he asked after entering the office.

"Just need the pin number," the woman spoke up as Natasha turned back toward her, an idea coming to mind. "Zero, seven, twelve."

Wyatt sat next to her and reached for her hand, and the warmth of his touch had her sputtering, "Sorry, no." She'd given the date on the video they'd watched at the hotel, July twelfth, but the date stamp on the footage had read as 12-07. It was more customary abroad than in the U.S. to have the date before the month. "*Twelve*, Zero, Seven." She swallowed. "That's the pin."

"Well, I'll go meet with my manager, and we'll process everything." The woman did a quick perusal of Wyatt as if imagining what he was like in bed, then stood and left the office, closing the door behind her.

"What number was that?" he asked once they were alone.

"The date on the security video. It's a guess."

He squeezed her hand. "And knowing you, I'm betting a damn good one."

She hoped so. "You call Jessica?"

"Yeah, I had Jessica alert Director Spenser about the palm

scan." He tipped his head to the side. "Everything will be fine."

"And by everything, do you mean the fact I'm in this bank or this entire situation?" She clutched her chest with her free hand, the knot of emotion working its way into her throat. "The fact he's calling the shots, and I have to keep following them, makes me crazy."

"Everything as in everything." Given what he was going through, the man was still so strong. "Just because we're letting him make his moves, doesn't mean we won't be making our own. The best players study their opponents, get a read on them, then attack."

"And since when are you a chess player?"

"I'm not, but war is often a game of strategy, and I'm an expert at that."

"Thank you," she mouthed when her vocal cords didn't seem to work. "For *everything*, thank you."

He leaned over the arms of their chairs and kissed her. Her coconut-flavored gloss, courtesy of the hotel, transferred to him as well, and when he pulled back, he tasted his lip. "That's good."

"Not supposed to eat it," she said with a smile just as the woman opened the door.

Wyatt shifted back into his seat, and some of the tension she'd been carrying seemed to have melted away with that kiss.

"Everything is all set," the woman announced.

Relief washed over her. *Thank God.*

"So, are you going to be transferring all of the money, or only some of it?" She sat across from them at her desk and opened her laptop.

"All of it," Natasha said as confidently as possible and

315

reached into her pocket for her phone to get the account number Harper had provided her in case of such a transfer.

"So, where would you like the one hundred and fifty million to go?"

* * *

"ONE FIFTY." WYATT HAD REPEATED THE AMOUNT OVER AND over again in disbelief after they'd left the bank.

"That's half the amount The Knight transferred out of the account in Sweden." She peered at Wyatt in the back of the town car, the partition up between them and the driver as they made their way to the airport. "Since nothing is ever a coincidence with this guy, I have to assume the money we're now in possession of came from that hack in Sweden."

"But why in the hell would he want you to have it?" His hand turned into a fist of frustration on the leather seat between them, and she set her palm on top of his to try and calm him down.

"Three hundred million is what he made off his hacks over the years. If that was his own money he actually transferred out of Sweden, he must have had to electronically break in because his assets had been frozen or something. But as to why he wanted me to have half of his money, I have no damn clue." And she usually never understood The Knight's moves until it was too late. She couldn't let that happen this time.

He reached into his pocket with his free hand and produced his phone, an incoming call from **Boss Lady.** "It's Jessica."

"Nice name."

They'd filled Harper in before they'd started for the airport, but they weren't expecting a call from Jessica. He held the phone slightly away from his ear so Natasha could listen in.

"Hey, glad I caught you before you got to the airport," Jessica said. "Ever since you guys got back from Pyramiden, I've been working on trying to get the video footage the Russians claimed to have of Roland Nilsson being tortured."

"I'm guessing you did?" Natasha asked.

"It took a personal request from POTUS, but President Bennett managed to secure the footage. And get this, Roland was tortured and beaten to death, but the abductors never once asked him for intel. Nothing about the data center in Sweden," Jessica announced.

"I didn't think The Knight would need him to hack the data center." Natasha's instincts had been right.

"But it still makes no sense as to why Roland was taken. If he wanted you to make the connection to Cyber X, the fact the seed vault, data center, and the weapons facility were all Felix's clients would have been sufficient enough, right?" Wyatt pointed out, following Natasha's line of thinking.

"There's more." Jessica was quiet for a moment. "The Russians discovered that someone else watched that footage. The surveillance cameras were hacked. The Russians couldn't trace the source of the hack, but my money is on The Knight, and he wanted to watch Roland being tortured."

"That means Roland's death was personal." Natasha closed her eyes, trying to understand how the security specialist fit into The Knight's plot of revenge.

"Asher and Knox are doing a deep dive into Roland's past as we speak. If there's something there, we'll find it. Hopefully, by the time you're back in Montreal, we'll know more."

"Thank you." Natasha's gaze moved to the window as they turned onto the final road leading to the airport.

Wyatt finished up with Jessica and put his phone away. "This is good news. It might be the break we need. A clue he didn't plant."

He was optimistic, but over the years, Natasha had learned that too much optimism in regard to defeating The Knight usually led to one thing . . . someone getting killed.

CHAPTER THIRTY-TWO

MONTREAL

AFTER AN UNEXPECTED DELAY IN MIAMI, BY THE TIME Wyatt and Natasha had arrived at the hotel in Canada, it was eleven at night. The competition was still going—no rest for the hackers if they wanted to place in the top three.

Wyatt set down their luggage, pulled out his phone, and opened Twitter. He'd had to create an account so he could keep up-to-date with the competition, but even more so to keep up with Gwen.

He'd gone with @JohnDoe2021. Somehow, he already had three followers, all who had XXX in their names.

He flicked the screen of his mobile. "Gwen was just tagged in the last announcement. She's in second. Neck and neck with Jasper."

"Impressive." Natasha stood off to his left and stole a peek at the screen.

"Twitter," he grumbled. "I swear being on here can take

you to a dark place. Feels about the same as going through terrorist cell phones."

"So, why are you still on there?"

He side-eyed her. "I guess it's less scary than going on Gwen's Instagram account." The thought made him immediately tense. "All those guys making comments about her looks on her photos. It makes me a bit—"

"Ragey?" Her lips trembled as if fighting a smile.

"Yeah, a bit."

"Did you take the time to read her responses? Because I did. And if anything, you should feel better about how she handled herself. She put all those assholes in their place."

"Really?" A sense of pride sent a thrill up his spine.

"Really." She reached for his mobile and tossed it onto the bed, then looped her arms around his neck. "From what I can see, you have a hell of a daughter. Looks like she takes after you. Blood can be strong."

Twenty-plus years.

Would she even want him in her life?

"Whatever you're feeling right now, I assure you it's normal."

He brought a fist beneath her chin. "Gwen doesn't need the bounty or a job from Felix. Her mum has plenty of money. Why is she doing this?" It'd been a question in his mind since he'd learned she was in the competition, but he hadn't verbalized his concerns.

"Well, since it appears she's very much like you, I'm guessing she wanted to pave her own path. Not be tied to money she didn't earn. Or live the life of a debutant." She brought one palm to his cheek, and he turned his mouth so his lips brushed the inside of her hand.

While he and Natasha were en route to the hotel, Harper had texted that she had news. But he'd much rather ignore responsibility and make use of the condoms they had left over.

Spend hours kissing every inch of her. Learning every freckle. Every sensitive spot. To bask in the warmth of that sun he'd never realized he needed until he met a woman whose light was so bright it was impossible not to see it, to crave it.

But The Knight was still out there playing his sick game. More people could die.

And one of them could end up being Gwen.

"We should probably head up." He begrudgingly stepped out of Natasha's reach and texted Harper they were on their way.

"Are you as nervous to hear what they found out as I am?" she asked once they were in the lift.

"I just want this over with." He faced her, catching his eyes in the reflection of the mirrored wall behind where Natasha stood. "I want a chance to get to know you." *And Gwen.*

"You don't know me yet?" Humor touched her tone. "You spent half the flight asking me questions. I think you know me better than anyone now."

"And I want to know all the things you refused to talk about on a plane full of people."

"Oh?" She arched a brow as the doors dinged and parted.

He stepped closer to her. "You can't cram thirty-five years of your life into six hours, and I'm greedy. I want to know everything. All there is to know about this rambly," he said while brushing her long hair to her back, "and awkward but badass woman."

"You might regret that," she teased, her eyes shining as she smiled.

"My only regret is not getting to know you sooner." And

it took him a psychotic hacker and discovering he had a daughter to realize that.

CHAPTER THIRTY-THREE

"LET ME GET THIS STRAIGHT." WYATT BLINKED IN astonishment at what Jessica had announced over the secure web call in Harper's suite. "You're saying Roland Nilsson went to Seattle for an interview with Cyber X before the op in Romania back in twenty-nineteen, then landed the job along with a sign-on bonus after The Knight supposedly died in the fire?"

"Yeah, and it gets better." Jessica's blue eyes gleamed. He knew that look. She was onto something. "Shortly after the initial interview, Roland flew to Bulgaria. Could he have been taking a vacation? Sure. Why not?" She added her usual sarcastic flair when speaking. "But the timing to the Romania op is too suspicious, especially because he booked a one-way trip as if he didn't know when he'd be coming back to the U.S."

"Did he cross the border and go into Romania when he got there?" he asked.

"Not legally, but yes. Looks like he was trying to cover his tracks and hide the fact he'd been there. Another check mark in the suspicious box. And it took all day for us to scour the old CCTV footage to prove he was even there. We managed to confirm his presence outside a hotel less than an hour away from The Knight's home a few days before your boots hit the ground." Jessica paused. "Then, a day after our op, Roland was back on a plane out of Bulgaria."

Natasha settled into the desk chair next to Harper and gripped the leather chair arms. Wyatt set a hand on her shoulder, worried she was blaming herself for missing this, and that was the last thing he wanted.

She lifted a hand to cover his and squeezed as if letting him know not to worry, that she'd be okay.

It was only the three of them in the suite. The guys were all in position, keeping an eye on their targets, one of which was Gwen.

"Jasper informed me of The Knight's location in Romania about a week before your people were sent in," Natasha said. "He had concerns, though. He thought The Knight might relocate. Looking back, I guess he was hoping we would jump on it, somehow cut through the usual red tape, and send in a team ASAP, which would make sense if Jasper was also working with Cyber X."

"And our guys were dispatched because it takes forever and a day to get approval for anyone else," Jessica said. "Plus, our people wouldn't have to worry about coordinating with the Romanians since we don't technically exist."

Wyatt's gaze cut to Jessica. "We had toyed with the idea someone hacked The Knight's fail-safe to detonate the explosives when we arrived in Romania, ensuring we witnessed his supposed death. What's Roland's background? Would he have been capable of doing that?"

"He had a double masters in computer science and chemical engineering," Jessica answered. "And here's the kicker, he worked for one of the cyber companies who had to close its doors after losing credibility due to repeated hacks by The Knight. Roland lost his job, and his wife ended up leaving him."

"So, if someone told Roland he could take out not only a dangerous criminal but the guy responsible for flipping his life upside down . . ." Wyatt turned away from the computer, processing the news. "What if Jasper's role was to tell the CIA the location, and Roland's job was to be in position and wait for an expected CIA team to show—then hack The Knight's fail-safe and detonate the explosives to ensure The Knight died."

"And our people were there to witness it all to get the Feds off Cyber X's back," Jessica pointed out.

"So, we're saying everyone and everything connects back to Cyber X?" They'd thought Roland Nilsson had been a pawn in The Knight's game, a victim. And maybe he had been, but if he blew that house in Romania where someone on Echo could've gotten injured or killed, then he no longer pitied the fucker.

"Looks that way." Natasha stood and stepped to the side, catching Wyatt's eyes. "Maybe Cyber X made a deal with The Knight to drum up business for them?"

Jessica removed her black frames and leaned back in the desk chair. "They provided the targets, and he made money off selling the intel. It would have been a win-win for the both of them."

"Wait." Natasha's eyes widened. "That three hundred million stolen from the data center in Sweden . . . what if The Knight and Cyber X shared their earnings from the hacks, and they kept it pooled together for safe keeping as cryptocurrency?"

"Why would The Knight split the money? Sounds to me like he did all the work." And Wyatt couldn't see either side trusting the other *that* much to manage an account of that kind of cash, either.

"I'm not sure yet. We don't have all the pieces to this." Harper's voice was soft, thoughtful. Wyatt recognized she'd slipped into her brainstorming mode, running ideas and possibilities like computer code.

"Regardless, we need to figure out why The Knight transferred one hundred and fifty million to me," Natasha said. "Some sort of clue to let me know Cyber X's guilt in all of this?"

"A hundred-and-fifty-million-dollar clue?" That seemed crazy, but they were dealing with a psychotic criminal who clearly enjoyed slowly doling out pieces of the puzzle to Natasha.

Honestly, this was all starting to give him a headache. The case served as a reminder to appreciate the ops where a target package was provided, and all he had to do was hunt and kill. Being in a full kit, carrying forty kilos of gear in the Afghanistan desert for two days without rack time, was preferable to chasing The Knight.

This job did come with one incredible perk, though, and that was spending time with Natasha. She was a brilliant officer who could go head-to-head with this terrorist arse no problem.

"Or maybe The Knight managed to lure Felix and Kate Ward to Montreal by promising them a chance at redemption for trying to kill him?" Harper suggested. "Getting back their stolen millions must be appealing, too."

Natasha's shoulders slumped, the creep of doubt, or blame, appearing to sneak in, so he brought his hand back to her shoulder for support. "But this is all speculation."

She was right. They couldn't get ahead of themselves.

There was still a lot to figure out. "We need concrete evidence tying The Knight to Cyber X."

"And to confirm Jasper and Roland were truly working with the Wards," Harper added.

"You manage to get a better angle of the woman at the hotel in London?" Natasha asked.

Harper shook her head. "She knew what she was doing. She never let the cameras get a good look at her face the day she was at Jasper's hotel. But I assume she was sent by Cyber X."

"What about Kate? Could it be her wearing a wig?" There was something Wyatt had never liked about the woman from the moment he'd set his eyes on her at the salsa club. Her background had come up clean, but maybe that didn't mean jack shit. "Can we find out if she was in London that day? She has the same height and build as the woman on camera."

Jessica placed her glasses back on. "I'll look into it now."

"What I don't get is why all of a sudden Cyber X would want The Knight taken out if they'd been working together in the past?" Natasha asked, and Wyatt had felt the tremble in her body when she'd spoken. The dip of unease. He couldn't blame her, but he'd do his best to help her get through this.

Natasha turned in her chair, and he let go of her. "We need to talk to Kate and Felix. Or Jasper. What if they can identify him?" Hope filled her voice, but he knew exactly what Jessica was about to say.

"Sorry." Jessica's response was immediate. "We don't have authority to operate here. We can't take them in for questioning."

"So, we're supposed to wait until The Knight's big move to find out what in the hell is going on?" Natasha was back on her feet. She brushed past him, strode to the window, and stole a glimpse outside between the drawn drapes. "It's obvious he wants revenge against everyone involved in the op in Romania. He feels betrayed."

"He tortured and murdered Roland," Jessica said, her voice steady. Years of experience in such difficult cases gliding through. "But he wanted Jasper at the competition. And clearly, since Felix and Kate Ward still showed up despite everything going on, The Knight wanted them here as well."

"We also need to find out how the Wards hired The Knight to begin with," Wyatt noted, and Natasha let go of the drapes and faced the room. "For a job like that, you don't just trust some guy off the Dark Net."

Natasha swept her hair to the side and twisted the long locks into a braid as she worked through a thought, her eyes on the floor. "Perhaps it was someone from their past they knew and trusted?"

"I'll do a deep dive into the Wards' background and take a closer look once I determine whether Kate was the woman in that hotel in London," Jessica said.

"And where are we at on piecing together all the photos you found online taken that night at the salsa club?" Wyatt asked Harper, a sense of hope filling him that they were finally figuring everything out.

"I'll have enough images strung together by morning, so we can look through them." Harper spun her chair back around to focus on the screen.

"Would The Knight show his face if Felix and Kate could recognize him?" Natasha asked, raising a good point.

"He may not have let them see him, but he could've been there." Wyatt closed his eyes and thought back to the night at the club. "Shit." His stomach roiled, and his eyes flashed open. "There was a guy in a hoodie offering Gwen a smoke outside. He left when I came out and never looked up. I'd been so used to seeing hoodies I didn't think anything of it."

Had the son of a bitch been right there? *And* talking to his daughter?

"Who wears a hoodie at a salsa club where the place is hot and sweaty?" Harper scoffed. "If he was in the competition, he wouldn't hide his identity, he'd want to show off the fact he successfully completed that Twitter challenge. He could be our guy. You remember anything else? I can try and find him in the photos."

"My height. Jeans. Plain black hoodie." Wyatt rattled off a few more details he could think of.

"This could be the break we need." Natasha met his eyes, a slight smile at the edges of her lips. Hope.

"And you were right," Jessica said a moment later. "Kate Ward was in London on July twelfth. It has to be her who met with Jasper. But none of this is enough evidence to get POTUS to put his neck out there and have the Wards arrested."

"I think we need more manpower." Wyatt looked to Jessica. "Can you send Bravo?"

"I was talking to them about that earlier, in fact." She removed her glasses and pinched the bridge of her nose before placing them back on. She looked tired. Wyatt remembered when Jessica would work for days straight during an op. Then again, she was pregnant with not just one but two babies. Hell, he got tired just thinking about it. "But Luke and Asher are being pains in the ass. One of them wants to stay behind in case I need help as if we don't have ten other guys working at Scott and Scott who—"

"She's six months pregnant with my babies." Asher came into view of the screen, ducking his head down and scowling at the screen. Wyatt hadn't even realized he'd been in the conference room. "I have every right to be worried. Tell her. You're a dad, you get it, right?"

Shit. He did get it. Asher was right. "Luke should stay back. With Eva pregnant, he can keep an eye out on the both of you."

Asher twisted his head to the side to look at Jessica. "See?"

Jessica rolled her eyes and mumbled, "Fine." She pointed to the door. "Go round up the guys. You'll need to drive." She fisted the material of Asher's long-sleeved gray shirt and tugged him closer to her. "These babies need a dad." Still clutching his shirt, she glared at Wyatt. "Don't let anything happen to this guy."

"Roger that," Wyatt said with a smile. "Bravo should stay at a different hotel and probably keep their distance from us."

Natasha came up beside him. "As careful as we have been about covering our tracks with security cams at the hotel, I wouldn't put it past The Knight to have figured out I have more than Wyatt here working with me."

He glimpsed his Casio. *Damn it.* "The light on my watch just turned red but only for half a second."

He started for the safe to grab a gun, but Natasha yelled out, "Wait!"

Wyatt pivoted around, his heart beating wildly at the idea of The Knight in their room.

"By the time you get there, he'll be gone." Natasha came closer with a palm in the air as if a request to consider her words. "If he planted a listening device, we could use that to our advantage."

His gaze dropped to the floor as he processed what she was saying. "Set a trap," he said with understanding, looking back up at her. "What if he suspects that?"

"Your watch blinked for what, half a second?" Natasha

challenged. "You could've easily missed that. Most people would have. You go running to your room, he'll know you figured it out. Surely he's got his own camera now positioned in the hallway outside our hotel door and will be watching our moves."

"She's right," Jessica chimed in. "He'll also cover his tracks to ensure we can't see him on the hotel cameras."

"He's damn good. If he looped the feeds, I can't tell." Harper was on another laptop, checking their hotel's security cameras. "You sure you saw the light turn red?"

"And are you sure your spyware didn't go on the fritz?" he shot back.

Harper smiled. "Hell no."

He held his palms in the air as if to say *Well, you know my answer, then: the light was red.* And great, no chance he'd be making love to Natasha in their hotel room again, not with that son of a bitch listening in.

Natasha closed her eyes and cursed. "It's pretty late, and if he really did just go into our hotel room, he had to have known we weren't in there. And surely, he monitored our flight arrival."

"Which means he may know about us," Harper said without lifting her gaze from the screen as she worked. "Well, I've got our identities covered if he tries to run our names or faces."

"But it's a good thing we've got Bravo coming." Wyatt let go of a deep breath. "He won't be expecting them."

CHAPTER THIRTY-FOUR

FIRST PLACE. LEADING BY TEN POINTS. ALREADY BEING called the Most Elite Hacker in the world on social media even though there were still twenty-four hours left in the competition.

How was this happening? How was Gwen kicking Jasper's ass? Jasper was supposedly one of the best hackers out there, and now he was being bested by his daughter.

"What if The Knight comes after Gwen because he thinks she's a worthy adversary?" He peeled off his shirt and tossed it onto Harper's bed Saturday morning. "It's too hot in here," he complained when Natasha shut and locked the bedroom door, giving them some extra privacy.

He'd begun pacing back and forth when he'd learned Gwen had taken the lead an hour ago at eight in the morning.

Wyatt and Natasha had reluctantly gone back to their hotel to get some sleep to keep up with appearances if The Knight had bugged their room, but they hadn't wanted to stay long, so they'd come back to Harper's suite.

"I don't think that's The Knight's end game. He wants payback for Romania, and Gwen doesn't fit into the equation." Natasha motioned for him to sit, but he couldn't stop pacing.

Sweat dotted his back. The heat was too damn high in the room.

"Gwen's been working from her hotel room," she said as a reminder. "And you have four more guys who will be here soon for backup."

Bravo Team was only an hour out, and Natasha was right, it'd be nice to have almost the entire team in town to help.

Liam could be on overwatch as an extra sniper if needed, plus he had a ridiculous number of other skills he'd bring to the table. Asher as leader, assaulter, EOD expert, or breacher, would be a great addition. And although Knox was their best medic, he also knew how to deactivate a bomb if The Knight had plans to go kinetic on them. Owen was basically good at everything, and if shit hit the fan and they needed a rapid extract, the man would commandeer a jetliner if that's what it took to save their arses.

So, having the nine of them there, why in the bloody hell was his pulse still going so damn fast? It was racing like one of those horses at the tracks his mum used to secretly bet on.

"She needs to quit this competition so we can bring her in. Have her here with us." He stopped walking and faced her, his nerves tangled the fuck up.

"Do you think she'll walk away from the competition when she's less than a day away from a five-hundred-thousand-dollar bounty?" Her eyebrows slanted as if an idea struck her. "That's how we talk to Jasper!" She reached for his arm, an excited smile on her face. "You. You're the, uh, missing link." Her smile broadened. "Don't you get it?"

"No." He shot her a puzzled look.

"Your alias Link. Jasper knows Link is one of the best hackers out there, and if Jasper has to win the competition because of whatever game The Knight is playing, he might be open to your help." She let go of him and lifted one shoulder. "It doesn't hurt that he was also clearly attracted to you at the bar."

"So, I'm supposed to do what, exactly?"

"Invite him into the back of your ride to talk. I'll be inside waiting. Finn can drive. We question him in the back of the SUV. MI6 will probably be following, but since he'll willingly get into the back of the car, the agents will only follow. Then we lose their tail."

"You're so sure Jasper will go with me?" He knew they could get him to talk once they were alone, but he wasn't so sure he could get him into a car without using a gun. Of course, that's what contingency plans were for. "He may not trust me since he saw us together at that club."

"We have to at least try and if not—"

"Use my gun without anyone noticing."

She grabbed her mobile. "According to these tweets, Jasper has been working out of that firehouse. Probably keeping himself surrounded with people to prevent being killed by The Knight."

The firehouse. It'd been an unforgettable night because he and Natasha had reconnected, and she'd strutted right up to him and kissed him, taking him by surprise. Not even a week had passed since that night.

"Before we go out there . . ." She traced a line down the center of his naked chest with her index finger. "I'm sure Harper wouldn't mind seeing you like this, but just in case, you may want your shirt."

He clutched her wrist and brought her palm to his mouth, momentarily forgetting everything going on in the world. "Thank you for the heads-up."

A soft blush touched her face. "Well, when you're half-naked, my thoughts get a bit muddled, and I imagine you might have that effect on others as well. And we need Harper at one hundred percent."

He allowed their hands to fall and dipped in for a kiss.

"You're vibrating," she announced against his mouth.

He hesitantly pulled back and cocked a brow. "Am I?" He wanted to stay close to her, but he grabbed his mobile from his pocket. Personal, not work phone. He looked up at her, a knot forming in his throat. "It's Charlotte."

"You going to answer it?"

He gulped but brought the phone to his ear.

"Wyatt?" Charlotte's voice was breathy upon answer.

"Yeah, are you okay?" His forehead tightened, eyes on the carpet.

"No. My son follows his sister's Twitter account. He said she's in some type of hacker competition. I'm on my way to Heathrow. Are you in Montreal? You said you were going to Canada, but . . ."

Shit. "Yeah, I'm here."

"You knew she was involved in this, didn't you? That's why you called me last week. How could you not tell me?"

Was she kidding?

"Have you seen her? Is she okay? Does she know who you are?"

"I have seen her, but no, she has no clue who I am." *Thanks to you.* "And you shouldn't come here. Stay in London."

She was quiet before whispering, "Is she in trouble?"

"She'll be fine, but if you come here, it'll only create more problems." A headache he couldn't handle was beginning to creep up on him.

"I'm coming. I have to, but if you think for one minute

you're going to have my child hate me again by telling her the truth, then I—"

"Hate you again? What are you talking about?" His gaze journeyed to Natasha, and a sense of calm washed over him with her there.

"I wasn't completely honest with you."

Not a surprise. "What are you saying?" He didn't have time to deal with Charlotte, but if there was something he needed to know about Gwen to keep her safe . . .

"Gwen got into some trouble when she was sixteen. She hacked into the school's records to expose fraudulent spending. She did it again at her new school the next year. Arthur managed to sweep it under the rug and made her promise she wouldn't get involved in that hacking nonsense anymore, but it looks like she hasn't stopped. I don't know, she called herself a hacktivist. Arthur demanded she stop, or he'd cut her off when she was eighteen, and that's when she decided to go to school in Toronto. She said she'd only stop when we were finally honest with her. She didn't want to live in, um . . ."

He thought back to Gwen's tweet. *A house of lies?* He looked up at Natasha, worry in her eyes

"I think somehow Gwen knew the truth." Charlotte paused. "I think she knows Arthur's not her biological father."

Wyatt immediately went to the bed and sat, his legs feeling like he was back at BUD/S during Hell Week, numb and sore. "I don't understand."

"Gwen's really smart. She'd once asked if she was adopted when she was ten because she had nothing in common with us." Pain sliced through her tone, but could he even feel bad for her?

"I, um." He tore his fingers through his hair and took a deep breath.

"I'm sorry. I'm so sorry for everything."

He hesitantly stood, worried his knees would give out. "You shouldn't come."

"Is-is she in danger?" Charlotte's voice was timid. Mouse-like. Gwen was nothing like her mum, was she? The woman he'd met at the salsa club had a strong backbone. "I'm coming. If you're there for your security job, that means there could be trouble. And Gwen won't trust you without knowing the truth first."

His stomach dropped. "What are you saying?"

She paused. "We need to tell her, Wyatt. She needs to know you're her father, but we do it my way."

"But you don't know for certain."

The silence ate up the space, and his heartbeat quickened with every passing moment. "Another lie?" The blood rushed from his face. "You didn't just tell Arthur there was a chance she was mine, you told him she *was* mine."

"I had blood work drawn after Gwen was born. Tests run," she confessed. "You were already married to Clara at the time, and we decided it'd be best if you never knew." She was crying. Regretful tears. But this was . . . "Arthur didn't want you back in our lives. He was still so angry at the time."

"Charlotte." He dropped his eyes closed, every fiber in his being locked tight. Anger, pain, and hurt ripping through him.

"Cancer changed him, though. He told me I should tell you. Tell her. But not until after he was gone. He wanted to live his last moments as her father. He didn't want her to hate him for lying."

Arthur raised her, he was her father in all the ways that counted. But what caused Wyatt the most pain was that he'd never been given the choice to raise her himself. The decision had been taken from him.

When he opened his eyes, liquid burned his gaze, obstructing his view of Natasha.

Were these tears?

"But you didn't tell me after Arthur died," he grit out. "You kept up the lie."

"I wanted to after the wake, but then you just up and left, and Gwen doesn't need another father who will leave her. And after the wake, she and I grew close again, and I realized if she learned the truth, she'd never forgive me. I'd lose her again."

He cupped his mouth, worried he'd lose his cool. Yell or cry, he wasn't sure. He wanted to do both.

Natasha stood off to his side and smoothed a hand up and down his back, attempting to soothe his nerves that didn't feel quite fixable.

"My flight gets in at eight thirty tonight. I'll let you know when I'm there." Charlotte ended the call before he could say more.

He blinked back unwanted tears he refused to let fall and turned to face Natasha. "They both knew. All these years, they knew Gwen was mine, and they lied."

CHAPTER THIRTY-FIVE

"You sure you're good?" Natasha stood in front of the bedroom door, blocking Wyatt's path to the living room. She needed to ensure he was truly okay after the bomb Charlotte had delivered. He'd had less than two minutes to process the truth before Harper had knocked on the door, saying she had news. She'd shot Harper a silent request with her eyes and a tip of the head to give them a second.

"I'll be fine," Wyatt assured her.

But would he be fine? He was paler than normal. Eyes a touch red. The veins at the tops of his hands more prominent from repeatedly clenching and unclenching, angrily tucking his fingertips into his palms.

Gray had done the same thing after the helicopter crash, and whenever she visited him, he'd be in bed, hands clenched at his sides as if channeling all his frustration, prepared to hit an invisible enemy.

Natasha took a tentative step his way and secured her arms around his body before he could protest, before he could tell her they had no time. Harper had an image of the guy in the hoodie from the salsa club, and yes, they were needed in the living room, but Wyatt also needed one damn minute.

"You can squeeze me. Tight as you need to," she offered. He buried his face in her hair near the side of her neck.

His heart pounded fiercely against her chest, but he didn't cry. He didn't let go. He just quietly held on to her.

"We should go," he announced as he pulled away, his voice deep. "Thank you." His brows pulled tight, and she nodded.

"So, um, what do you have?" Wyatt asked Harper once they were in the living room.

"The image I pulled from Instagram was pretty pixelated since he was in the background of a selfie, but I worked my magic and managed to get a cleaner shot." Harper magnified the view, and for some insane reason, Natasha closed her eyes.

"Natasha?" Wyatt placed his hand on her shoulder, and that simple act immediately gave her strength. This man had flipped her world upside down these last few days, and most likely, long before tonight.

She swallowed, pushed away her fears that this would be a dead lead, and lifted her gaze to the screen.

A pair of close-set, dark brown eyes stared back at her. Brownish-black hair peeked out beneath the hood on the man's forehead. A long, straight nose. Thick slanted brows. No remarkable features, but she recognized him instantly.

Natasha's shoulders sagged under the weight of disappointment. "I know him. And he's dead. Well, I thought he was."

"What do you mean?" Wyatt's hand connected with her back this time. Gentle strokes up and down. Comforting and calming.

She turned to the side so she could look back and forth between both Harper and Wyatt. "That's Alexander Rothus, a deceased businessman. The owner of the house in Romania where your team was sent to try and apprehend The Knight. At least he *was* the owner of that house. He died in a car crash in twenty-sixteen. Or so I was led to believe. He had no heirs, so the property was turned over to the city and had remained vacant. Well, supposedly vacant."

"But the CIA believed it was actually The Knight who'd been living there in twenty-nineteen?" Wyatt asked, and she nodded. "You're sure this guy in the hoodie is a match for Rothus?"

Natasha set her focus on the screen, doubt in her abilities to perform the job creeping into her mind. But . . . "Yes, it's him." She inhaled through her nose and let the breath out slowly. "After the Romanians cremated the body and labeled him as an unidentified squatter, I did some digging."

Wyatt pulled the chair out next to Harper and offered Natasha a seat, but she needed to stay upright, to keep her feet grounded as she faced the fact The Knight had fooled her again.

"Originally, the Agency assumed The Knight must have chosen the house because it was empty, and for the off-the-grid type location with those pre-existing tunnels. And most likely, he paid someone under the table to look the other way while he lived there. I wasn't able to verify who he paid off, though. But I did double-check Rothus's background to ensure The Knight wasn't actually Rothus, and he'd faked the car crash." *I triple-checked even.* "Since the crash happened in twenty-sixteen around the time the case fell into my lap, I'd been suspicious it may not have been a coincidence."

"Fake his death, then a few years later, come back and

temporarily hide out on that property in the middle of nowhere . . . maybe." Harper pursed her lips in thought.

"He'd have to be damn certain no one would recognize him." Wyatt addressed one of the concerns her COS had countered as a plot hole in Natasha's theory back in 2019 about Rothus being The Knight.

"Rothus did own multiple properties when he was alive. It's possible he never called that one his home. But since I wasn't authorized to go to Romania and poke around without getting fired—"

"You couldn't show Rothus's photo to anyone in town," Harper finished for her. "What about CCTV cameras?"

Natasha's shoulders slumped. "The closest towns to his house didn't have the kind of tech I needed to try and see if Rothus was walking around alive after the car crash but before your team went in. And even when I ran the image we had of Rothus, there weren't any hits internationally, either. Or any alternate aliases connected to his face."

"I'm betting your boss shut this theory down, then?" Harper knew all too well how things went at Langley, and she'd been right.

"Yeah, and he did have one point." Natasha had returned to Langley after visiting Wyatt in Colorado and had pitched the idea about Rothus as The Knight to her boss, Dan Jessup. He'd shut her down within minutes, forcing her to move on to a new case.

"It was the fact you even had a picture of Rothus, right?" Wyatt asked. "If Rothus was The Knight's real identity or even an alias, he'd never leave a legitimate photo of himself online to be traced."

"Well, it looks like your boss—I'm betting you were dealing with Dan the Man Jessup—was wrong." Harper swiveled in her chair, setting her eyes on Natasha.

"Don't even think about beating yourself up. That arsehat of a boss probably reassigned you, then threatened you to back off The Knight or else, right?" Wyatt spoke up, attempting to dispel her doubts, to remove the blame that was going to eat at her.

Bottom line, looking at this new photo of a supposed dead man at the salsa club, meant she should have followed her gut and kept pushing her theory.

"I guarantee that even now if I run the photo of this guy in the hoodie—Rothus or whatever his real name may be—through our facial recognition software program, we'll turn up with zero leads," Harper said as she turned back to her computer and began emailing the image to Jessica. "However he got to Canada, he'd have found a way to protect his face from getting flagged."

"Which means there's absolutely nothing you could've done differently after that op in Romania, especially with Dickhead Dan in charge," Wyatt remarked.

Dan Jessup wasn't that bad, but he hadn't been as stubborn as her in pursuit of the truth.

"And having a photo of The Knight probably wouldn't have helped you find him before." Wyatt braced her shoulder. He'd slipped back into strong operator mode, pushing his personal issues aside for the sake of the mission. How many times had he done that? How many times had she?

"But that doesn't mean having his photo now won't do any good," Harper said. "Since we know The Knight is connected to the Wards, we can better sift through the Wards' history and see if he's in any photos. Maybe get a real name."

"Didn't Jessica spend all of last night combing through their past?" Wyatt asked as Harper reached for her phone. "That woman has a crazy good memory about on point with Liam, so maybe she'll remember seeing him."

Natasha looked to Wyatt as Harper phoned Jessica and began explaining everything they'd learned so far.

Wyatt scratched the back of his head, his eyes falling to the floor. "If there's such a thing as a photographic memory, Liam's got it, but still nothing compared to Elaina."

"Elaina, right. The adorable girl they adopted." Natasha smiled. "Alexa told me all about her."

"I swear Elaina is psychic, and Liam is gonna have his hands full when she's older and starts dating." His voice thickened as he said his last words, and his hands went back to that familiar clenched position at his sides. He was thinking about his own daughter now. Eyes drawn closed. Battling emotions that raged quietly beneath the surface.

"Jessica thinks she may have come across a photo of Rothus when he was younger last night." Harper's words grabbed their attention, and Wyatt's hands relaxed at the news.

He was calmer in operator-mode. In his element. She supposed she could relate.

"Jessica's looking something up now, but I was just thinking—you said the guy in that house was on fire when you entered, right?" Harper looked to Wyatt since he'd been the one to try and brave entering the home as flames ate the structure, trying to get the man out.

God, she still owed him for that. His bravery. His heroics to forge ahead against all odds. He'd risked his life to try and bring The Knight out alive for her.

"Yeah, he was covered head-to-toe in flames. I couldn't get to him without dying." Wyatt glimpsed Natasha, apology in his eyes, and she squeezed his bicep, a plea not to blame himself for anything.

"If he was engulfed in flames, how could he have possibly escaped, even if there was a tunnel, without massive scarring? I'm not familiar with the recovery process for burn victims, but if he did survive, wouldn't he have some burn scars? Discoloration or change in the texture of skin, at least." Harper pointed to the screen, Alexander's picture pulled back up. "This man's skin in this recent photo is flawless. Face. Neck. Hands."

"Best plastic surgeon in the world?" Wyatt proposed.

"I don't know." Harper wasn't buying it, which meant . . .

"You think Wyatt saw someone else on fire that day." Natasha released Wyatt's arm and looked toward the drapes that hid the view outside as she worked through an idea.

"Maybe the Romanians did cremate a body, it just wasn't The Knight's," Wyatt said, his tone grave. "It's highly likely he wants revenge if he lost someone he cared about that day in the explosion."

"Which means the Wards believed Roland successfully killed The Knight that day. Maybe they even paid off the police to cremate the body quickly." Shit, that was it, wasn't it? "The Wards wanted him cremated because The Knight's real identity could connect back to them."

"And I think I know why," Jessica announced over speakerphone. Natasha had nearly forgotten the line was still connected. "I'm sending you a twenty-year-old photo now. Let me know what you think."

Natasha gripped the back of Harper's chair as Harper clicked open a secure email from Jessica.

"The photo dates back to two thousand and one," Jessica explained. "It's from Kate Ward's yearbook at the boarding school she attended in Sweden. Look at the man standing behind her."

Natasha leaned in over Harper's shoulder as she enlarged the image so they could better see. *And holy shit.* "That's him. That's Rothus."

"According to the yearbook, his name is Alexander Balan," Jessica said. "He was the computer teacher and also the chess coach. The photo was taken when Kate won the European chess championship."

Chess, of course. "What else can you find out about Balan?"

A crackle popped over the line as if Jessica had exhaled a deep breath. "Nothing. I ran his name, and he's a ghost."

"Except this picture." How was that possible?

"Balan must have erased his identity. When I uploaded the recent photo Harper sent me into our database, I got Rothus for a match." Irritation weaved through Jessica's tone. "The only reason I managed to even get ahold of this photo is because this coming summer is the twenty-year reunion of the graduating class of two thousand and one, and the coordinator for the event digitized their yearbook as a gift to those students. Kate was a sophomore at the time of the chess championship in the yearbook, so she wouldn't have received a copy."

"This is a damn lucky break." Wyatt reached for Natasha's hand and interlaced their fingers.

Was this what hope and optimism felt like?

"I guess Balan overlooked that detail," Jessica said. "I'm thinking Balan not only took Kate under his wing in chess club, but he saw potential in her as a hacker. She was probably his protégé while at school."

Natasha lifted her gaze from the screen, an idea coming to mind. "What if Kate is the brains behind everything, and Felix is just the face and name? The business was in trouble, so Kate reached out to her old coach for help. He was someone untraceable who she trusted."

"But when Balan went too far . . . Kate realized she had to

put a stop to him," Wyatt added. "And isn't the queen in chess actually the piece with the most power?"

Natasha frowned. "I've spent five years chasing The Knight, but what if Kate has been calling the shots all along?" She glimpsed Wyatt as he squeezed her hand a little tighter. "But we have to stop Balan before he calls checkmate."

CHAPTER THIRTY-SIX

"Are you sure this will work?" The last thing Natasha wanted to do was question Wyatt and his team, but her nerves were stretched thin, especially after discovering the true identity of The Knight and his connection to Kate Ward.

"My guys have run ops like this more times than I can remember." Wyatt's strong hands held her cheeks, warming her, calming her. His eyes. His touch. His smell. He could calm an army of Spartan soldiers and get them to surrender with a simple but powerful look.

They were back in the safety of Harper's bedroom. They'd gone to their hotel room to keep up the act in case The Knight was listening in. They'd even kissed a few times, which was weird and somewhat stilted since neither of them was comfortable with the situation. But they didn't have any choice but to act as normal as possible if it meant they had a shot at finally outsmarting the bastard.

"You can trust me."

"I know." She smiled. "And I do. It's him I don't trust."

And now *her*. Kate Damn Ward, who she'd dubbed The Queen in her mind.

Every death, every terrorist attack, was now on Kate's hands. Her greed for wealth, her desire to be part of a company of unparalleled expertise and fame in the field had caused her to use whatever measures necessary and without regard for human life.

In Natasha's mind, she was as much a psychopath, if not more, than Alexander Balan.

"Balan feels cheated. Jasper probably never would've found him if he hadn't had an assist from Kate. I think Balan kept Jasper alive, unlike Roland Nilsson, because he wants to prove to him that he's the superior hacker." She paused. "Once he's proven that, *then* he'll have Jasper killed."

"But he can't do all of this alone," Wyatt reminded her. "He hired mercenaries to abduct Roland, and surely, he has people in Montreal as well." His hands went to her biceps, and he gently squeezed. "Plus, Harper has scoured every CCTV camera in and around the convention hall and our hotel. He's keeping his face down. He knows where not to look. But I also think we can't get him on any cameras because he's not alone out there."

"He showed up at the salsa club. He called me from the convention center when I was at the mill. And no way did he have someone else break into our hotel room last night. We can't know for sure if he has a team here. He could've just covered his bases by manipulating all the CCTV footage in the area." She didn't want to be pessimistic, especially when they were so close, but she had to be a realist. Cautious when it came to The Knight.

She'd learned her lesson, and he'd fooled her one too many times.

No more being made a pawn in his game of revenge. And as for Kate, it was time she was dethroned.

"Regardless, if he hired someone on the Dark Net, it won't hurt to have Jessica try to find out who." His thumbs moved up and down her arms, his continued attempt to ease her. "And with any luck, maybe Balan's hired guns will even come to us tonight. Someone has to be watching Jasper. Most likely Kate and Felix, too."

"And Balan can't be in three places." It made sense, she supposed. The Knight wasn't playing the same game as he had in the past. And maybe like Svalbard, this wasn't a solo mission. Alexander Balan was a computer genius, but had he ever even pulled a trigger? "You're right."

She turned away from him, and he let go of her. Eyes on the mirror above the dresser, she dragged her focus from her reflection to Wyatt standing alongside her. "How much do you think Felix knows?" Her mind was going in so many different directions as they waited to roll out to the firehouse where Jasper was competing.

"He can't be an idiot, especially since the FBI looked into him."

She checked her watch, the one Gray had given her, and faced him. "Charlotte's plane gets in soon."

Wyatt hadn't mentioned Gwen since he'd ended the call with Charlotte. Natasha had been waiting for him to bring her up.

"I don't see any reason why The Knight would be watching Gwen, but he's most likely got eyes on me, which means I need to make sure I don't have a tail when I head to Gwen's hotel later." He walked over to the bed and dropped down. "Do you think Charlotte will tell her tonight?"

"Do you want her to?" Natasha sat beside him and planted a hand on his muscular thigh.

"I think so. But I also need to clear the air about what's going on with her and Felix, without also divulging classified intel."

"That might be tricky." She wished she could go with him for support, but no way could she go anywhere without The Knight's notice, and she didn't want to further endanger Gwen. "It feels like weeks ago when it was being considered we bring Gwen in to see what she knows."

"You mean when Harper suggested we turn my daughter into a source?" He lifted a brow, still sour about the idea ever being presented.

"Harper and Jessica were thinking like CIA officers when they brought that up. Try not to hold a grudge," she said, keeping her voice soft.

"I get that. If they hadn't saved my arse more times than I can count, and I didn't trust them with my life, then maybe I'd still be angry. But *you* didn't put the mission first." He angled his head, his blue-gray eyes thinning. "Do you think it's dangerous caring about someone?"

"What do you mean?"

"The 'greater good' thing," he said and shook his head. "I mean, what happens if I had to choose between saving someone I love and stopping a terrorist attack?" Regret darkened his eyes.

"You stop the terrorist attack." Her lips rolled inward as she thought about how to explain herself. "As hard as that would be, if you were to save one life over the many, the person you'd save would forever live with those other deaths hanging over them. The guilt would be worse than death." She took a shaky breath, her bottom lip nearly wobbling. "It's the job. It's why we've been chosen to do what we do because when it comes down to it, we'll make the choice that's best for the nation."

"It's easy to say that now, but it's harder to live it." He stood and braced the back of his head with both palms.

"Well, fortunately, there's another reason why we're in these jobs." She rose and came behind him, finding his eyes in the mirror, and his arms relaxed to his sides, but he didn't turn around. "We won't let ourselves get into a situation like that."

"Don't fall in love, then?"

Her eyes remained connected with his. "No. Protect the people you care about and take out the bad guys before they can get near your loved ones."

"You're starting to sound like an optimist." He pivoted to face her, his brows slanting.

"No, that's ten years on the job and being a realist. The Knight is the only person who was able to look past my legend and find out who I really am."

He shook his head and palmed her cheek. "That's not true." He leaned in closer, his mouth near hers. "I see the real you."

CHAPTER THIRTY-SEVEN

It was almost nine o'clock, and after sitting in the back of the stretch limo outside the firehouse for over fifteen minutes, Natasha was getting worried Wyatt would come outside without Jasper.

"You need to relax."

She eased back into her seat and peered at Finn sitting in the driver's seat. "I didn't say anything."

"All that fidgeting you're doing says you're worried." He looked back at her and smiled. "Wyatt's got this. Don't worry. And if Jasper won't come willingly, then he'll stick a gun in his side and make him." He acted as if this was a typical Saturday night. Then again, his team was probably used to much more intense operations than interviewing a hacker in the back of a limo.

"I normally work behind a computer." She sat farther back on the seat and picked the lint off her jeans. "I go out in the field every once in a while, but clearly not enough." *I wouldn't be a ball of nerves if The Knight wasn't involved, though.* Of course back in Russia in Boris's hotel room, she'd been confident, unwavering in her pursuit for the truth to see if The Knight had performed the weapons facility hack.

But now, well, it felt different. Probably because she was on vacation and operating without official authority. If this op went sideways, she was going to have her ass handed to her by her boss, if not POTUS as well. Plus, she was also terrified her actions could get someone she cared about hurt.

"We've got this. Don't worry. You have no idea how many times we've hunted down bad guys and won." He smiled. "I mean, Chris almost getting eaten by a polar bear in Svalbard was unique, but—"

"What?"

His smile stretched, exposing his white teeth.

"Are you trying to distract me with a made-up story?"

He held a palm in the air, his brows lifting. A glint of humor in his eyes. "The story is true, but yes to the distracting part. Is it working?"

She scooted off her seat a little. "Yes. Now, tell me more about this bear."

"Captain America has no problem putting a bullet in human flesh, but an animal? Nope. He almost got himself captured by the Russians instead of shooting the bear."

She allowed the insane scene to unfold in her mind. "So, what happened?"

"One sec." Finn brought a hand to his ear. "Roger that." He tipped his head to the side, and she caught sight of Wyatt and Jasper on approach to the vehicle.

Finn closed the partition to keep his identity hidden from Jasper before the side door opened.

Jasper slid onto the seat opposite her, and Wyatt stepped in and sat next to Natasha. "Lock the doors. Lose MI6." Wyatt's order had been over comms to Finn, but the gun in his lap meant Jasper hadn't come willingly.

The limo pulled away from the curb, and Jasper clutched his backpack, disdain in his eyes as he focused on Natasha. "You bitch."

"Bite your tongue, or I'll cut it off," Wyatt hissed, his jaw clenching, the 9mm still tight in his grasp.

Jasper shifted on the leather and relaxed the death grip he had on his backpack. "You're going to get me killed."

"Maybe if you hadn't made a deal with Kate Ward, you wouldn't be in this situation," she shot back, letting him know she was aware of his betrayal.

Jasper's chin jutted forward in surprise.

"Don't bother lying. I know Kate came to your hotel in London in July of twenty-nineteen. What I don't understand is why? You're better than this. You've been taking criminals down for years." Hell, he was named The Smoking Gun for a reason.

Jasper leaned forward, his eyes shifting from hers to Wyatt's gun as he rasped, "And what was my reward for all the work I did exposing arseholes? I got arrested!"

"That was your own stupidity, Jasper. MI6 cut you a deal," she reminded him, "and we paid you."

"Oh." He guffawed. "Sure. I was everyone's pet monkey." Sitting back, he added, "The CIA was no different."

"Tell me, Jasper." She sought his gaze, hoping there was still some good left in him. "What really happened?"

Jasper looked to the window as they made a sharp turn, then another. Finn was working to ditch MI6.

"Tell her," Wyatt ordered, his voice thick with an authoritative command.

Jasper's shoulders slumped, but he kept his eyes on the glass. "When you brought me in to help catch The Knight, well, I *was* able to track one of the hacks back to the source.

355

When I saw how rich the woman was, I decided to see if she wanted to cut a deal."

"How'd you make the connection between The Knight's hacks and Kate Ward?" Wyatt asked, his voice less tense. Leaning in, he whispered to Natasha they'd lost the MI6 tail but picked up a new one, and hopefully, it was by someone The Knight had hired.

Jasper's gaze cut to Natasha. "You don't know?" He cocked his head as if he were about to try and cut yet another deal now. Not going to happen.

"Don't test me," Wyatt snapped. "Talk."

"Kate Ward *is* The Knight." Jasper swallowed. "Well, one of them. Alexander Balan, the man who dragged us all here, he's the other one."

She didn't want to reveal her shock, to let Jasper have any small victories, so she did her best to hide it.

"At first, Kate was the only Knight. Then she realized it'd throw the authorities off if two hackers used the same online moniker and coding. It also provided her with an alias for half the hacks, which would throw off investigators, such as yourself, looking into the case," Jasper explained, maintaining eye contact with Natasha. "From what Kate told me, she asked this Balan guy to not just help, but to consider it a challenge between them."

"Like a chess game," Natasha whispered in understanding, everything coming together now. "That's why it appeared as a game of escalation. They were going back and forth, trying to outdo one another."

"Kate's competitive, and I guess, Balan is the one who made her that way when he was her coach and teacher back in school." Jasper scratched his forehead. "She brought him in on her plan around January of twenty-sixteen, a couple months after she first started."

And that's when Alexander faked his death as Rothus, and a month later, the case fell into my lap. "They never split the money," Natasha said in realization. "Kate earned that hundred and fifty million herself."

"The day we thought Balan died, Kate bled his accounts dry. I don't know where she transferred the funds to," Jasper said.

The data center in Sweden. "And she told you all of this incriminating evidence?"

"I threatened to turn her over to the CIA if she didn't tell me. Also, she wanted me to help her find Balan since he was always on the move. For me to do that, she had to share everything she knew. Plus, she needed help locating his stash of money. She didn't want millions sitting around going to waste. I told Kate I would agree to the deal only if she stopped her game." He lifted one shoulder. "See, I'm not a bad guy."

"You took money in exchange for silence, so yeah, you are," Natasha scolded, rage burning through her. "You could've ended this a long time ago if you'd come to me first."

"I just wanted my life back, a life not dictated by others." He covered his eyes with his palm and leaned back.

"What happened?" Wyatt asked.

His hand fell to the top of his backpack with a heavy thud. "Kate claimed she'd tried to put an end to everything even before the FBI showed interest in her company in twenty-eighteen. She hacked competitors and made money selling the intel back to them, whereas Balan sold intel to terrorists. As far as she was concerned, he'd crossed the line."

Like the Black Hawk crash in Algeria, Natasha remembered.

"Kate said she finally quit when the FBI started actively

looking into Cyber X, but Balan refused. And he stopped hacking for profit after that. He did it just to prove he could. To prove he was better than her or something." Jasper paused to take a breath. "Kate thought it was fate I found her because maybe I could help bring him down. Live up to my Smoking Gun name." He shook his head as if pissed at himself, and good, he should be more than just pissed. "I thought I was doing the right thing. She assured me he would die. Justice would be served."

"What was the plan?" Natasha's hand tightened on her lap.

"Kate said she knew another hacker who might be willing to help kill Balan once we located him," Jasper began, his breathing evening out to normal. "I was to alert the CIA of Balan's location once we found him, and her guy would be outside the home waiting for the CIA to send in a team."

"Why wait for us?" They had their theories, but she wanted confirmation.

"Kate wanted the CIA to know the man in the house was The Knight to put a stop to their investigation. You know, so she could breathe easy again."

"So, Roland Nilsson was waiting around Romania for our people to show." That'd been her guess. "And you put a clock on us by suggesting The Knight might move soon, ensuring the government rushed the op."

Wyatt grimaced, probably disgusted by the idea his team had been pawns in Kate's game.

"How'd you find out Balan didn't really die that day?" she asked.

"At first, I thought the message I got last week was a joke from Kate. A sick fucking joke. Because someone had died in that house in Romania. Both Kate and I thought Balan was dead because she paid off the Romanian officials to cremate the body and label him as an unknown squatter."

"You just didn't know it wasn't *his* body," Natasha said. "Any idea who else it could've been who died?"

Jessica and Harper had spent all day trying to find out more about Balan, but they'd come up empty.

"My guess is that it was his brother. Kate had said Alexander was close to him. Find his brother, find Balan, she'd said. His brother was probably already at the house with Alexander before Roland arrived."

The death of his brother would definitely escalate Balan's anger. If he'd been inside his house and died that day, Balan would want revenge, and he'd patiently wait for the right moment to bring all his targets together.

Jasper combed his fingers through his blond hair. "His brother was living under an alias, but he didn't cover his tracks as well. They were originally born in Romania, and based on his brother's different aliases, he stuck around the country but moved from time to time, which is probably the only reason Balan ever risked coming back to Romania for any period of time. But honestly, if Kate hadn't known Balan's alias had been Alexander Rothus when she first reached out to him in twenty-sixteen, I doubt we would have been able to find him."

"How'd Balan convince you to come to Montreal?" *He clearly found you while in hiding without a problem.* "Why not just run and hide somewhere else?"

"He said I had to enter the competition, or he'd have my family killed. He also said he'd forever hunt me down if I didn't show." His voice was low, dull, a touch remorseful.

"And what'd he tell Kate?" But she already knew the answer, didn't she? "He'd expose the truth, right? Let the world know what she did. I'm also betting she wanted back that three hundred million Balan transferred out of her account. Money she kept hidden from her husband, I assume."

Jasper nodded, and Wyatt's attention veered to the window as they began to slow down. He brought his hand to his ear as if listening to someone over comms.

"You all must have a plan, right?" No way would Kate show up in Montreal without a strategy in place, would she? "How are you going to stop Balan? He didn't want you talking to me because he wanted me putting the pieces together without help. He doesn't like cheating like he must've believed you cheated in tracking him down in Romania because you had Kate's help."

Jasper tossed an angry hand in the air. "He's been three steps ahead of us at every turn. It's like he knows our moves before we do."

God, could she relate. But she wasn't about to sympathize with him. He'd used her, taken advantage of her. He was just as bad as Kate and Alexander, and it made her skin crawl to be sitting across from him.

"Because Balan had a long time to set this up," Wyatt said as the car rolled to a stop. "Now, get out and act like we never had this conversation." He pointed to the door.

Jasper lightly clutched his throat. "He's going to kill me. Are you going to stop him?"

Wyatt cocked his head and echoed her own thoughts, "You think we should care about your life?"

Jasper fixed his attention on Natasha as he reached for the door handle. "I'm sorry."

Not that she believed him, but she couldn't help but respond, "Too bad you can't apologize to all the people who died because of Kate and Alexander." She shook her head. "Their families are the ones you owe an apology to."

Jasper's jaw tightened, and he pushed the door open. He swung his gaze over his shoulder. "I'm not going to win this competition. There's this chick, Gwen, and she's better than me."

Natasha stuck her arm out to block Wyatt from leaping forward at Jasper's use of the word chick about his daughter. "Was that part of the deal?" she asked him once Wyatt settled back into his seat. "Are you supposed to win?"

"He said if I couldn't even win the competition, then there was no reason to keep me alive." His eyes cast down to the limo floor. "I'm assuming he wants some sort of rematch with me. Maybe with Kate, too. Then probably kill us. I, uh, was hoping to buy myself some time by winning this thing to come up with a plan to take him down."

"You could've started by telling us the truth," Natasha said, her voice like a sharp blade cutting through the air.

"He said he'd kill me if I talked to you. And now since you ditched the MI6 agents who'd been tailing me and you're about to leave me alone out here, I'm guessing you knew that. I'm bait, huh?" Jasper stepped outside but ducked his head back in, eyes straight on Natasha. "My death will be on your conscience. You'll have to live with that."

"As much as I hate you," she began, "I'm not going to let you die. No, you belong in a prison cell."

Jasper grunted. "Sure."

Once the door slammed shut, Finn scrolled down the glass partition. "That was intense."

Wyatt touched his ear. "This is One, Bravo Four, do you copy?" He paused to listen. "Roger that, Four." He looked at Finn, then Natasha. "Liam's on overwatch. He has two tangos following Jasper. One on foot. One in a car."

"And if Balan's hired guns do kill him?" There were no guarantees.

"You said so yourself that he didn't want Jasper talking to you because he wanted you to solve the puzzle without help. You're part of his game. Chances are Balan already knows you've connected the dots," Wyatt began, "and besides, he won't murder Jasper when Jasper's his smoking gun. He wants the world to know the truth, and Jasper is part of that truth."

"How can you be so certain?" She gulped back her own doubts.

"As flimsy as this may sound, I'm going with my gut." He released his gun and brought a fist beneath her chin. "And it looks like I need to ask Gwen to lose to Jasper to buy him a few more hours to live."

CHAPTER THIRTY-EIGHT

"What if Jasper dies because of us." Natasha paced in front of the window in their hotel room.

"Jasper wouldn't talk." Wyatt stabbed the air. "And if you ask me, that prick deserves what he's got coming."

"Just because he clearly betrayed me by working with Kate—taking her money to set up The Knight—doesn't mean he deserves to die."

"Yeah, well, maybe he does." He turned his back and glimpsed the time. Charlotte had checked in to her hotel, and he'd given her instructions to get a two-bedroom suite. With any luck, Charlotte would be able to persuade her daughter to stay with her.

"Well, your stunt to try and lure The Knight out tonight by picking up Jasper failed. Jasper's back at his hotel, and we don't have a clue as to who The Knight really is." Natasha kept her voice level and void of dramatic flair. If Balan was going to believe this argument was real, they couldn't overdo it, and if there was a camera in addition to a listening device, they had to keep their body language as realistic as well.

"We have learned something from this puzzle he's left

behind for you." Wyatt faced her, doing his best to act sort of dick-like without going too far. "Kate and Jasper are guilty. And Jasper's a fraud."

"And we'll take them down, but I—"

"Can't have their deaths on your hands?" He huffed an exasperated breath. Was that too much? "If it weren't for Kate, none of this would've happened." He raised a hand. "I need some air."

"Don't go. Please." She'd told him on the plane she'd acted in a few plays in high school, including *Macbeth*, and the woman was damn good. She could've fooled him right now with her puppy dog eyes and quivering lip.

He crossed the room in quick strides and snatched his jacket. "I just need to take a walk."

"Don't be angry. Please."

He slowly went back to her. "We're both stressed, and I'm frustrated. I didn't mean to yell. Why don't you meet with the team upstairs and see if they have any new leads?"

"Yeah," she said, her eyes connecting with his, a wickedly sexy gleam there. "You sure you don't want me to come?"

Oh, I want you to come. All over my cock. My hand and my mouth, too.

Yeah, his dick wanted hot, make-up sex, not realizing his not-so-Oscar-worthy act was a performance for a ruthless hacker.

But they needed The Knight to believe he'd duped them.

His watch had only showcased a red dot indicating his room had been breached for a half a second. So, Balan was damn good, because Wyatt could've easily missed the color change, and he wouldn't have known the arse hacked his security measures in their room. Balan could've heard, maybe even watched, him make love to Natasha.

The idea had him wanting to bury his fist through the man's skull over and over again.

But no, this was a break, one they desperately needed, and they'd use it to their advantage.

"I'll be back in an hour or two." He held her eyes for a moment, then left and rushed to the lift, knowing Balan probably also had a camera in the hall and was watching him.

And now . . .

Well, now he had to face Charlotte and Gwen.

If Gwen was anywhere near as stubborn as Wyatt, he wasn't so sure she'd back down and lose the competition.

What Wyatt had said wasn't all an act, though. Part of him wished Balan and the Wards died an ugly death. Preferably by his hand. Maybe Jasper, too.

Once Wyatt was on the street, he checked his mobile for status updates from Bravo. Nothing had changed since they'd spoken an hour ago. Bravo was still in position tailing the hired guns The Knight had watching Jasper. Two men were in a black Range Rover parked outside Jasper's hotel. And with any luck, those two men would be The Knight's downfall.

Wyatt tucked his phone into his back pocket and hopped onto a city bus at the designated stop on the corner.

It took three bus changes, a taxi, and walking several blocks to ensure if he had a tail, he lost it before he made his way to Charlotte and Gwen's hotel.

The idea of facing both Gwen and Charlotte together had his stomach twisting and his heart beating wildly, his ribs trying to contain the emotions that pounded relentlessly with each step closer.

Once inside the hotel, he checked Charlotte's text for her room number.

I can do this. He'd been in the service for nearly twenty years, so he should be able to handle this. The moment he'd officially be introduced to his daughter shouldn't scare him more than the first time his boots touched the ground in the Middle East. Of course, he'd been excited to kill terrorists back then. Maybe he'd even liked it.

Alone inside the lift, he brought his palms to the wall and bowed his head.

No, I don't like killing. But . . . Was that a lie? Yes and no. When he took out the life of a killer, someone who made it their life's work to murder good people—well, yeah, he felt good about it. The world would be better with them gone.

Hi, Gwen, I'm your father. I'm also a sniper. I get paid to kill bad people, and I like it. Yeah, that couldn't be his opening statement.

Shit, first, he needed to explain why he was even in Canada, right? And he still had to discover what Gwen's relationship was with Felix Ward, see what she may know. Hopefully, she didn't know anything. The less she knew, the safer she'd be.

A few seconds later, the lift doors parted, and he made his way to Charlotte's suite. He was in the same clothes he'd worn to talk to Jasper. Dark denim jeans, black sneakers, a long-sleeved black shirt beneath his army green jacket, and a plain black ball cap. Nondescript and casual.

He brought both palms to the frame of the door. *Man up and knock.*

If Natasha had been at his side, he wouldn't be such a damn mess. She had a way of calming him. She understood him. He never felt guilty about his line of work around her— that he sent bullets downrange to kill men before they knew what hit them. A shot center mass or a headshot. A quick and clean kill.

On their return trip from Grand Cayman yesterday, Natasha had confessed to having taken three lives during her career. He'd confessed to quite a few more. No shock or disdain from her.

What would Gwen think of him, though?

She was a hacktivist, her mum had said, so did that mean she was also a pacifist? Would she hate his profession? He'd met his fair share of people who'd rather spit on his boots than sit across the dinner table from him, considering him to be just as repulsive as the terrorists he eliminated. Or maybe they were worried he might snap one day.

God, his insides hurt at the idea his own flesh and blood would be unable to handle the sight of him.

I'm losing my mind. He hadn't even introduced himself, yet he was setting himself up for failure. Setting up the moment to be a catastrophe, which wasn't normally like him.

He pushed off the doorframe to the room and knocked before he could turn and walk away like some damn wanker.

Charlotte opened up a few seconds later, her lips pressed in a tight line, her ash-blonde hair restrained in a tight knot at the top of her head. A fitted black pantsuit, her heels still on. The slight smudge of mascara beneath her eyes the only evidence something was wrong.

"Is she here?"

Charlotte stepped aside and nodded. "She just brought her stuff into her bedroom. She wasn't happy about changing rooms."

"Figured." He let go of a deep breath and closed the door behind him once inside.

"Whoa. What's he doing here?" Wyatt lifted his eyes to find Gwen striding through the living room with a finger pointed his way. "What's going on?" Her gaze darted to her mum as she pinned her arms over her chest, her stance defiant. She was in jeans with rips in the knees and an

367

oversized white T-shirt hanging off her shoulder, the cast of the *Avengers* on the front.

Liam's adopted daughter, Elaina, liked to joke his teammates were real-life action heroes. Granted, it was just a comic book story, but if Gwen liked the *Avengers*, who were a group of vigilantes, maybe she'd support his work. Who the hell was he kidding? Gwen was twenty, not twelve.

"Gwyneth." Charlotte lifted both palms in the air. "This is an old friend of mine."

Wyatt hesitantly stood alongside Charlotte, not sure what to do with his hands, so he left them heavy at his sides, the tension building and locking tight in his shoulders. "Hi." Was that the best he could do? Really?

"And he's a liar." Gwen's blue-gray eyes, ringed with black eyeliner, sought his gaze. "But you look familiar, aside from that night at the club." She allowed the angry position of her arms to relax as she closed the space between them. "He said he was Link."

"And who is Link?" Charlotte asked.

"He's an ex-boyfriend," she shot back with easy confidence, no worry about pissing off her mum by dating a hacker, "*and* Link's the guy who taught me everything I know."

Of-fucking-course. Because what were the odds? And did he need to kill Link?

Gwen's eyes narrowed as she stood less than a meter away. "I've seen you before this week, though." Her long lashes fluttered down, then she snapped her fingers. "Dad kept one drawer in his office locked, and I was curious why. I picked the lock when I was sixteen."

His heartbeat took a brief pause as he waited for her to continue, wondering what in the hell she was about to say.

"It was a photo of Dad and you. You were teenagers."

Her eyes opened. "That's why you looked familiar the other night." She stumbled forward another step instead of backward. "But it feels like more than that." She stared at him as if entranced, and he bit down on his back teeth, fighting to keep the truth locked tight until Charlotte was ready.

But had Arthur really kept a photo?

"Why is he here?" Gwen turned her attention to her mum. "What's going on?"

"Wyatt works in private security, and he's here for work."

"Wyatt." The way Gwen said his name, it was as if she were testing it out, seeing if it was legit and not another lie. "And why are you here for work?"

This would be the hard part. "I'm tracking down a hacker, someone who hurts people."

Her eyes widened in surprise. "And you think he's in the competition?"

"No, but he's in Montreal," he answered as honestly as he could without giving too much away.

"The only real arsehole I know here is Felix Ward." Gwen turned her back and went to the mini bar and grabbed a Corona. He did his best not to act like an overbearing father and snatch the beer from her hand.

"Gwen explained to me the real reason she entered the competition," Charlotte said. "I still don't like it, and God forbid anyone back home hear about this, but—"

"Mum." Gwen popped open the beer and strode back to stand in front of Wyatt where he remained awkward and stiff, still in shock he was even there, and still surprised Arthur had kept a photo of the two of them locked in his desk.

He'd spent his life thinking Arthur hated him—the picture was a curveball.

"What happened with Felix?" And if it was bad, so help

him, there'd be two men he planned on killing. Felix Ward and Alexander Balan.

Gwen took a sip of her beer, then let it hang by her jeaned leg. "I applied for an internship at Cyber X Security, and when I went for the interview, he decided to handle it personally." She shook her head. "The prick said I could have the job if I slept with him."

His pulse spiked at her words, and his hand bunched at his side.

"After I kneed him in the nuts, he threatened to report me for assault. Can you believe that?" She drank more beer.

Pride at her ability to stand up for herself cut through, but not long enough to kill his anger for Felix.

"I couldn't help but wonder how many other women he did that to. How many more would he proposition after me?" Her free hand went to her chest. "I couldn't let it go."

Charlotte moved to stand in front of the telly, then sat and braced her thighs. She didn't seem as troubled by Wyatt at the news, but maybe she'd had more time to process. Maybe this type of behavior by dickhead men in power was far too regular for women in general?

"So, I entered the competition. He called me shortly after and threatened to ruin my reputation if I didn't drop out. He said no one would ever hire me." Her jaw tightened almost the same way Wyatt's did when pissed. And he was pretty sure he was doing it now, too. Grinding down on his back teeth as well. "But screw him, I wasn't about to cower in fear and bow out. The night he issued that Twitter challenge to show up at the salsa club, I decided that'd be my chance to get some proof he's a scumbag."

Felix had been pissed she showed, but damn, Wyatt had misconstrued things.

"Felix blocked his number after he'd called me that one

time, but I managed to find it out. I texted him after I left the salsa club and told him to pick me up. I said we could talk things out."

Damn. She'd set a trap. More pride surged inside him. She really could handle herself, couldn't she?

Gwen set her beer on the coffee table and crossed her arms over her chest. "I tried to record our conversation at his condo, but when I got back to my hotel, the recording was scrambled."

"What are you planning to do?" And did she need his gun?

"Win the competition tomorrow, then announce to everyone what kind of man he is," she said, confidence returning to her voice.

Shit. "Felix will be dealt with, I promise you."

"What are you planning to do?" Charlotte eyed Wyatt warily, a look of fear momentarily crossing her face as she stood and approached him. "You're not going to kill him, are you?"

"Why would he care enough to want to kill him?" Gwen looked back at her mother. "It's not like he's my . . ." She let go of her words and slowly turned back toward Wyatt.

Fuck.

She'd pieced it together in a matter of seconds.

Two tentative steps closer brought her directly in front of him. "Same eyes. Similar cheekbones." She slapped a hand to her mouth and blinked rapidly in shock. "You," she practically breathed out. "You're him." Her eyes fell to the floor. "Why didn't you want me?" Gwen's gaze slowly lifted, her bluish-gray irises becoming glossy.

His heart broke. It fucking shattered. "I, um."

If she knew the truth, Gwen would hate her mum. He'd plant a wedge between them, and there may not be any going back from that. She'd hate Arthur for keeping the truth from both her and Wyatt, too.

"I need you to lose the competition tomorrow," he said instead, not sure how to answer her question without destroying everything she'd ever known and believed about her life.

"What?" she cried, her shoulders trembling as she fought to keep her tears trapped inside of her like a Montgomery was taught to do.

Charlotte sought his gaze, pleading with him not to reveal the truth. To keep his mouth shut, but . . .

He took a calming breath and focused on what he could control—the mission. "I need you to stay away from the convention hall tomorrow. Jasper Kenyon will die if he loses to you. And believe me when I say I wouldn't mind if he died, but the person who wants him dead is dangerous. Very, very dangerous."

"How can you ask me that?" Gwen wiped a few tears from beneath her eyes and stared at him, a mix of anger and pain competing for attention. "You're my dad, and the only reason you've decided to come into my life now is to try and save some guy?" Her voice broke, and he nearly fell to his damn knees and told her everything. "You don't even care about me. You weren't going to tell me the truth if Mum hadn't shown up." She turned and started for her bedroom, marching with fierce steps before shooting one last glare over her shoulder his way. "Get the hell out of my life. You didn't want me, and I sure as fuck don't want you." The door rattled as it slammed shut, and he bowed his head the moment she was out of sight.

"I'm sorry." Charlotte grabbed hold of his bicep. "But thank you," she whispered.

He slowly brought his eyes to her. "You said Arthur

wanted me to step in for him. How do you expect me to do that when she hates me? When there's a lie between all of us?" When she didn't respond, he shook his head. "I have to go. Please, talk some sense into her. Get her to drop out of the competition."

She released him. "She's as stubborn as you."

"Just do it." He went for the door and swung it open. "If you want to keep Gwen safe, keep her in this room, okay?"

"And if I can't, will you keep her safe?"

"I'll die before I let anything happen to her." He squeezed the emotion down his throat. "You have my word."

WYATT PUNCHED THE WALL INSIDE THE LIFT, CONNECTING HIS fist with the metal. He needed to alleviate some of the pain in his chest and direct it elsewhere. Pain in his knuckles would be a vast improvement.

"She hates me," he announced the second Natasha answered his call when he was standing out on the street. "I couldn't tell her the truth. I let her walk away from me believing I abandoned her, that I didn't want her." He brought his back to the brick exterior of a shoe store down the street from the hotel.

"You let her hate you instead of Charlotte and Arthur." She hadn't asked why. She understood him. "Oh, Wyatt."

He hit the back of his head against the brick, enjoying the dull ache it caused in his skull because it gave him a second to transfer the pain away from his heart. "Are you with Harper?"

Stupid question. Of course, she was with Harper. She wouldn't have answered if she'd been in their hotel room with The Knight listening to their call. He wasn't thinking straight, which was dangerous.

"Yeah, Jessica just called, though. And you were right. Balan did hire help. The two guys Bravo Team is following—they're not alone. She thinks Balan has four people here, but we don't know where the other two are."

Work-talk. This he could do. He needed a distraction from what had gone down at the hotel.

"We got a break, though. The two men trailing Jasper split up. One stayed at the hotel, and the other left in the Range Rover, so Liam followed him."

"Where to?" He observed the starless sky. A blanket of darkness overhead.

"The mill where Balan led me to when I first got here," she said, her voice shaky. "No one else was there. But the thing is, Liam saw the guy rigging the place to blow up."

"Why would he blow up an abandoned factory?"

"My guess?" She paused. "He's going to kill Jasper and the Wards. Burn them alive the way his brother died. He wants to watch them suffer."

Four guys hired. Three people to keep an eye on each target to ensure they didn't flee Montreal. The fourth man to rig the explosives.

"Maybe that was his plan all along," she said. "The challenges between him, Kate, and Jasper were merely a ploy. He had no intention of allowing them to prove they were better. In his mind, he's the best."

"He just wanted them to think they had a chance." Wyatt removed his ball cap and slapped it against his leg. "He's going to bring them to the factory and burn it down."

"Everyone will be at the convention hall tomorrow. I bet he's planning on taking them from there directly to the abandoned mill." At least Gwen would be safe if Balan was only targeting people directly connected to the op in Romania. "We'll have our guys at the mill waiting. We'll take the son of a bitch down then. He'll be there since he'll want to watch."

She was quiet before saying, "But why am I here? I'm still not sure exactly how I fit in."

"You're most likely the only one he views as a true opponent." His breath floated in the cool air in front of him. "Maybe the last game he wants to play is against you." His stomach tightened. "But I won't let that happen. This ends tomorrow, and if Felix happens to get killed in the crossfire, then so fucking be it."

"I'm guessing Gwen talked to you about him?"

He started walking as he shared with Natasha what Gwen had told him.

"We'll make this right. We have to." She was talking about Balan. Felix and Kate. Jasper, too. But with a heart the size of Natasha's, he also knew she was talking about Gwen.

And as much as he wished he could make things right, he knew the only person who could set the record straight was Charlotte, and he wouldn't hold his breath.

He couldn't destroy Gwen's love for Arthur, have her hate the man who raised her, a man who was no longer there to defend himself, could he?

After ending the call, Wyatt picked up his pace and hurried back to his hotel and to Harper's suite. The moment he saw Natasha, he halted in place with her sympathetic eyes pinned his way, and Harper and A.J. quickly went to the bedroom and left them alone.

"Wyatt." Natasha's soft voice stamped out his muddled thoughts. "I know what you're thinking," she said while striding closer to him, "but you can't let Gwen hate you. You think you're doing the right thing for her parents, but you're her father." Her lower lip trembled, her eyes welling with liquid. "She needs you just as much as I do."

His chest hurt. Absolutely every part of him hurt. "I, um . . ." His voice broke, and he stumbled back like a drunk despite his soberness, then dropped to the floor and covered his face.

It was only when Natasha wrapped her arms around him and hugged him tightly to her, that he finally let his guard down.

. . . And he gave in and cried.

CHAPTER THIRTY-NINE

IT HAD BEEN ALMOST FIVE YEARS SINCE THE KNIGHT'S CASE first landed on Natasha's desk. While other people had been out celebrating Valentine's Day in 2016, Natasha and the rest of a newly formed FBI-CIA joint task force were at Langley, being briefed on a new case.

She'd been on her first date in a year that day. A CIA analyst had asked her to dinner. It'd been a casual *Hey, neither of us have dates, so what do you say?* kind of night. She'd happily left the overpriced restaurant and returned to the safety net of being forever single to focus on her career. But she never imagined she'd wind up in a five-year relationship with a hacker. A five-year commitment to take down not one, but apparently, two people.

One of the most valuable lessons she learned at the Agency was situational awareness—be cognizant of your surroundings at all times, practice the art of reading people until you can anticipate their every move, and examine your environment for oddities, things that don't add up. To do that, you need a baseline to go off of. You need to memorize every inch of your home to ensure nothing has been tampered with.

Pay attention on your route to work, to the baristas at your local coffee shop, to the grocers at your store . . . make sure everything is as it should be, and you can usually keep yourself safe. And for CIA officers and FBI agents, it helps to solve crimes if they can identify any interruptions to that baseline: the man with the coat and backpack in a crowded tourist area on a July day, the flower vase in your home two inches off from its normal spot, the man who maintains your pace when walking, which is not natural for people to do.

But Kate Ward hadn't raised any flags for anyone at the Agency. She hadn't done anything to prompt Natasha to believe she was the mastermind. Good grades in school, stable home life growing up, steady relationships, brilliant coder, a savvy businesswoman. Her baseline had remained constant. No abnormalities. No deviations.

Kate had fooled the CIA. Tricked the FBI. And manipulated Alexander Balan, one of the best hackers in the world.

So, as Natasha sat in the audience at the convention center that Sunday, waiting for Felix and Kate Ward to announce the three finalists in the competition, she was questioning herself and her abilities as a CIA officer.

With every passing second she waited for Felix to talk, she questioned every decision she'd ever made, every course of action she'd taken during this five-year-long case. She drew up images in her mind, played scenes out in her head over and over again, trying to figure out how she'd missed the truth. Why hadn't she seen the pattern that there'd been two hackers rather than one?

She momentarily closed her eyes as her stomach rumbled, her nerves pinching and squeezing. Anxiety could manifest itself as physical pain in the human body. It wasn't always deep panicky breaths—it could be teeth grinding or tension in the shoulders and neck. And right now, her pain was nearly unbearable.

You couldn't have known, Wyatt had said earlier today. *Stop blaming yourself.* She replayed his words in her head, hoping they'd comfort her. *Today is the day we nail both of them. It's finally going to end.* He'd held her cheeks and dipped in for a kiss after he'd spoken before they'd left for the auditorium.

She sought out Wyatt in the room of over a hundred people. He was sitting in the second row from the elevated stage, four rows in front of her. Chris, who had on a baseball hat, was parked on the other side of the aisle in the back of the auditorium. And the rest of Bravo and Echo Teams were in their designated positions.

Unfortunately, Gwen had also shown up. She was in the front row next to her mother, who'd dressed in all black like she was attending a funeral. Nobles probably weren't used to events like these.

Wyatt hadn't spoken to either Gwen or Charlotte since he'd left their hotel last night, so they weren't sure what Gwen had decided to do about the competition, and at this point, Natasha wasn't so sure if it mattered. The team was pretty confident whatever Balan had planned would go down today.

"We'd like to call to the stage the three people with the best scores." Felix was at the podium, motioning with a flick of the wrist for the contenders to stand as he called their names.

Jasper, Gwen, and a third guy climbed the three steps to get to the raised platform. Kate stepped alongside her husband and directed the three hackers to the chairs lined up off to the right of the podium.

Kate's long black hair was in a tiny ponytail, her eyes

covered in heavy dark makeup. She had on a silver-gray pantsuit, whereas Felix was in jeans and a pressed white button-down shirt. Two criminals on stage. Jasper made three. But where was Balan?

"I'd like to say something." Jasper remained standing in front of his chair.

"Can it wait until we make the announcements?" Felix looked to the crowd, plastering on a fake smile, but Jasper ignored him and strode up next to the podium, forcing Felix to step aside.

"I am withdrawing from the competition," Jasper said, his voice shaky. His eyes moved straight to Natasha, and she shifted in her seat, worried about his game plan.

Something had to have happened since she spoke to him in the limo last night.

Balan got to him.

Jasper reached into his pocket, his hands trembling as he produced a notecard. "In good conscience, I must withdraw from this competition, and I will not accept blood money."

Blood money. Natasha's pulse jumped, and she gripped the blue chair arms.

"I think that's enough!" Felix attempted to take the microphone from Jasper, but he wouldn't relent.

"I'm known in the hacker world as The Smoking Gun, but I failed to reveal evidence that would put our hosts, Felix and Kate Ward, in jail." Jasper had spoken fast and frantically, trying to get the truth out quickly before someone stopped him. "I kept it hidden for my own financial benefit, and I intend to rectify that here and now. The Wards are responsible for destroying their competition—other security companies, as well as—"

"Stop!" Kate lurched forward and grabbed Jasper's arm, and that was when Natasha saw the gun.

Jasper had traded his notecard for a Glock, turning his back to the audience and aiming the firearm at Kate.

The Knight's hired men must have given it to him.

The people in the audience screamed and rose from their seats in a panic.

"Turn on the fire alarms," Wyatt's voice popped into Natasha's comm, an instruction meant for Harper. He was on his feet, his gun still concealed, as he started for Jasper.

"No one on stage move!" Jasper's voice boomed through the microphone. "It's rigged to blow with any change in weight."

Wyatt immediately stopped in front of the steps of the stage. "Everyone, hold your positions," he ordered to Echo and Bravo Teams over comms.

The audience continued to scatter, and the alarms began shrieking overhead. Natasha rushed toward the stage, maneuvering through the terrified people filing out in disarray.

"Gwen!" Charlotte stood near the stage steps, her eyes on her daughter.

"Mum." Gwen remained frozen on the stage, her palms up in surrender, same as the others up there.

"Move, and you all die." Jasper shoved Kate to the ground and used his gun to nudge Felix to sit next to her on the floor.

The third hacker remained standing next to Gwen, sweat dripping down his cheeks. Panicked. Probably on the verge of pissing his pants.

"I'm sorry," Jasper said, eyes on Natasha. "He has my parents and sister. I-I have no choice."

Wait . . . if Balan planned to eliminate all of his targets here, why rig the mill with explosives?

She tried to control her heart rate, to maintain a steady

hand. To think clearly. "It's going to be okay. We'll figure this out." Natasha came up alongside Wyatt, the 9mm he'd provided in her hand. "What exactly does Balan want you to do?" she asked Jasper.

Jasper wiped the back of his free hand across his brow. "I'm sorry," he said again, but his apology was directed toward Gwen and the other innocent hacker.

Gwen set her focus on Wyatt. "Get Mum out of here. Please!"

"I'm not leaving you." Charlotte started for the steps, but Wyatt grabbed hold of her and yanked her back.

"Get her out of here." Wyatt turned Charlotte over to Chris, ignoring Charlotte's continued protests as Chris forced her toward the exit.

The rest of the auditorium was empty now, and the alarms had been shut down, probably remotely by Harper.

"Police and first responders are en route," Harper announced over comms. "They've been ordered to stand down once they arrive and wait for the bomb squad and a negotiator to arrive, but wait . . . shit, I have two officers in tactical gear on the security cameras already inside the building."

Wyatt eyed Natasha, his 9mm in hand, and he shot a grave look her way. "Change of plans," he mouthed, and she nodded in understanding. She hid her gun from view, and Wyatt focused on his daughter. "You're going to be okay. I promise."

"Put your guns down!" Natasha turned at the sight of two officers shouting in unison. "Get on your hands and knees."

"This stage is rigged to explode!" Jasper called out.

"You bastard," Kate roared Jasper's way. "I should've killed you. Loose ends are . . ."

"What in the hell is going on?" Felix worked the top two buttons free of his shirt as if he couldn't get a decent breath.

"You," one officer said as he neared Wyatt, "Gun. Down. Now."

Wyatt glimpsed Natasha out of the corner of his eye, and he gave her a quick nod. She followed his lead and lowered to her knees. Palms behind her head.

Natasha tracked Wyatt's gaze, his eyes on his daughter up on the stage, tears cutting down her cheeks.

"He's trying to help! He's innocent," Gwen came to Wyatt's defense.

The officer closest to Wyatt stowed his weapon, then tugged Wyatt's arms behind his back. He slapped cuffs on Wyatt's wrists and jerked him to a standing position.

"Stay put," the second officer said to Natasha and the others. "Help is on the way."

Natasha stared into the officer's green eyes, a shiver rolling over her spine.

"Wait! You're leaving? He's gonna kill us. You can't leave!" Kate called out, frantic.

"Everything will be okay," Wyatt said to Gwen in a calm voice, his Adam's apple moving with a hard swallow before the officer pulled him back.

Wyatt locked eyes with Natasha, a silent request to keep his daughter safe.

"I don't understand," the hacker at Gwen's side yelled out once Wyatt and the officers were gone, tears in his eyes. The kid couldn't be more than twenty like Gwen.

Gwen slowly sank to the floor, her eyes positioned on the door through which Wyatt had left with the two officers. "Why'd they only take him? Why'd they leave us?"

Jasper slid down the side of the podium, keeping his back to it, the gun in his hand.

"Don't worry, we won't lose him." Harper paused. "But shit, Balan is—" Her words died in Natasha's ear, the comm going dead. Her communication with the team had been severed, and when the door off to the side of the stairs connecting to the backstage opened, she knew why.

Alexander Balan, The Knight, was there.

"IT IS NICE TO FINALLY MEET YOU IN PERSON, CHANDLER." Balan casually threw out the words, no longer trying to conceal his heavy European accent, which also emphasized his formal manner of speaking English. He dropped a black duffel bag at his feet, and Natasha instantly went for her firearm, standing quickly, the gun aimed his way.

Balan didn't pause. No hesitation. He knew she wouldn't dare shoot him with the stage rigged to explode.

Dressed in a Canadian police uniform, Balan took off the Montreal PD hat and tossed it. He swiped a hand over his hair back and forth twice.

The stereotypical lanky look of a computer nerd she'd had in her mind wasn't a match for this guy. He'd changed since he was in his twenties and was Kate's teacher. More muscles on his tall frame where there hadn't been in the past. A trimmed beard that'd never been in any photos of his alias as Rothus. If it weren't for the cold, dead eyes that met hers right now, she'd swear it wasn't even him.

"Your comms frequency is jammed as long as you're within fifteen meters of me. You can take that little device out of your ear if you'd like." He cocked his head, and when she didn't follow his directive, he shrugged. "You look surprised to see me, Natasha. Did you not expect we would meet here in person like this?"

She kept her arm steady even though her insides shook, and her pulse intensified.

"Put the gun away." His voice, so eerily calm, chilled her. "You cannot shoot me, and you know it. You hurt me, and we all die."

The unpleasant truth of his statement had her lowering the gun to her side.

Balan's lips stretched, showcasing crooked teeth that were tinged yellow, then he faced the stage. "Hello, my dear Kate."

"You son of a bitch." Kate slowly stood. "You were supposed to die."

Balan ate up the distance between where he stood and the edge of the stage, his eyes lifting to meet Kate's. "I taught you everything, and I am dismayed by the way you decided to repay me."

Natasha could shoot him. His back was to her. But what if . . .? No, she couldn't take the risk. She had to play the long game, to believe Wyatt's team would come through for them.

"What'd you do, Kate?" Felix hissed.

Kate faced her husband, an ugly twist to her lips. Her forehead tight. "You stupid ass. If you didn't need to stick your dick in every woman that crosses your path, maybe I wouldn't have had to save the company."

"And you could not have done it without my help." Balan pivoted to the side to put eyes on Natasha as well. "The FBI thought *you* were The Knight," he said to Felix. "But you were a pawn in your wife's game. She has been using you since the day you laid eyes on her." The bastard kept his tone so freaking casual it made Natasha's skin crawl. "Did you actually think you earned first place in that competition where you met Kate?" He snickered. "I taught your darling wife how to be one of the best hackers in the world."

Natasha kept her gun in hand, prepared to use it when the time was right, and if she couldn't manage to shoot him, she could knock him on the back of the skull, at least.

"Let those two go." Natasha tipped her chin toward Gwen and the young man at her side. "They're innocent."

"Collateral damage, I'm afraid." Balan's cold eyes met hers.

"Like your brother was?" She'd either intensify his anger with her question, or she'd distract his focus. If she could try and control the direction of the conversation, control what happened next, maybe she could gain the advantage somehow. "How did you manage to get out of your house without burns? The operatives said your brother was engulfed in flames, and yet, your skin appears flawless. Did you choose yourself over him? Was that what happened? Does the guilt keep you awake at night knowing he died when it was supposed to be you?"

"I am not a coward. I would not make such a choice." He rolled his shoulders as if attempting to dispel his anger. "He was innocent. He shouldn't have died."

"You must have cared deeply about him, or you wouldn't have arranged such an elaborate plan of revenge. So, why'd you let him die?" She was poking a bear, and she had no idea if he'd be the one to draw blood.

"I did not let him die," he said, each word punctuating the air as if he stabbed a finger her way. "I always traveled using tunnels. I was on my way home when my fail-safe was remotely hacked and triggered. He was dead before I got to him." Mourning and regret eased into his tone.

Natasha took a step closer, wondering if there was even a fraction of humanity inside of this man. Was there a way to tap into his love for his brother to try and get him to back down? "Please, let them go. Like your brother, they're not part of this." She had to get Gwen out of there. If something went wrong, if their plan failed . . . no, she couldn't lose Wyatt's daughter.

Kate sprung toward the stairs, prepared to flee when Balan spun her way and shouted, "You will die if you take one step down. The bomb activated the second the five of you were all on stage. Give or take a few kilos, if the weight on the floorboards goes up or down, the bomb goes off." He cocked his head, eyes set on Kate.

"Do what he says," Felix pleaded with his wife. "Don't kill us all."

Kate lowered her heel to the floor, took a step back from the stairs, and leveled Balan with a glare. "If you had just stopped like I asked, we'd all be fine. Rich and happy." Her voice was softer now. "You taught me everything I know, but you took things too far, Alex." She tipped her head, a plea in her eyes, an attempt to get Balan down from the cliff of crazy.

Balan smoothed a hand over his bearded jaw and repeated *Rich and happy* over and over again as if he were a parrot. "I never did it for the money."

"The game," Natasha whispered. "That's why she had to make it a challenge. The money wouldn't have been enough, would it?"

Felix slowly stood and faced his wife. "I asked you years ago if you were somehow connected to The Knight's cyberattacks. I know our company is good, but come on, that Knight character never once targeted our clients in the past. Sort of hard to believe we'd be so lucky unless *you* were involved somehow." His brows shot together. "You denied it when the FBI poked around, but it's true, isn't it?" He grabbed hold of Kate's shoulders and shook her.

"You bankrupted us. What choice did I have?" Kate

pushed at his chest, attempting to get him to back off. "And you're no saint. Don't pretend you're any better."

"I'm not a murderer!" Felix released his wife and stumbled back onto one of the chairs.

"You two done yet?" Balan adjusted the sleeves of his shirt. The detonator had to be small, most likely strapped to the inside of his wrist.

"Why'd you bring me here?" Natasha asked when he grabbed his duffel bag and set it on a chair in the front row. "Why all the clues, *Balan*?"

He stilled at the mention of his real last name but only for a moment before he unzipped the bag. "You figure that out with Jasper's help? I thought he did not say anything to you in the limo last night."

"I didn't need Jasper."

He retrieved a laptop, a smile crossing his face. "You knew I was listening, right? You knew I had been in your room." Balan shook his head as if impressed. "Nice work, Chandler. You got me on that." He balanced the computer on his palm while typing.

She glanced at the stage, ensuring no one moved. No heroics that'd lead to the place blowing up. Gwen had her knees to her chest, her arm around the guy next to her since she appeared to be steadier than him. She was tough like her father, no surprise there.

"All of this time, I had been playing a game with Kate, but you were my only worthy opponent." Balan set the laptop on the chair and dipped his hand back into his bag. "It is time for part two."

Natasha's stomach dropped. "Part two?" Her brows lifted in surprise at the chess game in his hand. *You've got to be kidding me.*

"I assume you have now realized those two cops that

arrested your British friend were actually my guys. He is in that lovely abandoned mill. He is tied up, and the place is rigged with explosives like this stage."

The clothing mill clearly hadn't been chosen only because it was abandoned but because of the proximity to the convention hall. And now Wyatt was there.

"No!" Gwen popped to her feet. "Please, don't hurt him."

Shit. Natasha glared at Gwen, willing her with her eyes not to reveal her relation to Wyatt, hoping to hell she got the message. Balan would only use that knowledge against them all.

"You know him?" Balan arched a brow. "Unexpected. I do like a good surprise." He grinned. "I was wondering why you threw your lead in the competition, Gwen. You were so far ahead of Jasper." His attention turned back to Natasha. "Is that why your friend went to Gwen's hotel last night? It was to ask her to lose?"

"Yes," Natasha sputtered, relieved she could turn this into a direction that would better suit the narrative of Wyatt's relation to Gwen as being strictly work-related.

Balan swapped the chess game with his laptop. "Look at the screen."

Wyatt was tied down in a chair on the top floor of the mill, near where she'd stood last week and talked to The Knight on the phone. Hands cuffed behind his back. Mouth covered with tape.

Her heart stuttered at the sight, but Wyatt's team could handle this. His team wouldn't let anything happen to Wyatt.

"If you lose the game of chess, you must choose between killing everyone on this stage or your friend at that mill. Five lives versus one." His accent dipped lower, almost soft. He was so screwed up in the head. "You choose to save him, and you and I will leave before the explosion. I refuse to allow you to make yourself a martyr. I am giving you the choice I never had. I did not get to choose between saving my brother and saving myself."

"No," Gwen cried out. "Don't do it."

"And would you have chosen him? Would you have traded your life for his?" Natasha's hand tightened on her gun, wishing she could shoot him in the head right now and end this, to make Gwen's worry and fears go away. To get her to safety.

"Yes. Despite what you think of me, I am a man of honor." He set the laptop back down, and it pained her to lose sight of the screen. "But I was betrayed, and my brother was killed, so the offenders must die."

Natasha shot Jasper a look as he lifted his firearm and aimed it at Balan.

"Fuck you!" Jasper squeezed off a shot before Natasha could react.

But the chamber in Jasper's Glock was empty. Nothing.

"Did you actually think my men gave you a loaded gun earlier?" Balan maintained his calm, eerie tone. "I'm always ahead. Always better. And you have probably never held a gun before to know the difference."

Jasper slouched in defeat and let the gun clatter to the floor.

"It'll be okay," Natasha mouthed to Gwen, and even though they'd never met, she hoped Gwen would trust her knowing she was working with Wyatt.

"Now, ready to play?" Balan motioned for Natasha to sit.

He opened the game of chess and balanced the board on the chair arm, then set up his pieces.

"What if I win?" She positioned her gun in her lap and clutched the knight piece, her stomach roiling.

"We can negotiate the terms *if* you win after the game."

"Five years," she said under her breath.

"The first three and a half were quite fun." He smiled without looking up at her. "Now, you go first."

She was going to lose.

There was no point going against a chess master.

This wasn't her game.

"You are disappointing me," he said ten minutes into the game. This was probably going to be the shortest chess match he'd ever played. "I thought chasing after me all these years would have made you a better player at the game."

"It was never a game to me," she said with a shaky voice.

His eyes gleamed with his next move. "And that is checkmate," he announced.

"No!" Kate jumped to her feet. "Let me play, I can beat you!"

Balan ignored her and set the game on the floor. "Who is it going to be?" He retrieved his laptop. "Someone you care about, or a bunch of hackers? The decision is yours." He cocked his head, his expressionless eyes meeting hers.

Natasha bowed her head as she slowly stood, gun secured in her right hand.

"You must choose." His brows knitted. "Who are you going to save?"

"Why not make me choose only between myself and him? You said you didn't have the option between saving yourself or your brother—why not make this situation the same?" she asked, attempting to buy a few more seconds if Wyatt and his people needed it.

She slowly dragged her gaze to Wyatt tied to the chair on the screen and then to Gwen, who was now on her feet, her arm outstretched with a plea. A plea to save who? Herself or her father?

"I'm not ready to lose you yet." God, he was obsessed with her, wasn't he?

"Save the people on the stage." Natasha kept her voice even, her tone flat, same as Balan had done since he'd arrived.

"Interesting." He hit a few buttons on his laptop without delay, and the view from the camera at the mill went black. She really needed to get her hands on that laptop. "It's done."

"No!" Gwen fell to her knees, tears hitting her cheeks. "How could you let him die?" She lifted her eyes to Natasha's, anger filling her gaze.

"You don't look sad." Balan filled Natasha's line of sight as he stood before her, now obstructing her view of Gwen. "You didn't care for that man? Was it all an act, part of your cover?" His brows slanted inward. "Or did you anticipate that move?" he asked, something akin to pride cutting through his tone.

She tried not to react at the sudden appearance of the red dot on Balan's chest.

That was her cue. A message it was now safe to take him down.

She swung her forearm up and forward, connecting her elbow to his face in one hard blow before she smacked her gun against his temple. A bullet pierced the air and nailed Balan in the thigh a moment later, dropping him to his knees.

In one fast move, Natasha flipped Balan, face to the floor, and buried her knee into his back, securing his hands behind him. "You don't have to make a choice between someone you care about and innocent people if you never put your loved ones in danger to begin with like you did with your brother."

She swept her gaze to the sound booth at the back of the auditorium near the ceiling and gave a nod of thanks to Roman, who'd been positioned there the entire time.

"And by the way, my friend at the mill isn't dead." Tears filled Natasha's eyes as she let Wyatt's daughter know the truth. "He's alive. I didn't kill him." Well, she had to assume Wyatt hadn't been in that building when Balan detonated the explosives. She had faith in his team. And any other alternative would be unacceptable.

Gwen's shoulders trembled, and a broken sob left her lips.

"It's safe to move off the stage. The bomb has been disarmed," Roman announced over the auditorium speakers, and relief swelled inside of her. Owen and Knox had been positioned inside the building for backup before Jasper's surprise announcement, so it was probably Owen and Knox who helped disable the explosives. "Damn it. You can't leave the auditorium yet!" Roman's tone became grave as if this was unexpected news to him as well. "We have another problem."

Natasha had been on the verge of asking Wyatt's status but . . . another problem?

Balan's chuckle had chills rushing from her shoulders down to her fingertips. "I'm always playing several moves ahead of everyone."

"No, we have to get out of here!" Kate exclaimed, panic settling in as she made her way down the stage steps.

"Stop!" Roman roared. "The doors have been lined with Primacord. Plus, sticks of dynamite have been placed on every other door. Multiple charges have been set to detonate simultaneously. If we open one door, they all blow."

Natasha looked toward the five other people now off stage as Balan struggled beneath her. "Do. Not. Leave," she issued the command in case the Wards or Jasper got any damn ideas and decided to risk it. Her eyes connected with Gwen as she took cautious steps closer to Natasha. She couldn't let anything happen to her.

"What can I do?" Gwen asked, ridding her cheeks of the last of her tears.

"Grab his laptop." Natasha pushed her knee harder into Balan's back when he tried to shift free of her.

"After the bomb beneath the stage was disabled, our guys came to get you only to discover the doors were rigged." Roman paused. "I'm so sorry we didn't know before."

"And where are we at on disabling them?" she asked as Gwen crouched next to Natasha with Balan's laptop in hand.

"I wouldn't disarm the doors if I were you," Balan barked out. "Not unless you want to kill a few hundred people. How many curious onlookers do you think are crowded on the street, wondering what's going on in here? How many people think they're safe because they're *outside*?"

Natasha jabbed her knee harder into his back. "What are you talking about?" she bit out, her rage and anger for this bastard intensifying. She was done with his games.

Balan shifted his neck, bringing his left cheek to the floor instead of his right. "You disarm the doors, and you automatically trigger another bomb. There's a car rigged with explosives outside."

Jasper knelt in front of Balan and fisted his hair, bringing his head off the ground. "You're full of shit." He pointed to the door Balan entered. "Those doors will blow outward. We'll be fine in here. Detonation cord like that is used for breaching doors all the time." His eyes met Natasha. "And you know that. Have your people just set them off—we can take cover on the stage far away from the blast."

Even if Balan was bluffing, if anyone was near the exterior of the building, they could get killed or hurt. And Natasha wasn't prepared to take the chance Balan was lying about the other bomb, anyway.

"Go ahead, kill a bunch of people," Balan said, his tone

casual. "But you're right, you probably won't be hurt if you're far enough away. At least you'll be safe."

"Let's do it," Kate insisted with a nod. "Balan could be lying. We should save ourselves."

"We have his laptop," Natasha reminded everyone around her. The same laptop he'd used to detonate the explosives at the mill. *Wyatt.* She still needed his status, but at the moment, she had to keep Gwen alive, as well as everyone outside.

"I don't think he's lying about the other bomb." Gwen turned the screen around to show Natasha a split view of the doors rigged with explosives, as well as a late model red Honda Civic in a parking garage.

"Red Honda Civic," Natasha shouted to ensure Roman could hear her. "I think it's in the convention center's parking garage. It's close enough in range to be synced with the detonation initiator here." She turned to Gwen. "Can you get a look at what level the car is parked on?"

Gwen shook her head no.

"You have a signal up there? Can you get out word to Harper?" she asked Roman.

"Yeah, I'm on it. I'm not leaving you, though." Roman's voice was low. His stubbornness on point with Wyatt's. "There are six levels of the garage to clear."

Wyatt's teammates would somehow need to get to the parking garage unnoticed by the police.

Harper and Finn were in a mobile unit outside, and she assumed Chris was with them since he'd escorted Charlotte to safety. Someone needed to warn the police to evacuate the area in case the bomb went off.

"If those doors blow, that sound booth is right above them —you can't be in that box. Get out," she pleaded with Roman at the realization.

She didn't hear Roman's response, her focus flying to

Gwen as she announced in a shaky voice, "This program running is heavily encrypted."

"Shut it down, Balan," Natasha commanded, but she knew it'd be a cold day in hell before Balan would do such a thing. "You don't have to do this."

"It's you or those people outside. The garage is far enough away, so you should be fine from the blast." His hollow laugh milked the air of oxygen. "Save yourselves, or save them." She brought her hand around to the gunshot wound on his thigh and pressed. His mouth tightened, but he swallowed back the wince.

"We choose ourselves." Felix attempted to snatch the laptop from Gwen, but Natasha lifted her arm and aimed the gun at him.

"Back off or you get a bullet in the leg, too," Natasha yelled. "Anyone who tries to get out those doors gets a bullet. Are we clear?" Her gaze journeyed back to Gwen before she glimpsed the four other people standing around her in a panic. "We have five of the best hackers in the world right here." She swallowed. "Prove to this asshole you're better than him. Hack his program and disarm the damn car bomb!"

CHAPTER FORTY

ELEVEN MINUTES EARLIER

"SHIT! I THINK WE'VE BEEN MARKED. GET—" THE mercenary's head snapped back as the bullet nailed the guy center mass.

Before the second hired gun could draw his weapon, he was taken down as well.

"All clear," Bravo Four, Liam, said over comms. "Three is coming in to get you out of that damn chair."

"Sorry about that, brother," Asher said on approach, then removed the tape from Wyatt's mouth and freed him from the chair.

Asher had been parked outside the convention center when shit hit the fan. The hired guns had pulled away from the building just as the rest of what appeared to be all of Montreal PD rolled up, and Asher had tailed the vehicle.

The fake officers had taken Wyatt to the clothing mill where Liam and A.J. had already been in position. Wyatt's team had anticipated Balan was going to bait his targets back to the mill. What they hadn't expected was the stage to be rigged or for Jasper to whip out a gun.

A.J. strode into the room a few seconds later, covered head-to-toe in tactical gear. "Let's get out of here before this crazy bastard blows us all up."

"Harper's got the footage of you tied to this chair looped on Balan's surveillance feed." Asher checked the first downed body to see if he had a pulse. Nothing. "Here's your piece he took off ya." He handed Wyatt his 9mm, then Asher checked for a pulse of the second tango. "We're ready to roll." When Wyatt couldn't get his feet to move, Asher came before him and wrapped a gloved hand over his shoulder. "Hey, don't worry. Natasha will know you're already out of here if this place blows."

Wyatt lifted his eyes to find Asher's. "But will Gwen?"

He'd hated leaving Natasha and Gwen, but Roman had been in the sound booth on overwatch keeping an eye out. That didn't change the fact that every step he'd taken out of the auditorium had been painful and gut-wrenching.

"If Gwen's anything like you, she'll be fine," A.J. said before Asher could respond. "We should go. Liam's pulling the SUV around." He flicked his wrist, motioning for them to get a move on.

A minute later, the guys piled into the SUV. "He's going to make her choose between them and me, isn't he?" Wyatt gripped the handle of the passenger side door as Liam tore away from the abandoned building. He closed his eyes, the rage cutting through.

"He's one twisted son of a bitch, that's for damn sure." A.J. slapped a hand over Wyatt's shoulder from the back seat. "But this all ends today, and maybe you two take a real vacation when this is over."

"Harper's calling." Liam hit speakerphone on his mobile

mounted to the dashboard. "We're heading back. What's the status?"

Wyatt tightened his grip on the handle, his nerves frayed.

Gwen. Natasha. They had to be okay. There were no other options.

"Owen and Knox have been working on disabling the bomb beneath the stage. A similar setup to Romania," she explained.

Harper and Finn were parked outside the convention hall in a mobile unit, serving as the eyes and ears for all of Bravo and Echo.

"We need to consider getting a K9 for the team," A.J. said. "We checked that building and didn't find any explosive materials."

"Security was tight. We weren't able to canvass every inch of that place," Harper reminded them. "And since these guys dressed themselves up as officers, they could have walked right past us armed with explosives, and there's no way we could have known."

"It'd still be nice to have an animal on the team. A dog would've known the officers were fakes, I guarantee it." A.J. released Wyatt's shoulder and leaned back. "I bet I could be a K-9 whisperer."

"Gotta agree with him," Asher chimed in. "But if anyone can talk to a dog, it's Chris, our resident animal lover. I mean, he got the polar bear to back down."

"Shut up," Chris grumbled over speakerphone. He must've had to stay outside after taking Charlotte out of the auditorium.

"We still haven't located the other two men dressed as police officers. They're either still inside, and I just can't see them," Harper began, "or they're outside blending in with the hundred cops there now. They could be Balan's getaway plan."

How had this gone so sideways?

The son of a bitch was always two moves ahead of them at every turn.

But they couldn't let him win.

"Jessica had the CIA reach out to the authorities. The police are doing their best to check all officers' IDs, but it's chaos over here," Harper said. "I'm worried you're not going to be able to get back inside once you're here. Every law enforcement agency in the city is parked outside this building."

"We have three guys inside," Asher said, his voice low but confident. "Roman's got them covered. Owen and Knox are there, too. Nothing will happen to them."

"And . . . sounds like he just blew the fucking mill!" A.J. yelled, the ground rumbling beneath the SUV, the blast booming from behind.

Wyatt caught sight of flames darting into the sky in the rearview mirror. "We're running out of time. We need to get that—"

"It's done," Harper exclaimed. "Owen just called. The stage bomb has been disarmed."

Wyatt clutched his chest. Was this what a heart attack felt like? This was good news, so why the pain? The dizziness? Why did it feel like there was still something wrong?

"Love can do that." Liam side-eyed him as he drove. "You'll be okay."

"*They're* okay," Asher reminded him.

"Have Roman take down this sick prick." Wyatt let go of his chest, trying to believe it was truly over.

"Yeah, okay, but—"

"What?" Wyatt brought his hands to his legs and leaned closer to the mobile, waiting for Harper to continue.

"Son of a bitch!" Harper cursed. "Balan must've overridden the surveillance cameras inside, and I missed it."

"What does that mean?" Liam asked. "Missed what?"

"I'm sorry. The prick is better than me." The line crackled from a deep, shaky exhalation. "I know where the two other mercenaries are, and they've been inside rigging the auditorium doors with det cord and dynamite. Owen and Knox went to the auditorium, but now . . ." Harper paused. "Roman just took the leg shot," she announced, changing gears for a moment. "Natasha has him pinned to the ground. Everyone is safe on the inside."

"But now they can't get out. Can Owen and Knox disarm the doors?" Wyatt's hand turned into a fist atop his leg as he waited for whatever news she was about to deliver.

"Hold on, waiting for more information from Roman," Harper said, her tone low as if she were trying to hide her nerves so Wyatt wouldn't lose his bloody mind.

"We just parked down the street," Liam informed Harper as he turned off the engine. They were as close as they could get with the police having barricaded the area.

"I need to get in there." Wyatt surveyed the street off to his left. Curious observers crowded outside, waiting to find out what was going on at the convention center, with phones in hand, recording the scene.

"Our people on the inside aren't going to be able to just waltz out of that building with their weapons. So, you really think you're gonna be able to get in?" A.J. asked.

"Jessica's got her contacts on their way from Canadian Intelligence, but—"

"My daughter is still in there," Wyatt cut off Asher and

unbuckled to turn and look back at him. "Natasha is in there. You expect me to sit and wait?"

Asher's gaze connected with his eyes. Asher was in love. He was going to be a father soon. Didn't he understand?

"You tore through a crowd of onlookers and cops in Berlin to get to Jessica when she had a bomb strapped to her chest," Wyatt said, not that Asher would ever forget that moment. "You think I'm not willing to risk absolutely everything to do the same?" He tucked his 9mm back under his shirt and shoved open the door.

"Wait! Hold on." Wyatt halted at Harper's words. "There's another bomb inside a red Honda Civic in what appears to be the convention center parking garage. If the auditorium doors are detonated or disarmed, it automatically triggers the bomb in the car," she rushed out in a hurry, the calm gone from her voice. "We need to evacuate the area!"

No, this can't be happening.

"Are you damn kidding me?" A.J. hissed. "How in the hell did Balan manage all of this?"

"All that matters is stopping him. Bravo Two and Five are making their way to the service exit to see if they can get to the garage without being noticed by the police. Let's hope the prick only rigged the auditorium doors and nowhere else," Finn said over the line, speaking up for the first time.

"Balan probably covered all his bases, but it's worth a shot," Wyatt said to Finn.

"But we can't exactly go flag down the bomb squad. The authorities have no idea who we are," Asher pointed out. "Get the CIA to call and alert them for us. I can help the boys diffuse the bomb in the Civic in the meantime. We don't have time to wait."

"We'll work on a way to get the crowd dispersed and far

away from the parking garage somehow, too," Chris said. "I'll come up with something that won't get us arrested."

"Natasha and the others inside are going to attempt to shut down Balan's program using his laptop. With any luck, the bomb will be disarmed before Asher even gets there," Harper announced as Asher exited the vehicle. "But if something goes wrong with those doors, Roman is in a bad position."

"Tell him to get out of there," Wyatt demanded. "That's a damn order. We're not losing any people. Understood?"

"Roger that." Harper's words shook with worry.

"And I still need to get inside." Fear shot through Wyatt as the rest of the team exited the SUV along with him. Small black dots filled his line of sight as he moved. He told himself this wasn't a case of choosing to protect the masses over the few as he ran to get to the convention center, arms pumping hard at his sides. He had his team there for support. They could save everyone else. He had to save Natasha and his daughter. If they were in that building, then so help him, he needed to be in there, too.

The people on the streets became a blur as Wyatt eyed the building off in the distance. His boots pounded the pavement, adrenaline surging with every step closer.

He pushed and shoved through the crowd that was beginning to run the opposite direction as him—*away* from danger. Good, whatever Chris and the guys were doing was working.

But no way would he let anything happen to Gwen and Natasha. No damn way.

He hadn't come to the realization that he was capable of love only to lose it now.

This wasn't the end. It couldn't possibly end like this.

"You can't be here!" An officer secured a hand around Wyatt's arm after he'd hopped over a blue police barricade.

But Wyatt yanked himself free and darted ahead, eyes set on his target, on the entrance doors just ahead.

"It's not safe," the officer hollered. "Get back!"

"All stations, come in." Wyatt barely heard Harper's words over comms. "The explosives in the car have been disarmed. Repeat, the explosives have been—" Her words died as the ground rocked, and a blast echoed in Wyatt's ears.

CHAPTER FORTY-ONE

THE GLASS EXTERIOR WALLS OF THE BUILDING SHATTERED. Fragments flew into the street. Sirens erupted from nearby cars. Flames licked and stroked the air around the front of the convention center. The det cord and dynamite wouldn't be responsible for all of this—the bastard had to have used thermite charges as well with how fast the fire was burning through the metal.

Wyatt pressed his hands to his ears and shook his head. His knees gave out as he tried to stand, but he pushed through the pain. He had to get inside. This wasn't supposed to have happened. The car bomb had been disabled, so why—

"Get back!" someone shouted from behind. "It's not safe!"

Disoriented, Wyatt flung his comm onto the ground, his ears ringing from the blast. He examined the building, identifying potential breach points. Only the front of the structure appeared to be damaged, but the auditorium doors were just on the other side of the fire, which meant . . .

"You can't go in there." Two people grabbed hold of him, yanking him backward.

"Let go," he growled out, prepared to reach for his gun, but a third guy jumped in to stop him now.

"I have to get in there," he cried, tears in his eyes. The nearby smoke burned his throat as he struggled to breathe.

"You need medical attention. You're bleeding," one of the men hollered over the wail of sirens and alarms.

Wyatt looked back to find three uniformed firefighters holding on to him. Men refusing to let him get to Gwen and Natasha. "Give me your gear. Let me go in. There are people in the auditorium."

The guy on his left side finally released his arm. "It looks like the blast came from outside the auditorium. The doors, maybe. The blast blew outward, probably not too much damage inside the auditorium." He brought a radio to his mouth as Wyatt processed what he was saying. "What's the status?"

"We've recovered multiple people alive inside," someone announced over the radio. "They're okay. We're exiting the left side of the building now."

Wyatt's shoulders dropped at the words spoken over the radio. "I need to go." Adrenaline pumped through him. His heart piecing back together. Hope building inside of him.

"Let go of him." The firefighter tipped his head. "Come with me."

They quickly rounded the building, and Wyatt stumbled and fell to his knees at the sight of Natasha and Gwen twenty meters away. Roman exited the building just behind them, along with the Wards, Jasper, and the other hacker.

But where in the hell was Balan? Hopefully, fucking dead.

Gwen's eyes connected with his a moment later. "Wyatt!" she called out and yanked free of the firefighter's grasp to sprint toward him.

"She your daughter?" the firefighter asked, offering an assist to rise.

"Yeah," he choked out, "she's mine."

Gwen flung her arms around Wyatt, taking him by surprise, and he buried his face into her shoulder and hugged his daughter for the first time in his life.

He lifted his eyes to search for Natasha a moment later, but he didn't let go of Gwen.

Natasha was talking to the police officers, and whatever she was saying had them not only handcuffing Jasper but both Kate and Felix as well. Another officer immediately brought a radio to his mouth and began running Wyatt's direction in a hurry.

Roman was nowhere in sight. He'd most likely discreetly vanished from the area, something he was good at, so the cops wouldn't question him.

"Are you okay?" he asked Gwen as Natasha started their way.

"I was scared." Gwen stepped out of his arms. "But the other bomb, it didn't go off, right? We disarmed it in time?" Her bottom lip trembled, and tears had her eyes glistening.

"Yeah," he said as Natasha returned, and he pulled her tight to his side, so grateful they were both safe.

"Balan got away." Natasha's tone was thick with regret. "Seconds after we disarmed the car bomb, the auditorium doors blew. We had a feeling that would happen, though, so we distanced ourselves as far away from the doors as possible. I had hoped you all warned everyone to clear the area."

"Natasha threw herself on top of me like a shield," Gwen spoke up.

Wyatt sucked in a sharp breath at her words.

"But, um, when I was back on my feet, those two other

fake cops had Balan, guns drawn. I couldn't get off a clean shot." Tears crept into Natasha's eyes. "I tried, but I couldn't take him down." She pressed a palm to her face. "He got away, and it's my fault."

"Ma'am," the firefighter who'd brought Wyatt to Natasha and Gwen spoke up, "the police are looking for him. Don't blame yourself. Sounds like everyone out here owes you and this young lady a debt of gratitude for diffusing the other bomb." He nodded. "You all need to get checked out in an ambulance, though. Let the police handle the rest."

"You, um, do have pieces of glass in your face." Gwen lifted a hand to Wyatt's cheek, a tender look in her eyes, and it was as if she were seeing him for the first time.

"I'll be fine." He tipped his chin, motioning for them to walk. "What'd you say to the police?" he whispered into Natasha's ear as they slowly walked out front.

"I had to show him my credentials. I had to let them know Balan got away, and I didn't want to risk Jasper or the others walking free," she said, her voice soft, still plagued by guilt.

He caught sight of Harper and Finn lingering off to the side of the barricade, attempting to blend in with the crowd.

"We're lucky everyone had been notified to get away. No one out here appears to have gotten hurt from the blast," the firefighter said as he helped Gwen up into the back of the ambulance. "Your dad was ready to walk through fire to get to you. You're lucky to have him."

Gwen looked at Wyatt standing outside the ambulance next to Natasha as if there were a million things she wanted to say but couldn't.

"Excuse me, we're family," Harper called out, pointing to Wyatt, and the firefighter nodded and let Harper and Finn cross the barricade to get to the ambulance.

"Roman touch base?" he asked Harper, making sure the

man purposefully disappeared and hadn't been grabbed by Balan's men.

"Yeah, he's good. And he begrudgingly followed that order of yours with only seconds to spare before the blast," Harper said, her voice low.

"So, everyone appears to be good." Finn lifted his eyes to Gwen, then peered at Wyatt.

"Balan got away." Natasha faced Harper, her shoulders trembling.

Harper motioned Wyatt and Natasha out of earshot of the firefighter and medic. "Roman told us. Our people are canvassing the streets."

Wyatt surveyed the area. Every first responder in Montreal was probably on their way there, but . . . "Shit. There!" He threw a hand out and pointed down the street in the distance. "That's the only police car leaving the scene. Balan's probably in there," he said just as the car rounded the corner, and he lost visual contact with the vehicle. He brought his hand to his ear, ready to alert his team, but his comm was gone.

"I'm on it." Harper tapped her comm. "All stations, come in."

Wyatt eyed Natasha as Harper updated the team. "I need to stop him. Will you stay with Gwen?"

"No, don't go." Gwen yanked her arm free from the medic who'd been trying to take her blood pressure and jumped out of the back of the ambulance. "Don't. Please."

"I have to." Wyatt kept his voice as calm and steady as possible. "You're okay now. I'll never let anything happen to you, I promise."

"Wyatt." Natasha grabbed hold of his bicep, urging him to look her way. "I want him as bad as you do, but if you go chasing after him here," she said, lowering her voice, "you could end up arrested. There are too many eyes on you. You can't just shoot him in broad daylight."

"And I don't care," he grit out.

"And if you go to prison, you can't be her dad," Natasha reminded him.

Wyatt's gaze flicked to his daughter, and Gwen nodded, her blue-gray eyes tight on him. A plea for him to back down.

Wyatt brought a palm to cover his eyes and took a deep breath. "Give Balan's location to the authorities," he said to Harper as he brought his hand back to his side, "but have our people tail them."

"We need him alive if possible." Natasha had said the words as if it pained her to do so, but she was right. Even though he wanted the cocksucker buried six feet under, he was more useful alive. God knew how much intel Balan might have collected over the years on the terrorists he'd sold intel to on the Dark Net.

Harper nodded before she and Finn took off toward the thick of the crowd.

"You've been after him for so long." Wyatt reached for Natasha's hand. "Why take the risk of losing him?"

"Because you're worth more to me than him." She brought her lips to his, a gentle kiss in the middle of chaos.

"I guess I was right about you two," Gwen said softly. "But you really should be the one getting checked out, Wyatt." She arched a brow. "Glass in your face, remember?"

Would he ever be Dad to her?

"This is nothing. Don't worry," he said, his heart squeezing with relief that Gwen and Natasha were unscathed. "And did you really help disable the bomb?"

Gwen shrugged as if it were no big deal.

He wanted to pull her in for a hug again, but he didn't want to overstep, this was still all so new. And after everything they'd been through today . . . "I'm so sorry you got involved in all of this."

"You did tell me not to come today." Gwen pointed to the ambulance as a stubborn directive for Wyatt to get checked out, but until he knew Balan had been taken down, he couldn't worry about glass in his face.

"I'm getting a call." Natasha reached into her pocket and produced her phone. "I don't recognize the number." Her brows drew together as she lifted the mobile to her ear. "Hello?" She paused as her eyes met Wyatt's, and she mouthed, "It's him."

They moved out of earshot of the medic, and Natasha placed the call on speakerphone.

"I guess our game is not over yet," Balan said. "I could have killed you. Many times over the years. But it looks like that girl, Gwen, has given me a reason to live. If it were not for her handiwork back in the auditorium, those other hackers would never have decrypted my program. I think I would like to challenge her, see how good she really is. Give you a chance to hunt . . ." Static interrupted his words.

Sirens wailed in the background.

Pops of gunfire as if shots were pinging the frame of his car.

Metal hitting metal. A crash?

Shouting and then more gunshots.

Then the line went dead.

Natasha's gaze lifted to Wyatt's, her face going pale. "You think he's dead?"

"I don't know." And as much as Wyatt knew they needed Balan's intel, part of him really hoped he was gone for good.

Wyatt caught sight of Charlotte running toward them as Natasha sputtered, "This time, I need to see his body."

* * *

"What are you going to do now that Balan is dead for real this time?" Wyatt held Natasha tight to his side a block from the convention center, far enough away from the police and the scattered onlookers curious about what had happened over an hour ago.

Natasha looked up at him. "Go get my ass chewed out by Headquarters. Hope I still have a job after."

The Agency had already called Natasha three times since the explosion, and Alexander Balan had been declared dead by the Canadian authorities, but she hadn't answered yet.

SWAT had AMF'd Balan—aka *Adios, motherfucker*. If Balan was going to die, Wyatt wished his people could have done it, but Natasha had been right, his team would risk exposure by engaging in a gun battle in the middle of Montreal while the streets were swarming with police and civilians.

Balan's men had refused to pull over during the police chase, so SWAT forced them to engage once they got them just outside the city and away from any innocent bystanders. The drivers had resisted arrest, and a gun battle had ensued. All three had died.

Wyatt had managed to get Natasha as close to the crime scene as possible without drawing eyes from the authorities, and she'd sobbed into his chest—tears of relief, tears for the lives lost, and possibly even tears for the evidence they may have lost because he died.

But maybe with Balan finally dead, and Natasha's chase for him over, they could be together?

They still had to address one issue: her father was about to be appointed Secretary of Defense, and Wyatt would report to him. But if Knox could work for his father, the president, then surely Wyatt could date the admiral's daughter.

Date? Was he really thinking about dating at a time like this?

He hadn't thought it would ever be possible to marry and settle down, but maybe this was exactly what he should be thinking about. His head was finally out of his arse.

"You know, I do have an in with the president. Also, CIA Director Spenser. I could put in a word so you avoid that arse chewing." He cleared his throat. "Then there's your dad. Surely he won't let anything happen to your job."

"I don't want favoritism, especially because of Dad." Natasha's green eyes lifted to the sky.

She was stubborn, and damn did he like it. "My people will need to get the hell out of here and soon. We've already shown our faces far too much for our liking." His guys couldn't stick around to give their side of the story to the authorities. They weren't even technically there. MI6 had disappeared quickly, too, but the agency would probably have the Canadians send Jasper back to London soon.

"I hadn't planned on staying, but since I had to pull out my credentials, I'll need to do some ass kissing and begging of forgiveness from the Canadians since I operated here without permission."

"I think stopping that bomb and saving everyone today should earn you a pass," he said with a reassuring smile.

Her lips pressed into a tight line, worry crossing her face. "Everything is going to be okay, though, right?"

"Yes." He planted his hands on her biceps. "It's going to be more than okay."

Her eyes cast to the ground between them. "Five years of chasing him. It's just hard to believe he's gone." She pulled her focus to his face. "But, um, I would've chosen Gwen, you know." Her lip wobbled, and she covered her mouth as tears sprung to her eyes. "If I really had to make a choice back there when you were at the mill—you or Gwen." Her entire body trembled beneath his touch now. "I would never have been able to live with myself, but I also know you'd never be able to handle living with me choosing you over her." She broke into a sob, and he pulled her against his chest, holding the sides of her head tight as she cried.

Tears pricked his own eyes. He expelled a deep breath, trying to find his voice. "Thank you for caring about me enough to kill me."

She half cried and half laughed at his choice of words. "I just never want to have to make a choice like that again. And then with the car bomb and—"

"Shhh." Still cupping the sides of her head, he pulled her back so she could see his eyes. "We're all okay. And we won't let anything like this happen again. No having to choose who to save."

"So, don't fall in love, then, and we don't risk it?" She arched a brow.

"It's too late, I'm already falling," he whispered, the intense emotions nearly suffocating his ability to get the words out. "We just need to continue being badasses to prevent such a choice from ever having to be made." He pressed his mouth to hers and stole a kiss before the sound of someone clearing their throat had him stilling. A deep, Asher-like throat clear. "Go away," Wyatt grumbled.

"I have bad news."

Wyatt dropped his forehead to Natasha's, not prepared to hear whatever Asher planned on saying.

"Word is, the Feds won't be able to hold the Wards in jail for more than forty-eight hours. And Jasper's claiming Balan forced him to lie and hold the gun, and that he'd been in severe distress. His family being held hostage adds some credibility to his statement, too," Asher said, his voice low and bitter. "He's not fessing up. Similar story with the Wards."

"This is bullshit," Natasha hissed, and Wyatt took a step back and let go of her. Both Asher and A.J. were standing off to his side, grim looks on their faces despite the big win they had today. "We needed Jasper. With Balan dead, we have to have him. He's the smoking gun in all of this."

"We'll just have to get Jasper to talk," Wyatt said with a firm nod.

"And have Jasper get off with some deal?" Natasha shook her head. "No, there has to be another way. And surely, Balan wouldn't go down without ensuring the Wards and Jasper got what's coming to them, right?" Her eyes were red from crying. "His laptop got tossed during the blast, but I'm sure the Feds can recover something of value from it."

"We won't let Kate and Jasper get away with this." Wyatt squeezed her arm. "Where's the rest of the team?"

"Doing damage control to make sure our handsome mugs don't end up on the six o'clock news." A.J. scratched his beard, then angled his head to the side, and Wyatt followed his gaze to see Gwen on approach alongside her mum. He wasn't sure how Gwen had even found him since he'd thought he was safely tucked out of sight of the convention building. Maybe they just had a natural connection?

"We'll, uh, be over there somewhere doing something." A.J. jerked a thumb over his shoulder.

Natasha started to turn as if she were going to leave, too, but Wyatt grabbed her wrist. "Stay. Please."

"Yeah, okay," she whispered.

Gwen had a firefighter's jacket draped around her

shoulders, and she fidgeted with the zipper as she neared Wyatt.

"Thank you for keeping her safe," Charlotte said once they were in front of him.

Gwen lifted her eyes to his face. "Mum and I decided it'd be best if I go back to London. Withdraw from school this semester."

"We're leaving tonight." Charlotte added a firm nod, a silent request not to stand in the way of the decision.

He threaded his hand through his hair before covering his mouth, trying to find the right words. He hadn't prepared for this moment, the goodbye.

"Glad to see you got fixed up." Gwen smiled, her eyes lingering on the bandage above his brow. "But, um, listen." She took a closer step forward. "I need some time to process everything."

Now wasn't the time to drop the truth on her that he didn't abandon her as a baby, but when would be the right time?

"Maybe you can come visit me in London," Gwen offered in a small voice.

Wyatt closed his eyes and took a breath. He'd been through the emotional wringer lately. "I'd like that," he said after gulping and opening his eyes.

"Good." She chewed on her bottom lip, her nerves showing. "Glad you're okay, and, um, thanks for nearly walking through fire to try and get to me." A smile crossed her lips. "See you around." Once Gwen turned her back, Charlotte nodded her thanks, and damn did it feel so fucking horrible for this to end with her walking away.

But Gwen was alive, and she was prepared to give him a chance, so it wasn't really the end, was it? Waiting for her call would be brutal, though.

"Wyatt?" Gwen turned and faced him, hugging the jacket closer to her body.

He cocked his head and studied her, doing his best to keep his arms at his sides and not reach out to stop her from leaving. "Yeah?"

"Try not to die. Okay?"

He swallowed and worked the words loose around the knot in his throat, "I'll do my best."

"She needs to know," Natasha said once Gwen was gone. "She deserves the truth."

"I know, but first, she needs time." He tucked his hands into his pockets, and Natasha's phone began ringing.

"Langley. Again." She pursed her lips together. "I don't know how long this whole mess will take to wrap up. But after it's over, can I see you? Will you visit me in Virginia?"

He smiled. "Nothing in the world could stop me from coming for you."

"Not even my father?" She smirked, and her smile erased some of the pain in his chest.

"No, not the admiral. Or your brother." He lifted his hands from his pockets and pulled her into his arms when her phone stopped ringing. "Not even the president himself could keep me from you."

"Is that a promise, sailor?" Her light green eyes gleamed as he leaned in closer.

"SEAL's honor," he said with a smile and met her lips with a kiss they both needed.

"Ahem."

Wyatt cursed under his breath. "What now?" He forced his lips away from Natasha to see Asher and A.J. standing there again. "You guys, always with the interrupting."

"Now you know how I feel whenever I'm with Jessica, and Luke shows up," Asher grumbled before his lips tilted into an apologetic smile. "Boss Lady called while you were talking to Gwen. She's ordering us out of here. The jet is being prepped. We gotta go, brother."

"But the—"

"I'm sure Natasha can handle everything," Asher cut off Wyatt.

"POTUS called," A.J. added. "He needs the best of the best—aka Echo Team—in Venezuela. It's urgent."

"Best my ass." Asher rolled his eyes. "Bravo Team all day. Any day."

"Is it always like this with you guys?" Natasha asked when Wyatt faced her again.

"The comedy show?" Wyatt stared into her eyes, a bit worried now. "Or the ops?"

"The constant spinning up," she answered as Asher and A.J. continued their back-and-forth on which team was superior.

"Yeah, it is." He gulped. "Is that okay?"

"You mean, am I okay with falling for a hero?" She hooked her arms around his neck. "Yeah, I think I can handle that," she said before her lips brushed against his.

CHAPTER FORTY-TWO

New York City, One Week Later

"You seriously called the two of us here for this?" Wyatt's eyes widened at the sight before him. "What makes you think I'll be able to help you assemble two cribs?" He leaned against the interior of the doorframe in Asher's home and grinned.

A.J. was already in the twins' bedroom looking around as if he didn't have a damn clue how to help. Pieces of the cribs were strewn all over the carpet.

"Well, you can strip and reassemble a rifle faster than anyone I know," Asher said, eyes on Wyatt. "These beds shouldn't be hard for you." Asher had his jeaned legs stretched out on the bedroom floor, a set of instructions on his lap. "And A.J. is here for the comic relief."

Based on the number of parts in the room, the assembly process would not be so damn easy.

"Maybe try flipping the instructions over to the side in English." A.J. laughed.

Wyatt pushed away from the doorway and removed his jacket. "And I hate to admit it, but Liam has about a half a second on me. I'm pretty sure he's been practicing just to gain that time over me, too."

"Probably has something to do with that wager I made him last month when we were bored and waiting to spin up for an op." A.J. grinned.

"What wager?" Wyatt asked.

"I bet Liam he couldn't strip and assemble a long gun faster than you." A.J. squatted next to Asher and snatched the instructions. "I'd assumed you had it in the bag. You know, prove Echo is better."

"I'm thinking we need some sort of matchup," Asher said as Wyatt set his jacket on the white wooden dresser by the door. So far, it was the only piece of furniture in the room aside from a white rocking chair. Pairs of animals were framed on one of the light yellow walls, a Noah's Ark theme.

And now all he could think about was the fact he'd missed out on Gwen's life and that she still hadn't called him.

He had to remind himself that it'd only been seven days. And had he not just gotten back from an op in Venezuela yesterday, he probably would've lost his mind sitting around the city staring at his mobile.

"I'm game for that." A.J. tossed the instructions back at Asher as if they were useless and grabbed a skinny white piece of wood off the floor.

"Anytime," Asher said with a teasing smile. "So, uh, how's Natasha?"

"Talked to her last night when we got back. She's good. Just frustrated." Echo Team had to rescue two Americans who'd been illegally detained by a private militia group, and fortunately, the mission had been a success. A walk in the park compared to chasing down The Knight.

"Did she take any heat about being a badass and going rogue?" A.J. asked, his tone casual.

"Nah. Director Spenser covered for her. He said she was working undercover for him to prevent any leaks. Good thing we have him in our pocket." Wyatt smiled. "She'd quit before she let her father step in and bail her out."

"Is that weird that her old man is working with us now?" Asher cocked a brow.

"Yeah, but no stranger than having Knox's dad as POTUS," Wyatt quipped.

"Touché, brother." A.J. tipped his head to the side. "You tell her you love her yet?"

"He just met her." Asher glanced at Wyatt. "Well, I guess you've had a few bump-ins in the past. Come to think of it, that's sort of how we all roll, right? We fall quick and hard."

"Except you and Knox." A.J. peered at Asher. "You boys waited too damn long to make a move." He discarded whatever he'd been holding and sat in the rocking chair, which was a bit snug for his frame.

"So, do you?" Asher angled his head to the side, waiting for Wyatt to answer. "And does she know?"

"I haven't told her," he admitted, but his feelings for her were undeniable.

"So, A.J.'s right. You do love her," Asher commented. "I knew beneath that rough exterior there was a softy."

"Softy my arse." Wyatt grinned.

"And look who's talking." A.J. pointed at Asher. "That MMA fighting shit you do is just an act to hide the fact you're the biggest teddy bear of us all."

Asher flung a piece of wood A.J.'s way, but he snatched it in front of his face.

"Yeah, well, Jessica doesn't want me fighting anymore.

She wasn't too happy to find out I stepped into a cage back in December." Asher reached for the instructions again.

Wyatt grimaced. "Sorry again. That was my fault." After far too many rounds of whiskey, he'd thought it would be a good idea to let off some steam at an underground fight club.

"Not just a softy, but you're whipped, too." A.J.'s lip quivered as he attempted to suppress a laugh.

"Says the guy who hasn't even looked at another woman since you met that FBI agent last fall," Asher shot back. "And you're too chicken to actually call her up and ask her out."

"Yeah, what are you waiting for, anyway?" Wyatt asked.

"I may have done some research. A bit of Googling and—"

"You Googled her?" Wyatt's brows shot up in surprise.

A.J. rolled his eyes. "Yes, and it looks like she just got divorced a few months ago. I figure there's like a waiting period before you can date again, right?"

"Maybe if she lost her husband in a tragic accident, but . . ." Wyatt cocked his head, smiling. "Damn, you really like her, don't you? You don't want to be a rebound."

"Shouldn't we be talking about Natasha?" A.J. pointed to the crib parts on the floor. "Or skip to the part where I make fun of you two as you attempt to put these things together?"

And back to the cribs. "Why'd you call me instead of someone who has done this crib assembly thing before?" Wyatt squinted at Asher. "Who asked you to distract me?"

He did need a distraction, though. He was anxiously waiting for Natasha to lock up her case before he went to visit her.

The account Balan had hacked in Sweden had belonged to Kate Ward, and given the money was a close match to what had been financially gained off the hacks over the years by The Knight—plus, with Kate having no way of proving how else she may have acquired the three hundred million—it'd been enough for the FBI to hold the Wards. Unfortunately, Kate and Felix were only placed on electronic monitoring while the Agency and FBI worked to get more evidence for the case.

As for Jasper, he was back in MI6's custody. His family and sister were safe, and apparently, Balan had lied to him, and they'd never been in danger. But as for what MI6 planned to do with him, Wyatt wasn't sure. The idea of Jasper working for any government agency again as a free man made him sick, so with any luck, Natasha would find more evidence to send him away as well.

"So, fess up. Who told you I needed the distraction?" Wyatt asked again.

"Who do you think?" Asher pointed to A.J.

Of course. "Yeah, well, we're going to need more of the guys for this. And if anyone can make sense of the instructions, it's Roman."

"Tell him to bring beers. I'm all out," Asher ordered while getting onto his knees and snatching the instructions again.

"You're *still* looking at the Mandarin side of the instructions," A.J. said with a laugh while Wyatt grabbed his phone.

"A lot of beers," Asher grumbled.

"You ever imagine this would be our lives?" Wyatt asked, taking a moment to appreciate the situation before he phoned Roman and corralled the troops for an assist. "That we'd wind up on a crib-making mission?"

Asher's gaze cut to Wyatt. "No, but now I couldn't imagine a world where this wouldn't be happening." He grinned from ear to ear. The big guy was a softy, wasn't he? "I'm gonna have twins."

"And I have a twenty-year-old daughter." Wyatt squeezed the phone in his hand, his thoughts drifting back to Gwen.

"Maybe after Natasha's wrapped up her case, you two will have some time to make a baby. At the very least, get a hell of a lot of practice in," A.J. commented.

"You know," Wyatt said with a nod, "that's not a bad idea at all." He eyed the crib parts, "But first reinforcements and—"

"The beer," Asher finished with a laugh.

CHAPTER FORTY-THREE

"YOU REALLY CAN'T TELL US ANYTHING ABOUT WHAT happened?" Natasha's mom passed the bowl of mashed potatoes to Gray, who was sitting beside Jack at the dining room table in Natasha's townhouse in Virginia. "I mean, you have pink highlights in your hair—what's that all about?"

She'd forgotten about her hair. She'd need to find time to swing by the hair salon at some point. "Does she always push you for details?" She eyed her father sitting at the head of the oak table, which her grandfather had made with his own hands before he passed years ago.

"Yes." Even out of uniform, her father still looked like an admiral. Spine so straight, it was as if someone had pinned his shoulder blades back. Always slightly slanted brows, a look of caution in his brown eyes. The chest candy didn't have to be present to give off the authoritative feel, the commanding presence came across in his tone of voice, in his often scrutinizing and protective stare.

425

Wyatt had met her dad before, not while her father served as admiral in the Navy, but during Wyatt's top-secret work for the president. And now her dad was Secretary of Defense and Wyatt's direct boss. They'd yet to tell the admiral they were a couple, and she wasn't sure who was more nervous about the conversation. Her or Wyatt? Even the idea made her palms sweaty as she sat at the table.

Her dad was a loving and caring man when it came to his family. And he was protective of his men in the Navy. But how would he feel about someone who worked for him dating his daughter? He'd never been a fan of Dale and her together, but this was different, and she hoped that when the time was right, he'd approve.

She wouldn't change her mind about being with Wyatt, but it'd be nice if her family accepted him.

"How about we talk about your house hunt since my case is classified." Although, she wouldn't mind venting about the case that still wasn't quite closed even though her greatest adversary, Balan, was dead.

"I think we might put an offer on a place here in Arlington," her mom said while cutting her steak. "Hard to believe we're leaving Texas, but this new promotion for your father is exciting." Her green eyes moved to Gray. "If only I could get you to move here from California, then we'd all be together again."

"And now you'll be heading to San Diego soon, too, I guess." Natasha glanced at Jack. He sat as regally as her father. Stiff back. Perfect posture. But like Gray, Jack had a hell of a sense of humor, and the moment he wasn't in the presence of the admiral, he'd let his shoulders slouch and sit in a more relaxed position. "How does it feel to be out from under the CIA's thumb?"

"It's nice to be out of Moscow, that's for sure." Jack took

a swig of his beer. "We'll see if I regret the decision after a few weeks of working with this guy." He elbowed Gray in the ribs.

Gray chewed on his steak and said, "Sorry this trip has to be so short. I've gotta head abroad for a few weeks."

"Can you, at least, tell me where you're going and what you'll be working on?" Her mom raised a brow, eyes on Gray, her fork hovering over her plate.

"Just going somewhere to kill a few baddies. No big thing." Gray winked.

She rolled her eyes and huffed out a breath. "How'd I end up with two kids who put their lives on the line on a regular basis?"

"You raised them right." Jack's straight white teeth flashed as he smiled.

"And speaking of kids—"

"Don't start, Mom," Gray grumbled around a mouth full of food.

"I was talking to Jack. I've lost all hope with you, Gray." Their mom's green eyes flicked to Jack, who was more like a brother to Natasha than a friend. "If you have kids, can I adopt them as grandbabies since it doesn't appear my offspring will ever have any?"

"Offspring?" Gray took a bite of one of their mom's famous buttery rolls and then released a slight moan of ecstasy. "Man, I do miss this food."

"Then move here. I'll cook for you every night." She squeezed her husband's hand and smiled. "Wouldn't it be nice to have both our kids under one roof again?"

"No," her dad said with a shake of the head. "They're too old to live with us."

"That's not what I meant." She reached for her fork again.

"But anyway, Jack, tell me, do you plan on getting married again and having kids?"

"That's a bit personal, Mom." Natasha studied her plate, her stomach growling, but she wasn't in the mood to eat.

After being away from Wyatt for almost ten days because her case wasn't locked up, she was growing a bit anxious.

Wyatt was safe in New York, though, thank God. His operation had been quick and successful, but they'd agreed to wait to see each other until she'd wrapped up her case and had enough evidence to put Kate away for good. Now, she was beginning to regret that decision.

"I'm almost forty. Not sure if I'll ever get around to having kids." Jack's voice was a bit lower and more rumbly than normal. Her mom must've hit upon a sensitive topic for him. "Sorry to disappoint you, Mrs. Chandler."

Before her mom could say something absurdly ridiculous, which she certainly would, the doorbell rang.

"Saved by the bell," Gray said with a smile as Natasha stood.

"Be back." Natasha checked the time on her G-shock watch as she left the dining room to get to the front door.

Normally, she was a stickler for security, always checking her cameras before answering the door, but with her family in the house, she didn't bother.

She pushed aside the curtains alongside the front door to glimpse out the window. "Wyatt," she whispered, surprise slicing through her at the sight of him standing outside.

After a few deep breaths, she swung open the door.

Wyatt had a travel bag next to his booted feet, and she slowly dragged her gaze up his jeaned legs to his black fleece jacket and then on to his handsome face.

"Hi." Wyatt secured his hands around her hips in one fast movement and pulled her into his arms. She surrendered to his passionate kiss, insanely happy to have him there. The world felt right again. "I know we agreed to wait," he said a few moments later, his mouth still near hers, "but I was losing my bloody mind. I had to see you."

"I'm glad you came." She lifted her chin to find his eyes. "I missed you."

"Ten days was too long. Better than our usual few years, I guess." His voice was husky, his arousal pressing against her, and she bit down on her back teeth. The need for him intense.

"Ahem."

"Shit," he said on a sigh. "You're not alone." Wyatt pulled back and turned away from the door, probably to adjust his hard-on.

"Dad." She gripped the nape of her neck and squeezed at the sight of her father standing off to her side.

"Admiral Chandler," Wyatt said upon facing them again.

Natasha stepped aside, allowing him to enter, and Wyatt extended his hand toward her father.

Her dad shot Natasha a curious look, which meant he had witnessed their kiss. "A word in my daughter's office, Pierson."

Shit. He didn't waste any time.

Wyatt lifted his brows when her eyes caught his, a touch of nerves on display. That made the two of them.

He followed her father down the side hall, and she snatched Wyatt's bag off the doorstep and locked up, only to find Gray and Jack standing in her living room, both looking curious and puzzled.

"Who is that?" Gray jerked a thumb toward the hall where her father and Wyatt had disappeared.

Her cheeks warmed as she set Wyatt's travel bag down and entered the living room. "Clara's ex-husband. The SEAL from Dale's wedding." *And boom, here goes.*

"How long have you been seeing him?" She was surprised Gray even remembered Wyatt from the wedding, as hammered as he'd been.

"Since the Algeria op?" Jack spoke up, clearly putting two and two together now.

Natasha glimpsed her mom exiting the kitchen with a wineglass in hand, and great, now it'd turn into an inquisition party. It was her job to interrogate, not be interrogated.

"Since Montreal," she finally admitted, even though, if she were being honest, her feelings for Wyatt started the night of Clara and Dale's wedding eight years ago, she just kept putting them on hold.

"He was with you in Canada?" Gray folded his arms, standing defensively, but all she could worry about was what was going on with Wyatt and her dad. And most likely, Wyatt was getting both the admiral and her father in there. Both equally intimidating.

"Yeah, he helped me. If it weren't for him . . ." *If it weren't for him, I don't know where I'd be.*

"What'd I miss?" their mom asked.

"Tasha has a boyfriend," Jack said, concern etched in the lines of his brow.

Natasha's eyes moved straight to the hall when her office door opened, and her dad stepped out. *That was quick.* And she wasn't sure if that was a good or bad thing.

"He's all yours." The admiral peered at Gray with a nod, and Gray motioned for Jack to come with him. The same curious look was in her dad's eyes, the one he always wore, so no help there on getting a read on him as to what he thought about Wyatt.

"Oh, come on." Natasha dropped into the lounger in the living room and cursed under her breath. "Give the guy a break."

"This is what we do," her dad said when the office door closed, and Gray and Jack were alone with Wyatt saying God knew what. "And it's been a long time since we've met someone you've dated. We have to make sure you don't make the same mistake you did with Dale."

"More money wasted on a wedding?" she bit out, slightly annoyed at the turn of tonight's events. She wanted Wyatt alone, damn it, not scared off. Of course, what was she thinking? This was Wyatt. He wouldn't back down.

"No, sweetie, we don't want you to suffer another broken heart." A glimpse of her dad's tender side had shown up. "I like him." It was like he was complimenting a chef at a restaurant the way he'd spoken so casually, though. "And he's a Navy man, so there's that. Plus, he's agreed to move down here so he doesn't interfere with Natasha's job, or take her away from us."

"Dad." She stood from her chair, but her anger dialed down at the realization of what her Dad confessed. Was Wyatt really planning on moving to Virginia? They hadn't talked about that during the hours they'd spent on the phone each night since he'd been back from South America.

"I wasn't so sure about the whole nobility thing, at first, but—"

"Wait," her mom interjected. "What?" She looked back and forth between her husband and Natasha.

"He's a lord." Her dad waved a dismissive hand in the air. "But also one of the best snipers on the planet, and since he's saved our baby girl more than once now, looks like I can trust him to keep her safe."

Her mom blinked in astonishment and polished off the rest of her chardonnay. The "saving our baby girl" comment probably inducing her reaction. She liked to pretend Natasha really was a telecommunications specialist instead of a CIA officer. It helped her sleep at night to ignore the reality of Natasha's dangerous line of work.

There was a bit more back-and-forth with her parents before Gray and Jack exited the office. They'd taken longer than her father.

"Wyatt, you okay?" she asked when he started her way, jacket resting over his arm.

"Better than ever," he said, his tone rich and deep.

So damn sexy, aren't you? Cocky, too.

"Well, I'm Marion Chandler, Natasha's mother, and it's so very nice to meet you." Her mom offered Wyatt her hand. "Would you like to stay for dinner? We were just getting started."

Wyatt looked to Natasha for permission. "I'd love for you to stay." She reached for his hand, damn curious about what else her overbearing protectors had asked Wyatt. "You sure you're okay?" she whispered before they went into the dining room.

He released her hand, slipped it to the small of her back, and brought his mouth to her ear. "I will be as soon as we're alone."

"SHOW ME." WYATT HAD HIS BACK TO HER CLOSED BEDROOM door. Shoes and socks off, but the rest of him fully clothed. "Show me exactly what you were doing to yourself when we talked on the phone last night." The deep timbre of his voice reached right between her thighs as if it'd been his hand instead.

Natasha peeled off her jeans and kicked them free of her ankles, then sat with her back to the headboard and removed her Texas A&M sweatshirt.

"Is that all you had on when you were touching yourself last night? Driving me wild with all those little whimpering sounds you made over the phone?" Desire thickened his sexy accent.

Her nipples pressed against the ribbed gray tank top she had on, no bra beneath. And she knew it probably drove Wyatt nuts now knowing she'd been braless at the dinner table beneath her sweatshirt with Jack present. In all fairness, bras sucked, and the cotton material of her alma mater sweatshirt was thick enough to hide her nipples.

"Yes," she practically breathed out, squirming a touch with Wyatt's eyes pinned on her body, the need and want for him having built over the last two hours while she impatiently waited for her family to leave. All of Wyatt's touching her beneath the table had robbed her of speech as thoughts of what they'd do together once they were alone had filled her head.

"Just the tank top and panties?" he asked as if needing more confirmation from her, or maybe wanting her to say the words.

"I was only in a tank top while I touched myself."

He took one step from the door, removed his long-sleeved white shirt, and tossed it, allowing her to take in the sight of his hard chest, the ink on his arm, the wall of abdominal muscles flexing as desire pulsed between them.

"No panties, then?" His heated gaze was like a command she so desperately wanted to follow, and she shimmied her hips, removing the pink silk material. "Spread your legs." There was a growl-like sound that left his mouth as she followed his order, eager and anxious to have him fill her, to plunge deep inside now that they were alone and she was free to scream out his name.

"And what were *you* doing when we were on the phone

last night?" She slid her finger along the seam of her wet sex, drawing his eyes, and she tipped her head back to rest against the black leather headboard.

He worked at his jeans. Painfully slow movements as if he were enjoying watching her squirm with excitement and need. Once he was free of both jeans and boxers, he wrapped a hand around his shaft and slid his palm from root to tip. She nearly drew blood from her lip as she watched his large hand work up and down.

"How much longer are you going to make me wait?" She squeezed her legs together around her hand, worried she'd get off before he ever even climbed into bed with her.

"I just want to watch a little bit more. Payback for all that moaning you've been doing on the phone that had me losing my bloody mind waiting for this moment." Still gripping his length, he strode closer to the bed.

He finally joined her, his feet on the floor, and she took that as her cue to take charge.

She discarded her top, snatched a foil wrapper, and tore it open. They'd already had three nights of foreplay over the phone.

Wyatt rolled the rubber over his hard-on. "Ride my cock," he rasped in a throaty voice.

Her thighs tensed, and her shoulders trembled at his words. He secured his hands around her hips, and his fingertips bit into the flesh of her ass cheeks.

Moving onto her knees alongside him on the bed, she then repositioned herself so her legs were wrapped right around his body.

His lips met hers in a crushing and hot kiss as she lowered down onto him, and he groaned at the contact as she took him inch by inch.

A mewl left her mouth as he bottomed out inside of her.

She clenched the walls of her sex and shifted up before slamming back down again.

Her heartbeat, her breathing, her movements were perfectly in sync with his as they made love.

"I'm so glad you're here," she cried out while grinding against him.

"Me, too, Sunshine."

Sunshine, she could get used to that.

Her fingertips buried into his shoulders while she lifted herself up and slammed back down over and over again.

"You feel so good," he said between kisses. "I missed this. I missed you."

She linked her ankles around his back so they were as tight together as humanly possible, and she rubbed and moved, hitting her sensitive spot, creating more friction and heat. Then she arched her back and gave in to her orgasm, unable to hold back.

He released seconds later, kissing her as his climax crashed through him. "God, that was incredible. You're incredible." He brought his forehead to hers, his hands supporting her back to maintain their position. "Let's do that again when I catch my breath."

"Yes, please." She slowly disconnected their bodies, and he discarded his condom in the en suite while she put on her pink silk robe.

He grabbed a pair of gray sweats he'd brought with him and slipped them on before they headed into the kitchen for wine.

"You still haven't told me what they said to you," she said as he poured two glasses of white.

"How could I?" He smirked. "The moment they left, you basically attacked me."

True. The second she locked her front door, she'd hopped

into his arms and had her mouth on his. "And you loved every minute."

"Damn right."

"So?" She took the glass he extended and perched a hip against the island counter. "What'd they say?"

"It was nothing I couldn't handle. I think Jack was the most protective of you, surprisingly."

"Probably because he's been protecting me, literally, for years while I've been with the Agency. He's a family friend, too, so his need to watch out for me has spilled over into my personal life. I'm not sure he'd even know how to stop." He stepped in front of her, and she placed a palm on his smooth chest. "He means well."

"I expected the inquisition, I just didn't expect it tonight." He lifted his glass between them for a sip of the wine. "But I'm glad I got a chance to meet your whole family. To be honest, I'd been nervous."

"And now?"

"I feel better," he admitted, and based on how well dinner had gone, she had assumed everything was good, but she wanted to hear it from him.

"Dad mentioned you might move here."

"I was thinking about it. Aside from Colorado, which is more of a vacation home, I don't really have a permanent address." He set his wineglass aside, and she did the same. "What do you think?" His hands went to her hips, and he pulled her closer to him, his back now flush to the island. "Do you want to give us a chance?"

"Was that ever even a question?" she challenged, her voice light, her body relaxed from the orgasm.

"I just like to hear you say it." He smiled. "But just so you know, I asked your dad and brother for permission to marry you. You know, for when the time is right."

She blinked in surprise. "What?"

"I have no idea when we'll all be together again, and I'm a guy who likes to be prepared. I *will* ask you to marry me at some point, and I'd like to do it right. Have their blessing first, which I managed to get."

Her chest tightened, tears threatening. "I don't know what to say." She took a deep breath and let it go, hoping to slow her pulse. "Does that mean you've moved past the whole, you're-only-good-at-shooting-and-sex thing?"

"Oh, I'll still be doing a lot of shooting. Even more sex, but I can't imagine doing anything if you're not in my life."

"So, you've learned you're capable of love?"

He brought his forehead to hers, his grip on her hips tightening. "I have a good teacher." His breathing was shaky when he whispered, "Thanks for not giving up on me."

"You, too," she said softly. His hands slipped between them to untie the knot of her pink silk robe. "Ready again so soon?"

"I'm always ready with you." He palmed her breast and pinched her nipple, then slipped his other hand between her legs, sliding a finger along her sex, discovering how wet she still was for him. "Damn, Tash. You were made for me, weren't you?"

"I'm beginning to think so." She pressed her mouth to his, but their kiss was interrupted by the doorbell. Always with the interruptions. That needed to change.

"Who the hell is at the door this late?" A sense of alarm pierced his tone. "You got cameras, right?"

She checked the time. Eleven at night. "Yeah." She pointed to the small display screen out in the hall, which showcased the view from the camera positioned outside her front door.

He started for the screen as she knotted her robe. "Who is it?"

"There's an envelope on your doorstep. I don't see anyone there." He grabbed a 9mm out of his travel bag. "Stay back just in case."

"We can rewind the footage before you open the door," she suggested, her pulse picking up at the sight of his gun, at his concern there was danger lurking outside.

Balan was dead, but did Kate Ward discover her true identity and send someone after her? She doubted that, but . . .

"Just stay back, please," he insisted, then opened the door. Moving outside in bare feet, he did a quick perimeter sweep before returning with the package. He locked up behind him, stowed his gun, and faced her. "It's lightweight. Something the size of a chess piece, maybe." He tore open the package.

She stumbled back at the sight of the small white knight in his hand as he let the 8x11 yellow envelope fall to the floor.

"Even in his death." Her shoulders trembled. "I moved since the last time he found me." *Looks like I'm moving again.* Balan was dead, but his delivery man had her address, so . . .

"It's not just a chess piece." He twisted the bottom and lifted the top, separating it into two pieces. "It's a thumb drive. He must have arranged for it to be sent if he ever died."

"I don't understand."

"I think we should look at it. Your personal laptop in your office?"

"Yeah." Once in her office, she sat at her desk and placed the USB stick into her personal computer. She couldn't risk uploading a device from Balan into her CIA laptop. "Why is he doing this?"

He pointed to the screen. "Two folders. Try the first one."

She clicked it. One MSWord file. "Oh God."

Wyatt leaned over her shoulder and read aloud, "If you're reading this, that means I'm dead, and you won the game. I am a man of honor, though. Here is everything you need to ensure Kate Ward goes to prison for a long time. The bank account information and where the rest of the money is hidden has also been included. Congratulations on checkmate. Best regards, Alexander Balan."

She leaned back in complete shock. "I don't understand. Is this real?"

"He doesn't want Kate running free. It makes sense, I guess. Plus, he's crazy, so . . ."

She clicked on the second file, still not sure if she could believe this was truly happening. There were hundreds of documents inside the folder. "Is this real?" She flipped through the documents one by one. "This is all of it. Every hack. Every terrorist he worked with." She gripped her chest, her heart beating too hard and too fast.

"Looks like you're going to have enough to take down not just Kate Ward, but you've got a list of terrorist arseholes to go after as well." He gripped her shoulder and squeezed.

"It's over," she said, tears streaming down her cheeks. "It's finally over." On Balan's damn terms, but at this point, she'd take it.

"Looks like you're going to be busy." He spun her chair to face him, then knelt in front of her and gathered her hands between his palms. "But there was something I wanted to ask you."

"Yeah?" She sniffled, more tears of relief rushing out.

"Come to London with me. After you turn over the evidence and the Wards are locked up . . . will you come with me?"

Her lip trembled as she repeated his words in her head, making sense of his question. "Does that mean you're going to talk to Gwen?"

"I need to give her time, but I can't handle the lie between us." His eyes became glossy. "And it's time I face my own parents again. I have some things to say, and they need to know I'm not so fucked up." He shot her a crooked smile. "I mean, if you fell in love with me, I can't be so bad, right?"

She half cried and laughed at his words, then pulled her hand free from his touch to palm his cheek. "How do you know I love you?"

He brushed the tip of his nose to hers before bringing his mouth near her lips. "Because I fell really hard for you, and I'm hoping you feel the same as me." He paused. "Do you?"

"Of course," she said as more tears flowed free. "Of course, I love you."

CHAPTER FORTY-FOUR

London, Three Weeks Later

The Montgomery home in London looked different than the last time Wyatt had visited. Of course, it was winter now instead of fall when he'd been there for Arthur's funeral. Yet, there seemed to be more life outside today. Flower beds that could withstand the winter surrounded the home, adding pops of color he hadn't remembered. He was planning to talk with his daughter, though, so maybe it was hope filling him when last time it'd been grief and pain.

With Natasha at his side, he had the courage to walk up to the door and face his daughter. He still wasn't sure what he was going to say, but he couldn't wait any longer.

He'd spoken to his mum on the phone last week. She confessed she'd been curious over the years about Gwen, but she'd been too afraid to push. It'd take him some time to get over that fact, but he wanted to forge a new path, a new future, so holding grudges and placing blame wouldn't do anyone any good.

441

And nothing would stop Wyatt from soldiering toward Charlotte's front door. He refused to miss out on another twenty years of Gwen's life because of some misguided notion he'd be as shitty of a father as his old man.

"You can do this." Natasha squeezed his hand as they walked down the cobblestone path, the clouds pulling overhead, rain threatening.

"Thank you for being here."

She peered over her shoulder at him. "And thank you for waiting until I could come with you."

When Natasha turned Balan's USB drive over to the CIA, the Agency had scored not only enough evidence to put both the Wards and Jasper away, but Balan provided significant intel that enabled multiple target packages to be put together to take down HVTs around the world. Bravo Team, along with A.J. and Roman, happened to be mid-assignment taking down a target now.

Wyatt wasn't about to thank Balan, but in all the craziness, at least some good had come from it. Plus, Natasha managed to convince the government to take the three hundred million from the hacks, which included the hundred and fifty Balan had transferred to Natasha, and divide it between the victims' families who'd been affected by Kate Ward and Alexander Balan over the years.

It wasn't blood money anymore, it was college tuition for the children of the soldiers who died in the helo crash in Algeria. It was cancer treatments paid in full for the wife of another victim of Balan's. It was money the fallen CIA officer's spouse chose to donate to wounded warriors. And so much more.

Natasha had been a champion for those people. She was truly a bright spot in what could be a dark world.

Wyatt squeezed her hand tightly once they stood in front

of the double doors. "I really do love you," he said before ringing the bell, his heart skipping a couple of beats.

"I love you, too," Natasha replied just as one of the doors creaked open, revealing his surprised-looking daughter.

"I, um . . ." Gwen took a step back, and Wyatt glimpsed the luggage off to the side of the door. "I was just coming to find you."

"What?" His brows lifted in shock, and he had to restrain himself from reaching out for a hug that'd probably be awkward for both of them.

"Your face healed." Gwen smiled, then blinked a few times and stepped aside, offering them entrance.

"That's a lot of bags," Natasha commented.

Gwen blushed and tucked her blonde hair behind her ears. "I was hoping to stay in the U.S. for a few months."

"You were?" He couldn't seem to shake the shock.

"I didn't know where you were living, but I had a feeling if I found Natasha," Gwen began, "I'd find you."

"I'm not exactly listed," Natasha said with a smile.

"Yeah, but you should probably do a better job at hiding where you live. I found you pretty quickly." She shrugged. Gwen really was a computer whiz, wasn't she?

"How'd you know my last name?" Natasha asked, a touch of pride in her eyes.

"That evil hacker guy called you both Chandler and Natasha while we were in the auditorium, and I figured you were CIA, so . . ." Another shrug. A touch of modesty in the curve of her lips, in the slope of her shoulders.

"You didn't hack the Agency, did you?" He didn't want his daughter getting arrested the second her plane landed in the U.S.

"What, um, are you doing here?" Gwen deflected.

Wyatt tucked his hands into his coat pockets, attempting

to formulate the words he probably should have practiced before he'd come.

"Your mom here?" Natasha asked.

"In the kitchen." Gwen pointed to the hallway behind her.

"I'll go say hello. Why don't you two talk?" Natasha wrapped a hand over Wyatt's arm, offering her support, then she left the entranceway in pursuit of the kitchen.

"Want to take a walk?" Gwen sidestepped him without waiting for a response, grabbed her jacket, and opened the front door.

He followed her outside, and they began walking along the path toward the back of the property. He remained quiet, still not sure what to say, or how to go about expressing his thoughts.

"I read the follow-up story about what happened in Montreal. The papers said both Kate and Felix Ward will be going to prison. Jasper, too. But they wouldn't be in jail as long as Kate."

"You read the newspaper? You don't get your news online like most people your age?"

"I can be old school when I want to be."

Maybe Wyatt was the one deflecting now. He wasn't sure if he was prepared to talk about Balan's quest for revenge or the people who'd been responsible for nearly killing Gwen and Natasha.

"Felix wasn't as ignorant as he let on," he admitted, "but he's also dealing with some other lawsuits." Wyatt had a feeling Gwen already knew this part, too. "Some women at Cyber X stepped forward about Felix's inappropriate behavior." The idea was too horrible for him to even say aloud. It not only repulsed him, it awakened his sniper brain and made his trigger finger itchy to know Ward had tried to get Gwen to sleep with him in exchange for a job.

"There's a group of women at Cyber X who will be taking over the company now, right? An awesome and diverse group of kick-ass ladies. Thank God some good came from Felix's fall from fame," she said. "But um, how long are you in London for?"

"As long as you want me to be." And that was the truth. He would put aside his position as Echo One for as long as Gwen needed him to. He couldn't miss out on her life. His mum and Charlotte had been wrong about him. He would have chosen his daughter above all else, even at eighteen.

"I honestly would like to get the bloody hell out of here. Maybe spend a few weeks in New York before I rent a flat near wherever you're living. There are some great schools in D.C. I could transfer to in the fall."

He blinked. More surprise moving through him.

She wanted to get to know him. Rent a flat and go to school nearby. Was this really happening?

"My twenty-first birthday is next month. I can't imagine a better place to celebrate than the Big Apple."

Twenty-one. New York. A birthday.

He was going to have heart failure at the idea. What if . . .

He couldn't think like an operator right now. Besides, it was only early February. He had time to come up with a plan for her birthday, a way to ensure her safety.

"I'd absolutely love for you to come to the U.S.," he finally admitted as she pointed to a bench at the back of the house on a patio area. He took a seat and twisted to the side to face her. "Why, though?"

She fidgeted with the zipper on her jacket before peering at him. "Mum told me the truth two days ago. She told me you never knew about me, not until right before you came to Montreal."

445

The blood rushed from his face as if he were fast-roping from a helo upside down. "She did?"

"She said Dad wanted me to know the truth after he died, and she almost did it, but then she freaked that I'd hate her and him." Emotion cut through her words, and it was a machete to his heart to hear and see her hurting. This was the last thing he wanted. "I know why you didn't tell me back at the hotel." Her lips pinched tight as if she were fighting tears. "You were going to take the blame and let me hate you, so I wouldn't blame him . . . because he's gone."

He closed his eyes, trying to channel the strength he'd need to get through this.

"He wanted you to be in my life, though. He asked me for forgiveness, and then he told me to ask you for forgiveness as well."

He opened his eyes at her words. "I don't understand."

"There was a letter Mum was supposed to give me after he died. Dad wrote it when he was sick. She gave it to me the other day."

Wyatt covered his mouth with his palm, trying to wrap his head around it all.

"He also said he forgives you for leaving. And that what happened with Mum wasn't your fault." She grew still for a moment, tears beginning to trickle down her cheeks, her blue-gray eyes shimmering. "Mum told me what really happened back then. She said Dad had been cheating, and she was angry. She, um, used you." She swiped the backs of her hands over her cheeks.

"We were all very young." He swallowed, hoping his voice would continue to work. "Younger than you are now. Not as mature as you are either, so it would seem."

"Would you have wanted me if you'd known the truth

back then?" She blinked away the rest of the liquid from her eyes.

"Yes, but I also know Arthur gave you a life I don't think I could have. Your mother was right to worry about me. I was wild and hated being tied down to the life of a noble. I joined the military, and I never really had a permanent address."

"You don't need to justify what they did."

"But if I had you in my life back then, I know in my heart, I would have made you a priority." *Because I'm not my father.* "We can't change the past, though. And it looks like your dad did one hell of a job raising you."

She smiled, another tear escaping. "But blood appears to run thicker." Her attention lifted to his face. "Maybe I'm more like you."

Now he was going to cry in one bloody second, but he did his best to maintain his composure. To stay strong. "I don't know where you got your computer smarts from. I'm good, but I'm much better at shooting."

Shit, he still had to tell her he was a professional sniper. She didn't need to know his kill count, but . . .

"Oh," she began, her smile stretching, "you should see me with a gun. Not so bad myself."

He clutched his chest at her words. She really was his daughter, wasn't she? "I could take you to the range back in the States."

"I'd like that."

"And maybe we could go grab ice cream?" He remembered she liked his favorite place in London as well. "Or pizza? Whatever you'd like to do."

"We can bring Natasha along with us. I don't want to leave her with Mum. That'd be just plain evil."

He laughed. "Natasha's pretty tough. She can handle herself."

Gwen stood, and he rose as well, his legs a little shaky. "You know, I might have taken a peek into your old service file."

He arched a brow. "My file?"

"Just a quick look." She did that humble sort of innocent shrug again. "Looks like you're quite the hero."

"I wouldn't call myself that."

"And what would you call yourself?"

Now? Now I'm a dad. He'd only ever been a Teamguy, and Echo One. But now he was a father. He was a man in love with a beautiful and talented CIA officer. He had a lot more than he'd ever believed he could have. More than he knew he wanted.

"Hm. Looks like you're humble," she said when he didn't answer. "I like that." She started walking. "I'm thinking I'd like to do the kind of work you do when I'm a bit older."

He froze at her words. "Are you serious?"

She popped up one shoulder and grinned. "We'll see."

"So," he said as they began walking again, and his heart damn near exploded in his chest when she reached for his hand, "will you, um, tell me more about you?"

"Like what?"

"You know"—he glanced at her and smiled—"everything."

* * *

W YATT HAD SECOND-GUESSED HIS DECISION TO GO TO HIS parents' house a dozen times on his way there. This wasn't even the home he grew up in. His parents had finally downsized last year. Of course, their definition of downsizing still meant buying a home in the ballpark of ten million pounds. But maybe he made the right move in confronting his parents.

Because after a thirty-minute, one-way conversation where Wyatt had vented about anything and everything that had ever crossed his mind, he actually did feel a little better.

His father removed his glasses and set them aside before standing from the chair. "You're just like my mother, aren't you?" His words weren't cutting or defensive, the typical way he spoke to him over the years. It was also as if his statement was a declaration of surrender.

His dad's gray eyes lowered to the floor, and his hands went into the pockets of his brown tweed jacket. "Your grandmother was like you. Carefree. Free spirit. She hated being tied down. Hated being a lady, and as much as she loved my father, she regretted the life she was forced to lead because of it." His tone was crisp. Decisive. Accepting. Or maybe forgiving, but for what, Wyatt wasn't so sure. "Pop was always afraid she'd leave him. Lived his life worrying about it."

"But she didn't." Wyatt didn't know where his father was going with this story, but he'd always been closest to his grandmother. She'd said they were kindred spirits, and he supposed there was a lot of truth to that because they were very similar in nature. Only, he'd left, when she hadn't. "What are you trying to say?"

"I saw how much you were like her when you were growing up." He pinched the bridge of his nose and lifted his normally cold eyes up. Today, they were lighter, less gunmetal and gloom. "I think I spent most of your young life worrying that you'd leave me the way Pop always worried she'd leave him. Because I saw so much of her in you."

Wyatt turned away from his dad, processing his admission. The truth of his words cut through him. It was as if his father had been wearing a mask for years and had finally taken it off.

After Wyatt's divorce with Clara, he'd spent his time dedicated to work, believing he could never love. He pushed everyone away to prevent any type of pain. He never thought he'd be able to relate to his father, but maybe he could. Maybe he was more like him than he thought. Taking preventative measures to safeguard his heart like his dad had done with him.

Had his father cared so much he'd accidentally built a wall between them? A strange sensation, a feeling of calm, had his skin tingling and the tense muscles in his body relaxing.

"I put distance between us, expecting you to hurt us by leaving, and maybe I was the one who actually pushed you away." His father confirmed his theory. "I'm sorry. The way I've treated you over the years was wrong. And to hell with what people think, you're my son. Even if you're a Pierson now. Ink and all."

Wyatt slowly faced him, his throat thickening at the break in his dad's voice. Chills forming, a rare sensation for him. He wasn't sure what had caused the change of heart, but he'd take it.

"And I was worried you'd hurt Gwen, too. You'd find out she was your daughter, and you'd leave her." Wyatt grimaced at his mum's words. "But I was wrong, wasn't I? Because you're here, and you brought someone you care about with you. You found love."

"You planning on marrying her?" He followed his father's hand as he pulled a box out of his pocket. "If you want to ask her, well, you can do it with this ring if you'd like."

Wyatt took the small leather box from his father, feeling

like he was moving in slow motion. This entire day was some kind of dream.

"It was your grandmother's ring," his dad continued. "She wanted you to have it if you ever found someone who, uh, didn't make you feel so tied down. Her words."

Wyatt stared at the diamond, which was surrounded by pale green emeralds, the same color as Natasha's eyes.

"Thank you." He blinked back the tears that tried to break free and tucked the box into his coat pocket. He hadn't even taken off his jacket when he and Natasha had arrived, assuming it'd be a quick visit. "And yes, I plan on asking her. I also plan on having more children."

His mum's face lit up at the mention of "heirs" as she'd call them.

With the ring in his pocket, there was only one thing on his mind now, though. And he was too impatient to wait. He knew what he wanted and it was a life with Natasha.

"Can you excuse me?" he sputtered, then hurried out of the room without giving his parents a chance to say more. "Natasha," he called out in search of her.

She was sitting at the breakfast bar in the mammoth-sized kitchen. "Are we fleeing?" she asked around a bite of a Danish.

"Just out to the back." He grabbed her jacket since she'd removed hers, and they quickly made their way outside.

"This place is stunning, by the way." She zipped up her coat, her eyes moving to the gardens on the back property. So many flowers. How had he never noticed all the flowers everywhere he went before? "And you really grew up in a house five times the size of this one?"

They approached the edge of the terrace, the London skyline in view.

His mum had given them a grand tour of the place when

they'd arrived, boasting that President Reagan once stayed in the house during his presidency. Natasha had smiled and nodded as if impressed, even though he knew she wasn't materialistic or into such details, but she'd been polite and made a show of being spellbound for his mother.

"Yeah, but, um." He faced her and took her hand, too anxious to do or say more than what he had planned.

"What is it?" Her smile was like a promise of love and hope, a reminder there was good in the world.

"This thing between us, it's crazy. I mean, we met at our exes' wedding eight years ago, and back then, I never would have imagined I'd be standing here in London with you, let alone be the father of an almost twenty-one-year-old."

The first few drops of rain came slowly, and she ignored them. The water hit her cheeks. Her lashes. Her lips. She simply stared at him as if mesmerized, and he felt the same.

"Should we go in?" he asked, but she shook her head. "I guess it's sort of perfect to be standing out here in the rain." His voice was low but shaky. Nerves and excitement coiling inside of him. "My grandmother told me to find someone who makes me feel like sunshine after a rainy day." He looked up at the sky as the heavens opened up on them, the rain crashing harder, and she chuckled, not giving a damn. "So, here we are in the rain, but you're the sunshine. You're my light." He wasn't a romantic, but damn this woman had him all out of bloody sorts in the best possible way.

He lowered to one knee, bending the other leg back as he let go of her right hand so he could reach into his pocket. She kept her eyes on him, and if there were tears there, he couldn't tell since the rain continued to pour down her face.

"This was my grandmother's ring, and I was hoping you'd wear it." He let go of her left hand to remove the diamond from the box, then held it above her ring finger.

"What do you say? Would you spend the rest of your life with me?" Tears mixed with the water on his own face as it rained. "Will you marry me?"

Her lower lip quivered, and she nodded. "Yes," she cried.

He slid the ring on, and she urged him to stand, then flung her arms over his shoulders. He clutched her tight to his body before pulling back for a kiss.

Standing outside on a cold and wet day in the city in which he was born . . . he'd never felt so bloody happy.

EPILOGUE

Situated flat on his belly, elbows propped up, legs stretched out behind him, Wyatt was in one of his favorite positions. Well, one of his favorite non-sexual positions. Behind his rifle on overwatch.

On the rooftop of a restaurant, which ironically happened to belong to Asher's sister and mom, the smell of garlic, oregano, and other delicious Italian scents wafted all around him even though the kitchen had closed an hour ago.

His target and reason for being there? The club across the street. His daughter's first stop in her night of celebrating her twenty-first birthday party.

"This is Echo One, all stations, radio check."

"This is Bravo Three, that's a good copy," Asher responded over comms, followed by the rest of his teammates announcing they were in position. He had over half the guys with him tonight, and if he'd needed all of Bravo and Echo, they would've suited up without question.

Everyone happened to be in the city, and that *may* have been a strategic plan on Wyatt's part, nudging Harper to choose this weekend for when she threw the triple baby shower party.

Harper had organized the event for three of the couples expecting: Eva and Luke, Jessica and Asher, and Emily and Liam. The babies were all due at different times that year, but it was hard to get the entire team and their families together at once.

Somehow, after the gifts and the baby excitement, the party last night turned into a Bravo-Echo face-off in terms of who could out drink the other and still be able to walk straight (not shoot straight, they weren't that crazy).

We need a real matchup. Bravo versus Echo. It's time we settle this, A.J. had urged after Bravo wiped the floor with them in their ridiculous drinking competition.

We're all here. How about Sunday? Asher, the other instigator in all this, had pitched the idea.

Nah, brother, who is gonna judge? We need unbiased people. A.J. had then turned to Natasha, a grin on his face as he struggled to remain standing, bracing the table off to his left inside Harper's flat where the party had been. *Didn't you say your brother is wrapping up a job in Syracuse? Maybe he can come down on Sunday, bring some Army buddies with him. They'll be unbiased.*

Ha! Chris had shouted. *They'll probably want to face off with us themselves.*

Not a bad idea, Captain America, A.J. had slurred. He'd removed his cowboy hat and placed it on Chris's head, which he'd never do if he was sober. *First, we brothers face off, then we have a good ol' Navy versus Army football game.*

"All stations, be prepared. Target's limo should be arriving outside the nightclub soon," Luke announced, interrupting Wyatt's memories from last night. Hopefully, he made it to tomorrow's planned events and didn't wind up in jail tonight for clocking some guy who decided to get handsy with his daughter on the dance floor.

And was Gwen really twenty-one?

Wyatt had taken time off from operating to spend time with Gwen, and of course, Natasha. Even though Balan was dead, the fact he'd known Natasha's address and provided it to God knew who . . . they decided she ought to move.

Last week, they made an offer on a row home a block away from where Knox and Adriana lived. The whole having-a-permanent-address thing wouldn't be so bad, especially since he'd be living with Natasha, and Gwen would be fifteen minutes away at uni starting in the fall.

"Can you believe I'm getting married this summer?" And had Wyatt really spoken his thoughts out loud?

"At this point, I should've given in and bought a monkey suit already. All the rentals are adding up with you guys tying the knot every five minutes," Chris griped over the line. He was positioned inside the club, and the beats the DJ spun popped into Wyatt's ear over comms.

"Yeah, well, maybe you'll be next," Finn said, and Wyatt waited for someone on his team to knock that idea out of the park in about two point five seconds.

"All the bad guys in the world would probably retire before Chris settles down." And, of course, it was A.J., their quarterback for tomorrow's impromptu Army–Navy game, to speak up.

"You said the same thing about Wyatt," Finn reminded A.J. "And look at him now. A summer wedding. A daughter. A happy life."

He was happy, wasn't he? How'd he get so lucky?

"Not to break up this riveting conversation, but we've got

incoming," Roman announced, and by his tone, you'd have thought they had an inbound RPG headed their way instead of Wyatt's daughter's limo.

"What's the count again?" A.J. asked.

"Four guests entered the limo outside Gwen's hotel," Luke answered. "Two guys in their late twenties."

"Damn. I don't know what I'm gonna do if I ever have kids. This shit is more intense than being on the Iranian border and having brought a knife to a gunfight." A touch more of Alabama cut through the line as A.J. dragged out his words.

"Well, maybe if you get up the nerve to ask out a certain someone, you might——"

"What's that?" A.J. cut off Asher. "I can't hear ya, brother. Must be a bad connection."

Wyatt bit back a laugh before growing serious, remembering the gravity of the situation.

His daughter. A nightclub. Alcohol and guys.

"Echo Four, when they get out of the limo, can you get some photos of the two guys and head back to HQ. We can run their images through facial recog and get their stats," Wyatt requested.

"Roger that," Roman answered.

"This is Bravo One, the doors are opening. They're getting out."

"Echo Three, they should be coming inside soon," Wyatt alerted Chris.

"Roger that. I'm just sitting at the bar watching a few women that look like they're mostly naked—well, does body paint count as being dressed?" Chris paused for a beat. "Anyway, they're doing some trapeze thing. I'm surprised Gwen would pick this club. It's filled with a bunch of snooty A-listers, overpriced drinks, and——"

"Damn it," Wyatt cursed over the line. "All stations, come in. Gwen's not in the limo. What in the hell is going on?" His mobile phone began ringing seconds later before he had time to make sense of how his boys lost his daughter. "Hey, Natasha. I'm, um, a bit busy right now. Can I call you back?"

"Did you just discover Gwen's not in that limo?" she asked with a laugh, and he sat back in surprise.

"Natasha," he playfully growled out. "Babe, where is she?"

"Gwen asked for my help in ditching you and your guys. She had a feeling you'd be playing the role of overprotective operator on her birthday."

"Why are you on her side and not mine?"

"Because I was twenty-one once and had to deal with Gray and the admiral. And Gwen's smart and strong. She'll be fine, I promise," she said far too casually given his daughter was out in the city somewhere. "Now, round up the boys. We have two tables going at Jessica's place." Her order came out soft and smooth, and that irresistible voice got to him every time.

"Two tables?"

"Poker. I mean, right now, it's just us ladies, but if you boys want to join us . . ."

"You had this planned already, huh? A way to distract me so I don't lose my bloody mind tonight?"

Natasha chuckled. "I'm pretty sure you've lost your mind already since you're probably perched somewhere in the city with your long gun, am I right?"

He eyed his gun and scowled as if she could see him.

"Come on, head to Jessica's." Her tone remained light and relaxed, so different from when they'd been in Montreal when the problems of the world had weighed heavy on her shoulders.

She'd be heading back to the Agency on Monday, and although he knew her job was hunting down bad guys, same as him, he hoped she'd never have to deal with another arsehole like Balan again. But if she did, he'd have her back. Always.

"Just come," she pleaded again. "Maybe you'll even get lucky tonight."

"At poker or in the bedroom?" he asked, but she'd already ended the call.

One thing he'd never grow tired of was making love to that woman. The idea alone had his cargo pants tenting. "Abort mission, guys. Gwen had help from Natasha to lose us," he reported to the team. "I guess I gotta learn to let go."

"You sure you can do that?" Asher asked, surprise in his tone. "I mean, we can Charlie Mike and find her. I got my sources."

He took a moment to consider the idea, then he removed his jacket and pushed up his sleeve to look at the ink he'd gotten as a reminder of Arthur.

His eyes lifted to the sky. *I won't let you or her down. I'll keep her safe. I promise.* He hoped Arthur could somehow hear his thoughts. But he had to know, right? Arthur had to know Wyatt would take care of Gwen like his own daughter, because she was, in fact, his.

He took a deep breath, doing his best to conceal the emotions in his voice. "As much as I'd like to, I gotta give her some space. Do that trust thing I hear kids always asking their parents to give them."

"Well, look at you being all wise and shit," A.J. remarked. "Or . . . did Natasha call you and give you no other choice?"

He closed his eyes and smiled. "Something like that."

* * *

AFTER THREE HOURS OF WHAT THE BOYS ON BOTH BRAVO AND Echo had described as being like a mini-version of Hell Week at BUD/S, they were flat on their backs, eyes on the sky trying to catch their breath as the judges decided on which team won the Bravo-Echo matchup.

Aside from swimming in the freezing New York waters, which would be crazy to do in March, they'd raced, carried heavy objects together as a team while marching, climbed and jumped over stuff with eighty-pound gear strapped on, shot at targets from various ranges, stripped and reassembled rifles, and more.

Natasha and the rest of the ladies had sat comfortably in their camping chairs, bundled in their jackets, coffees in hand, while they watched the boys in the insane competition.

Bravo and Echo Teams were in cargo pants and T-shirts. And the sweat had their shirts clinging to their rippled and muscled bodies. The dampness had to add an extra bite of cold, but they seemed oblivious to the temperature.

Gray, Jack, a few other guys from her brother's tactical security company—plus some Army guys from Fort Drum— had loved every minute of the event.

Gray had snapped out orders to Echo Team: do better, run faster, work harder. Jack had taken charge of Bravo, pushing them the same. Basically, they'd enjoyed tormenting a bunch of SEALs and egging them on.

"So, what do you think?" Back on his feet, A.J. snatched his cowboy hat from the chair and placed it on, then helped Wyatt up off the ground.

Wyatt glimpsed Natasha, his breathing still labored, and she grinned at him. "You all are nuts," she mouthed.

But it'd also been freaking hot. Ten extremely fit and good-looking Navy SEALs completing an obstacle-like course in a field not far from the shore. How had they even pulled this off on such short notice?

"We have the results." Gray waved a hand in the air, and all the guys gathered around him, waiting for the announcement.

Natasha went to Wyatt's side, and he pulled her tight against him.

"Well." Gray looked up, that mischievous look in his eyes Natasha knew all too well. "It's a tie. Five votes for Bravo. Five for Echo."

A.J. removed his hat and slapped it against his thigh. "Now that's some bullshit. No way are we ending this on a tie," he said as the rest of his teammates grumbled.

"Well, you can't argue with math," Natasha spoke up. "You guys had the same times on pretty much everything."

"Yeah, yeah," A.J. griped and put his hat back on.

"If we're going to get technical, I'm pretty sure Knox had a half a second on Captain America during that race." Asher crossed his arms.

"It was nose and nose," Jack said, a massive grin on his face. Yup, he was loving this.

This was only the second time Wyatt had seen her brother since they'd met that first night in Arlington. Gray had been working nonstop since then, and she was beginning to worry that maybe he'd never settle down. Too work-focused like she'd once been when working Balan's case.

But The Knight was dead. The chase for him was over. And something beautiful had come from all that darkness. The rainbow-after-a-storm kind of beautiful. Wyatt had said she was his sunshine, but she was pretty sure he was also her light.

Natasha glimpsed her watch, the one she wore every day, before her gaze slid to the engagement ring. *I'm so lucky.*

"I can break the tie if you'd like," Gwen offered, striding up to the crowd of Army–Navy guys.

"Same." Jessica stepped up next to Gwen.

"Sure. One vote for Bravo from Jess since you're carrying the Big Guy's babies and Gwen will vote for her old man." Owen shook his head. "Another tie."

"Well, you clearly have to settle this," Natasha teased, looping her arm behind Wyatt's back.

"You sure you guys didn't make this tie happen on purpose?" Liam challenged. "I bet they did, didn't they?" He nodded and faced his wife, Emily. "Babe, your brother's a Marine, maybe he can settle this."

Emily rolled her eyes. "Sure, you want to FaceTime him while he watches more of this insanity?" She looked at Natasha and laughed.

Alexa had been right about Emily. She was awesome. And their adopted daughter, Elaina, well, she was pretty incredible, too. Gwen had even babysat her while Liam and Emily, and Wyatt and Natasha, had gone out on a double date last week in D.C.

"Well, we bloody well have to do something." Liam's Aussie accent moved through the chilled air.

"You know," Harper said, stepping forward so she was between the sailors on one side and the soldiers on the other. "It is possible you're both just awesome. *Equally* awesome."

The guys on Bravo and Echo exchanged a look with each other, then simultaneously shook their heads and said, "Nah."

"Well, I give up." Harper went back to the chairs they had set up, and she settled next to Owen's wife. "You're a bunch of crazies, in my opinion."

A.J. turned back toward Harper. "And you know you love us."

"How about we move on to something more important?"

Gray stepped forward. "And we play a little football. Have a real matchup."

"This is what I've been waiting for." Natasha bit into her lip, and Wyatt nudged her in the side with his elbow. "But take it easy on your leg, Gray." She stared at her brother, waiting for him to acknowledge her concerns, and her brother wrinkled his nose as he shot her a playful, close-mouthed smile, which basically meant *Not gonna happen.*

"And who are you betting will win?" Jack strode up next to Gray, facing her and Wyatt.

"Yeah, who?" Wyatt's hand slid down to her ass, and he squeezed.

Natasha turned to the side to catch his eyes. "You did admit to me in Montreal that playing football is not one of your many talents."

"That was also in reference to real football." A puff of cold air carried Wyatt's words.

"And I'm supposed to believe you'll be better at American football?" She couldn't help but laugh as she jerked her free hand toward Gray and Jack. "You're going up against a bunch of guys from the Lone Star State who can play as well as they can shoot."

"You got that right." Gray folded his arms. "I'll take it easy on you, no worries." And her brother was probably going to regret that once out on the field. Wyatt was stubborn and when pushed . . . well, hell, all the guys out there were probably similar.

Wyatt fully faced her. "Does that mean you're betting against me?"

She pushed up on her toes, bringing her mouth close to his, forgetting her audience. "Now, you know I'd never normally bet against you."

"But?" Wyatt arched a brow.

"This might have to be an exception."

"Damn straight," she heard Jack say. "And that's our cue to give you some space."

"Care to make a wager if I win?" Wyatt asked once the guys were out of earshot.

"Okay. If you win, I'll let you try that position in the bedroom you've been dying to test out."

His eyes widened, and a devilish, but sexy grin crossed his lips.

"Bro, you ready?" A.J. called out, and Wyatt lifted his eyes to the sky as A.J. strode closer. Always with the interruptions. "We gotta go kick some Army ass. You up for it?"

Wyatt smirked. "Hooyah, brother."

"And what if our kids choose to join the Army instead? Or become Marines?"

"You trying to give our man a heart attack before the big game?" A.J. quipped. "The poor guy didn't sleep all night with Gwen out in the city—thank God she returned to her hotel alone and at a reasonable hour—but still, the man might need a little bit of some inspiration instead. You know, maybe a hot kiss?"

Natasha threaded her fingers through Wyatt's hair and pressed her lips to his, and A.J.'s whistling grew faint as if he'd retreated.

"Mm. Was that for good luck?" Wyatt asked after their lips broke apart.

"You don't need luck." She patted him on the ass, gave him one more kiss, then he left to join his team in the huddle. "Now, this is going to be fun to watch."

Gwen came up next to her. "You give him a pep talk? His eyes are still bloodshot from staying awake all night worrying about me."

Natasha had also spent most of the night trying to distract Wyatt by having sex.

Gwen twisted sideways to fist-bump Natasha. "Thanks again for the rescue last night. I'm sure Dad flipped a lid when the limo showed up at that club, and I didn't get out of it."

Dad. Gwen had first called Wyatt that two weeks ago when they'd all been at the gun range, and he hadn't been able to wipe the grin off his face.

"Your dad is a good man. He's just overprotective. He means well." Natasha turned back toward Bravo and Echo Teams in their huddle. Their quarterback, A.J., had on a cowboy hat instead of a helmet. "But yeah, I wish I could've pulled off something like that on the admiral when I was your age."

"I guess you didn't have a badass CIA officer in your life to help you."

Natasha glimpsed Gwen. Her eyes were positioned on the soldiers as they moved into position opposite the SEALs. Gwen's gaze lingered particularly long on one of the guy's Gray brought down from Fort Drum.

And when the guy lifted his eyes, and his focus moved straight to Gwen, he smiled at her.

Gwen's cheeks immediately took on a rosy hue as she shifted her hair behind her ears.

And did Gwen have the hots for an Army guy?

Well, this will be interesting, she thought as Wyatt glanced back at them from over his shoulder, and Natasha and Gwen both waved.

"Let the game begin!" Harper exclaimed, standing off to the side of the men on the field.

A.J. lowered himself into position, preparing to receive the ball.

465

"Who do you really think is gonna win?" Gwen asked.

"Well." Natasha smirked, eyes on Wyatt, who was playing center as he snapped the ball to A.J. "I think I've highly motivated your father, so I'm gonna go with Navy." A.J. passed the ball to Chris just as Jack threw his weight onto him and tackled him to the ground. "But, um, I guess we'll see," she said before Gwen leaned against her, and they both laughed at the sight.

Chris was doing some sort of polar-bear-like growling move as he pawed at the air, trying to get free from Jack. The comedy of this all was priceless.

"And to think," Natasha said with a laugh, "they've only just begun . . ."

IF YOU MISSED THE LATEST BONUS SCENE, **STEALTH OPS #5,** it's available for download on my website. The next bonus scene will be available June 2020. Continue for more Stealth Ops info plus the playlist!

STEALTH OPS TEAM

Want more of the Stealth Ops team? A.J.'s book, *Chasing Daylight,* releases July 30th, 2020. Stay up-to-date on releases by heading over to Brittneysahin.com.

If you missed the latest bonus scene, **Stealth Ops #5,** it's available for download on my website (Brittneysahin.com/bonus-content/). Be sure to bookmark the page or join my newsletter so you don't miss out on the next scenes.

A new series starring Gray and Jack releases 2021. Stay tuned for updates!

**Learn more about Alexa (Natasha's MI6 friend) in *Surviving the Fall*

* * *

Stealth Ops Team Members

Team leaders: Luke & Jessica Scott / Intelligence team member (joined in 2019): Harper Brooks

Bravo Team:
    Bravo One - Luke
    Bravo Two - Owen
    Bravo Three - Asher
    Bravo Four - Liam
    Bravo Five - Knox (Charlie "Knox" Bennett)

Echo Team:
    Echo One - Wyatt
    Echo Two - A.J. (Alexander James)
    Echo Three - Chris
    Echo Four - Roman
    Echo Five - Finn (Dalton "Finn" Finnegan)

President in the Bravo Team books: President Rydell

President in the Echo Team books: President Bennett

PLAYLIST

Fight Song - Rachel Platten

10,000 Hours (with Justin Bieber) - Dan + Shay

Circles - Post Malone

Push My Luck - The Chainsmokers

One Thing Right - Marshmello, Kane Brown

Takeaway (feat. Lennon Stella), The Chainsmokers

Must Be The Whiskey - Cody Jinks

Liar - Camila Cabello

Don't Start Now - Due Lipa

Lover - Taylor Swift

BOOKS BY BRITTNEY SAHIN

Stealth Ops: Bravo Team

Finding His Mark

Finding Justice

Finding the Fight

Finding Her Chance

Finding the Way Back

Stealth Ops: Echo Team

Chasing the Knight

Chasing Daylight (7/30/20)

* * *

Becoming Us Series: *Stealth-Ops Spin-Off Series*

Someone Like You
My Every Breath

* * *

Dublin Nights

On the Edge
On the Line
The Real Deal
The Inside Man (4/30/20)

* * *

The Hidden Truths Series

The Safe Bet
Beyond the Chase
The Hard Truth
Surviving the Fall
The Final Goodbye

* * *

Contemporary Romance Stand-alone

The Story of Us

Thank you for reading Wyatt and Natasha's story. If you don't mind taking a minute to leave a short review, I would greatly appreciate it. Reviews are incredibly helpful to keeping the series going. Thank you!

www.brittneysahin.com
brittneysahin@emkomedia.net
FB Reader Group - Brittney's Book Babes
Stealth Ops Spoiler Room

Get the latest news from my newsletter/website (brittneysahin.com) and/or find me on Facebook in the groups: Brittney's Book Babes or the Stealth Ops Spoiler Room.

* * *

A Stealth Ops World Guide is available on my website, which features more information about the team, character muses, and SEAL lingo.

Made in the USA
Coppell, TX
22 September 2020